Apple Gill

D. BRUCE EDWARDS

Apple Girl

Matador
9 De Montfort Mews
Leicester LE1 7FW, UK
Tel: (+44) 116 255 9311 / 9312
Email: books@troubador.co.uk
Web: www.troubador.co.uk/matador

ISBN
978-1905886-623 (paperback)
978-1905886-715 (hardback)

Typeset in 11pt Book Antiqua by Troubador Publishing Ltd, Leicester, UK
Printed in the UK by The Cromwell Press Ltd, Trowbridge, Wilts, UK

Matador is an imprint of Troubador Publishing Ltd

To my own girls:
Jeanine, Tertia-Jayne,
and most of all
Susanne, their mother

AUTHOR'S NOTE

The situation of the 'Old Vicarage' is loosely tied to the edge of Salisbury Plain, where some charming *old world* houses nestle into the folds in the rising ground to the north. Jocelyn may have gone to school in Salisbury, but exactly which one is left to the imagination, as is the village of Tinsfield and its environs.

Exactly what is described as the training of Territorial Army volunteers is neither precise nor necessarily accurate, so apologies to any professionals.

The ability to sketch beautifully as can our Jo is not a figment of the imagination; one Charles-Antione Coypel (1694–1752) was capable of '(expresssing) a wide range of emotional moods', one such being a study 'Head of Potiphar's Wife' (c. 1737). Allegorical paintings are a common feature, albeit often seen executed on walls and ceilings of historic buildings (cp. Hanbury Hall (NT) in Worcestershire.

Jocelyn Anne, to give her both first names, seems to be a girl with traits a good many parents would envy (apart from her propensity for abandoning convention), but we can all dream.

ONE

"Jocelyn! Jo! Jo-oo! Where are you? Your supper's ready!" The shout came echoing across the orchard, reaching out to disturb her thoughts and bringing a frown onto her freckled face. On her back, knees in the air, gazing up at the slow moving clouds through gently moving branches of the apple; just to lie here, quiet, reflecting on her day, and wondering how she could best capture the magic of what she could see; peace and perfect serenity. Marvellous.

Allowing the summer evening breeze to brush over bare legs, devoid of stockings or anything silly like that, just cool naked down to her pants, that was the best part of it. She'd opened her cotton blouse buttons, and pulled it clear of her skirt. A perfect picture of late teen girlhood, with near full breasts under that simple bra and a penchant for tearing it off when she knew she'd be alone for a while. It helped, oddly, to concentrate on the essence of the place, to get into the right mood, become part of nature herself. And now she'd have to fasten herself up and tuck her blouse back in, for Mother always complained at her for sloppy dressing. It wasn't sloppy, as far as she was concerned, just freedom. She'd run naked as a silly school girl through the orchard if she felt she'd not be told off.

But, alas, the spell had been broken. Struggling to her feet, brushing dead grass off her grey college skirt, running her fingers through thick auburn hair, and slipping her feet back into the rather worn black court shoes, she wondered what was for supper. Not that she really felt hungry. At least she wasn't like that silly Amanda who looked like the proverbial lamppost and still complained of being fat. Fat! The girl didn't know the meaning of the word. Just because she felt the boys

1

weren't always looking at her. Jo took off at a run, and cleared the orchard gate in a single bound, skirt flying, before coming back to a sedate stroll as she came within view of the kitchen window.

"There you are. As if I didn't know. You won't be able to day-dream like that once you get to University!"

Her mother, her darling Mums, was putting out plates onto the large kitchen table.

"Spaghetti again! Mums – you'll get me fat." Jo pecked her mother on her cheek before slipping sideways onto her chair. "Where's Pa?"

"Still at the garage. Late customer, you know how he won't turn them away. And Tony phoned. Wanted to know if you'd care to go with him to see the latest film on Friday. Said you'd phone him back. Was that right?"

Jo frowned. She didn't much care for Tony, or any other moonstruck boy come to that. She liked her friends without entanglements, thank you very much. She was aware she turned boys' heads, but that was their problem. There were one or two who had tried to get too friendly – friendly, huh – pawing at her, and she'd given them short shift. Elbows and knees were effective weapons when applied correctly. Conversation, preferably both witty and intelligent, was much more in her line, or even a shared exploit like orienteering or a mild cross-country run. She wasn't averse to a weekend's camping out, either, but time wasn't on her side, what with exams coming up and, importantly, her project, her secret project.

"Don't know, Mums. I've still got some last minute revision to do. I'd rather go walking on Saturday with Pa if he's got time. No, be a dear and tell him I'm studying and can't be disturbed!"

She adroitly forked up a mouthful of spaghetti, while her mother sighed and resignedly reached for the phone. The things she did for her beloved daughter. Eleanor loved her girl deeply, saw in her some of her own traits, wild, her own person, tough as they came, a survivor. And as usual, felt a pang of sadness that she was their only child. How she and husband David would have loved to have had another – boy or girl – but with the hard time she'd had bringing Jocelyn into the world it just hadn't been worth the risk, so she'd had to agree to have the tubes tied. David had been so good to her, and she couldn't have wished for a more supportive – and loving – partner. She dialled, passed on Jo's reply, sensed the disappointment in Tony's voice, and rolled her eyes as Jo shook her head. Job done, she attacked her own plateful, just as she heard David's car crunch onto the gravel. Car door slammed, footsteps, a whistle and her husband was home. Tall, dark haired still, tanned, always that crinkled grin. He leant over her, kissed her neck, smoothed her wild hair down and kissed her on the lips as she twisted round to him.

"Lover! How's my pretty girl?" The West Country accent was ever a pull at her emotions.

"Fine and dandy, sorr. How's my rare old husband then? Made your fortune yet?" They were forever playing up to each other, and Jo thought it both funny and somehow comforting. She loved them both.

"Pa!" She wiped her mouth with the back of her hand, and put her fork down. She'd made short work of her plateful, while her mother had just started. "I'll get yours – you can have my seat, it's warm. I'm up to my room – then you two can canoodle as much as you like. Can you spare half a day on Saturday, Pa? I'd love to do some of the Plains walk again, clear my head for the exam week?"

David narrowed his eyes, pursed his lips, and thought. If he got John to hold the fort after mid-morning, perhaps he could risk it. It would be good to stretch his legs, especially in the company of his energetic daughter.

"If John will do a few hours for me, yes, I'd love to. What about your mother…?" He'd been massaging her shoulders as they talked and she was revelling in the feel of his fingers.

"I've got the garden, Dave. Lot's to do yet before we're tidy for the village do. You two go, you deserve it, both of you." Eleanor, in an unthinking moment, had agreed to host a village barbecue in their grounds, and she was blowed if she'd let some of those more snooty newcomer women think their garden was a mess. She had a week to get it spick and span. "Mind you, I'd appreciate some help on Sunday. Bargain?"

David laughed, and took Jo's seat. "Fine. Bet you it rains!"

"Rotter! I'll leave the rubbish for you to clear, rain or no rain!" She returned to her own plateful, while Jo, taking a glass of lemonade with her, went on up to her room. They heard her, taking two or three steps at a time, then her door closed with the characteristic slam. Eleanor raised her eyebrows at David, who shrugged.

"Is she going to survive the last hurdle, do you think?"

He took his first fork-full, savoured the sauce.

"Jo? She's your daughter, so she ought to. Yes, she'll survive. Very well, I should think. At least she's honest with herself. And quite serious about things. Quite why she's spending so much time in the orchard I'm not sure. Real thinker, that one." Eleanor paused, then her voice changed, and David looked up. "She doesn't seem to have any interest in boys, Dave. And she's *so* attractive, regardless of those freckles. Even I know that. Not that I should worry, at least we know she's not messing about, but it ain't *narturell*."

The brogue derived emphasis caused them both to smile. David knew what his wife meant, and leant back in his chair. She'd said as much before, though he wasn't overly worried; the girl knew her own mind. He'd a healthy respect for his daughter, and was sure she'd come to terms with the opposite sex in due course. So long as she kept herself in check. He'd have a word with her on Saturday, while they were out.

"El, dear, don't panic. She's only seventeen. Plenty of time yet. We shouldn't worry; apparently one of her form mates has been, er, *seen*, if you know what I mean."

"I don't want to know, Dave. And don't call me El!"

He grinned, knowing he'd provoke her. He didn't really much care for the shortened version either, preferring her earlier nickname – Tom – but that was even more confusing. Calling such a feisty woman Tom was daft. Just because she'd been known as a tomboy in her younger years, and her family called her that when she was at home. Even now her mid-brown hair was all over the place, she wouldn't spend money

4

at the hairdressers unless she had to. But her work-a-day dress still showed off a reasonable figure, and he wouldn't swap her for the world. He put his fork down, and pushed his chair back.

"Coffee?" Eleanor was asking.

"Hmm. No, a glass of wine, I think. Let's go and chill out. That's what Jo does! Will she want another drink?"

"Shouldn't think so. She's quite capable of sorting herself out."

"I know. White and cold?" David reached up and opened the cupboard for two of the thick-walled hand-thrown goblets.

"Yes – let's take that opened bottle – it needs finishing. Do you really think she's standing up to the exam pressure, David? I mean, all this business of her chilling out in the orchard. I just wonder, sometimes. She's *so*, so laid back. And she doesn't worry about her dress. I bought her some simple make-up the other day but she's scarcely touched it!"

David laughed. "I shouldn't panic about *that*. She doesn't need war paint! Just carry on keeping an eye on the feminine things dear, and only let me know if there's something awry. Come on, let's go see what attractions the orchard has!"

They linked arms and wandered off up through the garden, bottle and glasses in free hands. Jo watched them go from her bedroom window, bored with reading the set English novel for her next exam and trying to understand the lecturer's idea of criticism. She wasn't unaware of the concern they had discussed. Intuitively, her instincts were to reassure her Mums that yes, she did know about boys – young men really, she thought, but there were other more important things in her life. No one was going to mess about with her, so there was no point in encouraging them by getting dolled up. A wry smile crossed her face as she saw her parents go through the paddock gate and Pa sneaked a kiss, as Mums was preoccupied with the latch. She turned back to her desk and picking up her favourite soft black pencil idly sketched the apple branches onto paper. Come what may she *had* to capture that feeling. How? She had to be in the mood. No good taking sketch pad and pencil up to the orchard, she couldn't sketch lying on her back. The vision of blue sky, ragged clouds, the knarled bark, leaves, the young apples still hanging, showing all the promise of ripening fruit. It seemed impossible, yet she had it in her mind's eye, and somehow…

It was all connected up with her being there, so it had to be *her*. She pulled another sheet down, and did a broad outline of what could be her on the grass, seen sideways from above, through the tree, instead of her original idea of a sort of worm's eye view. No, that wasn't right. She screwed it up. Irritated, she tipped her chair on its back legs and scowled at the mirror across the room, tapping the pencil on her teeth.

The look of her straggling hair annoyed her, so she reached for her hair-brush and set to; brushing out the soft curls soothed her; then watching her image in the mirror she tried her hair in different ways, up in a knot on top, then swept back, then on the side, no, the other way, and then half up and in a sort of swirl. That was better. She moved her head to one side, tipped her chin down. Hmm.

In a careless way, she pulled her blouse back off her neck, but the button snagged, so she undid all the buttons and took it off. The white cotton bra, particularly the straps seen in the mirror against her lightly bronzed skin, also annoyed her, so she reached round and unfastened the strap, threw the offending thing onto her bed. Moving slightly, she got a much better picture. There. That's me! Self-portrait? She'd not thought of it before. Why not – all famous artists had had a go! Scrabbling about in the desk drawer, she found the charcoal sticks in an envelope that her college art lecturer had given her. On a larger piece of cartridge paper the first tentative lines were a bit scratchy, and horrid, so she rubbed at them and found the blurring effect suddenly pleasing. She caught the outline of her hair, the oval of her face, her curving neckline and the first swell of her breasts, eyes constantly moving up and down; as she worked she became more and more absorbed. Gradually her features took shape; she picked a smaller piece of stick, rubbed it on her sandpaper to get the right shape, tried getting the detail of her eyes, then her nose, her mouth; found she was losing the light but was loath to move. She tried a bit of careful rubbing, and with a bit of blu-tack, lifted off the surplus dust, instantly discovering a new way of changing the texture. Enthralled, she kept going, straining as the sun was dipping down, lengthening the shadows. Suddenly, she shivered. Naked from the waist up, sitting still, she'd got cold. Getting up, she shrugged into a sweater, pushed the sleeves up her arms and tossed her hair free, before picking up her handiwork and moving to the window to critically appraise her efforts. Solemn eyes and yet mischievous mouth stared back at her; long neckline, the still slightly unkempt hair. *It was her!*

She had to share her joy. A new found skill, a sideswipe at her known talent; suddenly she was brimming over with delight. Then she remembered, Mums and Pa were down the garden, and goodness knows what they were getting up to. Jo had no illusions about her parents. They were as deeply in love now as they must have ever been, and she had grown up with their love. Which is probably, she thought to herself, why I'm the girl I am.

With another critical look, she put her effort back on the drawing board on her desk, switching the old Anglepoise lamp on. A few lines needed grading down a bit, and perhaps just a teeny bit less, there, perhaps another few stray hairs on top, no, leave it. See what Pa says. She left it on the board and went back to the window. The sun had dipped below the tree line, and the orange after-glow against the deep green was ethereal. Surely they should have been back before now – it was gone ten. She raised the sash window and whistled. An answering whistle from her father. So they would be back shortly. Perhaps she'd go and put the kettle on.

* * *

Eleanor and David were indeed wandering slowly back. It was barely five hundred yards to the orchard fence, but they could have been on the edge of space. Without a word between them, they had walked, arm in arm, up through the vegetable garden, across the rough grass patch where the former owners had kept hens, and into the orchard. It wasn't a desperately productive orchard, but somehow it had woven a spell on all three of them, for the ancient trees seemed to have an aura of elemental productivity mixed with folklore. Suggestions that the orchard should be replanted, or even turned over to some other use, had been considered, but somehow, at the last minute, neither David nor Eleanor could bring themselves to the point of no return, and Jo had been adamant from the start she wanted it to stay. So stay it did, and here they were, soaking up the last heat of the summer day, swishing through un-mown grass under a canopy of swirling leaves and the few apples of the potential meagre harvest. Eleanor pulled at David's arm – there in the grass under that little closer planted group of seven smaller trees, a flattened patch.

"Jo. That's where she's been. You can see, Dave... Why there?"

David was just as puzzled. "Unless..." He looked critically at the layout. The orchard itself was quite large, well over a quarter of an acre the house particulars had said when they'd fallen in love with the place four years ago. An old vicarage, just the place for them and their rather bohemian lifestyle, it had been so run down as to be well below market value.

"Unless, the way the trees are planted here. See, in a sort of circle?" He paced round, and understood. Where Jo had been was in the middle. "Spooky. She's a girl, our Jo. Trust her to discover somewhere with a bit of..." He broke off, unsure. He couldn't bring himself to say imagery, or even symbolism, because he wasn't certain he understood. His the more practical mind; at one with mechanics and engineering; he left the artistic side to his wife and now, more recently, their daughter.

"Atmosphere?" Eleanor felt something, but she didn't quite know what.

"Hmm, something like that. Over here?" He moved over to where a dead tree had been felled and the bole left. It made a good seat. Eleanor cuddled up alongside him as he poured out the wine, less cold now, into the tall stemmed glasses. The part-bottle just filled them.

"Here's to us. And Jo's success in her exams!" They clinked glasses, and sipped.

"What will you do when she brings the first boy home, Dave?"

David blinked. He'd not thought. After a meditative pause, and another sip, he put the glass down carefully on the ground alongside the wood.

"What did your father say when you unearthed me?" He put an arm round her, feeling her warmth. She laughed. "Shan't tell you!" knowing full well that they'd been through all this times before, and that Dave always liked her telling him. It boosted his ego, but it also brought out the love in him.

He squeezed her, kept the pressure on.

"Hey! I'll pop!"

"No you won't. What did he say, again?" He was grinning, oh, how she loved that grin.

"That you were too good for me! He liked strong handshakes, and you've got that. And he thought I'd never find anyone, 'cos I was always too rough and ready, tearing about when I should have walked, you know, not caring about what I wore. Girls were always supposed to be prim and proper."

The mental picture of her mother, always dressed to kill, not a hair out of place, no wrinkles anywhere, superb figure, and then that dreadful day when she'd overdosed and they'd lost her. She'd not been able to come to terms with growing old. Eleanor was over it now, but the memory still haunted her. One reason why she was so careful with Jo. Not being too severe. She took a real swallow of her wine, put her glass down alongside David's, and turned her head so he could kiss her, gently, then hard and demanding. She had to break free, to breathe.

"Steady on, Dave. You'll have me all sexy. What will you say?"

The question hadn't gone away.

"Oh, I don't know. Something like, watch out, she'll eat

you for breakfast, or, you'll never stand the pace. Depends. I may tell him to get lost. And you'll tell her to watch her step!"

Eleanor chuckled. He was right. She wasn't overly worried though, for Jo wasn't showing any silly symptoms, unlike some of her friends. The girls she did bring home from time to time were almost brought in for psychotherapy, like she was supposed to talk sense into them. Her chuckle turned into a deeper laugh. Her, telling Jo's contemporaries how to behave!

David's hands were searching under her jersey top, and he was nuzzling her neck. The responses were inevitable, and lovely. Jo had been born just those right months from their wedding, and they'd been blessed with all the right feelings ever since that first time. She would always, always, feel with him, for him, whenever, wherever. The evening breeze had stilled, the air warmer, the long grass dry, and the scents of the end of the summer day were strong. The wine glasses tipped over, but they were beyond righting them. Thank goodness their land was so secluded.

A while later, and she felt the cooler air on bare flesh. "Jo will wonder where we are!"

"No she won't. She's our daughter, remember. But it is a bit fresh, I agree. Happy?"

"Always. Pity about the wine. You?"

"You're lovely, you know that. Inside and out."

"Stop it. You'll make me blush. Get yourself decent. I may not take you home, else!"

David laughed, stood up and watched her rearrange her long skirt. This was not the time to comment on what was worn and what was not, but if it made life easier, then great. He picked up the glasses and the bottle, took his wife's hand, and they made their way back through the gathering twilight. There was a whistle from the house. Jo, warning them it was time to come home. Bless her. He whistled back, a shrill single note.

* * *

The kettle was singing, the mugs in a row, and Jo was beaming all over her freckled face. "Good up the orchard, was it? Not too cold?" She could see her Mums was a bit flushed and Pa had that self-satisfied look on his face he couldn't disguise. And they thought she didn't know about these things? They should hear the other girls going on about their parents, or their mother's boyfriends, or whatever!

Eleanor felt herself going redder, and turned her head away, searching for the biscuit tin to hide her confusion. Jo had never been quite so direct before, and it came as a bit of a shock.

"Here, Mums, I didn't want to embarrass you. Really. Good old Pa. I mean, oh, sorry."

Now she was getting embarrassed, and poured the boiled water into the coffee mugs. Her father was trying to keep a straight face, but suddenly he couldn't bottle it up any longer, and burst out laughing. He reached out for his daughter and put an arm round her. "Hey, watch it! I don't want to scald you!" she said, putting the kettle down, rather awkwardly with an arm pinioned, and then reached up to stroke his cheek.

"Here. I've got something to show you." She pulled away, and picked up the cartridge paper in its half-rolled up state. She held the top and bottom edges, and pulled it straight so they could see the charcoal sketch. "Whatcha think?"

Eleanor was taken aback. Somehow, her daughter had captured herself perfectly, the expression, the eyes, the lift of her bust and the turn of her head, even the freckles!

"Darling! It, it's lovely! It's you, really, really you! You did that? When? Did anyone…"

Jo shook her head, auburn hair bouncing. "Tonight. This evening, while you two were…" She stopped, turning the sketch more towards her father. "Pa?"

He took a long, searching look, his head on one side, and then the other. "Bloody marvellous, girl. I knew you were clever with the pencil, but this is something. Your Mum's right. It really is you. Are you pleased with it?"

Eleanor was frowning. "Dave. Really, you shouldn't swear!"

"Oh. Sorry. Well, it is. Talent, that's what it is. We'll have to frame it…"

Jo carefully placed it back on the kitchen worktop, out of reach of the sink, watched it spring back into the half roll. "Yes, Mums. I'm pleased with it, as a first attempt. Sudden inspiration, 'cos I saw me in the mirror and I just wanted to *create something.* Took me a bit by surprise I s'pose, but then it just came naturally. Old Petersen gave me the charcoal sticks at the end of last term, but I'd never really tried them before. Should have been reading that stupid book, but it's *so* boring. Pa, do you think I should really do that English degree? Shouldn't I do History of Art or something? A bit more *me?"*

David looked across at Eleanor. She was thoughtful. When she was Jo's age, she'd been moved to try painting and had done some passable landscapes in oil, but never really persevered. Her mother's death had put such a strain on them all, and she'd had to go straight into a job in that bookseller's. Jo had a much better chance. She was bright, articulate, made friends easily and had had no trouble in obtaining the promise of a place at Uni, with exam results likely enough to be adequate. She was quick with her pencil, some wonderful sketches, and a few watercolours hadn't turned out too badly. One was hanging in the hall now. Lately, though, as she had turned another teen year, she had become a lot more adult, and as this evening had shown, a real thinker.

"Let's sleep on it, Jo," her mother said. "It's getting late. One self-portrait shouldn't dictate the world, you know. College tomorrow. Bed, I think. We'll think about it – no –," she held up a hand as she could see Jo beginning to open her mouth. "– I promise you, it'll be a serious think. That's lovely, Jo, darling, you're very clever. So we'll sleep on it. Okay?"

Jo had to accept her Mums word, so she picked up her precious roll, kissed her parents goodnight, and disappeared up to her bed.

David looked across the room at his wife. She smiled at him, a lazy smile. A 'come to bed' smile.

"We've made a wonderful girl, between us," she said. "Shame we couldn't do it again." There was a hesitant pause. "Never mind. Going through the motions is rather fun. Come on. Put the lights out. I'm going up."

Jo had propped up the portrait, rather haphazardly, on the chest of drawers then climbed into bed; and with arms over her raised knees, was studying it from across the room. Was it really that good? Her parents evidently thought so, and they didn't praise her work lightly, as she knew only too well. Maybe she'd try doing another portrait, perhaps Mums would sit for her. Pa wouldn't, he hadn't the patience. How had she managed to get it *so* right, first time? Some of her sketches she'd had to spend what seemed like hours, rubbing out, re-drawing, even scrapping and starting again, before she'd been happy with them. This had been right at first go. Strange, that. She heard her parents come up to bed, Mums first, her light tread on the stairs, then Pa with his two steps at a time and the careful click of the light switch. Her mind wandered off to what they'd been up to in the orchard, and she began to feel a bit strange within herself, as though she had a sort of inside itch. Silly girl, she thought, and looked across at her picture again. "Goodnight, Jocelyn Number two," she said, sort of out loud, and turning her bedside light off, rolled onto her side and curled up, falling asleep almost at once.

* * *

Dawn light flooded into her room at this time of year, waking her long before most folk would stir. She always slept well, mostly dreamless, and with the benefit of youth managed a long day effortlessly. So flinging back her bed-cover, Jocelyn did a neat half-roll out of bed and stretched, arms up, then down – strrrretch – almost to her toes, before coming back up slowly. This exercising was always her routine, followed by a rub down all over with her lovely soft fluffy towel. She dumped her nightdress and headed for the bathroom. No sound from her parents' room, but that was normal. Her father was usually the first to pad downstairs and put the kettle on. Ten minutes later, and she was back in her room, searching around for clean underwear and blouse. One more day at college, then it's the weekend. Hooray! She was looking forward to getting out onto the open Plain, moorland with that southern difference, open space, open views, lots of lovely sky, fresh air. As she bent down to step into her knickers, she saw the portrait, rolled half under the chest of drawers, which the bright morning sunlight had bathed in gold. She'd forgotten about it, strangely, but now it all came springing back, last night, the intense feeling, the success and the delight. Picking it up, she sat back on the bed, and tentatively opened the roll. Yes, she was still there, with a sort of slow smile to the eyes; oh gosh, did I do that? Jocelyn wasn't sure if she could believe herself. With care, she had another go at propping it up on the chest of drawers, but again it curled up and fell onto the floor.

In a fit of pique, she nearly kicked it under the furniture, but stopped herself just in time. Instead, she picked up her bra and reluctantly eased her self into place. How she detested bras! She couldn't go to college without one though. Boys were bad enough ogling her if she bent down or she had to lean over or something and her blouse opened, God knows what would happen if she showed nipples. She pulled a face, and found her clean blouse.

Brushing her hair out was another morning delight, and she took her time. That and the towel rub made her feel great. And hungry. Time for tea and toast. Picking up her shoes she padded quietly downstairs and into the high ceilinged kitchen. The stone floor was cold to her feet, but then it was all part of her attitude to life in general, put up or shut up, and she liked to feel in touch with her surroundings. Hence the not bothering with some things her classmates would go spare about, like having their meals prepared for them, *always* being carried about, getting parents to fund their mobile phones and making sure they had a snoggy boyfriend to twitch about with at a night club. These random thoughts flicked through her mind as she organised herself her toast and some of Mums's best Seville marmalade. She made herself tea in a mug with a teabag, and opened the back door to stand and breathe in the steely cool early summer morning air. It was barely half past six, and the birds were still doing a good dawn chorus thing. Great to be alive! Taking care not to spill her tea down her college skirt, she walked bare foot, across the strip of paving and onto the grass still damp with overnight dew, taking bites of marmaladed toast as she went. The blue tits scarpered off from the peanut feeder, but the chaffinches just moved out of reach. There were two blackbirds scraping about in the border and throwing leaves about with their beaks. Overhead, a vapour trail from an early outward-bound flight carved the blue sky in two. She did her deep breathing exercises in between toast bites and tea slurps, and completed the circuit of the lawn leaving dewdrop footsteps in the soft grass. Mums's herbaceous border was a treat, and some of the shrubs were just coming into reasonable flower. Should impress the locals next weekend, she thought, and having a free hand now with the last of the toast gone, deadheaded a couple of roses. Keeping the crunched up petals in her hand, she sauntered round to the small compost heap and chucked them, before her eye caught the curtain movement from her parents' room, and Mums was opening the window.

"Hi, ya, early bird!" Eleanor greeted her daughter from her eyrie. "How's the world?"

"Morning Mums!" Jo shielded her eyes to look up. "Bright and beautiful! Wish it were Saturday! Don't fancy college on a day like this!" She waved at her and went back indoors.

* * *

Eleanor ducked back into the room, and closed the window partially.

"Your daughter's about early, as usual. Will you take her into college today, Dave? I'm going to have another go at the decorating. I'll pick her up, when I do the shopping." Her husband was still contemplating the ceiling and stretching his toes before swinging out of bed.

"Sure. She'll attack me over this uni thing, though. What are we going to do about her? I thought she was settled but

15

now she's done this drawing she's suddenly all at sixes and sevens!"

"Shush, dear, she'll hear us. Let it rest till after the weekend, so we'll see if she's serious. It may only be a temporary flight of fancy. Plenty of time." Eleanor had started to dress, choosing some of her oldest clothes, pulling on a pair of really crummy jeans. David watched her, pulling a face. He didn't much care for her in trousers, partly because they hid her still gorgeous legs and partly because it didn't help disguise her middle-age tummy. She caught his eye, and had to grin.

"Sorry dear, but I'm only being practical. Think yourself lucky I don't wear trousers all the time! Come on, you. It's breakfast time, and your daughter's had hers."

"My daughter, El? She's yours as well. Why don't you say 'our'? Or is she only 'mine' when she's being different?" He put his feet to the floor and stood up. Eleanor looked at him, eyes narrowed.

"Call me El once more and I'll thump you! I should have been a Helen, then maybe you would have had a problem with 'Hel'."

"No, dear, you're not a Helen. 'Helens' aren't as nice as Eleanors. At least, not as far as I know. I think I'll go and get a shower. Leave me out a clean shirt, there's a dear. Shan't be long." David swung out of the room, whistling. Eleanor shrugged, and went to find Jo, who was sitting in the basket chair in the kitchen, thumbing through the old magazines. She looked up as her mother appeared.

"Hi Mums. Kettle's hot. Are you taking me in today or is Pa?"

"Your father. I'm going to splash paint about. That downstairs loo's been crying out for a face-lift for ages, and if Mrs Blounce and her mates get half a chance they'll be in and out of the house and the loo all next Saturday. Can't have them nitpicking about crummy paint. I'll pick you up, though, darling, and we'll come back via the supermarket. Normal time?"

Jocelyn thought for a moment. She didn't much care for acting as shopping trolley, but anything to keep Mums on her side.

16

"I should be out by half three. Last lecture's only a re-run of possible exam questions on that wretched so-called modern classic. So, meet you on the corner by the post box?" Then she had another inspiration. "Betty said something about wanting to see our garden. She's the green-fingered one with the classy parents, you know; her mum's the editor or something of that magazine, and her pa's a science research chap. Would you mind if she came back with us? I'm sure she'd get her mum or dad to pick her up? I need to keep some friends." This was a reminder that so many of her classmates had given up on her because she didn't smoke, or go to discos or have a trendy boyfriend. *And* she had freckles. Eleanor wasn't unaware, so had to make allowances.

"Sure. Do you want me to feed her – tea and buns, that sort of thing?"

"S'pose so. Yes, okay. Thanks, Mums. You'll do some showing off?"

Elaine laughed. Jo was so predictable. Invites friends over then expects her parents to participate in whatever was needed. She didn't mind, though, as the garden was her pride and joy. At that moment David appeared, freshly showered, ready for the day, and had caught the last phrase.

"Your Mum's always showing off! What now then, Jo? What are you cajoling her into now?" He was straightening his tie as he spoke. Eleanor explained, while Jo poured her father his large morning cup of tea and put more bread into the toaster.

"Well, sooner or later your Mum will be making a charge. You can't visit good gardens without paying, you know. Quite an idea, that. Gardens Open. Do teas as well!"

"Now, David. Don't get carried away. I know the garden's getting better, but I've still a long way to go yet. It's only four years!"

When they had moved into the property that never to be forgotten autumn, it had been virtually derelict with a wilderness garden, all four acres of it. Luckily the former owner hadn't done much to it since he had bought it from the Ecclesiastical Commissioners as a Vicarage surplus to requirements, and when he died, a recluse without family, David and Eleanor had struck lucky, the old man's estate wanting a quick sale. So they had been able to move from the modern semi in the main village to out here, and Eleanor had been pre-occupied with bringing the garden back to life ever since. The best of it was, she had found a natural bent; and even without any horticultural training was becoming an extremely good gardener, so holding down a part-time job as assistant in the village general store was at times very irritating when the garden demanded specific seasonal work. David was as proud of her achievements as she was of his success in bringing the house up to date without spoiling its character; between them the Old Vicarage was becoming a real asset. Thirteen-year-old Jo had taken it all in her stride and, if the truth were known, was lots happier than being in the modern box. At least she could feel the space and the quiet under the rise of the Plain behind them. Only occasionally the noise of mock battles of the army training bothered them, or the roar of Hercules aircraft on their run-ins for parachute drops. Otherwise it was heaven.

* * *

"Well, we'd best be off. All set, Jo? Are you taking that portrait of yours in to show off?"

David pushed his chair back, wiped his mouth on the back of his hand, a habit Eleanor still detested but couldn't cure, and reached for his jacket from the back of a chair. He liked being clean and reasonably smart without showing off. Selling cars was not the job on the top of the league table, but he did it well, giving his customers the best deals he could, always leaving them with the impression *their* vehicle was the best one around. What he could never do was appear to be superior, so he dressed down a bit without being sloppy. Eleanor habitually eyed him up and down, brushing specks off the jacket, occasionally straightening his tie; making him put more polish on his shoes. She had tried to do the same for Jocelyn, but Jo had her own ideas; dodged her mother's hands, itching as they were to straighten her blouse or get her to adjust her bra. At least she didn't have to tell her to take the reef out of her skirt, as Jo's contemporaries were prone to do, rolling inches up to show indifferent thighs.

"Go on then, have a good day, the pair of you. See you at half three, Jo – and your Betty. Will she mind being dragged round the supermarket?"

"Shouldn't think so. Tough! – She wants to come; she'll have to put up with it. I'll be nice to her. Thanks, Mums. Bye!"

* * *

The pair of them left Eleanor to the clearing up. Ten miles into town, it would be a clear run as it was still early, though the college where Jo was finishing her last few weeks being to the south meant the last couple of miles were solid traffic. David had then to return part way to the showroom and workshop complex of the garage that was just off the Bypass. His was probably the most responsible job in the outfit, ensuring the constant flow of vehicles in and out, buying well, selling well, and keeping the customer base strong and happy. Good thing was, the owner knew it, and paid him well to stay. He'd even been promised a part share in the business at the end of the year, if the turnover continued to rise. He whistled to himself as he opened the garage doors. Not everyone kept their vehicles indoors nowadays, but with a large workshop cum garage, it was easy and simple to tuck the car out of sight. You never knew who fancied their chances with a Jaguar, even if it was nearly vintage. His pride and joy; used because he loved driving a good bit of British engineering and it was solid and reliable, especially when maintained by the older mechanics. Eleanor's little shopping car sat alongside the Jaguar, a funny sort of greeny yellow colour he'd never really got used to but she seemed to love it. He much preferred the metallic grey. While he backed the car out, Jo had taken herself off down the drive to open the gates. The drive, pea gravel, was beginning to show weeds again, and she knew that was one job she'd probably get landed with. Mums had said raking was good for the bust, though quite why she needed to improve her bust she didn't know; she'd enough up front as it was. When taxed about it, her mother had explained it wasn't size, but the ability to keep a good shape. 'Not such a stiff bra needed,' she'd said, with a twinkle in her eye, and Jo had seen the sense of that so then didn't mind. She even enjoyed raking leaves off the lawn in autumn, leaving nice swathes of fine green grass for the blackbirds and the occasional thrush to scratch about on, competing for the best worms. She pulled the gates back, and bent down to drop the bolt into its slot, just as the postman appeared.

"Morning, Miss Jo! Lovely day again! Can I give you these, or shall I drop 'em in the door?"

He was a lovely chap, their postman, been on the round for years and years, knew all the intricacies of the houses, the gates, doors, post boxes, where to leave what, which dogs to avoid. Jo was one of his favourite people; she always had a lovely smile and a nice word. And she was a real good looker, too. He didn't let on she showed o'er much leg when she bent over dropping them bolts.

"I'll take them, Reg. Thanks." She gave a smile, and watched him stride on up the lane. As the Jaguar approached, she sifted through the half-dozen letters. Two for Mums. Two bills. What looked like a mail-shot thing, and one for her? Pa had stopped, was waiting for her to jump in. She waved her Mums's two letters, and raced up the drive to drop them into the door. No point in taking them to the garage for the day. David watched her in his mirror, skirt flying, with her auburn hair bobbing from side to side. His Jo. He'd do anything for her. Back she came, at a more sedate pace. Opened the car door, climbed in, settled herself down into the comfortable depths of the old leather upholstery.

"Okay, Pa."

"Got everything you need? Books?"

"Don't need anything today, just my bag, – last day before exams start next week; bit of a waste of time, really. I'm going to have a chat with Petersen. See what he says about my chances in Art. Just in case," she added hastily, seeing a frown appear on her Pa's face, as he pulled out of their lane onto the main Salisbury road. "I won't tell him I've changed my mind. Not yet, anyway!"

David grunted. Having told himself earlier he'd do anything for this lovely daughter of his, now he was thinking she should stick to her earlier decision to go for an English degree. He'd watched the ebb and flow of different interests over the past two or three years, as she'd progressed from wanting to be into horses – what girl hadn't – to being a model, which didn't last above a month, happily; a biologist, until she'd been introduced to dissection; and then a nursing career that had been abandoned for the longer lasting interest in languages, but mainly literature, strangely. But then she'd started sketching, and it became very obvious she was very good. She'd kept it as a hobby, until this sudden bombshell after just one thing in, what was it, *charcoal?*

"Why charcoal?" His query was voiced, out of the blue, without thinking. Jo was immersed in her letter, and hardly heard the question.

"Hmmm? Sorry. This is from the University; details of the courses. Want to know which slant I'd prefer. Good, isn't it – I mean, asking *me* what *I* want to do? What was that, Pa?"

He waited for a moment, watching traffic behind him, and the vehicle about to overtake.

"Silly bloke. I'll still be behind him when we get into town. Why didn't he stay where he was?"

David got quite irritated when other car drivers were impatient with no good cause. He was a careful driver himself, taking few, if any, risks. "I wondered why you used charcoal on that picture – sorry, portrait."

Jocelyn was surprised at her father's question. He didn't normally get so curious about trivia. Was it trivia? She liked that word. A lot of what went on around her at college was trivia. Why didn't some babies get christened 'Trivia'? It would suit one or two.

"S'pose it's because it was handy – better than a pencil. Bolder, quicker. More texture. Seemed right. Lots of artists use charcoal. Or red crayon. I think that inventor chap, what's his name, Leo somebody, used to use red."

"Leonardo de Vinci. Have you got the sort of stuff you'd need to do other portraits? Other than charcoal?" He eased the car round a couple of parked cars on the approach road to the college, and turned into the gate. Jo wasn't quite sure where this was leading.

"Why do you ask, Pa? You can drop me here, save you having to turn."

"I'd like to see what else you can do, Jo. Bit of fatherly support, like. Let me know. Have a good day, look after your mum, make sure she doesn't spend too much on biscuits!" He leant over and gave his daughter a quick peck on the cheek, at the same time as releasing the car door. Jo nearly fell out, saved by her belt.

"Hey, Pa. Are you that keen to get rid of me? I'll make a list, if you're going to spend money on me. Sure there isn't an ulterior motive? Nude pictures of Mums?" She was teasing him, but maybe, just maybe, there was a tinge of truth in her query. Her father laughed, an honest laugh.

"Go on with you. Be good!"

* * *

She was out, and the car door shut with that satisfying thud. He watched her go, waving to another couple of girls. A group of lads turned their heads and watched her cross the pavement. He noticed, but then, she'd turn any male's head, that one. He put the car back into gear and edged back onto the main road, conscious of the growing volume of youngsters coming in from all directions, most of them with no regard for traffic. It was always a relief to get out of the college precincts. At least, some consolation, it was an exercise neither he nor Eleanor would need to repeat by the end of the month, but, he reflected, ruefully, it also heralded the start of a new era, the launch of Jo into another phase. Oh well, we can't stop fledglings flying.

He reached the showrooms, tucking the Jaguar into its accustomed place in the corner of the car park. Sometimes it attracted some addicts to the marque, and gave him a chance to open conversations with potential customers. He collected his jacket from the back seat, carefully locked the car and went into the showroom and to his desk with an optimistic view of the day ahead.

* * *

Catching up with her classmates, Jo was safe from predatory comments from that group of lads. Three girls together were more than a match for the boys, whose attention, fortunately, was then taken by that leggy blonde from year twelve, who somehow just managed to keep her knickers out of sight. Betty and Tricia were good mates, and though Trish had a steady boyfriend, she was sensible about it. Betty, akin to Jo, looked disparagingly on the college lot, having been rather taken with a guy from her mother's office. Crazy, she knew, but he *was* rather sweet. He'd picked her up when she'd tripped and fallen over the waste bin next to her mother's desk on her last visit to the office. Smiled at her, and she'd melted. *Lovely!*

"Did I get an invite to see your mum's garden, Jo?" was Betty's first greeting. It was very much top of her agenda. Her sights were set on becoming a landscape gardener, first step to getting onto a television show. Her role model had long brown hair, just like hers, and those high eyebrows and oval face. She didn't quite see herself in grey trousers though. She was more the jeans and welly boots type. Her stepmother was going to help, though maybe she didn't know it yet, by getting her into the magazine. Betty was a very determined girl, and would happily use any opportunity to further her desire.

"Provided you're okay to help shift groceries, Bet. After college, supermarket run, then home for tea and buns and Mums's guided tour. You'll have to get a lift home, though." Jo tucked her arm into Betty's, and turned to Trish. "Do you want to inspect the dahlias too?"

Trish was not a garden girl nor really an outdoor one. True, she had a down to earth approach to life, which is why the three got on so well together, but she was into the hotel trade. Being a manager of the Hilton or some such was her ambition, albeit she had a long way to go, but doing bar work in her local pub was, in her view, a step in the right direction. The boyfriend also worked in the pub, and Friday nights they were on together. She had that tingling feeling at the prospect.

"No thanks, Jo. Not my scene." Then she had a thought. "You're having the village do next weekend, aren't you? Barbecue or summat? Will your mum want a hand with the catering? Reckon I could spare a few hours on Saturday. Be good experience. Yeah, I quite fancy *that*. Ask her, will you?"

Betty, not to be outdone, had to volunteer as well. Jo was pleasantly surprised, and rather taken with the idea of having her friends at the barbecue. She was sure Mums would jump at the offers, and said so. They shook hands on the deal, then split up for their first periods of the day, the last before the inevitable exams. Jo's was her History session, passing uneventfully, with no worries from her tutor about her getting a moderately good grade, then the free period when she could go in search of her Art lecturer.

Old Petersen, as he was affectionately known, wasn't really all that old, but had turned grey early and didn't get his hair cut all that often. A crumpled appearance, often in a tatty sweatshirt, a lined face, little goatee beard and bushy eyebrows, the epitome of an artist. A good one, too, a talented landscape painter; oddly he had taken to endeavouring to instil rudiments of art into recalcitrant teenagers. Jo was a favourite pupil of his, not only being an attractive person, both in looks and personality; she had that knack of putting onto paper what appealed to the eye. Technically, still had a way to go, but she was heading in the right direction. Flair – that's what she had. Flair.

He was musing about what he was going to do next month. He rather fancied Picardy, somewhere warm and sunny, and he'd do some modernistic stuff, bright colours and twirly. He hadn't actually got her in mind, but when the door to his extremely untidy and grubby little office was knocked on and then opened, to reveal a tallish redhead with that slightly haughty expression and lovely curling eyelashes above the aquiline nose, pert yet full lipped mouth, dimpled chin, he automatically had her dressed in a full bloused, full skirted French peasant dress. The artist in him sometimes got the better of his common sense.

"Come in, come in! Jocelyn – dear girl – want to spend a week in Normandy? I've decided to go and do some Van Gogh – I need a peasant girl who speaks English." Leaning back on the rickety stool he refused to let the Health & Safety wallah remove, his bright blue piercing eyes ran an appraising eye over the rest of her. "Get rid of that college kit and you'd be a sensation. In the right dress, I mean," he added, hastily, realising all too late the implications. Well, it was nearly the end of term and he was allowed moderate artistic liberties. "What brings the delightful Jo to my door on this febrile Friday? You are aware, like myself, that my flights are fanciful? Not that your company would not be a delightful addition to the temptations of pastiche and Pernod. But enough. You want something?" He brought the stool teetering back to a semblance of stability, and waved a hand to the other, almost equally unstable, armchair that was firmly labelled 'Petersen's Property'. "A seat, dear Jo. Take a seat. Before the establishment removes it. It has character, you know."

It was clear Petersen was in good form. Jo had not the slightest intent of taking offence from any of his remarks, quite the contrary; he had a manner she found refreshingly honest and flattering.

Settling herself gingerly into the armchair, aware it could collapse under her at any moment, she hesitated, looking at her hands, twisting them together, and brushing her skirt down over her knees in a subconscious gesture. Petersen, student of human nature as well as form, anticipated her.

"You want to take up Art."

The bald statement made her look up, astonished.

"How did you guess, Mr Petersen? I mean, I haven't really been *that* keen, have I? And I'm not all that good," she paused, twisted her hands again, looked at her lap, before blurting out "Except…" and she stopped again.

"Except?" He spoke quietly. She was nervous and he

mentally kicked himself; potentially he might have destroyed her need to talk to him, frightening the timid bird away from its nest. "Jo, you've done something you like, haven't you? Something to cling onto, in this god-forsaken world? Can I see? You've not brought anything. What's the catch?"

Now she'd come this far, she had to go on, without having really understood how difficult this was going to be. What would he think if she turned tail and ran, which she was minded to do? She gulped. It wasn't like her to refuse at the first fence. Petersen, turning half round on his stool and nearly tipping it over, managed to reach the tatty paper bag of jelly babies he lived on in between meals. He liked the colours and the ability to crunch the head off. He named each one before he bit, hoping one day persistence would see the end of bloody politicians. Especially ones who thought they were God's gift to culture. He rummaged in the bag and found the last red one, bit savagely at the head and mouthed something that sounded like 'Hair!' before offering the bag to Jo.

She had to smile. Her smile made her mouth crinkle up and her cheeks dimple. Petersen's eyebrows lifted a trifle in an unspoken query. He'd love to have a go at putting her in a landscape composition, sort of Reynoldesque. She took a sticky sweet, but didn't eat it.

"I did a self-portrait. Last night. I used the charcoal sticks you gave me. Mums and Pa think it's not bad. Thing is, I did it without thinking, and I was in the mood, and the light was right, and I'd not done it before, and it worked. Least I think it worked. And so I *feel* happy about it, and..." she tailed off, and he thought she *could* be blushing. Redheads weren't supposed to blush, but there *was* a tinge of colour.

"And you mean to say you didn't bring it to show me? Well, that takes the biscuit, coming here, chatting about a momentous change in your lifestyle, and not actually *showing* me the earth shattering creation that's caused this cataclysmic conference!" Jo, taken aback at the pseudo fierce tone of voice, tucked her head into her neck, before realising he was being sort of funny, Petersen style. She grinned at him, with the flooding back of her courage. She'd told him, and he'd said he wanted to see her sketch. So that was all right.

"It's charcoal, Mr Petersen."

"Oh, yes. So you said. Well, well done, girl. Yes. Of course. Here, you'll need this." He slid off the stool that fell over as he got up, but was ignored as he crossed the room to the shelf that was so chock-a-block with tins, tubes and pots the slightest tremor would have sent the lot cascading onto the cork floor. With amazing dexterity he removed an aerosol can without a label and gave it to her.

"Spray gently, foot away, all over. Don't sniff it; else you'll be drawing psychedelic monsters all night. Don't smoke either, or you'll be decorating the wall, rather bloodily. Use gently. As if you're putting your make-up on. Not that *you* need any, thank the Lord. Now go." He waved an arm, and then stopped. "Oh, one moment. When do I get to see this lifestyle change material?" She could see that behind the banter he was serious.

"Come to Mum's village barbecue next Saturday. Not tomorrow, next week. The Old Vicarage, Tinsfield." She was sure Mums wouldn't mind, but she'd better tell Pa not to take him seriously. 'Do you think I could be an artist?' That, really, was all she'd come to ask, but somehow it didn't seem all that important now. Almost rhetorical.

"The Old Vicarage, Tinsfield. I shall make it my most important engagement, young lady. *Then* I may consider the question. Now, if I might excuse you, for I am required by the thirteenth year. Unlucky for some." He smiled at her, offered her his hand to extricate her from the depths of his cushion clad armchair. Jo took it, and was heaved unceremoniously upwards. He stepped back, and let her go; as the door closed behind her he wiped his brow, said "Phew," and shook his head. What teaching did for you!

* * *

Jo, in a curiously similar gesture, wiped her forehead, feeling as though she'd perspired. Why had that conversation, exchange of banter, been so draining? Petersen himself, as a male, didn't bother her or give her any cause for concern whatsoever. He was so much a character, with his odd little beard. Taking a couple of deep breaths, she walked on down the corridor and on towards the next class, the only one of the day when she knew she'd have to concentrate, so thoughts of Art and artists had to go to the back of her mind for a while.

* * *

Her last lecture, such as it was, came as an anti-climax; she was reprimanded not once but three times for yawning. At the end, the young lecturer, a spotty, scruffy guy with an odd northern accent, swept up his notes and disappeared without saying 'good luck in the exams' which most of the others had. She saw Mandy thumb her nose at him, and giggled. Her feelings too, but it wasn't in her nature. She just pulled at an itchy bra strap and heaved a sigh of relief. The only two lads in the class watched her; one of them, Mark, grinned as she caught his eye, and pretended he hadn't seen her put her hand in her blouse. He was all right. The other, Claude, was a wimp anyway. Three minutes later, and she'd found Betty, propped up against the main noticeboard, clutching the briefcase she used as a school bag in both hands, looking faintly bored.

"Taken your time, Jo. What kept you? Exchanging pleasantries with Robin? I escaped early; Miss Scofield had a headache so she let us go. Any excuse!" She pushed herself away from the wall with her shoulders, tucked her case under one arm, and took Jo's with the other.

"Tea and buns, you said? I'm famished!"

"Not until we've been shopping, Betty. Mums won't feed either of us 'till we've earnt our keep. You love pushing trolleys about, don't you?" The two girls were of the same height, and though Betty was of thicker build, they were well matched.

"Brunette and Redhead!" came a voice. "Best of luck next week!" The Head of Year, uncharacteristically, called at them as they passed her office door.

"Thanks, Mrs Summers!" The girls replied in unison.

"That was rather nice of her!" Jo was surprised.

Betty revealed she'd spoken to her earlier, and in the course of conversation, mentioned she and Tricia were going to help at the Tinsfield village barbecue, whereupon Mrs Summers had become quite pally. "She lives just outside your village, Jo, didn't you know? She said she might turn up."

Jo groaned. That's all she'd need. Petersen, now Mrs Summers. Pa would never forgive her. It had all the makings of a full-blown college reunion, and she was about to up skittle the applecart with a change of Uni course. Oh well, couldn't be helped. Mums and Pa had still to agree, of course, but Petersen would convince Pa, she was sure, but only if he in turn was convinced. The two girls steered their way through the milling throng of the younger children waiting for parents and buses, round the corner towards the post box, and there, true to promise, was the little yellow-green car. Jocelyn's mother caught sight of them, and waved. Eleanor hadn't actually been waiting long, managing to get a parking slot before the younger mums arrived in sundry variations on the four-wheel drive theme.

"Hi there! Betty, isn't it? Jo told you we're doing the shopping run first, is that all right?"

"Hello, Mrs Danielleson. Thank you for letting me come and see your garden. I've heard so much about it from Jo. It's very good of you!" Betty, always very polite, had a winsome smile. Eleanor took to her, straight away. Perhaps it was all part of being mutual gardeners.

"Please, Betty, call me Eleanor. You can't call me 'Mums', but Mrs D is far too starchy. You can call Jo's father Mr D if you like; you certainly can't really call him David in case someone gets the wrong idea. Hop in. We're only going up to Asda. Jo, dear, let Betty get in the front. Good job the weather's held, though a drop of rain wouldn't hurt. Everybody in?"

Eleanor took off, at her usual break-neck speed. In the jaunt round the supermarket the two girls acted as gophers, Eleanor going down her list, "One of those, two, no make it three; special offer, oh goody, let's stock up. No, Jo, I don't think so. Too fattening – yes, we'll have that instead. Your father likes those; we've run out, better have a couple more.

Betty, do you have trouble with your mother when you go shopping?"

Betty raised her eyebrows at Jo, in mock horror. "Most of our groceries are delivered, Mrs D. My father likes us to shop on-line. But it is quite fun, isn't it?"

"Fun – oh yes, I suppose so. I wouldn't want to sit in front of a computer screen buying groceries. Far too modern. I might buy the wrong things, or too many or not enough. While I've got legs... oh – we'll try those. Pop a couple in the basket, Jo, dear. There, I think we're nearly done. Find a till, Betty, there's a good girl, hold these 'till we catch up." Eleanor was quite adept at ensuring a quick get-a-way by putting any of her shopping accomplices in a till queue in advance; all they had to do was keep dropping back one until the main trolley arrived.

At last, the expedition reached its climax, the laden trolley pushed out to the car and emptied variously into seats, boot and leg spaces. They all squeezed in and returned home in near record time. The gravel spun under the braking as Eleanor shot into the drive, and she looked at her watch.

"Not bad. Fifteen minutes. Not quite the world record, but it'll do. Sorry, Betty, hope you don't mind my driving. Mr D hates it, so I never get to drive the Jaguar." She had learnt very early on she wasn't to call it a 'Jag', far too common. Betty extricated herself from bags of sugar, rolls of biscuits and several jars of olives, vowing to herself that she'd be rather more circumspect in arranging her visits to the Old Vicarage. She was relieved in knowing *her* stepmother would collect her when she texted her to say she was ready. Jo was passing things to her mother, rather like a human conveyor belt, and Betty, intelligently, joined in to help empty the car in quick time.

"Now, girls. Tea, I think, and do you prefer buttered scones, toasted teacake or biscuits? There's some Jaffa cakes – or maybe chocolate digestives?" The questions hung in the air, but Betty chose.

"Buttered scones sound home-made, Mrs D. May I have my tea black?"

"Certainly dear. Very good. And, yes, the scones are all my own work – aren't they, Jo?"

Jo had taken refuge in her favourite basket chair, a trifle selfishly, but Betty was seemingly quite happy to perch on a stool. Eleanor busied herself with the kettle and mugs, reached for her scone tin and shoved it towards Betty.

"Butter's in the fridge, knives, spoons in there. Plates in the cupboard. Jo, stir yourself; she's your guest. Heavens, is that the time? Your father will be home any moment. What sort of garden do you have at home, Betty?" The quick fire conversation was unnerving Betty, and she had to try and recover her wits.

"Bedding plants, lots of short grass, a couple of pampas grass plants, that sort of thing. Dreadfully boring, we have a gardener guy once a week. Mother won't garden, and Daddy's too busy. Jo's description of yours sounded too good to miss, so I'm afraid I rather invited myself. Hope you don't mind. You know I want to be a landscape designer?"

Jo eased herself out of her chair. Designer, now, was it? Well, well, one up from mere gardener.

She wasn't going to be outdone. Opening the cupboard door she fished out three plates, then reached back and got a fourth for her father, due in any time, and spread them round the table.

"I may be changing my Uni degree, Betty. If Mums and Pa agree. I've got rather put off a pure English course. That silly Jeremy chap talks drivel. I couldn't stand that sort of thing for three years."

The tea mugs were filled, passed round, the scones buttered, and for a while the concentration was on the eats. Eleanor, wisely, avoided making any comment, and when Jo looked at her, she just smiled.

Betty was intrigued. "How come, Jo? What do you want to do instead?"

"History of Art. And painting, on the side. I've suddenly discovered that's what I want to do. Saw old Petersen today, Mums. Do you mind if he comes to the village thing – he wants to see my picture; I told him about it." She remembered her fixative spray, tucked in her bag, and rummaged for it.

31

"He gave me this, Mums, to stop the charcoal rubbing. Got to keep it away from heat and flames, it's inflammable. And sniffy."

Betty was more curious. She wasn't really into drawing as such, although she realised she'd have to draw plans and things, but there were computer programmes to help, she knew. "What picture's that, Jo? In charcoal? You never said?"

"It's new. The new *me. Inspired,* I guess. Don't ask me how, but I just did a portrait of me, looking in the mirror, and *I knew* I'd got something."

"Will you show me?"

Jo wasn't sure. She'd didn't want to risk ridicule, nor did she want Betty sounding off back at college next week. She regretted having mentioned it. Eleanor, the clever and intuitive mother she was, sensed the dilemma, and came to the rescue.

"I'm sure she will, Betty, once she's fixed it. But I think we'd better start round the garden, don't you? It's quite large, you know, if you include the rougher bits. Are you tagging along, Jo, or will you look after your father? He shouldn't be long." Her quick thinking saved the day, and Betty's attention was diverted.

"Oh, right. Sorry, yes. I'd like to see whatever you think, Mrs D. My mother will fetch me once I give her a call." She fished her mobile out of her skirt pocket, the latest neat fold-up thing. Jo's was a hand-me-down from her father, adequately plebeian. She didn't text people in quite the same way.

Eleanor never bothered, despite pleas from both husband and daughter. She'd catch up one day, she'd said. Now she eyed Betty's device a little suspiciously. "Does it take pictures?"

"Oh, yes, all the new phones do. Quite a cool thing, really. Can I show you?"

"Not just now, Betty, but thank you. We'll start in the front. Jo?"

"I'll stay, Mums. Less trampling on the grass. Don't mind, Bet?"

"No, no, it's fine. Guess you've seen it all before."

* * *

Betty and Eleanor departed on their tour. Jo relaxed, dropping back into her chair with another scone and the remains of her mugful. The late afternoon was moving into evening, the June day was still warm; the day and the conversation had been tiring, so having swallowed the last crumb with the dregs, she let her head go back and closed her eyes. Flies buzzing, the chirp of the birds, and the slight sighing sound of the breeze in the shrubs outside the kitchen door all contrived to lull her into a doze. A succession of mental images flitted through her resting brain, of curling cartridge paper, her picture, Petersen and his goatee beard, that boy Mark smiling at her, Betty pushing the trolley, her naked knees in front of her vision of the lace pattern of apple tree boughs. How was she going to capture that picture that kept appearing in her brain? Her project? She jerked, a bodily reflex, and woke to the sound of the Jaguar on the gravel.

Her father was as bright and breezy as ever. Flinging a briefcase onto the table, he reached into the depths of the basket chair and pulled the warmth of his lovely daughter onto her feet.

"How's my beautiful girl? Had a good day? Where's your mum?" He gave her cheek a quick kiss, and she hugged him back in return, getting a nose of stale perspiration and a bit of cigarette smoke.

"Pa! Mums won't like you smelling of people! Why don't you go get a shower while she's still showing Betty around our version of Wisley? Betty's mum is coming to collect her later, so you'd better look smart. I'll freshen up the tea and do you some scones if you like, ten minutes?" She pushed him away.

"Sorry, Jo. I detest it when customers smoke around me, but there's not a lot I can do about it, other than avoiding giving them discounts. Shower sounds a good idea. Save the scones, I'll just have tea – presumably we still have to eat? How long's the tour?"

"Oh, depends on how interested Betty is, s'pose. Another half hour? They've been gone a bit. I fell asleep, I think. That

sort of a day. Too warm, really. Go on, before they get back in –
Mums will have heard you come."

Her father picked up his briefcase and vanished upstairs.
Jo put the kettle back on and went prospecting. She found her
mother and Betty deep in discussions about planting regimes
in the long herbaceous border at the far side of the house.

"Mums! Pa's home. How's the tour, Betty?"

"Fabulous! I think your mum's done a super job, Jo – sorry
Mrs D, does that sound a bit patronising?" Betty actually
coloured up, and swung her long brown hair back in a rather
nervous fashion.

"Betty, do call me Eleanor. After all, we're both gardeners,
aren't we? And no, I don't mind being told I've done a good
job. Your father takes it for granted, most of the time, doesn't
he, Jo?"

"Pa's all right! We think she does a super job too, though
we do as well, we're the grass cutting, leaf sweeping, rubbish
removal experts; that's Pa and me. He's having a shower,
Mums, 'cos I told him to. He stank of smoke and sweat. *Not*
nice! When's your mum coming, Betty?"

They moved slowly up the length of the border as they
spoke, coming to the last group of perennials. "Eightish, I
think, straight from her office. It's the last day before the next
mag goes to the printers; she'll either be happy or frustrated.
Hope it's the happy mood; she's horrible when she's
frustrated! Are these phlox, Mrs – er – Eleanor? I *love* phlox.
Such a sexy scent."

Eleanor raised her eyebrows. "Sexy? I hadn't thought of
flowers being sexy!"

Both girls spoke simultaneously. "Of course they are,
Mums!" came from Jo, and "What about roses, Eleanor?" from
Betty. Eleanor laughed.

"Well, yes, I suppose you're right, girls. I shan't be able to
forget your comment, Betty, whenever I see these again!
Anyway, I think we've about covered things. There's just the
orchard, the paddock and the rough area. The orchard's Jo's
favourite place, right Jo?"

Jo did *not* want her retreat discussed, and just gave a non-committal "Hmmm" before diverting their attention to a snail she'd spotted. She pointed at it, and Eleanor seized it in two fingers and hurled it away over the hedge onto the road.

"Not good for my delphiniums," she said. "Okay, Betty? We'll go and find some more tea – or coffee if you prefer it. Or perhaps a cold drink?" The evening was still comfortably warm, and the rising heat from the garden gave the atmosphere a lovely summery smell. The three made their way back down the recently laid random slab paving towards the house. Jo linked her arm with her mother, while Betty was still looking around as they heard the approach of a throaty engined vehicle, and a low-slung sports car appeared up the lane.

"That's mum! She's before time!" Betty glanced at her watch. "It's only just gone seven. She'll be in a good mood then. The mag must have been put to bed early!" She had all the jargon. As the car came to a careful stop, with no skidding on the gravel, Betty waved. An answering wave came from a very elegant woman, headscarf, open necked blouse, extremely pretty from what Eleanor could see. As they approached, she opened her car door to swing herself out, short skirt showing all leg before she stood up.

"*Hellowee!* I'm Felicity. Betty's stepmother. Thanks *so* much for taking the trouble to show her your garden. She's mad about gardens, aren't you, darling?" A tall, willowy girl, perhaps in her late thirties; as she took her headscarf off and shook her hair free it cascaded out in a flowing blonde shimmer. Jo was fascinated. Although she'd seen Betty's mum before, she wouldn't have linked the two of them. Betty was so very different, and now she knew why. Stepmother! She just hadn't taken it on board. Eleanor, generally so very at ease with people, felt frumpish and a trifle off balance, none the less, she put out a hand, to have it touched rather than shaken. A very soft touch, too.

"Pleased to meet you, er, Felicity. Eleanor. Jo's Mum. The gardener, I'm afraid. Thank you for coming. I hope Betty's enjoyed her visit. We were going in to have drinks, have you time to stay? Please? Then you can meet my husband, David.

Has the magazine – er – gone to bed happily?"

Felicity laughed, and her face creased in a lovely smile. Suddenly, she seemed normal.

"Thanks for asking! Yes, it has. Everything in place, and I have a good feeling about it. So Betty will have told you that I'm horrid when it doesn't? Do you look at it? I'll arrange for you to have copies if not?"

Eleanor became embarrassed. She hadn't thought to find out what the title was, it was bound to be either 'Country' or 'Perfect' or 'Traditional' something; but Jo hissed at her, whispering the name in her ear, cleverly disguising matters by adding, out loud, "I'm reminding Mums that Pa will be wanting his tea. Sorry," which effectively set the conversation on a new track, about what he did, and how nice it was to live out here, and did Jo think the exams would go well? Betty hung back as the two older women went into the house, and pulled at Jo.

"I think my mum's going to be friends with yours. She doesn't always like people, you know. Something about being an Editor, I think it makes you stuffy. She'll love your dad. She likes rough types."

Jo swung round. "Rough types! Pa's not rough!" Her eyes were wide and angry.

"Whoops – sorry Jo. *Sorry!* I didn't mean rough, I meant…" a pause, then "Manly, then. You know, a proper *man*. Someone who can get on with people, and knows what's what. If you see what I mean." Betty's contriteness mollified Jo, and they followed their elders into the kitchen. Felicity had been introduced to David, and Betty had been right. Her stepmother was standing quite close to him, looking into his eyes, while Eleanor was looking out glasses and wondering if she should offer proper drinks or whether soft drinks or coffee would suffice. Her husband, smelling of shower gel and much the better for it, clean short-sleeved shirt and his summer weight fawn slacks, hair brushed back, was as good as a men's outfitters model. Having this gorgeous blonde haired creature to look at was an unusual Friday evening treat, and he had a job to keep his eyes off her rather too-evident deep cleavage.

She was talking to him, but his mind was asking itself questions it shouldn't, a male's natural inquisitiveness, and it was having an effect.

"...Isn't that right, David?" She'd posed a question, and he hadn't heard her.

"Er, um, sorry, Felicity. What was that again?" Looking over the top of her head, he caught Jo's eye, and moved his eyebrows a fraction. Would she cotton-on? He needed support.

"I feel we should encourage girls to do more practical things, David, they're all far too lazy now-a-days. Can't stand the pace, not like us. Look at your wife. I think she's marvellous, doing all that green-fingered stuff. I should get her in a feature, you know. Just the sort of thing our readers love. Women close to nature. Wonderful background shots here too. Would you mind?" She gave him a hint of a wink. "May I ask her?"

"Er, no, I mean, yes, of course. I'm in no doubt she'd be flattered. Are you sure?"

Eleanor had decided on soft drinks, after all Felicity was driving. She'd got out the glasses and filled a jug of water, while Jo dug some ice out of the freezer and fetched a new bottle of shop lemon squash from the garage store. Betty had collapsed into Jo's basket chair and found Eleanor's 'Gardener's World' magazine.

"Iced lemon, Felicity? David? What about you, Betty?"

It seemed she'd done the right thing. Felicity smiled at her. "Just right, Eleanor, thank you so much. After a warm day, nice to cool off." She took a glass, and sipped. "I'd like to come back and take a better look at your garden again, Eleanor, if I may. And I'd like to bring my garden Features photographer with me. Would you mind? Could be it's just the place for an autumn feature. We're always looking out for *different* places, and this is *so* handy." She was giving Jo an up and down look at the same time, taking in all the elements of Jo's particular beauty. "I think you'd all look marvellous in the photos. And Jocelyn is so *very* photogenic."

Betty, almost ignored by her mother, broke in. "Mother!

Can't you leave the magazine alone for a moment? Jo's my friend, not a model, and Mrs Danielleson has been very good, showing me over her wonderful garden, so don't you think we ought to let them get on with things?" It wasn't that she wanted to necessarily dash off, but she was sensitive to Jo's feelings. "We can always come to the village barbecue next Saturday, if they'd have us?" It was her way of saying she'd love to come back.

So Felicity turned back to Eleanor, eyebrows raised in that quizzical 'Can we?' look, and Eleanor had to say "Of course," while her husband, impressed with Felicity as a decorative item, and the possibility of seeing his two girls in this up-market lifestyle glossy, could only concur. He didn't want to appear too enthusiastic, but it did seem like a good idea. It was left like that, with Felicity sweeping an arm round her daughter and taking her out, sliding into her low-slung car seat with skirt well above her knees. Betty rolled her eyes at Jo, as if to say, 'Mothers!' and then they were gone.

"Phew. What a whirlwind. Eleanor, dear, I think this barbecue thing is going to be some occasion. What other devious social shenanigans are going to go on, I wonder? Some girl, that Felicity; I must say the daughter isn't much like her mother; how did you get on with her?"

Eleanor, with narrowed eyes, scrutinised her husband's expression.

"I saw you looking at her knees. And she was too close to you for comfort. You watch it, Mister. I'm not having her flash her socks at you. Jo, tell your father who else is likely to appear at this do."

Jocelyn had stood the can of fixative aerosol on the side ready to take upstairs, but she reached over for it, and showed it to her father. "I was given this by Mr Petersen today, it's to spray over my portrait to stop the charcoal rubbing any more. I told him about what I'd done, and he wants to see it, so I invited him to come as well. Hope you don't mind. He's a bit eccentric, but a real dear. Wanted to cart me off to Provence or somewhere to act as his model. He does some super landscape oils, real dishy stuff, like Van Gogh. I think he was pulling my leg, but it was a nice gesture. He's like that. Fun, and approachable without being pushy or wanting to look at your tits. You'll like him, Pa."

"Well, that's all right then, if you say I'll like him, then I shall have to do as I'm told!" Her father wasn't too sure about her expressions some times, but had to accept reality. "Just let's hope its fine. Have we contingency plans, Eleanor? The barn's not *that* big!" Part of what they had taken on with the house, garden and estate was an old wooden barn that they'd done absolutely nothing with other than remove an accumulation of rubbish. It stood empty, apart from housing a few mice and the summer invasion of swallows. They hadn't even looked at another old shed up in a far corner of the orchard.

"Weelll," she replied, slowly, "The W.I. lot who are doing the catering *did* say they would locate to the village hall if it poured with rain, but that place gives me the creeps. High time it was knocked down and we got a new one. The barn *would* take about fifty or so. Maybe we should have another look at it?"

"Not today," David said, firmly. "I gave up my scones in favour of supper, so what's to cook?"

* * *

After they had eaten, David being very good at impromptu meals and Eleanor only too happy to share the kitchen, Jocelyn excused herself and went upstairs with her can of fixative. She laid her portrait out on the part of the bare wooden floor of her room not covered in her lovely deep pile rugs, weighted the corners down with a couple of dirty mugs she really should have taken back downstairs, a small heavy book on Greek mythology, and the heel end of one of her walking boots. Then she opened the window wide, left the bedroom door open, took aim at the paper and tentatively pushed the button. The first squirt missed and she had to hastily mop the floorboards before the lacquer dissolved, but then she got the hang of it, spraying carefully across and back, until she'd covered every inch. At first, she wasn't sure if she hadn't ruined it, because it turned a sort of grey yellow colour, before realising it was just wet spray and it didn't take long before it dried back to the original cartridge paper colour. It certainly smelt, and she had to hang out the window and take deep breaths to clear her lungs. Old Petersen hadn't been joking. Perhaps she should have done it outside, but the breeze would have taken the spray away. Too late, but the job was done. She cleared away the things she'd used as weights, and taking the picture back to the window, examined it critically. It was funny, looking at yourself, she thought, especially when it's all your own work. At least it didn't curl up quite so much. She tried rolling it very carefully the opposite way that made it stay really quite flat. Good. Propped up against her mirror, it was fine. Time to get some fresh air. She pulled at her zip, dropped her college skirt and pulled off her blouse, then her bra, wretched thing; stretched her arms wide and up, then pulled her shoulders back. Freedom! She found an old gingham skirt and top that had seen better days and squeezed into them, but then, all she was going to do was see what Mums might like her to do outside until bedtime. She picked up the two dirty mugs and waltzed downstairs. Her father was immersed in the television, and she was sure he'd fall asleep. She didn't disturb him; dumped the mugs on the draining board, and went in search of her mother.

* * *

Jocelyn found her on her kneeler, systematically weeding the long herbaceous border near the gorgeous scented phlox that Betty said smelt sexy. Perhaps they did, she thought. Her mother looked up, then struggled to her feet, putting a hand to her waist and rubbing.

"I'm getting stiff. This border looked a disgrace, so I thought I'd get on top of it while I remembered. You look cool, darling. How's the picture?"

"Sprayed. I still like it."

"So you should, dear. It's good. What are you going to do next?"

"Would you sit for me, Mums? Pa might like a portrait of you."

Eleanor laughed. "Jo, I'm sure your father sees enough of me! But if you want me to, well, of course. When and where? How long will it take?"

"Don't know, Mums, how long it will take. Mine only took me half an hour. In the garden? When the light's right. Perhaps on Sunday? Pa and I are going walking tomorrow, aren't we?"

"I should think you could, provided the weather holds, but I don't want you up on the Plain if it turns thundery, which it might." Indeed, the evening had become sultry, and with a stretch of imagination there could be a line of clouds on the southern horizon. "There, that looks better. It'll do. Collect those weed piles for me, Jo, and compost them. I'll put the kneeler and my fork away. Time for a drink. What's your father doing?"

"Watching telly, or snoozing. He was rather taken with Betty's mum, wasn't he? She's quite pretty, in a scary sort of way. Thanks for showing Bet round, Mums, much better than me trying to explain things."

Eleanor coughed. She'd noticed, of course, but wasn't reassured by Jo's description of Felicity as 'scary.' She picked up her kneeler, kicked a bit of soil back into the border, and turned back to her daughter. "What do you mean by 'scary', Jo?"

"Short skirt and low blouse, I guess. Man traps?"

"Man traps! I like it!" She laughed. "What do you know about man traps, daughter of mine? You're only seventeen!"

"Nearly eighteen, Mums. It's what the girls at college call them. *Some* of them are awful, as though that's all they want, they don't even..." She broke off, not really wanting to tell her Mums what they did and didn't wear, because she knew she liked to be free of straps herself, but not to attract men, just because it felt better.

"Okay, Jo. I get your drift. Just let's keep your father out of harm's way, shall we? We don't want him straying. Let's get rid of those weeds. I'm ready for a drink."

Jo picked up one heap, dumped it onto another, and

managed to collect most of it to stagger across the lawn to the compost heap behind the laurels. Her mother tucked the fork and the kneeler into the little tool shed alongside, and the pair made their way indoors.

* * *

David was indeed snoozing away happily, but woke with a start and a grunt when Eleanor poked him.

"Hoi, you. You sleep in bed, not down here! Want a drink? I'm having a long port and lemon. *I've* been working! Jo wants to do my portrait now – any ideas?" Their daughter was making her own concoction of lime and lemon with a slurp of gin, but was all ears. Her father spoke flippantly, without thinking.

"In the nude, in the bath," before realising how silly it sounded. "Sorreee. Obviously in the garden, I would have thought. Deckchair, straw hat, that sort of thing? It's up to Jo, really. I'll have a whisky – no, make that a gin and tonic, lots of tonic. Thanks."

Jo made her father's drink, dunked some ice in it from the tray she'd brought from the kitchen, then carried on making her mother's. Eleanor collapsed into another of the big armchairs, grateful for her daughter's ministrations.

"Thank you, Jocelyn. Are you going to sit for a minute?"

Being called by her full name was a prelude to Some Serious Statements, so with a small degree of concern she perched on the arm of the settee, nursing her tall tumbler.

"Are you *really* keen on this art thing, Jo? You have hopped around a bit, you know, so you can't expect us to take you *too* seriously unless you can be convincing. And what sort of income do you get from being an artist? We can't support you forever, much as we love you. Don't get me wrong, though, we *will* support you as much as we can, whatever you do. But we do want you to feel happy about things, and not just because you think it's what we want. So you see our dilemma?"

Her long legs swinging, her hair awry, her parents

42

watching her as if she was some sort of alien object, Jo's mind was vacillating about like a frightened bird hopping around indoors where it knew it was trapped. She loved her parents dearly, didn't want to upset them, make them anxious, even, on her behalf, but the more she'd thought about things, the more difficult it was to continue on the smooth path to a steady degree, maybe a boring job in some distant office, fighting off voracious blokes. Yes, it would be easy to go along with; no, it wouldn't make her happy. Yes, her parents might think it was the 'thing to do'; no, *they* might get unhappy if it all went pear-shaped. She might be good at Uni; she might find it was just not her. She might even find she wasn't all that good an artist, that what she'd done was lucky, so she'd be better off going with the flow. She got off the chair, walked to the window, stared across the lawn, watched the remnants of the sun veiled in gathering clouds turn the garden deep pink; the sky was beautiful, shot with gold and red streaks of light. It was gorgeous! Could she capture it in paint?

"Pa, Mums, I *don't* know!" Jo's voice was high-pitched, tremulous. She was close to tears, with the beauty of the picture seen through the window welling up inside her, she wanted to capture the mood and the light and her feelings and she *couldn't!* What she meant was she didn't know how to put what she was seeing onto paper or canvas or whatever; her parents thought she couldn't decide what course to take.

"Okay, darling, let's leave it for a day or two. See what tomorrow brings, eh? Time you were in bed." Her father climbed out of his chair and went to the window, putting his arm around her. "Some sunset, that. Let's hope it's a shepherd's delight day tomorrow." He gave her a little squeeze. "Love you."

Jocelyn ducked out from under her father's arm, and ran out of the room, took the stairs two at a time, shut the bedroom door with a bang in her haste. The sun's last few moments above the hill and she might *just* catch it, at least the feel of it. Turning to find her large sketch pad, flinging her blouse off her shoulders, grabbing a soft pencil, sketching in the tree line, the best of the shapes of the clouds, a few squiggles for the shrubs, got her left arm out of her sleeve, desperate in her haste to at least *try* to put *something* down. The rosy glow was spreading, even as the light was failing, and the awesomeness of the effect was massive! Would she, could she, get the colour? A few cryptic notes on the edge. Yellow, straw, *gold!* Pink, rosy, that's darker. Purple? Drat this blouse. I can't draw like this. She dropped her pencil, got her arm out of the other sleeve and flung the blouse onto the bed. Crayons – where did I put those crayons? Quick, oh, heavens, *there they are!* She couldn't, the light had gone. *Damn, damn, damn!*

Eleanor and David had been put off balance by her precipitate flight from the room, David especially. Eleanor was more matter of fact about it. They both thought they had upset her by bringing the matter up for discussion, unaware of Jo's sudden inspiration from the dramatic sunset. David had turned back to his wife, eyebrows raised. Eleanor shook her head, mouthed "leave it". They'd waited a few moments, heard brief movements above, and then once silence descended, crept upstairs.

Jo did hear them though, poised with hands flat on the windowsill, catching every last subtle change of the ebbing twilight. She couldn't draw, or colour in, but she could endeavour to memorise the magic effect. At last all light had gone, and she shivered. Why she couldn't draw with her arms covered she didn't know, but there it was. The sheet of paper lay on the pad, a mass of lines. Would it come good? She couldn't do any more, not tonight. She slid her things off, dived into bed just as she was, rolled onto her side and was asleep in seconds.

TWO

It was raining, a steady, mid-summer grey, wetting drizzle of a rain, giving the whole garden that sodden drippy feel, with heavy drops from the trees erratically plopping onto shrubs, and paths, and Jocelyn; as she splashed barefoot through little puddles, ducked under the water laden branches of the buddleia and up towards *her* orchard.

She'd woken early, the grey light filtering through her window; listening, struggling to get her head round the unaccustomed background noise. It hadn't rained for weeks, certainly the flowerbeds and the lawn would be all the better for it, and the birdsong above the purling of the wetness welcoming.

"Lots to do!" she'd had said out loud, and flung back the single sheet, to sit up, a tousled haired slightly smelly chunk of feminity. Padded to the window, peered out at the greyness. There was her last night's effort, lying forlorn on the chair. She wrinkled her nose at it; not in the mood. Later. It was only six o'clock.

Caught a whiff of sweaty armpit, decided she *must* shower. "I'd wake Mums and Pa" she'd thought; on impulse, daringly, she'd gone downstairs, quietly, not a stitch on, to let herself out the back door. Stood, hesitantly, on the doorstep, and then ran for the cover of the shrubbery. Completely naked, the wet catching the fine hairs on her thighs and arms, running off her hair into rivulets down her back, gone up through the soaked wetness of the garden.

There was a forgotten old shed in the orchard, tucked away, abandoned to the elements. Curious they'd never seen fit to clear it out; but then, there was always too much else to do. Having picked her way through the profusion of too-enthusiastic weeds, scrupulously avoiding the nettles, that was where she now found herself, stupidly in her nothings, shaking the rain off her hair, using her hands to squeegee the wet from her limbs and bottom. She shivered. "I'm mad," she said out loud, and chuckled. "I must be, I'm talking to myself." Inside the creaking door, a fair amount of debris, old boxes, a rickety table, a scruffy broken armchair, lots of cobwebs. "Yuck!"

Should get this place cleaned up a bit, as a refuge, she thought, and encouraged by the brainwave, pulled at a few boxes to get some idea of what had been dumped up here. One was quite heavy, and opening the flap found musty fabric; it seemed like old clothes. With finger and thumb, treating the contents as though they were contaminated, she pulled out the top item. It looked like a waistcoat. She dropped it on the floor, and picked out the next one. Serge grey, a heavy skirt, with a banded top. Then a scrumpled chunk of satiny pink material, which turned out to be a dress. "This must have been here for *ages!*" Intrigued now, forgetting her state of undress and dampness, she pulled at the white lacy next piece. Well, it had been white, but now a sort of dingy cream. Shaking it out to loosen the folds, well away from herself, she examined it, head on one side. It *looked* like either a petticoat, or maybe a nightdress. She could see it was well made, and had some lovely bits of lace round the neck and sleeves. This she laid on the old chair, and reached down for the next. A rough old shirt thing, dumped onto the pile on the floor. Then another, blue and grey stripes. "How weird!" Finally, at the bottom, a bundle. She had to use two hands to lift it out, shaking the box loose, so it dropped back and tipped over. Ignoring it, she laid this bundle on the old dust covered table to unravel. A dark grey coarse satin, the folds were age stiff, but inside, a collection of what looked like underclothes, girls, well, women's anyway. A sort of top, with straps. Then a half-length skirty piece, now that *was* nice! Lastly, two panty things, with wide legs and rather long. Fascinating! Where on earth had these come from, and why hadn't they unearthed them before? She shivered again, her concentration on the box diminished.

She had had a silly notion of running round the orchard for a sort of naturalistic shower; now all she wanted to do was get back to the house and discover what Mums thought about these things. It must be nearly seven, or even later. She hadn't intended to be out this long. The rain had eased, but, and this was the problem, folk may be around and she didn't fancy comments being made about Lady Godiva or whatever. A nude eighteen-year-old rampaging around at seven in the morning might make the Sunday papers, and that *would* make Pa cross. On inspiration, she picked up the lacey nightdress thing, and considered. Oh, well, I'm going to have a *proper* shower anyway. She held it against herself, checked the size. It might fit? Carefully opening the hemline, she ran her arms up through it, shovelling it onto her forearms.

The material felt quite smooth and silky, smelt rather musty but that was all. Taking a deep breath, she lifted it over her head, letting the silk run down her body. Gently she tugged the neckline over the fullness of her bust, where it sat, lacey edged, in a vaguely eighteenth-century *décolletage*. The hemline reached to just above her knees, after she'd straightened out the skirt bit, and smoothed it over her hips, where it was a bit stretched. Well, her bottom was fuller than an eighteenth-century girl's would have been, *if* it were that old. Maybe it wasn't, else the fabric would have split. She shook her damp hair out, and held her breath for an instant, before peering out, seeing nothing but dripping trees and soggy grass, and making a run for it.

Only Reg, the postman, saw the fleeting vision of a ghostly clad girl dash across the paddock, but he was a broad minded, gentle chap with a lot of time for Jocelyn, so he grinned to himself and cycled on up the lane.

Jo's mother was down, and in the kitchen, producing scrambled egg. Not realising her daughter had gone out, not having tried the back door; she nearly dropped the basin on the floor when the vision of white appeared.

"Good gracious, girl, what on earth are you wearing, and where *have* you been?"

Jo dropped into her basket chair.

"Mums. That old shed, in the orchard, that we've never bothered with? There's loads of old rubbish in there, and a box full of old clothes, and I found this. Rather nice, isn't it?" She picked herself up, and did a twirl.

"Hmmm. You went up there starkers? In the rain? You're daft, girl. Go and take that thing off and get yourself showered. Then you can tell me what else you've found. Oh, and poke your father. It's time he was down if you're going out, though with the change in the weather it's not going to be very nice, is it?"

Jocelyn, never one for standing on ceremony, pulled the petticoat or whatever it was carefully over her head, and dropped it on a chair.

"Do you think it'll wash okay, Mums? It seems to fit, doesn't it? Might be fun to wear!"

Her mother wasn't overly sure. They'd have to look at the other items now; certainly that hovel of a place was overdue for a sort-out. Project for another day.

"No modesty, you. Go on upstairs. Breakfast in ten minutes. And don't forget to get your father up!"

Jocelyn duly took herself upstairs, treated herself to a luxurious shower, washed her hair, thoroughly towelled herself down, found suitable things to wear for a energetic walk over the Plain, and was just about to launch herself downstairs again when she remembered, she had to get her father up.

"Pa! Lazy bones! Mums' got breakfast ready – I've been up since before seven!" She'd opened the door, her father still apparently comatose. As she approached the bed, bent on poking him as suggested, he suddenly flung the bedclothes over her, wrestling her to the floor.

"Hoi! Rotter!" A muffled voice as she struggled up. "You've been waiting for me, haven't you!"

Her father let her up, chuckling. Playing games with his beloved daughter at weekends, when time did allow, was one of his delights. Going out with her on a hike across some of the nicest country in Wiltshire was another.

"Yep. Took your time. You've been out?"

"I have. Fancied taking an outdoor shower, but got sidetracked. The tumbledown shed? In the orchard – the one we've been going to tear to bits for ages? Well, I took refuge in there and found all sorts of things. Shall we have a go at it tomorrow?" Jo stood back and let her father dress. He'd promised himself his shower after they got back from their hike.

"Why not? Provided we keep your mother happy with what she wants sorting in the garden. This time next week, you know!" He combed his hair, grinning at her. "You didn't go out starkers, did you? One of these days someone will catch you, and then what?"

Jocelyn shrugged. "I'm no different to anyone else. It's up to them. Come on, Pa. I'm hungry, and Mums said ten minutes!"

* * *

After their companionable breakfast, the rain had ceased; the sun was breaking through the clouds to give the garden that wonderful streaked light that Jo so loved. She hadn't forgotten the aborted attempt to capture last night's incredible sunset, promising herself time to attempt to colourise her sketching. Here was another picture she'd have to try.

"Pa. I'm just going to get my sketch pad. Won't be a tick." They were all but ready to set out, a couple of sandwiches and a chocolate bar apiece, mobile phone fully charged, a route mapped out, the phone call to the Range Office to check the route was clear of any army activity, when Jo decided to take her pad with her. Just to try out a few ideas, nothing serious. Her father raised his eyebrows at Eleanor. She shrugged. Jo skipped upstairs, and her mother could then make her comments to her husband.

"She's trying to convince us, David. We'll just have to go along with this. Be patient. Maybe this chap Petersen will shed some light on her capabilities next Saturday. I mean, if he says she's good, then what do we do?"

"As you say, go along with it. I'm not going to force her

into something she doesn't want to do. Last night's discussion didn't get us very far, did it?"

Jocelyn had put her pad into her largest pocket, and stuffed a few pencils in as well. It took them a few minutes to lace on their walking boots and don waterproofs. Eleanor fussed round them, sure that it was foolish to undertake a hike after the overnight rain, but nevertheless they set off, taking the lane at the side of the estate, and up towards the rough ground. The terrain they had thought to traverse was not unfamiliar, though not known to many other than the locals. Perfectly safe under normal conditions, too, that was the beauty of the route. David liked to have a challenging piece of country, Jo happy to be with her father, and more than competent.

The first part was straightforward, taking the lane that gave access to the open ground. The sycamores that gave the lane a cosy tunnel-like feel were still dripping, the track sculptured with the effect of rivulets running through the fine silt covering, for all the world as though a tide had swept in and out. Footprints squelched into the softness destroyed the patterning; their passage disturbed the blackbirds and the unseen field mice had rustled away. The gate, a tired lean-away from its hinges, was unusually, unlatched, or rather the length of old string that kept the latch in place had been untied. Easing themselves through the gap, avoiding the ragged ends of barbed wire and the flailing overreach of blackthorn, they were now out into the pasture. An energetic haul up the lane, climbing away from the village below. Without words they paused to reflect on the view behind; house roofs merging with tree canopy, the ribbon of the Salisbury road and the march of overhead power lines and the mistiness of distant farmland. David glanced at his daughter. She grinned, reached for his hand.

"Come on, Pa. You're not out of puff, are you?"

He was just getting his second wind. Sitting behind a desk in the showroom all week wasn't conducive to maintaining his ideal condition of fitness. Maybe he should get out more often.

"Not really, Jo. It's nice to be out, though. Thanks for inviting me. Press on?"

"Uh huh – shall we do the fenceline then swing over towards the pines? I like that bit."

Tramping steadily on, keeping the Range boundary to their left, they passed one of the flagpoles where on live-firing days the Range wardens flew red warning flags. Today the halyards were tied neatly round the pole, no flag in sight. A vehicle track swung away across the grass towards the distant observation post, a flat roofed concrete mass crouching into the contour. The ground was drying nicely, a slight breeze giving accent to the clouds breaking and moving away to the east. The long grass, white topped, shimmering pale green and gold, rippled away in the drying breeze. A hesitant sun re-appeared, and they could see cloud shadows racing away over the ruffling grass. The distant dark green mass of pines marked the edge of the flatter ground and where the next valley began. Far over, the other edge of the grassland, a few figures emerged from nowhere and they could just see rucksacks, helmets.

"Weekend soldiers. Bet they're soaked. Camped out all night, I shouldn't wonder. Whatever turns you on. Not my scene."

"Pa! Where's your sense of adventure! You'd love it! I wouldn't mind. Perhaps I should volunteer as a part-time soldier. That would keep me out of Mums's hair!"

"Jocelyn! You're a girl, and your mother would go spare if she thought you wanted to do something silly like prancing about in uniform at weekends! Don't be daft!"

Jo laughed. "Only pulling your leg, Pa. And I know I'm a girl, fortunately. Doesn't stop you being a soldier or whatever, but I can't see the army being happy about someone who has a liking for wandering about without their kit on. Look – there's more of them!"

Another small group had suddenly sprung up, and the first group scattered. A few puffs of smoke, and then little cracking sounds like breaking brittle sticks.

"Rifle fire! The Range warden didn't say anything about this! Hope he's got it right. I know they'll be blanks, but even so. Come on, Jo, let's keep going. We'd better stay to the left, I think."

Tramping on, heading west, across ground more uneven to a part where armoured vehicles had previously exercised and some of the terrain evidently subjected to shellfire. They scrambled across some ditches, maybe what had been dugouts, then across a couple of craters, all now well grassed. Both Jo and her father were intelligent enough to know what they were up against, and certainly would not have picked up or even touched anything that looked remotely like ammunition of any sort. Within forty minutes or so the rough ground had given way to smoother grass, the last half mile towards the stand of conifers, the dark green a stark contrast to the overall pale blues and grey greens of the Plain. The country to the north had become clearer, the cloud cover had thinned and it was really getting quite warm. Jo unbuttoned her coat and flung it open; her father had already done so. Looking back, no sign of activity but she was sensible to the fact the group of Territorials could well have gone to ground.

"Reckon we could lunch amongst the trees, Jo, what'd you think? I'm getting quite peckish. Then do we go south again here, or over to the next valley?" The plateau of the Plain broke up into several little valleys at its southern edge, each with a good bit of timber cover, and an interesting route back towards their village, though it might mean a stretch along the road.

"Next one, I think, Pa. I don't fancy too much road. Tell you what, though, we can always swing round after the wood and do that circular bit, across the Down." The Down was a chalky barrow, giving extra height and super views from the top; it would add another mile to the walk, but still well within their anticipated timing.

"Fine. Yes, why not? So long as we get back mid-afternoon, don't want to leave your mother on her own too long, we did promise to give her a hand with the garden, remember."

The grass below the pines was fine and quite dry, the wood producing its own mini atmosphere of calm and with the growing heat of the day, a resinous scent. Jo sniffed.

"Lovely. I always think pinewoods smell nice, don't you, Pa? Park on that fallen one?"

The crumbling remains of a long felled pine had evidently seen quite a few lunches or meal breaks of one sort or another, scuffed areas clear of vegetation and tyre tracks, old and new, in the dried mud; a few pieces of litter, and a scattering of a couple of dozen small brass cartridge cases that had been left.

"Tut tut. I thought they were supposed to clear up behind themselves! Still, if it were for real..." Jo's father pulled his sandwich pack from his capacious waterproof's pocket, and sat down, while she tactfully disappeared behind the largest tree bole to 'make herself comfortable' as her mother would have said. Suitably re-adjusted, as she dug her lunch out of her jacket, she pulled out her sketch pad. So far she'd had no inspiration, but seeing her Pa sitting on the log... with his back to her... a pencil... a few tentative lines, hmmm. Rather good, but can't quite get the perspective... bother this jacket. She put the sketch pad down alongside her lunch, her pencil behind her ear, and took her waterproof jacket off. She was getting too warm anyway. The light jersey top wasn't a bother, and she pushed the sleeves up over her forearms. Her father, conscious she'd been out of sight for ten minutes, turned to look, and saw her, sketch pad now back in hand, evidently concentrating.

"Should have brought my camera, Jo!" he called across. "You look a picture like that!" True, she made a striking figure, auburn hair catching the glint of sun slanting through the trees, bare arms and a firm stance with one knee forward to support the pad.

She frowned; waved an arm at her father as if to say, keep still, and sketched in the background, trees, a few shrubs, the track, a few lines for the horizon, twirls for the few remaining clouds. The log was easy, then another tricky bit, getting proportions right. Concentrating on a bit of shading, crosshatch where the ground came up, a sort of code to allow the memory banks to function as and when she might detail the missing bits she'd have to leave now, managing to get some semblance of what she thought to achieve.

"All done. Thanks, Pa, just a sudden inspiration. Sunlight through the trees and all that." Moving forward to join him on the log, she dumped her pad on the ground and opened up the sandwiches.

"Are they all right? Mums' best ham and tomato?" She bit and chewed, hungry and happy at the same time. Her father picked up the pad, eying her sketch, holding it at arms length. "Here!" She nearly choked. "Not finished yet. Only an idea!" She coughed and spluttered, so David dropped the pad again and patted her back.

"Looks fine to me. You're trying to convince me, my girl, aren't you? You *really* want to ditch English and go for Arts? But can you imagine the problems of supporting yourself just on an artist's occasional comissions? Think, Jo, think. I can see you've got talent, but, how does one *live?*"

"On one's wits, Pa? Quite exciting. Keeps you on your toes. Hey – can you hear that? Sounds like a Hercules. On a Saturday?"

She had become aware of the recognisable drone of the aircraft, a not unfamiliar part of their existence so close to the Plain, now getting steadily louder. They got up and moved out from under the canopy of overhanging branches to get a better view, for despite it being a commonplace event, these lumbering giants of their sky always attracted a degree of strange pleasure. Like big bears, she'd once said. This particular aircraft was fairly high, but on a straight line approaching them. Then, as it was nearly overhead, little tumbling dots of men began to fall from the rear-loading ramp.

"Parachute drop, Pa! Look!" Indeed, the canopies were opening, and ribbed rectangles of olive nylon were swinging through the sky above them, slanting off towards the flatter ground to the south. David was concerned, with no mention made of this activity when he checked with the Range Warden. Had they got it right? Were they meant to drop here? Counting, hand over his eyes against the glare of the sun, about a dozen. The Hercules had gone, dipping down below their sightline towards the eastern side of the Plain. Jocelyn was watching where she thought the men were landing half a mile or more away, one down, two, three, six, all the canopies eddying and crumpling, being folded, already the small contingent were forming up and beginning to move away from them. Her father, watching the fall, tugged at her elbow.

"Jo! Look!" The urgency of his voice made her start. "That chap's off line. His canopy didn't open till now! He's going to hit the trees! Come on!" Indeed, Jo could now see the canopy wavering, the man pulling at his lines, body swinging, but too late. With a rending sound, he was into the upper branches barely a quarter mile away from them. Somehow he must have caught his feet, and with the cords all around, the fabric drifting down, it could be a real mess.

"He's in trouble. Where's his mates?" Jo looked back, they'd disappeared. Gone to ground, she supposed, but without checking they were all together? They began to run, instinctively, looking to give help.

"We'll have to do something, Jo." They reached the foot of the tree, peered upwards. The man was swinging, head down, his legs caught in the cords, and he looked in a right state.

"Can you hear us? Are you okay?" David shouted up, but there was no response. "I say! *Can you hear us?*" No response. "He must be unconscious, Jo. We'll have to do something, otherwise he might not survive. Can you get up there? I'll try and raise the Range office." He was dragging his mobile phone out of his pocket as he spoke. Jocelyn was inwardly terrified. The thought of jumping out of an aircraft must be horrendous, and to find you are going to land in a tree! She knew that was something she could never have done, and felt sick. But she couldn't walk away. Something had to be done, and plucking up what courage she could muster, she scrutinised the tree. It had to be the only deciduous one in the patch, an oak, but there *might be* a way. A lower branch on the other side swept within grabbing distance of the ground. There really was no time to waste.

"Pa! Have you got that penknife thing with you?" Her voice was squeaky, her pulse racing. Her father had his phone to his ear.

"There's no reply, Jo. Just an answer phone. I'll have to go triple nine." Scrabbling in his pockets with his free hand, he produced the gadget knife he always carried. "Here, catch! I'll be right behind you. Take care!" The call had gone through, and as she cautiously reached for the access branch, she heard her father giving a terse message. She pulled with both hands, swung, got one leg over the branch. "Thank heavens I wore jeans," she thought, and heaving her body onto the branch, started inching her way to the main trunk. Once she got to the bole, she gingerly stood upright, clasping the rough bark, and took hold of the next branch.

"Don't look down, Jo! You're doing fine. That branch above your left side?" Her father was underneath her. "The message is going through to the Range Control. We should have some help soon!"

Jocelyn looked up, and yes, there was a good branch, but could she get up? A foothold in the bark, where an old bit had broken away. She reached, pulled, stepped and made it to the next leg. Now it was easier, the branches were more numerous and she didn't feel quite as vulnerable. The leaves were cloaking her vision a bit. Another shout from below.

"To your left again, Jo! Not far!"

Again she peered up, and saw some of the parachute canopy waving about in the light breeze.

"Must be nearly there, Pa?" Her father heard the touch of fear in her voice. He guessed she was as frightened as he was, but tried to keep a reassuring tone.

"Jo – you'll have to cut what cords you can, to try and get him upright. Over to your left, I think you'll reach that thicker branch!"

"I don't know if I can, Pa! How long before someone comes?"

"Not long, Jo, but if he's got a cord round his neck or something…? Try, darling. Give it a go!"

Jocelyn could feel her arm muscles trembling, but her Pa was right, she had to give it a go. Once more she looked up, saw the next possible handhold, and swung herself round, nearly losing her grip, but scrabbling with her right foot, made it to straddle the bigger branch. Looking round the trunk, she suddenly saw the problem, and the solution. The cords were wrapped round the soldier's feet and the parachute material was caught above him. If she could cut those cords, then the canopy should still support him until help came. At least he'd be upright. There didn't seem to be anything round his neck, but his helmet was crooked. Perhaps he'd hit his head on the tree. He didn't look all that old. Ever so gingerly, she edged round the trunk, stepped onto a flimsy branch that nearly gave way and squeaked.

"Pa!"

"Okay Jo, I'm below. You can't fall, darling, Too many branches below you! Can you see the problem?"

"I think so." She gulped, tried another branch, took a few deep breaths and stepped onto it, managing to transfer her weight quite efficiently further round. Closer to the soldier now, she could see his face. Young, perhaps twentyish, but very pale. Oh Heavens! Could she reach? The next branch, further up, hold onto that, then maybe… She tried, and missed, swinging back to the trunk. Another deep breath, and another reach. Yes! Now, how to get at the knife, in her top jacket pocket. She had to balance, lean back onto the trunk, reach with her right hand. Mustn't drop it! Got it! With her teeth and one hand, she pulled the main blade open. Good job Pa kept it sharp. The soldier was now below her, still no movement. Some of the cords were across the branch she was standing on, so she inched forward, then felt insecure and moved back. Perhaps if she straddled the branch, leg on each side? Allowing her weight to help her, she lowered herself down, until she had the branch between her thighs, and she could grip. Now! The cords in front were tight, and after just two slashes, pinged away from her, one catching her on the cheek and stinging.

"Ouch!"

"Jo! Are you okay?"

She couldn't see her father, but tried to concentrate without feeling she needed to reply. The next cords were spread around and she had to use both hands to reach, grab and cut, so the thigh grip was all she had. "Going to have some bruises after this. If I get down in one piece!" Three more. One cut, it pinged away; two, that one was slack. Now, let's see. She cut, and as the weight of the soldier's trunk and legs pulled at the mess of fabric above her and the remaining cords, there was another rending tearing sound, and as she flattened herself back, almost dropping the knife, the canopy fabric brushed past her, blocking out her vision. Then it was clear. Her next tentative look down merely saw the camouflage fabric bundled over the branches. Now what?

"Pa? Paaaa!"

The shout from the ground seemed an awful long way away. "Can you get down? I think we're okay. Our guy's only ten feet up now, and clear. The 'chute's holding him. I can't see you, are you all right?"

Jocelyn, still straddling the same branch, folded the knife up and slid it back into her pocket.

"At the moment. Is he safe?"

"Yes. You did a good job, Jo. Can you get down?"

"I'll try. Where's the help, then?"

"Don't know. I'll come round the other side."

She craned her neck round, saw what she had to do, but didn't much fancy it. However, there wasn't a choice. She took hold of the branch with both hands, swung one leg over, and eased herself down, blind, trying to find the lower branch with her feet. Touched, felt around, got the other one, let herself slide, feeling her jeans fabric tear. Damn! With one hand still up, the other feeling for another hand hold. Got it! Facing back the way she came, and the next bit was easy, walking round, branch onto branch, then dropping onto the lower one, gosh, nearly there! The last branch was the sloping one that went almost to the ground, and edging down like a tight-rope walker, to the point where her father stood, and she jumped off into his arms, and burst into tears.

"Jo. Jocelyn, darling. Well, well done." Her father held her tight to his chest, patted her back and stroked her hair. What a girl! He couldn't have got up there, for one he didn't like heights, and for another, he wasn't as nimble as he used to be.

Then they heard the welcome sound of a helicopter, and Jo, disengaging herself, wiped her eyes as best she could, ran out from underneath the tree canopy, waving frantically. The Lynx helicopter was circling almost overhead, and immediately began to descend.

* * *

Within minutes, the four-man team had assessed the situation, one man was up into the tree and the others below, the still unconscious paratrooper cut free and recovered, and his condition ascertained.

Once the man's helmet had been removed, it was evident he'd had a fairly hefty blow to the side of his head, judging from the mess of blood matted in his hair, so no time was wasted in getting him strapped onto a stretcher and into the helicopter and away. Two men remained, a Captain and a Sergeant.

"Captain Adams. We're indebted to you, Mr…?" The officer was a weather-beaten thirty year old, rather a stern expression, the Sergeant an older man but with a pleasant smiling face. Both in battle dress, or whatever they now called it, Jocelyn wasn't really sure.

"Danielleson. David. And my daughter, Jocelyn. It's her you've got to thank. Your man was hanging upside down up there; it looked as if he was likely to suffocate. She cut him free, on her own. Glad you found us. I don't know we could have done much more."

"Well, all I can say is we're very fortunate you were here, though perhaps you shouldn't have been. Did you check with the Range Office?"

"Yes, we did. I must admit we were a bit surprised to see some action over there," David pointed, "and then the Hercules. The others who dropped just disappeared. I would have thought they would have counted heads?"

"I can't comment, I'm afraid, Sir, at least, not officially. Off the record, it's these weekend warriors. Not always as clued up as they should be. Don't get me wrong, good keen chaps, hey, Paul?"

"Absolutely, Sir, But this bunch, yet to see. First drop for most of them, nervous, see. One or two sometimes decide not to jump at the last moment. Could have been the case here, like. Our man may have changed his mind twice. Yes, no, I've got to go! Then he's not missed, you see, till afterwards. Bit awkward really. Did a fantastic job, missy. But for you, we may have had a nasty accident. Very unpleasant, it is, what with enquiries and such. He owes you, I think."

"All right, Paul. I agree with you, but no need to go on. Now, can I take an address, Sir, just in case? And would you like a lift home, or are you carrying on? I'm assuming you were out for a walk?"

David looked at his daughter. She was beginning to shiver, and had lost some colour.

"A lift home would be very acceptable. I'm a bit concerned for Jo – my daughter. She's been rather stressed." He put his arm round her.

The Sergeant, Paul, was already on his army radio. He didn't want to see the girl in shock either.

Captain Adams walked round the tree, peered into the branches, then came back to David and Jocelyn

"I don't know that I would have wanted to go up there particularly, if I'd been you, Miss Danielleson. You're certainly a plucky girl. Sorry that your walk has been interrupted. Any joy, Paul?"

"Yes Sir. Landrovers already on their way. In fact.... " As he spoke, the familiar sound of a Landrover could just be heard, and within a couple of minutes one vehicle had bounced over the grass towards them from the concrete road half a mile away. The other stayed on the road. The Sergeant helped Jo into the passenger seat, then he and his Captain and David piled into the back. Once onto the road, the other vehicle with Military Police insignia led the way, so with a blue light escort they were taken to the Officers' Mess, Jocelyn placed in the care of a very competent looking female Officer with the RAMC insignia and whisked away. David was reassured she would be well looked after, whilst he was taken to the Dining Room for a very welcome mug of tea. His concern now, as time was getting on, was to contact Eleanor, before she became anxious. Captain Adams was insistent that he used the Mess phone rather than his mobile, and having showed him where it was, left him to it.

"Eleanor. I thought I'd better let you know, we've had a bit of an adventure. I'm in the Officers' Mess, up at Larkhill. They'll be giving us a lift home; so don't be alarmed if we come back in an army truck. No, we're both okay. Well, sort of. Jo's been a bit of a hero – sorry, heroine. Tell you all about when we get back. How long? Maybe half an hour, okay darling. See you."

Returning to the entrance lobby, Captain Adams was waiting for him.

"Your daughter's in the car, Sir, ready to go when you are." He led the way, and rather than the anticipated army truck, it was a pool car outside, quite a respectable Rover with a civilian girl driver. "I'll leave you in Amanda's care, Sir. We'll be in touch. Many thanks." With that, he turned on his heel and disappeared. David found Jocelyn snuggled up in a blanket in the back.

"Darling – how're you feeling? You're not that cold, are you? Did they look after you?"

"I'm fine now, Pa. Really. I'm sorry I went wimpish on you. After all that. Maybe I should have cried properly, so..."

"Hey, Jo, enough. You did enough to keep yourself going. Let's just get ourselves home." He climbed in alongside her. Amanda, the driver, patiently waiting for instructions and very aware of what had happened, was diplomatic.

"Do you want me to take you right to the door, Sir, or shall I drop you close by?"

"To the door will be fine – will you know the Old Vicarage?"

"Yes, Sir. Fifteen minutes or so." And with that she pulled away.

* * *

Actually it took her twenty minutes, but smooth enough. Jocelyn stayed quiet the whole journey. A somewhat full day, what with her explorations in the nude in the morning, to this completely impossible to imagine ending to what should have been a good long walk. She'd been checked over by the army lady medic, all bruises examined, the scratches cleaned and dressed, given a hot drink, and generally looked after. She had asked about the soldier they had helped, reassuringly he was going to be all right, though a couple of days in the hospital would ensure no complications. It had been his first jump, maybe hadn't pulled his ripcord at the right moment, though the lady medic thought the drop was a wee bit early on the flight plan. More than that she wouldn't say. Jocelyn, grateful for the care lavished on her, hadn't felt she could press her further.

Now they were back home. Amanda popped out of her driver's door, opened the rear door for them, smiled and was off before they had properly thanked her. Eleanor met them at the door, full of concern.

"What have you two been up to? Brought back? I call that cheating! Jo – you look drained. David – come on, tell."

"In a moment. Let's just get our girl indoors. She's the heroine of the day, that one. I'm proud of her. I don't think she'll forget the day either. Come on, in!"

Eleanor was more than mystified. After Jocelyn had had something to eat and, more importantly, to drink, David explained. A Hercules, a parachute drop that was misplaced, an off-course first-timer and the way in which he'd been tangled up in an oak tree, and how an eighteen, well nearly eighteen-year-old girl had scrambled desperately to his aid and most probably saved his life. Eleanor was horrified, and then intensely proud. Her daughter, rescuing a soldier out of a tree!

"Oh, Jocelyn! You might have hurt yourself or been killed or something! David – what do you think you were doing, letting her do such a daft thing?"

"Darling – if we hadn't done something, the guy might have died. He was all wrapped up in his canopy and cords, hanging upside down, unconscious, none of his mates about, and I certainly couldn't have done what Jo did. So just be

62

proud of her. She's a great girl, is that one."

The great girl in question was asleep. She had succumbed to a more than eventful day. David looked at Eleanor, and grinned. Eleanor's face was a picture. Then she saw the humorous side of it all and smiled with him.

"What do we do with her?"

"Let her lie. I can't pick her up and carry her upstairs like I used to. She needs a power nap. Oh, and by the way, she sketched me while we were having our picnic lunch. Look...' He pulled Jo's sketchbook out from her flung jacket, and opened it. Eleanor peered at it, seeing instantly the reality of the day, the place, and her husband's pose.

"She is good, isn't she? So did you manage to talk things through with her?"

"No. A parachute drop got in the way."

"Oh well. Another day, then."

"Yes. Another day. And Jo?"

"You go up, dear. I'll keep her company till she surfaces. Sunday tomorrow. Gardening day?"

"Hmmm. Sure?"

"Why not? We promised. Got to have the place spick and span to impress the neighbours. I think it may be something of an occasion, Eleanor, my darling. Just let's hope that we can get our girl through her exam week. Go on, dear."

Eleanor touched her husband's hand, drifted hers across his face, and left him to his vigil. The sleeping Jocelyn, so peaceful in her armchair, breasts rising and falling as she slept, bedraggled hair, was such a special, precious girl. And yet she was at a crossroads, poised to be launched out onto the world at large, and they would have to let her go. David flopped into the other armchair, and let these thoughts chase round his brain. Would they have the strength to allow her to follow her inclinations, to give way to the strengths of *her* feelings, and support her? Should they try and keep her on line for that University degree and at least as good a chance as anyone for a meaningful income, or go along with the abandonment of sense, at least as *commonsense* suggested? Or was she going to be so good, so much her own person, that she'd survive anyway? He just didn't know. She was *his* daughter, and he'd had to have confidence in her, allowing her to risk her life in a tree. Or should he have kept her on the ground like the most sensible, cautious parent would have done?

As he pondered, he was staring at her, drinking in the wayward beauty of her, relishing his relationship. *His* daughter. He loved her. Adored her. And she stirred, woke, saw her father and smiled at him.

"Pa, sorry. I didn't..."

"I know. Jo, you need your sleep. Get yourself to bed. Gardening tomorrow?"

"Hmmm, I think I might like that. Has Mums gone to bed?"

"She has. Half an hour ago. High time you were there too. Go on with you, darling. I'm mighty proud of you, you know." He felt his eyes pricking. As Jocelyn unravelled herself from her chair, she stretched up and brushed his prickly cheek with her lips.

"Love you, Pa. Thanks for being you. Night night."

THREE

She was climbing, climbing, the helicopter was pulling the tree up; she had a pair of scissors and was trying to cut the winch cable. A grinning soldier was sitting on a branch alongside her, sketching her with *her* pad. Then she slipped and the ground came up to meet her. She woke up, perspiring, and feeling just a little sick. Attempting to recall why she had such a vivid nightmare, the room seemed to come in on her.

"Mums! Mums!" She yelled. She didn't want to wake up like this, feeling so strange. Her mother heard the cry, and bounded back upstairs from putting breakfast on the table.

"Jo, darling! What's the matter? Been dreaming, have you? I'm not surprised!" She sat on the bed edge, to put an arm around a bewildered daughter. "Where's your nightie, you silly girl? I think a shower, don't you? Come on, Jo. Time you were up." A combination of humour, concern and tact got the confused girl out of bed and into the bathroom. Eleanor stayed with her until she was sure that Jocelyn was back on an even keel.

"We're gardening today, remember, Jo. Put something appropriate on, won't you, darling? Breakfast is ready. Your father's gone exploring, up to the orchard, to have a look at that old shed again. Perhaps we'll turn it into a summerhouse or something. Anyway, more important things today. Are you okay, now?"

"I think so, Mums. P'raps I'd better not have too much breakfast. Just in case."

"It can't be that time of the month, can it? How's your tum?"

Jo thought, and it *did* seem just a *teeny* bit fragile. Surely not. She knew she wasn't far off, according to the diary she kept, end of the week, which had been nauseating as it was the barbecue weekend when all her friends would be about. So she just shook her head.

"I knew it. That escapade yesterday caused havoc. I'll clobber your father for putting you up that tree. Daft, plain daft!"

"But Mums, that soldier could have *died!* I *had* to do something! An early period's nothing. Anyway, if it means I'm clear by your do next weekend, then so much the better!"

Eleanor was stymied. Her daughter was right, of course. A man's life, even at some risk. She cuffed her daughter's head, lightly, and then kissed her cheek, finally putting the large towel round the damp and naked girl. She hugged her.

"Just you make sure you do what you have to, Jo. See you downstairs." She had to juggle her feelings between too much tender loving care and being too aloof to her daughter's needs. At least Jo *did* look after herself in that department.

* * *

Round the breakfast table, David summed up his findings. He still wasn't sure why they hadn't cleared out that old shed before, but it was as if it had been blocked out of their thoughts. Very strange. An eerie feeling, being in there, as though he'd been intruding, and it had been a relief to get back out into the open air. The morning was still, not a whisper in the leaves, like the garden was holding its breath. No sun yet, just a grey mantle of thin cloud. He was sure it would turn warm. The bulk of what was in there he'd dismissed as rubbish. The boxes Jo had been through were quite old, made of straw-based cardboard. The building itself was sound, the roof not at all bad. A few ideas of what its original use had been were bandied across the table. Eleanor's idea was an old man's refuge from a nagging wife, David snorted and thought it had been the gardener's den, but Jocelyn was far more imaginative, and suggested a venue for illicit dalliance.

"Illicit dalliance! That's a bit eighteenth century!" her father commented. "Bit of a grim hole for that sort of thing.

Not exactly a rose covered arbour. I've thought of a good use for it, provided we do something about the windows. How about a studio?"

"Studio!" Jo and her mother spoke in concert, Jocelyn with sudden enthusiasm, Eleanor with surprise. David grinned with pleasure at their mutual reaction. He'd thought about it on his way back down the garden. Jo needed somewhere of her own if she was going to sketch, or paint, or whatever, and she loved the old orchard, so why not? New, larger windows, maybe even a bit of glass in the roof. It was roomy enough, once they'd got rid of the debris. And, if it had been the venue for some age-old romance...? His girl was a romantic, even though she didn't show it openly. So what better?

Jo's nightmarish waking was forgotten. She wasn't sure about the monthly thing, but had taken suitable precautions. She hated it, but there wasn't much else she could do but grin and bear it. Mums watched her, she knew, and was happy about that, feeling the care, and comforted by the protective aura. Her father was blessed with some sixth sense about his daughter's condition, and he also watched her carefully. Her reaction to his suggestion was encouraging. It was also a turning point, his acceptance of her wish to expand her artistic talent.

"Eleanor?"

"Depends on Jo. What do you think, darling?"

"It's a super idea, Pa. Oh, Pa, yes. Yes, yes, yes!" She got off her stool, went round to her father and put her arms round his neck, kissed him. "My *own* studio! Great! Oh, thank you, Pa. Thank you! When can we start?"

"Not so fast, young lady. Your mother's garden takes preference today, and then you've a week of exams, whatever happens after that. You can't abandon two years' work just because we've said yes to your concept of being an artist! We expect results, my girl. Finish your breakfast!" He patted her hand, holding it briefly before sending her back to her stool.

Jocelyn's mind was in a whirl. Her parents had agreed. She could *really* plan to paint. Her mother looked at her indulgently. She and David had talked, or rather, whispered, into the small hours, and finally decided to give their daughter her head. The things they did for her! But she was their only daughter. Eleanor felt a twinge of sadness, recalling that fateful day when she'd known the prospect of having an expanded family had gone in order to stay alive. For Jo, for David. So it was only right to sacrifice any selfish ideal and go along with her beloved girl's dream. And in her heart of hearts, she felt it was right.

* * *

Breakfast over; delicious home-made bitter marmalade on home-made toasted bread, good coffee in the super hand-thrown pottery mugs, Jo in a state of euphoria; Eleanor outlined her plans for the day.

Apart from just plain tidying up, clearing rubbish, weeding, mowing lawns and trimming edges, there was gravel to rake – Jo's bust developing task – and shrubs to prune into disciplined shapes.

David summed it all up. "Have you got our Ground Force T-shirts?"

"No, David. But I have one that says 'Head Gardener'."

"I know. I gave it to you." He pushed his stool back under the table. "Come on then. Let's get cracking."

Once outside, Jocelyn's spirits rose still further, the overcast sky burnt away by the gathering strength of the midsummer sun, the day still smelt fresh, and the blackbirds were already busy doing their own bit of gardening, turning leaf mould over in the herbaceous border in the search for worms. Her Mums was sizing up the shrubs, while her Pa retrieved the wheelbarrow from behind the little tool shed. He also came back with the rake, and grinned as he handed it over to Jo.

"You don't need this for the bust development, madam. You're sizeable enough now!"

Jo blushed. "Pa! Really!"

Her father's grin broadened. He knew she would actually be inwardly pleased at the subtle – or not so subtle –

compliment. Now that they had the question of her change of direction sorted, the feeling between the three of them was great. Jocelyn took the rake, and threatened to 'spank' him with the handle. He laughed, and took the barrow off to pick up the growing heap of prunings Eleanor was producing. Jo went off to her gravel raking on the front drive.

* * *

She'd managed to get all the way down the one side, but it was pulling at her tummy. Not such a good idea, this, she thought, and suddenly felt queasy again. Silly girl, she told herself. Should have had more breakfast. Looking at her watch, it was elevenish. Time for mid-morning break. The rake she propped up against the big laurel bush, and rubbed her wrists, wriggled her blouse round and tucked it back into her jeans. Distantly she heard her Mums; sounded as though Pa was getting a telling-off about something. Perfectly normal. She stretched, and her blouse popped out from her waistline again. Bother. That's what comes from having too much up top, she thought, then grinned to herself. Better than some, so don't despise the size. Oh, that rhymed! She pulled the rest of the fabric out from her belt and let it drop naturally, a sort of shirt look. At least it was cooler, as the day was warming up. The sound of an approaching car intruded on the otherwise peaceful morning, and she frowned. Mums didn't like unannounced visitors, especially on a gardening day. It broke her concentration. Jo walked slowly towards the gate, curious as to who was coming up their dead-end lane. An open topped thing. Sports car – blonde hair – oh no, it was Betty's mum! On her own? At least she wasn't driving fast, quite sedately actually. What on earth does *she* want? The car had slowed right down to turn into the drive.

"Mrs Downs! How nice to see you!" Jocelyn was nothing if not polite. "Does my mother know you're coming?" At least that should warn her, she thought.

"Felicity, please, Jocelyn. Mrs Downs sounds *so* stuffy. I used to be a 'Sheridan' before I did the silly thing like getting married. Still am in the magazine world. I brought some copies for you. Sorry Betty couldn't come, she's out riding. Passing this way; just thought I'd call in. Hope it's not inconvenient?" She had an amused expression, and Jo sensed she was teasing her, which made her slightly cross. Looking down on 'Felicity' from the advantage of the sloping lawn, Jo couldn't help notice the short skirt above – well, yes, they were *nice* knees, and a too open blouse. At least she had a bra. What to do? Thank her and send her on her way, ask her to wait and grab Mums before Pa sees her, or do the polite thing and ask her in for coffee. Oh, Lord!

"No, not at all, er, *Felicity*. How good of you to remember the magazines!" I sound like Eliza Doolittle, she thought, and grinned.

"That's better, Jo. You look lovely when you smile! Can I get past the armed guard?" She laughed, and Jo had to admit, she *was* pretty. Pa will be livid if he doesn't get a chance to ogle her.

"I'm sorry, Felicity. Just that Mums is in gardening mode, and not always polite. I'll go and warn her. Do please come on up. We'll make some coffee or something." Without waiting for an answer, Jo dived into the shrubs and short-cut to the back of the house. Mums was still wielding her secateurs with enthusiasm; Pa was nowhere to be seen, thank heavens.

"Hello, Jo, dear, finished the drive?" Her Mums was all sweaty and red faced, not at all in 'meet visitor' mode.

"Not quite, Mums. It's not doing my tum much good. But, you heard the car? It's Betty's mum, Felicity. You know, the one with blonde hair and short skirt? Pa's delight? I've had to invite her in; she's brought those magazines she promised. I'm sure she fancies him. What do we do?"

Eleanor laughed, pushing wayward hair out of her eyes.

"My, my, you are protective! Jo, your father can look after himself – he's welcome to feast his eyes if she wants to show off. Worry not. Bit of a pain, though, having to break off. At least it may curb my extravagance in the shrub-cutting department. I was getting quite carried away. Where is this Gorgon?" She stuffed the secateurs into her wide gardening skirt pocket, and wiped her hands down the sides.

Jocelyn pointed back to the house. "She'll be by the front door, I expect. I told her to wait. Should I find Pa, then, or keep him out of trouble?"

Chuckling, Eleanor started back towards the house. "No – go and tell him his girlfriend's here – see what he says! I'll deal with madam!"

Jocelyn went to find her father. She thought he'd be doing some of the routine weeding on the long beds beside the hedges, but no, the beds were already neat and tidy. She whistled. Nothing.

Strange, she thought, where's he gone? So she crossed the paddock towards the orchard, and whistled again. And an answering shout.

"Here!" He must be in the orchard. "Sorry, Jo, I couldn't resist it." She found him, covered in dust and cobwebs, with a heap of debris piled up outside the shed. Studio, she thought, think 'Studio'.

"Does Mums know you've escaped, Pa? Are you dodging the weeding, or did she say you could play?"

"Oh, she'll guess. I've done my bit, anyway, at least until she dreams up something else. At least I've made a start. There's some other stuff I think we ought to look at – those boxes there, and that old wooden crate. Anyway, what brings you up here? I thought you were tied to the gravel?"

"Felicity's here. You know, Betty's mum, well, step-mum. The blonde with a 'come hither' look and too short a skirt? Mums sent me to tell you to come and ogle. I think she's got an ulterior motive. Felicity, I mean. Just watch, it, Pa. She's dangerous."

David had to laugh. His daughter, telling him to behave. He had to admit, though, she *was* a pretty shapely woman. "You want me to show myself, Jo? Anyway, why the surprise visit? She's not brought her magazine crew, has she?"

"Nope. The excuse is the free copies of her thing, but *I* think she's come to see you."

"Rubbish. If she's got an ulterior motive, it's not me. 'Specially in this state. Okay, lead on. Let dog see rabbit, or

71

should I say Bunny girl. No doubt your mother will have to get the coffee going – no bad idea, that, anyway. Time for a break." He took his daughter's hand, and the two went together back across the paddock.

* * *

"Felicity! How nice to see you! To what do we owe the honour? Will you come in and have coffee or something? Jo's gone to fetch David. We're gardening, as you can see. Sorry about the state I'm in – not expecting visitors." Eleanor managed to combine pleasantry with a mild reproof. Felicity had to hand it to her; she was well versed in repartee.

"Not coffee, thank you, Eleanor. Makes me too hyper, but I'd love a glass of your lemony thing. I brought you these." She handed over three copies of her magazine. "I've bookmarked an article in that one. It's the sort of feature that I would love to do on this place, if you'd let me. See what you think. We can always give you a different name and fudge the location a bit, so readers won't have the foggiest where you *actually* live. We all do that, you know. It's all in the photos, really." She paused, as Eleanor led the way into the house. "Your Jocelyn. She's a *very* pretty girl. She'd look well in the photo shoot. And Betty's very fond of her, so it seems. Talks of nobody else, hardly. Love the garden."

Eleanor thought Felicity was rather overdoing things a bit, prattling on. But the woman sounded genuine enough, and why else would she spare her time on a Sunday morning just to deliver magazines her mailroom could well have sent out?

"Here's David, and Jo. Have a seat, Felicity. I'll go get the drinks." Eleanor passed her husband and Jo as they came into the front room, David in his stocking feet. She scowled at him, then winked, out of Felicity's line of sight. She caught Jo's arm, and dragged her back. "Leave her to your father," she whispered, and the two went into the kitchen, leaving David to face the 'Gorgon'.

"David! *Lovely* to see you again. And looking so *outdoorish!* Makes a man *very* attractive to us office-bound females. You

72

must show me round the estate." Her eyes didn't leave his. A faint waft of her scent as she re-crossed her legs, with a more than adequate display of thigh. He plumped for a chair slightly askew from hers and pulled a small table forward ready for the drinks. God, she was a temptress.

Heaven help her husband. He decided to divert the conversation.

"Your husband not about then, Felicity? Isn't he an outdoorish type?"

"Goodness, *nooooh.*" What an emphasis! "He's a bit of an academic, you know. Spends his Sunday doing the crossword and tinkering with his computer. Does cut the lawn, I'll give him that, but otherwise, no. You're *far more...*" She was interrupted by Jo bringing in a tray, so David didn't manage to discover the comparison. "Jocelyn. How nice. Thank you *sooooh* much!"

The tray had three coffee mugs and a tall glass of lemonade, home-made, complete with ice and a slice of kiwi fruit. It was all Eleanor could come up with, but it seemed to work. Felicity took her glass and sipped.

"Heaven. Absolute *heaven!* And *home-made.* Marvellous." She sipped, elegantly, and waited until Eleanor re-appeared. Jo went and stood by the window, then on inspiration, returned to stand behind her father's chair, and put a hand on his shoulder. A light touch, but he knew what she was thinking. He had to try and hide a smile.

"Listen. This idea I have, of a feature on this place." David wasn't sure he liked 'this place'. Seemed a bit derogatory. "Can I have someone about next Saturday? Sort of, well, undercover? I'd *love* to come too, of course. Betty can come with me, I'm sure you'd find her useful. Would you mind?"

It sounded as if it were cut and dried. Jo squeezed her father's shoulder, and looked across at her Mums. Eleanor shrugged. "If you think we're *really* worth the effort, Felicity. Of course it'll be lovely to have the support. And I'm sure we'd be very happy to have Betty's help, eh Jo?"

"Sure, Mums. The more the merrier. If it gets tedious, we'll escape to the studio!" She had to get that one in, just to gauge the reaction. She wasn't disappointed.

"Studio, Jocelyn? How interesting! What do you do?"

"She draws, sketches, paints, that sort of thing," David interjected. He was beginning to come to terms with his daughter's talent and quite liked the idea.

"*Really! Well! Fanceee!*" Felicity didn't need to be quite so affected, Jo thought. She'd be quite a pleasant person most of the time otherwise. "Are you any good?"

"Show her your self-portrait, darling?" Eleanor wanted her to show off, let Betty's step-mum know her daughter *was* good. Jo wrinkled her forehead, not sure, but her father reached up and patted the hand on his shoulder.

"Yes, why not? I think it's good!"

So Jocelyn, reluctantly, went upstairs and returned with her portrait. She propped it on the mantelpiece so Felicity could see it across the room. As she did so, her likeness seemed to smile at her. So it must have been the right thing to do.

Felicity unfolded her long legs and stood up, put her head on one side, looked across at the portrait and then back at Jo, stepped forward a pace, and repeated her actions.

"You did that, Jocelyn?"

"Yes."

"You *are* good. It's not only you, but it captures your – *liveliness*. Forgive me, Jo, but *yes*, you're good. Very good. May I see something else?" Her demeanour had changed. She was expressing a professional interest and the social animal had become submerged. Jocelyn, pleased and yet not pleased with her meagre portfolio, couldn't think, but her father came to the rescue.

"Yesterday, Jo. Me on the log, you know, picnic time. Before…" He stopped; maybe not a good time to revive *that* incident just now. Jo's heart skipped a beat. She'd pushed yesterday out of her mind, at least that bit. She'd far rather think of running next to naked back down the garden in the cool of the morning.

"Where's my sketch pad then, Pa? It did come back, didn't it?"

"In the kitchen."

Jo went out to find it, and when she was out of the room, David couldn't help boasting.

"We had an incident out on the Plain yesterday. Went walkabout, got involved in a parachute drop that went wrong, and Jocelyn saved a guy from strangling himself in a tree. Proud of her."

His voice cracked a bit, remembering the close call. Felicity was intrigued, before realising maybe now wasn't the time to probe. No doubt all would be revealed.

After a brief silence, Jo returned. The sketch pad cover was a trifle the worse for wear, but the sketch in question was okay. Her attempt at the light across the garden the other evening had suffered, although maybe recoverable. She handed the pad, folded with the picnic scene on the top, to Felicity.

Felicity took it, and held it at arms length.

"Hmm. How long did this take you, Jo?"

"Ten minutes. Maybe less. It's only a sort of *aide-mémoire*; I'd use it to do something properly. I have to be in the mood."

"How long have you been – sketching – painting?"

"Not long. I'm afraid I got fed up with pure English at college, and started doodling. It sort of came from there. That," – she pointed to her self-portrait – "was done late evening, after I got bored with revision. I haven't shown it to anyone else yet, but our college art lecturer will be coming next Saturday to have a look. I wouldn't take it to college. He's very supportive. I like him; he's got a great sense of humour."

"Well, Jocelyn, all power to your elbow. I think you've certainly got talent. Good luck with it. I look forward to seeing more. But I must go; I've intruded too long. Do have a look at that article, you two; I hope we can produce something we all like. Okay for next Saturday, then?"

Eleanor looked at her husband. He spoke for them both.

"We'll give it a whirl, Felicity. Thanks for coming, and all your comments on Jo's work. It's very encouraging. We weren't sure, but it seems she's doing all the right things. I'll see you out."

* * *

Jo and her mother looked at each other, and simultaneously burst into giggles. Felicity was all very well, but a bit over powering. Jo went to the window, watching her father seeing her into her car. She was doing her short skirt, long leg routine, and then she saw her father stoop down and apparently listen to something Felicity was saying. She looked quite animated, and put a hand on her father's cheek, like implanting a fingertip kiss. Oh, my, Pa! She turned back to her mother.

"Pa won't get mixed up with her, will he, Mums? She's a bit too – um – *sexy* for my liking."

Eleanor laughed. "No, I shouldn't think so, dear. Don't take actions at face value. He's far too fond of us girls to mess about with the likes of her. Despite her dress or lack of it. Worry not. Want some lunch, or is it too late? We've still got a bit to do yet. Oh, and don't moan about him starting on the old shed. I actually suggested he took a look, just so we know what we're on about."

"Oh, I'm not moaning, Mums. Far from it, but we must have the place decent for next week."

Another burst of laughter. "Oh, Jo! Jo, darling. Most of our visitors won't notice if the grass was pink. They're only coming because it's the thing to do, or because it's a meal. Provided we talk to the keen gardeners and explain what we're doing. It'll be fine. You'll see. Tomato sandwiches, Jo, dear?"

* * *

Later in the afternoon, Eleanor did a re-assessment of the garden's condition, and held a council of war. Most of what she had wanted to see done had been; David having spent most of the post-lunchtime in mowing the grass. Jo finished the gravel rake, having completely forgotten about tender tummies, and stole ten minutes to do an unobserved sketch of her mother clipping away at a rampant cotoneaster. It was teatime, and the heat of the day still shimmered over the hedges. Jocelyn was commissioned to organise a tea tray, which gave Eleanor another chance to discuss Felicity's visit.

"Jo's a bit concerned you don't get swept up by that man-eater, David. I know she's a shapely thing, but you will take care, won't you? Put her mind at rest? She's very protective."

David pursed his lips. Well, she was a bit of a dish, and he, frankly, liked looking at her, but so what? He certainly wasn't about to rush off to check out her underwear, and in no way was he going to leave himself open to recriminations. But what she'd said to him when she left was intriguing. He couldn't talk about it at the moment; he'd have to see what developed.

"Darling, who do I cuddle? Who do I take up to the orchard when no one's looking? Worry not. She may be useful, though, so bear with me. We've got Jo's future to consider, given the change in circumstances, and she's very impressed with what she's seen, so maybe she'll be able to come up with something. Oh, and the new studio. I'll get our maintenance guy from the garage to come up and give us an opinion on the structural condition. How much should we spend, do you reckon?"

"What it takes, David. Within reason. What do you think to getting it finished for her birthday?"

"End of the month? Hmmm. Well, we can but try. A few BB pencils in a pretty parcel in reserve?"

Eleanor punched him. "Horror! You'll do better than that for your precious daughter, if I know you! Here she comes, shush."

* * *

There was something very Edwardian about taking tea in the shade of their big chestnut on the edge of the newly-mown lawn. The oak garden seats, a present from David's parents some years ago, the old Victorian cast iron table, a rather tatty sun-shade umbrella thing, and the rattle of china cups.

"You should have a stripey blazer and a straw boater, David. And we'll put Jo in a flouncy dress and ribbons in those gorgeous curls of hers. Cucumber sandwiches?"

"Now that's no bad idea, Eleanor. Sets the scene? Can you cope? Jo? What'd you think?"

77

"Rather nice, I think, Pa. Yes, nice. If Mums can cope, as you say. Don't know about getting a dress organised, though. Have you any ideas on that front, Mums?"

"That thing you romped back in yesterday, Jo? If we put you in an underskirt, and add some bouncy sleeves? You didn't see her, did you, David? She looked a treat, other than she had no underwear on, silly girl. Maybe she'll grow up, one of these days, eh, my girl?" Jo blushed. Maybe it was a bit silly, but, well, it felt good at the time. The dress, perhaps Mums was right.

"Let's go for it, Mums. I think it'll be fun. Where's Pa's blazer coming from?"

"Don't know, dear, we'll think of something. Another cup of tea?"

* * *

As the light began to fade, Jocelyn walked slowly back up to the old orchard. The scent amongst the trees, warm grass, a touch of the subtlety of the apples, magic, it was magic. She sat down on the log. Behind her, the empty shell of the shed, soon to be *her* studio. She still had that idea of a picture in mind. Well, a studio right here. She'd do it. She knew she would. Apples. Why? Why not? It had been a busy day, a busy weekend. An *exciting* weekend. A quick twinge of apprehension over the start of her exam week. Well, all over by this time next week. End of her school career. She hadn't got any real concept of what would happen if she didn't get a university place. She had a promise in writing, subject to grades, and she was lucky in that. Perhaps she'd smiled sweetly at the right chap on the selection interview panel. What was going to happen if she announced she wanted to abandon English for History of Art? She knew it was a despised course by some, seen as a simplistic way of getting a BA behind your name. So she'd have to get a First. She squared her shoulders, stood up, and meandered her way across to the small grove, her favourite place. She put a hand on the nearest apple tree trunk, and gazed up into the branches. It seemed to be a friendly tree. Like that oak she'd been up. A friendly tree, it saved a life, in a complicated sort of way. "I wonder how that soldier chap is getting on," she thought. Maybe they'd ring and let them know. Or maybe she'd get Pa to ring the Range Office. She hoped she wouldn't have any nightmares tonight. Not with that English Literature paper tomorrow. Oh well, better get back. The warmth from the ground rose around her as she crossed the paddock; the scent from the garden, the roses especially, and the faint rustle of field mice in the shrubbery. A flutter from a disturbed roosting bird, then the sudden coolness as she walked along the yew hedge path. Really, she was a lucky girl, and with super parents. So long as Pa... Well, no, he wouldn't.

"Mums! I'm going up. Where's Pa?"

Eleanor was finishing drying the washing-up.

"All right dear. You are okay, aren't you? Your Pa's in the lounge, probably asleep. Sleep well, darling. Night night."

Her father was, indeed, asleep. She blew him an unseen kiss and softly crept upstairs. In her room, she shed her clothes, remembered her mum's comment about her nightie, or absence of, and digging it out from under the pillow, slipped it on. In her mirrored imagination the nightdress metamorphosed into the old dress from the shed. It was a nice feeling. It would be good to have it restored, to wear something from a mysterious past. Once into bed, she lay on her back, sorting out her thoughts, only just aware of the rising moon. Lovely day. Poor Felicity. Dear Pa. Thanks, Mu... She was asleep.

FOUR

David surfaced just after dawn. The bedside clock showed a quarter to six, and it was Monday, at least he thought it was Monday. Yes, it was definitely Monday. The tousled hair beside him moved, and Eleanor struggled up to have her look at the clock, before subsiding and rolling over. Too early. David put an exploratory arm in her direction, to find a cosy shape to cup his hand over. Lovely time of the day, this, occasionally gentle cuddles got quite enjoyable. Not this morning though, unfortunately. He got a shove.

"Jo's exam week, David. You'd best get her up."

"Why me? Why not you? Mum's job, getting daughters out of bed!"

Eleanor used her toe to good effect.

"Ouch!"

"She loves you, David. She takes more notice of you. You'll need to ensure she's in the right state of mind. Take her up to the orchard; discuss plans for the new studio. I'll do a nice breakfast. You'll have to take her in anyway; I'm in the shop till after lunch. What's the weather doing?"

"Don't know. She loves you too, Eleanor. Oh, all right. We both love her. I'll go."

David rolled over, stuck his feet down and slid out without uncovering his bed mate. She cosied down again, grateful for the prospect of another hour's peace. Looking at her comatose shape beneath the bedclothes, he very nearly gave way to his basic instincts, but doubted that would actually make him very popular. Well, not in the short term, but once she was in tune, she seemed to appreciate what happened! Not this morning, however. He put his gardening gear on, given he was going to take Jo up the orchard. Before he left the bedroom he planted a kiss on what he could find under the duvet. All he got in return was a sort of grunt. Oh, well!

* * *

He pushed open Jocelyn's bedroom door, fully expecting to find her still asleep. She wasn't there!

Feeling the bedclothes, they were cold. She'd been up sometime, then. Where had she gone? There could only be one place. The back door was unlocked. Outside, he sniffed the air. Cool, but pleasant. It was going to be another nice day. Taking the yew walk, then across the lawn, into the paddock, he found the dew-shewn footprints. Looking ahead, he tried to see her, but didn't until he got to the gate. She was sitting on the old log. At least she was dressed, albeit short skirt and sweater, not like the other morning when Eleanor had told him she been up here starkers, daft girl! She looked up as he opened the gate.

"Pa! Fallen out with Mums? Couldn't you sleep?"

"You should talk! Why up here so early, Jo, my dearest girl?"

"Inspiration, Pa. Its so, *atmospheric!* Don't ask me why. It just suits. So quiet. Peaceful. Just the apples, growing away. And me." She was swinging her legs, bare to her toes, and looking up at the branches above.

"Sorry to intrude, Jo. Your Mother suggested I went through the ideas about the studio conversion. I'll disappear again, if you'd prefer."

"No, Pa. I didn't mean it like that. You're fine." She slipped off the log, and went close to him.

"Let's go look at the job, then." She stood on bare tiptoe and gave him a kiss. "Love you, Pa!"

He was touched. Putting an arm around her, gave her a squeeze. "Love you too. You will do a good job this week, won't you?"

She ducked out from his embrace, with a slight frown. She hadn't wanted to be reminded about exams, not here, not now.

She walked off towards the old shed. He followed, aware he'd been crass in mentioning the day ahead. In silence, they opened the door and peered inside. He'd left the other old boxes, but got rid of the rest of the debris outside, all piled up in a heap behind them. Jo pulled open one of the boxes. More old clothes, it seemed. As she lifted the garments out, David stood back and just watched. A couple of pairs of musty old trousers, grey serge; a coat, strange mid-brown colour, with large horn buttons. Then a dress, a pinkish fabric with a sheen of purple.

"Silk, Pa, I think." She dropped it onto the pile on the ground. Another garment followed, it could have been a sort of undergarment, a bit like a petticoat. Then a pair of what must have been 'bloomers'. "Yuck! Fancy wearing those!" She delved into the bottom of the box, and pulled out a blazer, with yellow and purple stripes.

"Pa! Edwardian teas! Just what you need! Try it on!" She offered it him. He wasn't too sure.

"Go on. It's still in one piece, surprisingly. Bit musty, perhaps. Try it!"

So gingerly he tried it on, and it wasn't a bad fit at all. Jocelyn laughed. He did look rather strange, wearing the blazer over a jersey and with gardening trousers. Her father was not impressed.

"Okay Jo, so it fits. We'll take this back, so your mother can see it. But I came to show you what I had in mind. Look, if we put a window in here, and possibly in this side of the roof, put in a new floor, and then strengthen the door, will that give you what you need? Furniture, of course. You say. Will there be enough light?"

Jocelyn was sure there would be. She helped him out of the jacket, and folded it. The shed would make a good studio. Rather a grand name for a converted shed, but she'd see what happened.

* * *

The dreaded exam day got underway. Breakfast, a change into

more demure college kit, the ride into town, all familiar weekday routine, but with one exception. It wouldn't happen next week. It would all be over. As she waved to her departing father from the college access road, she could feel the pressure building.

"Hiya, Jo!" Betty yelled from the door. She seems confident, thought Jocelyn. All right for her, she's got it made; her mother could put her into a job with the publishers, no sweat. I couldn't sell cars for toffee. Nor do I want to spend my days selling groceries and newspapers. *I want to paint!* The inner declaration gave her a bit of a boost.

"Hi, Betty! Good weekend? I gather you went riding? Your mother called."

"Yeh. I know. She's got eyes for your Pa, Jo. She thinks he's sexy, she said so. Poor Daddy doesn't always come up to expectations, I guess. Sorry, Jo. I gather she's volunteered me for your do next Saturday. She wouldn't know I wanted to come anyway. It's all right, isn't it?"

"Sure, Bet. I may need some moral support. All *sorts* of people will be turning up – including our Mrs Summers, *and* Petersen! And your mum, with her magazine snoop; she does seem keen on getting us to allow a feature thing. Are you all set?"

Betty snorted with some derision. She didn't have the same set of papers to take; her subjects, Maths, a science and a resources paper wouldn't stretch her. Jocelyn, with her English papers, was in for some heavy writing.

"What will be, will be, Jo. Are you serious about this art thing? Is that why you've got old Petersen coming? Oh, and tell your Pa he's not the first my mother's been after!" Then came the revelation Jocelyn had, in part, expected. "My real mother went off with some foreign chap yonks ago. Not seen her for ages. Don't *really* know her as a mum. Felicity's okay, I suppose. She *does* love me, I think. Thought I best tell you, just in case. I'd best go, Jo. See you at lunch? Bye!" She gave Jo a touch on her arm, and ran off, her short college skirt bouncing and flashing her legs. "Takes after her step-mum", said Jo to herself. "Look out, Pa!" She walked slowly on, and into her first exam.

Nothing further was said about either Felicity or her father during lunch break, both girls were far too keen to swap comments on the severity of the first set of exam papers. Betty had the rest of the afternoon off, but Jocelyn had an hour's paper to deal with before she could take the bus back to her father's garage. Then, at last, she was free, and tomorrow, just a half day to survive.

As she walked across the garage forecourt and into the showroom, she was considering how best to warn her father about Felicity. She had no intention of seeing him upset her Mums. When he caught sight of her, David pushed his chair back from the desk, walked across the carpeted floor, and took her in his arms.

"Well, daughter of mine? How's day one? You don't look too harassed! Cup of tea?"

"Thanks Pa, that would be nice. Day one's not too bad. Nothing I couldn't handle. Can we have a chat?" David looked sharply at her. A chat? Sounded ominous. Sitting in front of his desk, tucked into a corner of the glossy showroom, Jocelyn felt a trifle overawed. Almost as though she was about to spend mega money on a flash new car she couldn't afford. He was looking at her, curiously, seeing her as an eminently attractive young woman, rather than as the teenager he recognised when at home. Context was everything. Pity about that college uniform. He made a sudden decision.

"What's to do, then, Jo?"

"You know when Betty came the other day, and her *mother* collected her, and they didn't look like mum and daughter? Well, Felicity is her *step-mum*, and she's a man hunter, Pa, and Betty thinks she's after you…" Jocelyn was close to tears. "You will be careful, won't you, Pa?"

David leant back in his chair, looked at the ceiling. Felicity was an attractive woman. She oozed appeal, and who wouldn't respond? His daughter, bless her, was riding shot gun. Eleanor was a girl in a million; she was Jo's mother, and his life–long companion. No Felicity would change that.

"Jo, I'm as vulnerable as the next when a woman like that swims into view. But, please, Jo, give me some credit for knowing where the limits lie. As the art galleries would say, look, but don't touch. If she wants to demonstrate her assets, then I'll look, like you would look at a Cézanne. You like what you see, but you don't take it home and shove it under the bed. Or on top of it, either. Right? I admire your support for your mother, Jo, and your care for me. I really do. Please don't worry; you can thump me if you think I'm kicking over the traces. Okay?"

Jocelyn saw the point, and felt a bit ashamed. She should have known her father better, and said so. David laughed. "I love you, silly. Now, enough said. We've got an hour and a bit before the shops shut. Come on, girl, I'm going to spend some money on you. You deserve it. I'll just clear it with the boss."

* * *

In the Jaguar, weaving through traffic towards the town centre, Jo voiced her uncertainty. "Does Mums know you're taking me shopping, Pa? You know she normally likes to come with me?"

"No, dear, she doesn't. Spur of the moment decision. I'm sure she won't mind. You want me to call her?"

"No, no, Pa. I'm intrigued. What had you in mind?"

"Something to make you look like the smashing young lady you are. Something special for your wardrobe, Jo. Hopefully." He swung the car into the multi-storey car park. "Got any ideas?"

Jocelyn still had some doubts. It was so unexpected. "Not really, Pa. You've taken me a bit by surprise. You tell me. You're paying!"

David, now in a very happy frame of mind, chuckled. "True. Short skirt and low cut top? Sweeping long gown? Tweed costume? Whatever we agree on. I just want to treat you. Bit of self-indulgence on my part. Is that all right – not too patronising?"

"Pa, really! Of course not! Maybe a dress I could wear if I

come out with you and Mums on a special occasion – sort of an evening dress thing. So you can be proud of me?"

"Suits me. It'll be a surprise for your mother, too!"

* * *

Having trawled through at least four dress shops, David began to think he'd attempted too much, and time was running out. There had been one or two possibles, but he could see from Jo's face she wasn't positive about them, so they had moved on. Then they tried an out-of-the-way place, and, on a rack at the back of the shop, a burgundy coloured dress that suited Jo's colouring admirably. The right length, a well-cut bodice and with little sleeves, a surprisingly interesting diagonal pleated skirt front and she filled it perfectly. The shop assistant, at first rather dour at having to deal with a customer ten minutes before closing, became very enthusiastic when she could see Jocelyn blossom and become proud, more self-confident than she already was. She suggested the addition of a scarf, gossamer light silk with a subtle pattern dark brown on amber. Jo twirled, preened, and was in raptures. She saw herself through her artist's eyes, imagined herself painted by Reynolds and hung on a stately home wall. A picture of elegance and poise.

"Yes please, Pa. It's lovely! What do *you* think?"

David contemplated, but only briefly. It embodied his thoughts. His daughter, looking sublime, even without her hair properly done, and at the end of a difficult day, so it must be right. Jo was waiting, the shop girl was waiting, and the manageress in the background was poised to turn them out.

"We'll take it. Anything else you need to go with it, Jo?"

Jocelyn started to colour up. She fancied *proper* underwear to have to suit a dress like this, but she didn't dare go that far with her father. Mums would like to take that aspect on board. She would need a suitable pair of shoes as well, not something they could sort out this evening.

"Not from here, Pa, thanks. Hadn't we better…" The rest left unsaid. David paid, trying not to flinch, and they were away.

* * *

Eleanor hadn't had a good day. The village shop usually was a friendly place, the hub of rumour and speculation, often quite busy, especially on a Monday, but it had been slow, dreadfully slow, and two customers in bad moods had soured the place. She'd been glad to get home. Half an hour with her feet up, a cup of tea and a bit of a read of the magazines Felicity had brought. She tried to visualise herself, and, well, all three of them, playing up to the camera and with the backdrop of *her* garden. Scary, as Jo would say. Thinking of which, where were they? Glancing at the clock, gone six. Strange, they should be back by now. Hope nothing had gone wrong. No, David would have rung. Relax, girl, she told herself.

Ten minutes later, the Jaguar purred up the drive.

"Hi Mums!" A happy, smiling, Jo. "You'll never guess! Pa's had a blip, and I love him for it! Give me a minute!" She tore upstairs, clutching the bag tight to herself so Mums wouldn't see the name.

" David! What've you been up to? I expected Jo to be all doom and gloom, instead she's come back as though she's been given full marks." He was trying to keep a straight face, inwardly a little petrified.

"Wait and see, Eleanor. Can I have a cup of tea?" He didn't expect a reply, getting his own mug out. Eleanor was both mystified and perplexed. Her husband and his daughter! Brief silence from upstairs, followed by footsteps. Not Jo's run, steady footsteps, and the door opened, and... *who was that?* She saw a sophisticated, elegant daughter, looking the proverbial million dollars. Fabulous!

"David! You horror – you've taken Jo shopping, without *me!* Oh, David, doesn't she *look* super! Oh my darling – you super, super girl! But you need decent shoes. And a proper bra! David – you've done it now! We'll have to show her off, won't we? Be proud of her?"

"Darling. I've been – we've been – proud of her for ages. I just think we've neglected the decorative side of her; so used to seeing her in scruff college kit. I had a sudden inspiration, so here we are. You approve?"

"Of course I approve. I'd have liked to be with you, but I guess you've done okay. It suits, darling, it suits very well. Bless you!" Jocelyn was practising a shoulders back walk; her chest out, her bottom swaying, and David followed her with his eyes as his wife spoke. He'd done the right thing. She'd go through the rest of the week's exams in the right frame of mind. She'd do all right. He'd managed to give her self-confidence a massive boost. And she looked a dream. She came back to him, stood on elegant tiptoe and gave him a kiss. Her eyes were shining.

"Thanks, Pa. *Thanks!*" Then she slipped out of the room, before she could burst into tears.

* * *

Upstairs, she preened in front of the mirror, the same mirror that inspired her first self-portrait.

She'd have to do another, full length, in *her dress*. For her Pa. Not now, though. So slowly, and carefully, she reluctantly shed her dress, and laid it with tender touch on her bed. Dearest Pa! She couldn't bring herself to put on lesser things, not tonight. Instead, she wrapped the old silky dressing gown round herself, and went back downstairs. Her Mums did an hour in the garden; Pa immersed himself in the television, and so she read a bit and listened to the radio in the kitchen before supper and bedtime.

Back in her room, she picked up her dress and held it in front of her, showing off in the mirror, before adjusting it onto the hanger, smoothing it down, hanging the scarf over the neckline, placing it in pride of place on the hanging rail. Super. Longing to wear it *properly*. Then bed, and to dream of an exhibition, her first, wearing *her* dress, congratulations from everyone, and old Petersen proudly telling the throng of people she was *his* pupil, standing in front of that splendid painting of *her* apple trees. And she was identified as the 'Apple Girl'. She wasn't to know it, of course, but it was to be an allegory of intricate detail, a complex understanding of life, birth, pubescence, adolescence, love, sadness, achievement and demise. But the foundations of this feat had yet to be laid. Only the ghostly image was in her mind and the undeniable drive, yet the conditions that would give her the impetus and inspiration still had to materialise. That day would follow after many days, other images, other inspirations, when she would be in tune with the spirit of the place; it was in her fates to bring the concept to completion. She moved, rolled over, unsure of what was in her subconscious. Fleeting pictures of antique people moving in space, clad in familiar old clothes; merged and mingled with gay blazers and straw hats, with naked figures running through the trees; a blonde haired goddess with a extremely short skirt chased by a rake –wielding gardener, disappearing into a ramshackle shed. Then a huge aircraft roared overhead and she was being smothered by a parachute. How could she climb free? Her sketch pad fell, was falling, falling, she was spinning, she was crying.

"Jo! Jocelyn! Darling! Please, darling. It's all right. Darling, I'm here. What's the matter?"

"Mums. Oh, *Mums!* Funny dreams!" Her mother was sitting alongside her on the bed edge, the bedside lamp on dim, holding her shoulder, stroking her hair. Jo struggled to turn over and sit up. "It's so odd, everything so jumbled up. My head's spinning."

"Look, dear, you've had a jolly strange day, and not so unusual at this time of the month, is it? Do you want a drink? Have a read, straighten out your thoughts, and I'll bring you something up."

David was still in front of the television, half asleep. He hadn't heard Jo's crying. Eleanor decided not to worry him, and went on into the kitchen to fix her daughter a hot chocolate. When she took it back upstairs, Jo was calmer, doing what her Mums had suggested, reading a lightweight romance.

"Sorry if I worried you, Mums. After such a super evening. Does Pa know?"

"No, Jo dear, he's sleeping in front of the box. P'raps you should have your own telly up here."

"*No way!* I'll read a bit more, Mums. I'll be all right. Thanks for the drink. You spoil me."

Eleanor sniffed. "Yes, dear, we do. Just so long as you realise, that's okay. Now go to sleep. No dreaming! Good night!"

After the book had nearly fallen on the floor for the third time, Jocelyn gave up, dimmed the lamp right off and closed her eyes. This time there were no haunting thoughts, just a comforting feel of warm sheets and a soft pillow. Sleep, gentle and deep.

* * *

Eleanor gently woke her dozing husband, a practised art. It was nearly midnight.

"David, my darling. Bed?"

"Whasat? Hmmm. Sorry dear. Was I snoring?"

"Not that I noticed. Bit of a waste of television programming. You're not supposed to go to sleep. But we've had this conversation before. Come on," she helped him up. "Do you want a drink? I've just had to get Jo one." Drat, she thought, I didn't mean to let on.

"Jo? She awake?"

"Uh huh. I think she was having silly dreams, but she's okay now, hopefully."

"Problem?"

"Possibly p.m.t., she does seem to get more upset then. Your surprise tonight may have heightened her mental state. Just one of those things. Don't worry. Let's go up, dear. What about that drink?"

"Thanks, but no. I'm fine. Did I do wrong, taking Jo shopping?"

Eleanor thought he looked worried. "No, darling, not at all! She's over the moon about it; I know it'll boost her confidence for this week, *and* I know you love to show her off. She is your favourite girl, after all!"

"Eleanor, *you're* my favourite girl! I see you in her, except I don't have to fight for her like I did you!"

She had to smile. If only he knew! She'd fallen for him then, hook, line and proverbial sinker, and any fighting he had done to stave off other suitors was simply, in her view, purely cosmetic; certainly she'd never once regretted her actions.

"Come to bed, David." She gently tugged him out of his chair. "It's tomorrow. Another day. Let's just get this girl of ours through the week. And, don't forget, we're being invaded at the weekend."

"True." He followed her up the stairs, treading carefully to avoid any creaking. Her waist was beckoning, her hips swaying beautifully, ankles…

In their room, she swung round to him, taking his head in both hands, kissing, kissing.

"You know what I want! I'm your favourite girl, you said? Show me!"

So he did. Gently. She had nothing to do. He knew how, and when all her things were carefully laid on her chair, he swung her, her hair down and eyes wide open; laid her down across the duvet; savouring the sight of her, the anticipation of her; and despite the lateness of the hour, they were awake to each other for the depth of the passion of their belonging.

* * *

Before Eleanor finally drifted into subliminal bliss of her afterglow, she murmured into his ear.

"Gorgeous man. Do I suit?"

"As ever. You happy?" She'd cried, just a little, but he'd felt her move, and he was pleased.

"Haaapppey. I'll buy Jo her undies. Night, lov…" She was asleep.

David stayed awake for a short while. Even after such a wonderful conjoining with Eleanor, his mind wandered off; to the blonde hair of that flirtatious magazine woman, the careless way she flicked her skirt, those eyes that seemed to be suggesting… oh, damn the girl! Then Jocelyn, proud and elegant, standing so gracefully, and dreamt of her as an artist of renown. And slept happily until dawn and the birds woke him and Eleanor together. He put an arm over, pulling her to him, kissed her messed up hair, soaking up the warmth and womanliness of her. He could never get over his innate joy of her constant presence, and hugged her.

"Hey, lover, you'll suffocate me. No! Go and shower. You smell!" She wasn't serious, but it offered an excuse. Withdrawing an arm, he half rolled over and stuck his feet out. She made to pull the covers back, and he was in half a mind to tug them off her. P'raps not.

"You smell too, girl, but I love you. It's reminiscent of a night of passion, so what's wrong with that? Join me in the shower?"

"No jolly fear! Go get yourself wet, David, then see how that precious daughter of ours is."

* * *

Jocelyn was already awake, and quite clear headed. Okay, she had a bit of a tummy ache, but nothing she couldn't handle. Day two of the exam week. Surprisingly, she was unworried. Yesterday it had been a bit nerve-racking, with moments when she'd wondered how she'd get through the week. But then she'd had that wonderful surprise from Pa, and over there was *the* dress! A silly, fleeting idea of trying it on again – no! She sat up, pushed the covers back, stretched, and lifted her knees. The bruises from that tree climb were still evident on her thighs, and a trifle sore. Nothing more had been heard from the Range. She wondered how that soldier chap was. Then she heard the shower running and got of the bed, went to the window as she always did, opened the sash wider and sniffed the air, before going to see which parent was already up. If it were Mums, she'd share the shower. She dumped her nightdress on the bed.

"Pa!" They never bothered with door bolts. "Sorry!"

"Not a problem, Jo! Won't be a minute. Scrub my back if you like!" Meant as a joke, he was more than a little surprised and a wee bit embarrassed when she took him up on his request. A novel experience. Eleanor frequently did, but Jo? He kept his back to her, and she did a good job.

"Okay, Pa. Here's your towel. I'm not looking!" David chuckled. As if it mattered. He took the towel and wrapped it round himself, but couldn't avoid her. She was a shapely girl, but he knew that.

"Don't fret, Pa. I've no hang ups. I've got the same bits as Mums. But I need the loo – so..."

He took the hint, smiling. Eleanor gave him an old-fashioned look.

"Been ogling your daughter, have you? Shame on you! How is she?"

"Fine, I should say. Bright and breezy, says she has 'no hang-ups', if that's anything to go by. Your turn. You can scrub her back, or vice-versa. She did mine." He watched her face, but she kept her thoughts to herself.

* * *

Eleanor decided she could take Jocelyn into the college, especially as the day's exam didn't start until ten o'clock, giving her the opportunity to ensure Jo was still in a good frame of mind. Desultory conversation while she drove, then once at the college entrance, she asked.

"You happy with the state of things, Jo? I mean, exams, the weekend, your period?"

She got an old-fashioned look. "Sure, Mums. I'm okay. Really. Sorry about last night, but I'm fine now. Can we go shopping for shoes and undies? To go with Pa's dress?"

Eleanor thought that was funny. Pa's dress! "It's *your* dress, Jo, *not* your father's! Yes, I'd love to help choose shoes and things, so, what time do you finish today? Midday, wasn't it?"

"Mmm, but I'd promised to spend a bit of time with Betty going over tomorrow's general paper. P'raps half two, Mums? Maybe Betty might like to come, shall I ask her?"

Jocelyn was forever thinking of her friends, Eleanor

thought. No bad thing, maybe, but sometimes a trifle irritating. "Do you really want her to watch you choose your undies, Jo? I think we're best on our own, really, I do. Another time, dear."

"Okay, Mums. Just a thought. I'd best go. Don't want to be late. See you here at two thirty?"

* * *

The morning was a mixture of both easy and complex thoughts. Jocelyn, scanning her exam paper, did an inward somersault. First impressions were 'Oh my goodness', before a glimmer of light as she came back to reality. Of course she could answer the questions! Pa had every confidence in her. Mums was taking her shopping, so let's get on with it. Her pen had a life of its own, and the essay just rolled. Complex argument, but simply put. Then the quick answers. Ten lines each, no problem. Done!

She very nearly got up to go, before subsiding and lapsing into a dream. She was walking – gliding – into a super ballroom, on the arm of a charming chap, and all eyes were on her. Wearing her dress, dark burgundy, the best in the world; her painting, pride of place, on an easel on the stage.

"Miss Danielleson! Are you with us? Your paper please!"

The ballroom vanished, and the dress. At least she still had her school kit on.

"Sorry!" She handed the sheets up to the invigilator, that woman from the maths department, no sense of humour. Two of the boys from her group smirking at her. She frowned at them, and ignored the titter from another girl, that silly Adeline. Then her friend Julie came across and put her arm round her.

"Jo – it looked as though you were day-dreaming! The paper wasn't all that bad, was it? Come and have a coffee with me!" Julie was a tall, slender girl with jet-black hair. She was clever, too. Well, at least she always managed to give that impression.

"Thanks, Julie. Good idea. No, I think I did all right. Just that my Pa's just bought me this super dress, and I was imagining me at a dance thing. You dance?"

The two girls left the others swapping disaster stories and walked off to the students' lounge area.

"I do, actually. Not your nightclub stuff, you know, but *proper* ballroom. I love it. Takes you out of yourself, makes you feel great. You?"

"No, never felt the need. I don't care much for going out with boys, either. Tony isn't bad, neither is Elliot, I suppose. But they don't have much imagination. Where do you go?"

Julie was grinning. No imagination! She was sure they had. Most boys did, but not what Jocelyn meant. Shame really, for Jo was a good-looking girl, with a better figure than hers.

"Oh, all over the place, really. Dance classes are in the Athens Club, there's a super chap who does the Latin tuition. You ought to come. You'd love it, Jo. It's very professional. No silly stuff, I promise you. I'll introduce you, if you want. Anyway, can I get you a coffee?"

Jo and Julie spent a convivial quarter of an hour discussing the relative merits of dance and art, all thoughts of the past exam clean out of mind, before Betty found them. She looked gloomy, not at all the breezy girl of normality.

"Betty, Hi! You don't look a happy girl. What's up?" Jo was all concern.

Julie thought she knew, but she wasn't totally on the ball. "Didn't it go well?" Julie was referring to Betty's morning exam paper, but it was more than that.

"Nope. My mother's lost her cool, my father's gone off for a couple of weeks on some conference thing, and I *feel rotten!*" She collapsed into a chair, brushing her hair back off her forehead, and Jo spotted what looked like perspiration.

"*Betty!* Hadn't you best see the nurse? Julie, go and get Mrs Summers to phone Betty's Mum. I'll take her to the nurse. Oh, and if you see Trish – let her know will you?" Jo, forever the organiser, had a knack of solving problems in a crisis. Julie just had to nod and accept her instructions.

"Come along, miss. You'll be okay." Jo took Betty's hand, lugged her up out of the chair and with an arm wrapped round her friend, carted her off towards the nurse's room.

The nurse wasn't particularly sympathetic; too experienced, too well seasoned in the vagaries of teenage females to be overly concerned. She did what she had to, confirmed her own instinctive diagnosis, spoke to Betty's mother on the phone, arranged for her to collect her charge as soon as possible and, as Trish had turned up, left her to look after Betty in the rest room while she went off in search of a late lunch. Jocelyn, with her eye on the time, and now fully aware from the nurse of the simple and regular problems that Betty obviously was prone to experience, commiserated, mentally thanked her lucky stars she didn't wilt the same way, and went to find her mum. Trish was better at the handholding routine. Julie had to face another hour and a half's exam before she could go home. What a day!

* * *

"Hi Mums! You're looking lovely! All dressed up? For me?" Eleanor had made a special effort; after a grotty couple of hours in the shop, she'd gone home for a long soak in the bath, then inspired, had looked out some half decent clothes and spent a bit of time on some make-up. After all, she was going out with *her* daughter. Her *growing up* daughter. And her efforts were both noticed and appreciated. She smiled at Jo, and loved her.

"Yes, you super girl. How's your day?"

"Oh, Mums!" Jo flung open the car door, and dived in. She managed to give her mother a quick misplaced kiss on the chin and pulled the car door shut. "Let's go. Before some silly boy sees us. Poor Betty's suffering the monthlies, so the nurse says. So she couldn't have come with us anyway. Her mother's coming to fetch her. I had to get her to the nurse's room before she flaked out. Oh, and the exam was a doddle. I finished early and nearly walked out. Day-dreamed instead. Nearly fell asleep. Where are we going?" Her stattaco resume of the college day made Eleanor chuckle. She backed the car away from another vehicle that had inconsiderately pulled into the space in front of her, and then took off at speed. "Steady, Mums! Let's get there in one piece!"

Eleanor had some idea of where to go, but she still had an open mind, so once safely parked, and with arm tucked into Jo's they went to see what fortune had in store. They looked into little boutiques, into department stores, and even the cheapy shops. Then they went back on themselves, and finally satisfied with purchases both sensible and some more sexy than practical, returned to the car clutching a multi-coloured collection of bags. Eleanor was quite pleased with herself, for not only was her lovely girl now well equipped, she'd even appeared to appreciate pretty things, which for a girl careless whether she wore small things or not, was a definite step forward. *And* she'd improved her own wardrobe at the same time. She wasn't overly sure about one pair of the shoes Jo had chosen, but until they were worn with the dress she would reserve judgement. At least the other pair were fine, though she was puzzled why Jo asked if they were suitable for dancing. Dancing? Jo? Hmmm.

* * *

Once back home, Jocelyn couldn't wait. She tore upstairs, and flung all her college things off, to hear her Mums calling.

"Jo! Jo – you silly girl! If you're going to try things on, have a shower first, there's a good girl! Don't you want some tea first?"

Jocelyn paused. Yes, she could see the sense of that. So she tucked herself into her cosy dressing gown and padded barefoot back down into the kitchen. Tea and teacake. Then a thought, "This Edwardian tea party, Mums? Do you really mean it? With Pa in that stripy jacket?"

"And you in that converted night dress, looking very pretty? Why not, Jo? Don't you think it's a nice idea? I do. It'll be a talking point. Might even make us some pocket money. At least I can make scones and cucumber sandwiches. Shall we have a dressing-up evening? Unless you need to do some more revision?"

Jocelyn pulled a face. She didn't want to be reminded she still had some more exams to do, and as far as she was concerned it was all now far too late to think about revision. What would be, etcetera, she thought. "No, no more revision. If Pa's in the mood, Mums, I'm game. Pass the teapot. Then I'm off for a shower."

* * *

When David returned from a satisfying day, three positive sales and another two in the offing, he was greeted by a vision of loveliness. Jocelyn, showered, even lightly scented, hair assiduously brushed and pinned into some semblance of style, her new dress fitting beautifully over consciously comfortable but also rather agreeably appealing equally new underwear, did another twirl in her super shoes. Her father's heart swelled with pride. He didn't regret his action one little bit. If it meant Jocelyn was one step nearer becoming a dream young lady, then it was money well spent. Just a slight pang of regret that it maybe meant the close of a chapter, a change in lifestyle, but then, it was going to have to happen sooner or later. She was waiting for his approbation, oozing self-confidence, radiant and blooming. Eleanor guessed he'd fling her about, and wasn't wrong. Jo squeaked as he caught her round her waist and swung her off her feet.

"Lovely girl! Well done, both of you. You're a picture, my daughter. Eleanor – shall we take her out to dinner? Show her off?" In the back of his mind he really wanted to see how she reacted to her newfound interest in her appearance. Eleanor frowned at him.

"Not tonight, David. For one thing, supper's organised, for another *we* need to dress up, and we also have to have a table booked. Don't rush fences; maybe after all the weekend's shenanigans are over, and Jo's free of exam phobia – if she ever had it – make it a sort of celebration? What I'd like to do is have a look at our idea of the Edwardian tea party. So get yourself sorted, David, we'll have supper and look at the clothes you dragged out from the orchard hut. Jo, dear, much as I love you in that dress, you'd better get changed again. Supper in ten minutes, both of you!"

* * *

After a typical Old Vicarage summer evening supper, salad and cold meats, nothing 'heavy', Eleanor sent Jo back upstairs to get into the flimsy dress she'd recovered from the orchard shed. How that lot had ended up in a box out there was anyone's guess, but it was an opportune discovery. David she managed to persuade into his old cricket flannels and with open shirt and the stripy blazer, all he needed was the straw boater. She'd find one from somewhere. When Jo returned she'd found a suitable slip so the dress didn't look too revealing. Her mother approved; her father's raised eyebrows showed he wasn't sure he could cope with seeing his Jocelyn looking quite so ravishing.

"That what you had in mind, Eleanor? She looks as though she's posing for a page three!"

"Page three! What do you know about page threes, David? I was going to get those sleeves sorted, give her a high waist, and a few strings of those old beads. Not a lot we can do with her hair, and I don't suggest we change it – it's nice as it is. A ribbon, perhaps?"

"No, Mums, a flower. One of your gerberas from out the greenhouse? Or a rose or something?"

"Good idea, Jo. Yes, you're right. David?"

"So long as we make sure she's decent. I don't want her flashing her socks, if you see what I mean. After all, we don't really know who's going to turn up, do we?"

Eleanor had to laugh. Put Jocelyn into a pretty dress, and he wants to take her out to a posh restaurant and show her off. Put her in a flimsy see-through thing and that's not on!

"Don't sweat, Pa! I'll try and stay decent. It'll be a bit of a laugh. Anyway, it's only for a little while, isn't it, Mums? Till we run out of scones or sandwiches? You know Betty's coming over? So long as she gets over her fit of the vapours. I had to get her to the nurse today. She's suffering from too much mother – stepmother – and too little father. I'm a lucky girl, having you two as parents."

Eleanor and David exchanged glances.

"You'll make us blush, girl. So what's wrong with Betty?" David was curious.

"Oh, the usual thing. *You know,* girl problems. At least, that's what the nurse thought. I don't think her stepmother really looks after her properly. I know she *looks* as though she does, all beams and smiles, but I don't know, it doesn't seem right, somehow. Poor Betty. Hope she doesn't miss her exams. Oh, heck. That reminds me. Felicity and her magazine people are going to be here on Saturday, aren't they? Photos, Pa, of you and me in *this* rig! Oh Heavens!" Jo turned to her father. "Is this such a good idea?"

David hadn't forgotten, truly Felicity was *not* the sort of girl one could possibly put totally out of mind. Photos in costume was not a particularly pleasing prospect but they couldn't back down now. Eleanor agreed, but all she had to do was organise the supplies, apart from keeping an eye on the garden generally. Jocelyn decided it was time to call it a day, kissed her parents goodnight and went off to bed.

Having dumped her 'costume', but still with her decorative new flimsy things on, she preened in front of the mirror. Perhaps a decent bra wasn't too bad a thing to wear, and the time the shop girl took to make sure she had one that fitted seemed to have paid off. It pushed her up a bit, and she rather liked the new shape she had. Should she wear it tomorrow? The thought of tomorrow made her flinch. *Two* more wretched exams, and she quailed at the prospect before taking a grip on herself. After today, she should be able to cope with anything, remember, Jocelyn? She took her new things off carefully and laid them delicately on the chair. How different from her normal 'kick things off and leave them where they fall' routine! When Eleanor checked her daughter an hour later, she had to smile. Jo was fast asleep, albeit no nightdress, silly girl, but she saw the way her clothes had been laid. So they had succeeded. Jocelyn was on the way to becoming a young lady.

Across the other side of the valley, Jo's friend Betty was tossing and turning in her bed. Felicity, downstairs, was working away on her concept of the Saturday project, unworried. Having a stepdaughter who couldn't handle feminine problems was a nuisance; she was a wimp. Of far more concern was obtaining a good feature out of the Old Vicarage and that fascinating chap David. His daughter was a good-looking girl, too. No doubt Eleanor would come good, such a *nice* down-to-earth woman. She hoped David didn't get the wrong idea but flashing her pants was one way of ensuring attention. Results were all that mattered. Sketching away, she was getting her storyline well to her liking, but the pictures weren't in keeping. She hoped her photographer could see what she wanted. So long as it was Britten. He was the best, but she knew he didn't like working weekends. She scribbled a note to herself on the edge of her storyboard: 'Ring Britten'. Then the phone rang, making her glance at the time. Eleven. Yes, that would be her husband.

"Hi darling! All in order? Conference working well? How's the hotel?" She listened, attentively. He worked *so* hard, and deserved all the credit and respect the organisation paid him. She loved him, and was sorry she couldn't bring herself to offer him another child. Not her scene, and luckily he'd accepted things, given that Betty was part of his world. Betty!

"By the way, I had to bring Betty back from college today. She's had another of her silly turns. You will have to get her sorted, Alan. No, I don't think you need to come back, I'll manage. If she listens to me. Don't forget I'm doing a feature at the Old Vicarage this weekend. Good garden, interesting family. Lovely daughter, Betty's friend. It's a barbecue for the village. Should be quite a laugh. Right, yes, I'll go up and see if she's all right. Love you, darling. Speak to you tomorrow. Have a good day. Bye!" She made kissing noises at the phone before pushing the off button, sighed, put the papers down and went to see what Betty was up to.

Some few miles the other side of town, 'Old' Petersen was at home, in his bachelor flat, trying to make some semblance of order out of his plans – and thoughts – for the summer break. Though he did enjoy his work, trying to instil some artistic appreciation into his victims, as he called them, he looked forward to the six-week opportunity to regain his sanity. Most summers lately he'd managed to get in some serious painting, essential if he was going to maintain his self-esteem. A week in that hot, baking, vivid reds and oranges and blues of southern France – or should he try for Italy? He bethought himself of the conversation he'd had with that shapely redhead, Jocelyn, and inwardly berated the masculine side of him for rashly suggesting she accompanied him as a model, the sort of comment that could have really landed him in hot water. So okay, she was attractive, as models were expected to be; he wasn't going to waste his time and talent – and money, come to that, - on some wrinkly middle-aged colleague. Apart from Dylys, that is. With a sigh, he put down the regional brochure he'd unconsciously been studying, and shrugged. No doubt there'd be some willing French barmaid he could con into shedding some of her clothes for a Euro or two. Jocelyn – Danielleson, wasn't it – was looking to become an artist? She said she'd done a self-portrait, and wanted him to look at it, possibly other things as well? And he had promised to look in on that village barbecue thing on Saturday; so all was not lost. Idly he sorted through the travel brochures again, discarded a few, left the Provence one, the Italian one and, on a whim, the Moroccan one, on the coffee table, and reached for the red wine bottle.

* * *

In the Officers' Mess at Larkhill, the young Territorial Officer who had been the unfortunate victim of a bungled parachute drop three days previously, had been invited to dine with the residents, as a prelude to his departure back home the following day. After two days on his back in the Medical wing on the base, allowing torn muscles, strains, contusions and abrasions to sort themselves out, he had been given the all clear. Being the subject of discussion and debate over the rights and wrongs of weekend exercises; treated by some as an object of derision and by others as one of considerable fortune, rescued from almost serious if not fatal injury by a *'femme fatale'*; all added up to an unnerving experience. And now here he was, being wined and dined in traditional and extravagant manner, something totally out of the ordinary. His fellow medical students back in Edinburgh would not believe him.

Captain Adams had sponsored him, had briefed him on etiquette, and really he couldn't have had a more memorable evening. He'd still had to take some good-natured banter, happily avoiding the one officer who gave the impression that it would have been better if he'd either not jumped at all, or if he had, that his 'chute had totally failed. Fancy being hauled out of a *tree,* and by a wisp of a *girl!* What he did know was he was going to find that wisp and see what she looked like, and make jolly sure she knew how grateful he was. The port was circulating and his head was beginning to throb. Tomorrow. He'd find out where she lived, and try and see her. Then he'd have to get back to Lyneham to pick up his car. It was going to be a long trawl home to Norfolk.

* * *

Mrs Summers had finished roughing out the report on the year she would present to the Management Board, and collapsed into an armchair for a half hour's relaxation before she went to bed. Only another couple of weeks and she'd be clear of students; the college echoing and empty, a couple of days to finalise the year end, and then home to her beloved Wales. She leant back and closed her eyes, stretching her toes, moving her arms, clenching and unclenching hands, flexing her shoulders. Thoughts of some events at the college rolled, annoyingly, across her mind. Better now than in the middle of the night. She didn't always sleep well at this time of year. The bedsit was stuffy, despite the fan. There'd been that stupid lad who'd stolen a girl's bag; he'd deserved being arrested but having police at the college was not good. Then Jeffries had announced he'd wanted to resign at Christmas. No loss, really, his capabilities limited to destroying all interest his students might ever have in literature. That Downs girl with no stamina for her period; shame really, if it was going to interfere with the exam schedule. Then she recalled a conversation with her about the Tinsfield barbecue, and her promise to turn up. Well, if college girls were helping there, it would be churlish to ignore the event; it might even be fun. Time for bed, she thought, before I fall asleep in the chair.

* * *

Jocelyn, happily dreaming again of her debut in the art gallery, stirred, rolled over onto her tummy and the covers slipped down onto the floor. Her dream changed to being taken outside by a dashing young man with that dramatically black hair and super friendly eyes, where he proceeded to take her dress off and she hadn't got anything on underneath so she was cold and ran into her studio to get warm and she rolled over again and really woke up, and realised that she *hadn't* got anything on, and she *was* feeling the cold. She flapped an arm down the bedside and fumbled for the cover, dragging it back on top of her and snuggling down again. What a silly dream!

* * *

Trish slipped out from underneath her boyfriend's arm.

"No! Enough! I'm not going to! I don't care what state you're in! Just give over, will you! If you really care for me, then leave that bit alone! You're getting too enthusiastic, Brendan!"

She'd not discouraged him early enough and he'd got carried away. Okay, it was his car, and she'd had a good time with him in the pub, but it was uncomfortable and she'd no intention of losing her virginity in the back of a car even with him. She was losing her patience. Being fondled, caressed, snogged, fair enough, but that's as far as it was going to go.

Brendan gave up. Trish was a peach of a girl, and wonderful company. He'd thought he was only responding to her inclinations, but it seemed he'd got it wrong. So, okay, he'd got too much respect for her to push. "Sorry, Trish." He took his hand from between her thighs, and pulled her skirt straight. She had to grin, and kissed his cheek.

"Take me home, Brendan. Then you can sort yourself out. Look, if you want to be useful, come with me on Saturday to Jo's place. Village barbecue, teas, they need professional help. Then we'll see."

Not that she'd any intention of changing her stance, and he knew it. He laughed. At least it would be different.

* * *

So the village event was going to be the centre of attraction. The local Woman's Institute Barbecue Committee had had a fruitful meeting, all i's dotted and t's crossed. The entire event was organised, all they had to do was to ensure Mrs Danielleson knew what they wanted, so Mrs Blounce and two of her cronies would go and see her tomorrow. The meeting broke up, with the ladies departing back to indifferent husbands as the last summer moon appeared over the hill and the village drifted into quiet.

* * *

Dawn, misty, heralding another fine day, brought Jo alive early, nothing unusual. Fragments of a dream she'd had bothered her, and though she couldn't piece it all together, it had involved her dress, that she had remembered. She scrambled off her bed, covers slipping off again, and she vaguely recalled having heaved them back over her sometime in the night. Early morning inspiration gripped her, slipping into *that* dress; grabbed her large sketch pad and a 3B pencil, sat on the chair by the window, caught the morning light and the reflection in her mirror. Deftly, surely, with eyes flicking up and down, she caught her outline, her hair, and with head to the side, the folds of the dress, the lines down to her bust, then her waist, ending where the dress was flounced out over her knees. Just enough. The vision she had was the colour, the glow from the warm light of an orange sun. The paper wasn't really quite big enough; as the only pad she had it would have to do. Holding it at arm's length, she viewed it critically. The eyeline wasn't right; her nose looked a bit squiff. She'd do it again later. She heard movement; hastily pulling the dress off over her head got it back on the hanger, just managing to achieve some semblance of normality before her Mums appeared.

Breakfast, and Pa's turn to take her in. It would be a grotty day, but then all downhill. The thought of spending more time on the latest drawing tonight would have to keep her sane; in her mind's eye she could see the finished picture; she'd give it to Pa as a thank you present for the dress. He seemed a bit pre-occupied this morning and her own thoughts kept her quiet, so the run was far less chatty than normal. She offered a cheek to his 'take care, have a good day' kiss, and saw him go. Dear Pa!

The exam papers were *not* to her liking, unlike yesterdays. Managing to catch Old Petersen in a good mood she sweet-talked a couple of pots of watercolour from his store without giving too much away. At least his curiosity meant he was sure to come on Saturday. By the time the clock had seen the collection of the second and last paper of the day, she was shattered. Half three, and Mums would be waiting. No sign of Betty today, which was bad news. Trish hadn't seen her either, though at least she had a bright smile on her face, saying with a sort of wink she expected to have someone else with her on Saturday, not saying who. Must be the boyfriend, Jo thought, as she pushed through the throng of the younger lot out of the gate, and looking for Mums.

"Makes a change for you to be coming straight home, Jo! No shopping tonight, unless we stop off at the pizza place to pick up some supper? Fancy a pizza?" This was an unusual occurrence.

Jocelyn looked quizzically at her mother. "What's up, Mums? Not like you to fancy shop-bought? Nothing wrong, is there?"

"No dear, not at all. Only it'll save time, and we've still to sort out a few things for Saturday. After all, the last two nights we've been pre-occupied, haven't we?" Jo was treated to a sideways smile, and a pat on her knee. So they had, *with her!*

"Sorry, Mums!"

"Don't be, Jo. Your father and I aren't, so long as we can keep the W.I. women under control. I've had a phone call. We'll be having an 'Official Visit' tonight. Best behaviour job!"

Drat, Jo thought. I shan't be able to colour in my picture. Oh, well, it'll keep.

So a stop to pick up supper in a box, and home to sample it. David wasn't best pleased, but, as he aptly described it, at least it was a refuelling exercise. It gave them an extra three-quarters of an hour, just adequate to look at the old barn and sort out in their minds what they'd do, before Mrs Blounce and her two cronies turned up. David, on his best behaviour, skilfully got them agreeing to a lot of what *he* thought were the best arrangements. Eleanor got out the best cups and brewed some proper coffee, decided against the shop chocolate biscuits and sacrificed her special home-made orange cookies. That turned out to be a good move. Conversation over coffee, and Jo evidently a girl who did *exactly* as her parents wished, put them all in a good mood, so introducing the idea of an Edwardian tea party after the lunchtime barbecue went down quite well.

"You'll be *in costume*?"

"Yes. Stripey blazer, straw boater. Lots of cucumber sandwiches, scones, we do rather need some more tables though. Perhaps card tables; and we haven't got too many tablecloths. I've got a large teapot, and a fair number of teacups, but maybe..." Eleanor raised her eyebrows at Mrs Blounce.

"My dear, I'm sure we can rustle up some extra tables, and cloths are *no* problem. You can have the crockery from the village hall if you wish. I think it will be a splendid addition to the event, Mrs Danielleson. You say your daughter will be a waitress?"

"Well, more of a hostess, actually. We've found a super dress for her. We discovered we had a cache of old clothes in some boxes in a shed, all rather amazingly, and the blazer my husband will wear came from there as well. No doubt we'll find out about it sooner or later, but it's a trifle odd. Suits the occasion, though." Mrs Blounce made no comment, and after a few more minutes the delegation took itself off, well pleased with its mission. The barbecue was in good hands.

* * *

Jocelyn excused herself and made a beeline upstairs. Eleanor and David thought nothing of it, uncorked a bottle and retreated up to the old orchard. From her bedroom window Jo saw them go and grinned to herself. Good, I have at least an hour! With a tinge of apprehension mingled with anticipation, she straightened out her morning's creation and with soft rubber and a bit of concentration put right the detailing of her eyes, nose and lips. She did a comparison with her earlier charcoal portrait, and was happy. It seemed to work. Now for the next stage. Having worked with watercolour before, she was confident, and using minimal water, added in bold colour before washing it down to the subtlety she had in mind. Reds, oranges, a hint of the darker burgundy. How long would it take to dry? Knowing a disturbance might spoil her efforts, and with firmness unusual in her, she left it to make herself a coffee. The evening was closing in, the sun had all but gone, and the garden scents were at their peak. Nursing her mug, Jo went out and walked slowly round the immediate garden. The quiet and the serenity of the place got to her, the success of her painting, the imminent end of her college life, and the way in which her Mums and Pa had treated her... so, so happy. They were gone a long time? Suddenly, she shivered. The sky was luminous velvet and the first stars had appeared. Dark edges to the treeline merged into a darker mass of the shrubs, and she shivered again. Flinging the dregs of her coffee away, she felt she needed to find them and walked purposely up the central path towards the paddock. Sure-footedly, she could travel the path blindfold. Reaching the gate into the paddock, she whistled. An owl replied. Was it an owl, or Pa? She copied the call and was treated to the silent flight of the bird against the sky.

"Mums! Pa!" She called, a tinge of anxiety. No answer. Walking carefully on, she crossed the paddock. The loom of the apple trees, the darker line of the hedge. She called again. "Mums! Pa!"

Still no answer. Now thoroughly alarmed, she blundered into the hedge, scratching her knee on some old barbed wire, found the gate and called again. No answer. They couldn't be there! She'd have to get a torch; it was far too dark. What was she going to do? Sure they'd come up here? Then, as she turned to retrace her steps, the lights went on in the house. A rush of relief, and she ran back down into the garden.

"Mums! *Where have you been?*"

Eleanor sensed the panic in Jo's voice and felt a pang of conscience. David came back from the lounge, hearing her. "Sorry, Jo. We wandered off into the lane, came round the long way. Such a lovely evening. Didn't realise we'd taken quite so long."

"Well, you had me worried. I've been up to the orchard to look for you, and scratched my knee."

She was calming down. Eleanor licked her fingers, and wiped the scratch.

"Ouch! Mums!"

"All right dear, its not *that* bad! Do you want a drink?"

"I've had a coffee."

"I meant *a drink!*"

"You finished the wine?"

"Uh huh. Port and lemon? *Small* brandy?"

"In a minute. I want to show you something." She skipped upstairs, hoping the watercolour would have dried sufficiently. The paper had crinkled a trifle, but it wasn't wet. Damp, maybe, but that was okay. She picked it up carefully by the opposite corners and walked steadily downstairs.

"Another sketch, Jo?" David was curious.

She turned it round, and held it against herself, facing them.

"Jo! You – in your new dress! That's brilliant! Well done my girl!"

"For you, Pa. Thank you for my new dress."

"I'll have it framed, for over my desk at the showroom. To remind me of a very pretty daughter!"

Jo almost blushed. All this praise, when she hadn't done anything other than follow her inclinations. Eleanor saw the embarrassment and cooled things down.

"Maybe Jo ought to make sure she's happy with it first, David. She'll want to show it to her college lecturer guy, what's his name, Petersen? He's supposed to be coming on Saturday. What else will you want to show him, Jo?"

"I haven't got all that much, really, not when I think about it, and 'cos of the exams a lot of the ideas I've had, you know, the little sketches, I haven't managed to flesh out. P'raps when I get back on Friday – I finish at lunchtime. Can you pick me up, Mums?"

"Should think so, dear. We'll get any last minute things at the same time. I'd like some help on the scone front, though. What time can you get back, David? You've managed to get cover for Saturday?"

He had to laugh, imagining the consternation if he said he'd have to work. After reassuring his darling wife that he'd get back as soon as he could, and that, yes, John would cover again but it was going to cost them a couple of nights baby-sitting, they called it a day.

* * *

On Thursday, Betty returned to college in a better frame of mind, Step-mum having unbent somewhat, more like the friend she ought to be rather than a starchy mentor; Trish had a discussion with Jo about suitable clothes she and Betty ought to wear at the barbecue, promising to borrow some suitable dresses and aprons and so on from her work; Jo's exam wasn't too bad, and even Old Petersen had sought her out to confirm he'd be with them just before twelve. It was all falling into place. The Daniellesons had a relaxing evening not doing a lot and retreated to bed early, although Jo spent a bit of time expanding on her sketch of her father on the log up on the Plain, which made her think again about the guy she'd rescued. She still had to get Pa to ring and find out how he was getting on.

Ironically, the subject of her concern had woken up that morning with a splitting headache, and the M.O. had suggested he ought not to risk his concussion by travelling home that day, which gave him added impetus to the thought of looking up his rescuers. Finding Captain Adams, he suggested he ought to offer his thanks in person. Fine by me, was the response; perhaps he could deliver the official letter of thanks for services rendered, but might it not be better to wait until the weekend? So he phoned his still anxious parents to advise them of his postponed return. At least he didn't have to get back to Edinburgh until the end of next month, which was something.

* * *

So the stage was set. Jocelyn dressed slowly on the Friday morning, a trifle numbed by the knowledge this was the last day she'd go to college as a student. The garden, as seen from her window, seemed to be holding its breath. Tomorrow all her mum's hard work would be under scrutiny, a backdrop to village politics, another place for the unthinking to congregate by habit; village events essential to some for social climbing. She knew all this, she also knew her Mums was apprehensive, on several counts. The garden was all-important and must survive. The family reputation was at stake, they must have everything organised, nothing must go wrong. The weather must stay fine. The Edwardian teas idea must be a success. As she reached the kitchen, her father came out of the front room, clutching her dress picture.

"Pa! It's not finished – you can't take it into work yet!"

"Okay, Jo, don't panic; I wanted to check the size so I can organise a frame. That's all right, isn't it?"

"Generally, you take the picture to the framers, Pa. All you need to do is select the sort of frame you want. If I can, I'll get it finished next week. There'll be plenty of time." She pulled a face. "I suppose I ought to find a job or something. Earn some pocket money. Any ideas?"

"Not off the cuff, Jo, but I'll give it some thought. You'd better have this back upstairs, then. I'll take it. You go and get your breakfast."

* * *

Later, after she had been dropped off at the college for the last time, she bumped into Julie.

"Hi, Jo! I was meaning to find you. Wondered if you wanted to come to the dance classes with me once we're clear of all this? Betty might be interested as well. What do you think?" Julie always had seemed a sensible girl to Jocelyn, consequentially she didn't dismiss the idea out of hand.

"I might, Julie. Good of you to ask, but I'll have to think about it. Can I let you know? Give me your phone number. Who else goes from here?"

Julie thought for a moment, and then listed some half a dozen names. Including Tony.

"Oh dear. Ummm. Anyone else?"

"Well, I think there's a couple from your village, Jo; and quite a few more middle aged. It's not a club in that sense. Don't worry; it's all very good natured. You'll be fine. Tony won't be any problem, if that's what's bothering you. Promise." She was sure of that, seeing as Tony was now *her* dance partner most of the time. "What time's your exam?"

"Heavens! Now! I'll have to fly. Thanks, Julie, I'll be in touch."

* * *

And then it was all over. The last paper. All sheets handed in, the die firmly cast. Strangely, she felt quite relaxed about it all. What was going to be was going to be, either she'd get some decent grades, or she wouldn't. In such a mood, she collided with Mrs Summers, on her way back to her office.

"Jocelyn! Please watch where you're going! I don't want any accidents so near to the end of the year! Have you completed your exam programme?"

"Yes, Mrs Summers, thank you. I'm just about to go, if that's all right. My mother's collecting me."

"Of course, my dear. I hope you do well. You deserve to. Don't forget you need to be back on Thursday week for the last day. Just to sign off." She paused. "The village barbecue – at your home, isn't it? I'll be there. Looking forward to it, in fact. Don't keep your mother waiting."

* * *

The last minute shopping was a pain. Eleanor went round the supermarket at least three times, peering at all the shelves. Should she take some of those, in case? What about a couple more bottles of lemonade? Are you sure we have enough flour for scones? Jocelyn became exasperated and in the end dragged her mother through the checkout with the determination of a husband.

"There's always the village shop, Mums, if we *do* run out. Which we won't. Anyway, isn't it the Blounce woman who's supposed to be organising things?"

"Well, yes, but…"

"No buts, Mums. Let's go home, I'm starving. And I want to try and finish that picture for Pa."

* * *

Once back home, and with some cheese and tomato sandwiches and a glass of home-made lemonade on a tray, Jo left her mother contemplating the scone manufacturing and vanished up to her room. With the dress picture clipped to her largest board, she set to work, painstakingly completing the detail. After a while, she got up and stretched, reasonably happy about the way it was going. It struck her, curiously, that doing *another* self-portrait was like saying she was in love with herself. Narcissistic, wasn't it? She took another look at it from a distance, and shrugged. It would do, and Pa obviously liked it, so it couldn't be too bad. So now what? Back to the orchard? Why not? Stripping off her college skirt and blouse, she rummaged through her wardrobe for an old dress. Better than jeans, it was still too warm.

"Think I've finished that one, Mums, I'm off up the orchard. You don't want any help with the baking, do you?"

"No thanks, Jo. It's a bit like a production line, I know, but I'll get there. No, you go."

* * *

Stretched out on the grass, she reflected on the week. Overhead, sketchy clouds from the mid-afternoon heat drifted slowly in and out of view between the leaf-laden branches above her, a mere suggestion of a breeze producing a gentle rustle. It was so peaceful and relaxing. She hitched her dress up over her knees and unfastened the top two buttons, letting the air cool her to the point of just shivering.

"Make the most of it, girl," she said to herself, it's going to be a hectic day tomorrow. The concept of a collage of the apples, sky, branches, somehow with her own figure involved, swum back into mind, and clasping her hands behind her head, she considered what it was that was so compelling.

She'd taken to 'chilling out' in this haunt of old fruit trees for some little while; there was just something about the place that gave her a nice feeling. It couldn't be put it into words, but she did think she could capture the feeling in paint; here it was that she'd decided to abandon English for Art and so far nothing had materialised that might reverse that decision. She had the promise of a 'studio', and she could see the old building now at the edge of the trees, awaiting time and materials to fulfil her father's promise; she'd managed to get a couple of things onto paper, including the 'Dress' picture -

oooh, *that dress!* and she'd got Old Petersen interested. Can't be bad, she thought; hitched her knees up still further, and laid back. Her eyes closed; the afternoon drifted on.

She was asleep. Auburn hair a halo around her relaxed prettiness, crumpled dress a foil to bare skin and curving limbs; a dream of a girl, in a dream of her own. Back, back, in time and space, in a meadow, deep grass and flowers of the wild. The stillness of the pasture, the distance call of chaffinch, the faint background whirr of insect wings, susurration of light breeze through young trees, all the natural essence of the country. She smiled in her relaxation, and her move to half turn and curl up brought her dress back across her thighs. The meadow edged with newly-planted hedgerow now had young saplings in rows, with a gap where she lay, as though purposefully, her space sacrosanct. A young man in grey serge trousers and a sort of blouse, hand in hand with a younger redheaded girl in a pretty white flowing dress watched her sleep. A call, the couple started and turned, as an elderly woman in a dark dress and with greyed hair waved at them from a gate, and the trio disappeared. Then a group of featureless men came, with collarless shirts and string-tied trousers with spades and timber, a horse-drawn cart beyond the hedge; within minutes a new building was erected, and the young redheaded girl stood in the doorway, all alone. The young trees were growing, leaves uncurling, covered in blossom, and beyond the brilliant blue sky clouds raced past, faster and faster, as blossom fell like snow, and she had to brush the petals away from her forehead. The girl in her white dress was older, very pretty, and there a man in a striped blazer and wearing camouflage trousers, was embracing her, kissing her neck, stroking her. A basket of apples, red and yellow, was picked up by another woman and taken into the shelter, as the other couple seemed to float into the mists of autumn. It was getting colder. The trees lost their leaves; she was being covered by their gentle fall. And she was falling, falling, enveloped in a cushion of leaves, a silk cover drifting down to blot out all sense. Darkness, soft darkness, and a strange feeling, like pins and needles, grew down her limbs. A hand reached down for her and she was floating as the light came back, the couple from the shelter were smiling at her, but her dress wasn't there. Was she naked? A beautiful new, dark red dress the colour of vintage wine lay on the grass, it fitted her perfectly, she was being led across the meadow, someone was calling her name, softly, softly, the petals were being brushed away from her…

"Jocelyn. Jocelinnn! Darling. Wake up, girl!"

The images faded, rushing away from her as though she was being accelerated into space. Why?

"Jo, dear! We've been calling you. It's past teatime. You must have been really fast asleep. Silly girl, aren't you uncomfortable?" Her mother was crouching alongside her, stroking her forehead. "Are you all right?" Eleanor put an arm under her daughter's shoulder, eased her up. "You look a bit pasty! I think we'd better get you back indoors. Come on, up you get."

As if she was sleep walking, Jo allowed herself to be escorted back to the house. How strange she felt, a detached view, where body was on automatic but mind in free-fall. Was it like being drunk? Once back in the kitchen, sat down on a stool and given a tall glass of Mums's home-made lemonade, bits of her began to glue themselves back together, and as Eleanor got out the hair brush and started to brush out those auburn tangled curls, sanity returned.

"I've had a silly dream, Mums. Rather nightmarish. Can't remember all of it, but it was *weird*. Back in time. People in those costumes, clothes and things we found. The apple trees being planted, the shed – studio – being built. *Weird!*" She repeated, taking a long swallow. "Ooh, that's better. Well, teach me to go to sleep up there. Can I go and have a shower, before Pa gets back? You won't tell him, Mums?"

Eleanor looked at her daughter critically. Her colour had returned, and the tone of her voice normal, the dimples as she smiled back in place. Down to her feminine make-up, she thought. Strange things, hormones. Jo was lucky really, having nothing too much to contend with in that way.

"Go, girl. I shan't say a word. Go and get wet. Enjoy! I

might even come and join you. I've just got to get this lot into tins." True, there was a fair old stack of scones on the cooling mesh stands on the table. Mums had *really* been cooking! She stood up, downed the last of the lemonade, pulled the old dress over her head and dumped it in the laundry basket in the corner. Eleanor raised her eyebrows, looking at a girl with all the attributes. Just as well she had no inhibitions, or was it?

"Join me, Mums? That would be nice. Mutual back scrubbing. See you in a mo?" Eleanor nodded, concentrating on packing scones into serried rows in her biggest tin.

* * *

Jo wandered upstairs, her odd dreams faded into a monochrome blur no longer worrying her. With shower on, small clothes bunged into a corner, just standing with the powerful cascade of heat down her back was intensely therapeutic. Her thoughts, oddly, clicked into place. All the pressures of the week had been so suddenly lifted with her relaxation, stretched out up there in the grass, that's what triggered such silly fantasy. Silly girl! Selecting the best-liked shower gel she started scrubbing herself down, then above the racket of the shower, she heard her mother come, stepping into the shower with her. Not a usual occurrence, but nice. Her Mums still had a good figure, tight tummy muscles on her rounded front, and Jo experienced a twinge of sadness. Of course, she'd only had me to stretch that tum.

"Wash your hair?"

"Uh huh. Your's?" Monosyllabic, but effective. Eleanor turned her back to Jo, and relished the feel of her daughter's firm fingers massaging her shoulders. Jo couldn't help it, running her hands around her Mums's front, feeling her softness.

"Hey, you. Careful! You'll be turning me on!"

"Turning you on? Oh, sorry!" Jo stopped, embarrassed.

Eleanor chuckled. "Don't you know? Dear me. I thought all you college girls knew about these things. Turn round. My turn." As Jo reversed position, Eleanor got her own back.

"Mums! Oooh. Nice. Umm. Feels good. Makes my tummy muscles go shiverery."

"Jolly good. You're normal, then. P'raps I'd better show you what else goes on, Jo. You know *anything?* I mean, I've not told you much, love, have I? Do you want me to explain, er, *things?*" She had had her hands cupped under her girl's front, and as the water continued to cascade over the pair of them, lowered them to run the palms along the inner softness of Jo's thighs. She felt Jo stiffen, and then relax against her breasts. There was a murmur, a sort of purring sound. Sounded good, and Eleanor dipped, stroked, found, and stroked again, carefully, gently, but insistently.

Jo felt, loved the feeling; relaxed and cosy, began to get some stimulus never before achieved, eased her position, wider, tiptoe, and suddenly a rush of electric ripples from the small of her back, down between her legs, and an urge to push her bushy bit up against her mother's hand and fingers.

Wonderful, gorgeous feeling; "Oo. Ooooh. OOOOOH! *What was that!!?*"

Eleanor recovered herself, rather surprised at the ease at which she had demonstrated one of life's central pleasures for a woman. "Good?"

"Um. I'll say. Magic, Mums. How did you do that?"

So Eleanor rinsed the lather off them both, turned the shower off, persuaded Jo to dry off, and when she had finished wiping the shower and surroundings down, took her daughter into her bedroom and in prosaic language, explained what was what. A topic they'd hedged round, assuming that Jo's peers would have shared all the appropriate knowledge. Jocelyn, aware of some things, but surprisingly naïve and luckily, uncurious about others, had all the gaps filled. She had to blush and squirm a trifle, but her Mums wasn't going to cut corners. Her daughter was as good as eighteen, metamorphosing into a vulnerable woman. Too pretty, too shapely, too *nice.*

"That feeling, then, was...?"

Eleanor nodded, gravely. "Reckon. Lucky girl. Don't misuse it, Jo. Too precious by far. We can't advise you, Jo, not once you've left home. And emotions can run high and get a bit out of control. Keep your distance, Jo. Don't sacrifice your purity for ten seconds of nice feelings. Easy to say, I know, but a real problem if things go awry. Especially if the other person isn't going to be much use. Your father, Jo, one in a million. Find someone like him and you'll make me a happy mother. Not yet, though. You've a few years yet. Is that your father now? Best get dressed, girl. Not a word! I'll tell him myself. I love you, Jo." Eleanor left Jo sitting on her bed, and went to throw something on.

Jocelyn gathered her thoughts, so tempted to just roll back, stretch out and muse over events, but no, she wanted to greet her father. Slowly, carefully, she dressed, pulled that nice silky slip out of the drawer, considered what she should wear. *The* dress? Too obvious. I know, she chortled, her Mums had worked miracles with that old nightie thing. The one the girl in her dreams had worn. There it was, on its hanger. White, shimmering, high waisted, with new ribbons, sexy even; welcoming, as she slipped it over her head, shivering as the light fabric shimmied down. The girl of her dream stared back from the mirror, and that shiver ran down her spine. The dress clung to her, absolutely right.

* * *

Her mother was quietly talking to her father as she entered the kitchen; he was looking quite serious but not cross. They gasped as they turned towards her; Eleanor'd thought she'd got the dress right, but not that right. It was stunning, emphasised every curve. The high neckline suited her, as did the high waist. If anything, it gave Jo more of a bust than was right, but then, if you have it, etc; and she did.

"David? Is *this* your daughter?" Eleanor chuckled.

"Of course. Who else would look so lovely? Jo, my darling girl, come and give your old father a kiss. You look rather delicious. Can I take you out tonight?"

"Take me out? Where, Pa? In this? It's too sexy by far. Everyone would think you were a sugar daddy!"

"And you know about sugar daddies, Jo? No, I didn't think we'd risk that dress. It's going to be a knockout tomorrow, though. No, the new dress; I've booked a table at Jonathan's. All organised. Celebration. End of your exams, Jo," and took her in his arms, feeling her warmth through the thin fabric.

He loved her, all of her. Eleanor had told him that she'd been filled in on some of life's essentials, and he had no problem with that. So long as she remained sensible, and he didn't think she'd be anything else. She was his daughter, for heaven's sake.

"Half seven, Jo. We've got an hour. I gather you two are all well scrubbed, so that just leaves me. I'll get on with it then." He swung her off her feet, with a bit of an effort, and put her down. "Love you!"

* * *

'Jonathan's' was a fashionable new up-market restaurant nicely placed on the edge of town with easy access, where David had managed to secure a first-rate table simply because the owner had been chasing him for a good new car deal, so he was confident of the best service. Eleanor, aware she was as much on show as Jocelyn, had given her hair a good brushing, put on the slinky dark green dress David had bought her last year; and was very happy she'd still managed to do up the zip. Jocelyn however, was the centre of attention; her mother conscious her daughter was struggling a little with this new-found phenomena.

As they were shown to the table, central to the window, in its own alcove, the Italian waiter all beams and smiles, tucking their chairs in, offering extravagant menus, Eleanor just managed to whisper in her girl's ear.

"Enjoy, Jo, remember? Let the evening flow. Your father's turning you into a woman, bless him. Goodbye schoolgirl, hello lady!"

"What are you two whispering about?"

"Nothing, David. What shall we have to drink?"

It really was a splendid evening. The restaurant had come up to expectations, the service impeccable, and more to the point, the bill less than anticipated. David had a sneaking feeling that he was being rewarded for doing his job, but wasn't going to argue. Jo was on a real high, glowing and not at all the worse for her very full day. To cap it all, one of the college lecturers was wining and dining a girlfriend – or perhaps she was the wife – and he hadn't recognised her. Probably just as well. On the way home in the Jaguar, she nearly fell asleep, until her mother leant over from the front and poked her.

"Jo! Wait till we get home! You'll only feel rotten if you doze. We're nearly back."

Indeed, they were home. Tomorrow was Saturday. Somehow she was upstairs. *The* Saturday. Oh Lord. Shoes off. No going back. Bed. Glorious bed. Dress on its hanger. Knickers off. She giggled. Bed. Oh, what a wonderful day. End of one chapter, and lovely feelings, thanks Mums. Pa – wonderful Pa. I feel full. And happy. Nightdress, can't be bothered. Bra, nearly forgot. She flung it onto the chair. Bed. Oh, I feel a bit woozy. Too much wine, Pa. Oh, busy day. Sleep. Hmmm. And she slept, dreamless sleep, until dawn woke her, clear-headed, confident and raring to go.

FIVE

Eleanor woke in a mild state of panic. *Saturday!* She flung herself out of bed and nearly fell over her shoes as she ran across to the window. What was the weather like? David heaved the covers back on, rolled over, glanced at the bedside clock and groaned. Only just six! His head felt fuzzy; too much red wine.

"Eleanor, for heaven's sake, woman. It's only six o'clock! Get yourself back here!"

"And have you distracting me? Far too much to do, David, I *must* get going. Really."

"Spoil sport." He stretched, yawned, stretched again, and gave up.

* * *

Ten minutes later there was good coffee on the go, and the aroma percolated up to Jo. She'd squeezed into an old pair of jeans, unusually for her, tied her hair back, and managed to find an even older sweater. Her double in the mirror looked like a nineteen sixties bopper. She grinned at herself, resisted the urge to do a pencil sketch. Enough of these ego trips. Coffee! She smelt coffee, and bounced downstairs.

"Good lord, girl, what *are* you wearing!" Her father was surprised.

"Morning, Jo! Sleep well?" Eleanor winked at her.

"I did, Mums. Morning, Pa, I'm wearing something entirely different 'cos it's a working day. What time are the troops arriving, Mums?" She reached for a mug and helped herself to the remnants.

"Hope they stay within bounds. Don't want them

wandering about, do we? At least it's a dry day."

With a hint of early morning mist, the garden had that spirit-lifting tinge of silver and blue across the dew-laden grass. It would be sunny, and warm. Just right, in fact. She moved to the window and looked out over her Mums's empire. Turning back to them, she smiled, that lovely dimpling smile.

"Thanks, you two, for yesterday. Marker point, I suppose. Well, what's to do? When do we have breakfast?"

"Barn, I think, first, then tables, chairs. Notices. Padlock on the paddock gate, Jo, should keep strays out of your precious orchard."

Pa's province too, Jo thought. He gets as much out of it as I do. She nearly giggled out loud.

"Presumably you'll do a garden check, Mums? Make sure no plant has strayed!"

Eleanor made to throw a croissant at her from the basketful on the table. Plants strayed indeed!

"The troops, as you call them, are scheduled for ten o'clock. First comers no earlier than twelve, according to the tickets. The entertainment at about two, two thirty."

"Morris dancers?"

"Maybe even the village band. And the primary school choir. And the poetry reading. We've been spared the W.I. drama group. Happily. Should wrap up by six, latest seven. We run teas from half three till five, or when the scones run out. Or the cucumber sandwiches. I'll need someone to slice the cucumbers, thinly, David. Plastic bread, I'm afraid, unless the Mrs Blounce comes up with masses of home-made. She mentioned it, but don't hold your breath."

"So are we all set? Who's going to check tickets? What about car parking?"

David pulled a face. Car parking was something he hadn't really thought about, but Jo was right to mention it. Silly, really, considering his job.

"Aren't some of your college friends coming? I don't suppose one of them would do tickets? I don't want to have you tied down to that job, Jo. I think we'll just quietly forget about car parking. So long as we keep the big gates shut so we don't get a drive full, they'll just have to park in the lane. Their problem, then. Agreed, Eleanor?"

"'S'pose so. Maybe we should put the W.I. cars on the drive, at the gate end?"

"What a good idea. That will keep them happy. Privileged parking!"

* * *

By the time the first W.I. car turned into the drive, just before ten to ten, the in-house gang had sorted out the barn, set out tables and chairs, and were now relaxing over the second coffee brew of the day.

Eleanor, mouth full of croissant, spluttered at Jo, "Dear -?"

Jo scowled at her mother. She wasn't much good at being the welcome mat, but just had to do as her Mums asked. Sliding off the stool, brushing crumbs off her front and fixing a smile in place, she went out to meet the day.

"Mrs Blounce! Lovely to see you! Aren't we blessed with a lovely morning? Would you like to come this way? We've just had our breakfast, but we might rustle up some tea or coffee? Oh – and we're only having your members' cars in the drive. Is that all right?"

Mrs Blounce was impressed; such a lovely girl, and *so* polite. "Dear girl! Thank you, but no. By the end of the day we'll have had all the liquid us ladies can cope with! We'll need to know where to *go*, if you take my point. Lead on, Jocelyn – if I may call you that – or do you prefer Jo?"

Jocelyn kept her smile nailed in place. A mental picture of a queue of resplendent ladies taking turns for the downstairs loo. Had Mums thought of that? Yes, of course, she redecorated last week.

"Jo is fine, Mrs Blounce. My mother will show you the toilet." She ushered her into the kitchen. Mums had removed the debris, and Pa had disappeared, unsurprisingly. Relieved of her charge, she ducked and ran for cover, finding her father skulking in the barn, musing on the state of the roof.

"Will we survive, Jo, my darling girl? I've been looking at the rafters. Bit woodwormey, I think. Oh well, so long as it stays on for today. Lord preserve us from too many Mrs Blounces. When are your friends due?"

Jo looked at her watch. Any time at all, she suspected. Betty, Trish and Julie; it would be lovely to have them around. Pa would love to entertain them too, and then the appalling thought struck her.

"Felicity! And her bloody magazine! She's coming! Does that Blounce woman know? No, she won't, will she? What are we going to do about her, Pa?"

Her father glanced sideways at her. "Do about her, Jo? Who? Mrs Blounce or Felicity?" He was grinning.

She could have kicked him; he was being *so* aggravating. "Just keep out of her knickers, Pa." Jo spoke without thinking, and instantly realising what she'd said, coloured up, biting her lip. Now she'd done it. Her father roared with laughter. His daughter, telling him that! As if!

"You haven't got a very high opinion of my faithfulness, Jo! As if Mrs Blounce would let me get anywhere near!" Now he was pulling her leg.

Jocelyn was still smarting. "Sorry, Pa. It just slipped out. I didn't mean it."

"I know, Jo. Don't worry. Felicity isn't at risk, neither am I. She's decorative, I'll admit, but then, so are you, my girl. Something you'll just have to get used to. Great pictures attract admiration, you know. Stay in the frame. Come on, you. Let's go do battle."

* * *

The three girls had arrived, all in Trish's Brendan's car that she'd borrowed; they were chattering away, reliving the last week at college; Brendan would be dropped off by one of his mates at any time. Betty was still fragile, but in one piece; Julie, always the sensible one, was more concerned with getting on with the day's arrangements. Eleanor welcomed them; it was lovely to see them, pretty girls all. And Jo still the prettiest of the bunch. Trish dragged out the waitress uniforms; they all dived into the front room, out of sight, to try them on. Black, yes, but with a demure pleat on the sides, a slight slit to ease movement and show just the right amount of leg, well-fitted waists, and a square cut neckline. Jo wasn't too sure about that.

"Scarves, Jo. These. See?" She draped one over the shoulders, tied it and pinned one end in place. A shimmering blue and purple, it gave just the right emphasis.

"Aprons?"

"Only if you think. They're a bit twee. Maybe if we use the extra scarves as a waist tie? Like this. See?" Trish certainly had the knack.

"That's rather good, Trish. I like it. Betty? Jo?" Overall, Julie was pleased, despite her skirt length being a trifle short. At least she was happy with her legs. Betty wasn't really too pleased at the waitress idea at all; the garden was far more her line, preferring the idea of being a sort of garden guide, telling people what plants were what. The dress was okay, though, so maybe she'd go along with it. Jo, as ever, looked quite alluring, but the scarf colours didn't seem quite right for her hair. At this point Eleanor popped her head round the door.

"My! What a collection of beauties! You'll have the local lads drooling. Perhaps we ought to charge extra. Brendan's here, Trish. Shall I send him in?" She laughed, at the expression on the girl's face and the alarm from Julie, who with her skirt round her waist was adjusting her slip to stop it showing. "Don't worry. David's putting him on ticket duty. That all right, Trish?"

"Sure. At least I'll know where he is. What do you want us to do?"

"Drinks, I think. Mrs Blounce's gang are the barbecue kings – I won't use the word queens – though they've recruited a couple of husbands as stokers, sorry, chefs. The kit's arrived and they're busy setting light to it. Not our scene, is it Jo? We can't stand half-cooked charcoal. Just be nice to people, smile prettily, you'll be fine. Betty – if you want to keep an eye on the precious bits, ensure we still have a herbaceous border at the end of the day. Stay in that dress. It suits you. When's your step-mum coming?"

"Just after lunch, I think. She's got some super photographer guy organised, but I know she doesn't care for half-burnt charcoal flavoured chicken either. What do we get for lunch?"

"That's a loaded question, Betty. Cucumber sandwiches? We've got them secreted away. Don't tell the gaulieter. Then there's loads of scones for later. You wait till you see Jo and her father at teatime. Surprise, even Mrs Blounce doesn't know. Can you speak Edwardian?"

"Edwardian?" Julie, back in one piece and more comfortable with it, was puzzled.

"Yes. Didn't Jo say? We have an Edwardian tea party organised for later. Jo in a fabulous dress and her father in a stripey blazer and straw boater, hence the scones and sandwiches. You girls will make super waitresses in those dresses. You wait! But we'd best get out there. Duty calls. Go say hello to Brendan, Trish. Betty – border patrol, but no scarf, I think. Jo, Julie perhaps an eye on the charcoal kitchen? Rendezvous back in the kitchen at, say half one? On your way, girls!" She turned and went.

"Hmm. Your mum's great, isn't she? A real organiser. Not at all starchy; my mother couldn't cope with all this, sadly." Julie's mother was an academic and a bit remote from the day-to-day. They weren't very close, not like Jo and her mum.

Trish sympathised, though her own parents pretty well left her to get on with things by herself, and Betty, with the high flyer step-mother, knew which style she'd prefer. But Felicity was, nevertheless, quite fun in her own way.

The girls went their appointed ways. Jo took Julie by the arm, and whispered in her ear as they approached the barn.

"You know I've got Old Petersen coming to see me today?"

Julie's face was a picture. "Petersen? Coming to see you? Whatever for, Jo?"

"My paintings, sketches rather. Just to see what he thinks. I may try to switch into History of Art rather than English. My

Pa's not one hundred percent sure, though he's coming round, so Petersen might convince him, if he thinks I'm any good. And Mrs Summers may appear as well." Her glance round revealed a few earlycomers drifting in. Betty was already on guard on the long border, and in the distance they could see Trish leaning over Brendan at the table on the drive. No sign of her father, but he would be keeping an eye on the barbecue lighting on the other side of the barn.

"Bit late to change courses, Jo. You might lose your place. Have you talked to Admissions?"

"Not yet. See how it goes. I'm not panicking. If I miss a year, then I do. I've got lots I want to do."

Round the corner of the barn there was the old oil drum conversion that was the village's community barbecue kit, with her father trying to help the two W.I. husbands get it properly alight. In the barn itself the buxom ladies were setting out their stall, cloths on old tables, stacks of plates, tray loads of sausages and chicken legs. Jo shuddered.

"Sorry, Julie, but this turns me over. Are you a fan of burnt bangers?"

Julie shook her head. "Not really. Too much of a tummy-bug risk, but I guess this lot will have got it sorted. Pre-cooked, by the look of it. Cheating, maybe, but a good deal saner. Do we help serve, or what?"

"S'pose so. We've got a while to go."

Her father had caught sight of her, and waved. "Hi girls. You look the part. Bob, Peter, meet my daughter, Jo. And Julie, isn't it?"

Both men, red-eyed from smoke, appreciated the sight. Truly, a sight for sore eyes! "Won't shake hands, girls. Nice to meet you. Don't come too close." Bob was the more forward; Peter never said much.

David stood back as the two resumed their blowing on the pile of reluctant charcoal. "What a game! There's been talk of bottled gas, but the die-hards won't hear of it. Roll on teatime, eh, Jo? How's the gate?"

"Trish's Brendan seems to be organised, Pa. How many are we expecting now?"

"The Blounce says sixty or so. Maybe more. There's always going to be last-moment types who wait for the weather. When's your art guy coming, did you say?"

Jo shrugged. "Any time, I suppose, but he suggested after lunch. Perhaps he's not a barbecue fan either. You know Mums has a store of sandwiches?"

David grinned. Oh, yes, he knew. "Don't let the smoke get at you. Go and watch the gate, Jo. Take Julie with you. These guys will only be distracted. You're too tempting a vision. Shoo!"

There were already quite a few visitors; many probably attracted by the curiosity factor, seeing what the Daniellesons had done to the old place, those with memories of the former owner, or even from when the last incumbent had been in residence. The picture of the two delightful girls walking together across the lawns attracted a few stares. Betty was standing guard on the herbaceous border.

"Seen my mother, Betty? Have you had any awkward customers?" Jo and Julie stopped to chat; avoiding the small group of young men newly arrived. She wasn't in the mood to be politely indifferent to blokes who only wanted the opportunity to gawk at her front.

"I think she's in the house, Jo. She's been out once, when I had to answer that chap," she nodded her head towards an older man still interrogating the dahlias - "about whether she used peat. Seems it isn't the 'in' thing to do. So, yes, he was an awkward customer. I'll cope. All good fun."

"Keep your cool, then. And avoid that lot if you can. My guess they're only here to look over the talent, which is us, I suppose."

"Risk we run, Jo." Julie wasn't overly bothered, but then, she was virtually spoken for. As well as Tony, she had a very well-to-do chap in tow, an excellent dancer, who worked in one of the law offices in town. Robert might even turn up later, once the office closed at lunchtime. "Let's go and chat up Brendan. That should keep them at a distance." The two moved off, leaving Betty to deal with another hovering inquirer.

The day was warming up. With the sun at full blast on the lawn and all shadows gone, even the shrubs were shimmering. A few of the more elderly ladies had found the chairs under the big tree; a young family were sprawled out on a rug they'd brought with them, the mother trying to keep a sunhat on her fair-haired girl while the boy was guzzling a Coke bottle. One more car crawled past the drive entrance, looking for a parking space. Another couple, hand in hand, were entering the gateway. The event was picking up, and could well be a record success.

"Who gets the profits from all this, Jo?" It was if Julie was reading Jo's mind.

"Oh, split between the Church and the village charity, Julie, *if* there is a profit. We lend the ground, the W.I. do the catering and the cricket club chaps run the barbecue and the sideshows, though most of them are W.I. husbands. We're going to try and make some money on the teas, though, to pay for some of the garden restoration. Not sure how Mums is going to get that past Mrs Blounce!"

They'd reached Brendan and his ticket table. Trish was standing guard. They both looked happy enough. It must be a very different Saturday for them, Jo thought.

"Trish. Brendan. You okay?" doing her supervision act.

"Sure, Jo. You two look smashing." Brendan made no effort to hide his appraisal, confident in his rapport with his Trish, "No wonder that lot turned up," nodding at the group who had succumbed to lying in an untidy sprawl near to the old ladies. They'd found some bottles, lager, no doubt, and Brendan narrowed his eyes. He'd deal with them if necessary, no worries. "There's always going to be someone who can't behave." Politely, he asked a newly-arrived young couple for their tickets, smiling at the girl. As they moved off, he turned back to Trish. "Wasn't she in the pub the other night? With her bloke? Seems familiar."

"Could be. Eyes off, Brendan. Trust you to remember. When's lunch, Jo? I'm getting hungry. Could do with a drink. Sure is a good day for this." She leant forward, putting her hands on Brendan's shoulders, so he reached up a hand and held one of hers. Jo looked at Julie, and winked.

"Tell you what, why don't you two go and find my Mums and grab some sandwiches – and there's a big jug of her home-made lemonade. We'll mind the shop for a while, but don't be too long. I'm waiting for my guests."

"What time do they start on the barbecue proper, then?"

Jo laughed. "When they've got it cooked! No, shouldn't be too long. Why, do you fancy burnt bangers?"

"I don't mind. What about you, Trish?" Brendan stood up and tucked his arm round her.

"Prefer Jo's mum's sandwiches, I think. Let's go and find her, then we can always move over to the barn. Half an hour?"

* * *

Jo sat on the vacated chair, and Julie perched on the table, swinging a long leg. Three more couples came in quick succession, then Reg, with his wife, all beams and smiles. Jo introduced him to Julie as 'their' postman. Reg had a soft spot for Jocelyn; she was always pleasant to him, always gave him the time of day, and he'd seen her frolicking about without a care. Great girl. They moved on towards the smoke and the odour redolent of beef burgers. Then Julie nudged Jo's elbow.

"Petersen – that's him, isn't it?" A solitary man wearing a panama hat and a red bandana scarf, using a cane like a swagger stick. "It must be, who else?"

"Oh Lord!" Jo's heart skipped a beat. Though she knew he was coming, suddenly she was nervous, with her future on the line. He would see what she had done, criticise her and tell her not to waste her time and his on childish drawings. He'd go away, laughing at her, Pa would be cross and laugh at the same time, she'd never get a studio, she'd be committed to a drudge life in some office or even a shop, at best a teaching job. "Julie. I'm scared. What if all this turns out to be just me inventing ideas? What would you do?" She couldn't not go through with it, but she was beginning to wish she hadn't told him about her dream. That's what it was going to be, a dream, a fanciful, silly girlish dream, dreamt up in the old orchard under the spell of the trees and being alone and half dressed.

Julie looked at her, concerned. Jo had gone pale, and her forehead looked sweaty "Are you okay, Jo? It's not *that* bad. He's a decent old stick, he wouldn't mess you about. Even if he did say you were no good, he'd be kind about it. Look, you take him off, go find your father or your mum. I'll manage here till Trish and Brendan get back. They won't be long." She patted Jocelyn's arm. "Really, Jo. You'll be fine."

He was within earshot, and smiling broadly, waved his stick at them and doffed his hat.

"Greetings, my lovelies. What a splendid sight you both are! Does the heart good to see such wonderful ladies awaiting me! Jocelyn, and Julie, isn't it? Such a wonderful day! I hope you are besieged with admirers, the pair of you! Reservations I may have had about this rural extravaganza, but the company herewith dispels all! Whither we go, Jocelyn?" Petersen was in fine form, his bright eyes twinkling away at them. "Have we a repast awaiting? 'Tis a fair step from the village."

Jocelyn had tried to swallow her apprehensions, but stumbled over her welcome. "Thank you for coming. I – er – wasn't sure, I mean, we'd not thought – oh, come and meet my mother," her Mums, a refuge in times of crisis. With a despairing glance at Julie, she made to lead the way, but Petersen was having none of it.

"Give me your arm, dear girl. Your company is reward enough for such a journey!" He resumed his panama, and with arm firmly tucked into Jo's, and swinging his cane, they made their way towards the house.

"Phew!" Julie resumed the chair just in time to smile sweetly at a posse of middle-aged ladies and their escort of two military-looking gentlemen. The Croquet Club delegation, she was told. She sold them tickets; surprised they weren't already in possession, but was further informed they 'had only come because their match had been called off at the last moment'. Such was village life.

* * *

Walking on with Petersen, Jo's nervousness wasn't going away. He was humming away to himself, looking about, and then glanced back at his escort.

"You are uncommonly quiet, my dear Jocelyn. Not quite your irrepressible self. The occasion a little fraught, maybe, or else there is disharmony in the ranks? No, I think not. You are concerned I should find you a scribbler, not a paragon? Hmm? You fear to be found wanting?" She found his gaze disconcerting, and felt her colour rising. "Ah. Close to the mark. A better colour, though the emphasis a fraction bright." His arm tightened on hers. "Not unexpected, but I am encouraged." They reached the kitchen door, and Petersen relinquished his hold so Jo could lead the way.

"Mums!" she called out, "Mr Petersen's here! Are you there?" There were two possibilities, either the sitting room, staying quietly out of the way, or in the dining room with the scones and sandwiches. "Mums?"

"In here, Jo!"

The dining room, then. Her glance back at her escort gave the unspoken authority to follow, and she moved through the kitchen. Panama in hand, cane discreetly in the 'at ease' position, Petersen tagged along behind. The house was cool, and smelt fresh after the stultifying warmth of the early afternoon behind them. A large vase of flowers in the hall was given a nod of approval; his glance took in the quiet discretion of three landscape paintings on the stair wall, amateur but well executed. Subdued colours, all blending, carpet, plain walls, a nice table. The two pieces of Mason's Ironstone gave just the right emphasis. Taste, he thought. Yes, a home of thoughtful caring. A lucky girl, this Jocelyn.

Jocelyn's mother was buttering the last of the ready-use scones. Serried ranks of pyramidal sandwiches were on oblong white plates under butter muslin covers. The dining room was another cool place. The table shone and the landscape theme continued with more watercolours – they must be prints – on the pale green walls. He would have darkened the shade a trifle. A sideboard, two good pieces of silver, a Wedgwood vase. Mrs Danielleson, wrapped in apron, looked up, her expression welcoming. She put down her knife.

"Mr Petersen. Welcome to the Old Vicarage. How good of you to spare the time! Can I offer you sandwiches and scones? All we have organised at present, I fear, unless you fancy charcoal-flavoured chicken – in the old barn with the rest of the melee. I have iced lemonade in the fridge. Jo – what about you?" Eleanor moved forward and shook his hand. "It's a bit of a nerve-racking day, I'm afraid, a first for us, hosting a village do. My husband's out there somewhere, keeping an eye on the barbecue and fending off the hordes. Not really my scene, I prefer the garden on my own. How's Betty coping, Jo?"

She was prattling on a bit, thought Jo, perhaps she's as nervous as I am. "Betty's fine, Mums. In her element, I'd say, but no sign of her step-mum. And Trish and Brendan are happy; Julie's doing a stint at the gate while they take a breather. I'd like some lemonade – I'll get it. Mr Petersen?"

"Edward, Jocelyn. Call me Edward, if she may, Mrs Danielleson?" So polite, so correct, Eleanor thought him charming. "Lemonade – yes, Jocelyn, that would be most acceptable. Sandwiches, much more to my taste. Barbecues, I think not. *So primitive.*"

"We'll go through to the sitting room. And please call me Eleanor. My husband is David."

It seemed so dreamlike. He had brought an air of Edwardian charm with him, putting them at ease and yet also on edge. As Jocelyn left to fetch the lemonade jug and glasses from the kitchen, Edward Petersen quietly and firmly stated his view.

"Your daughter is a fine girl, Eleanor. I have a very high regard for her, both as a pupil and as a person. She is determined, and likely talented. I will be pleased to assist her progress if it is your wish I do so. Also, please be sure she will be safe with me." His eyes were unwavering as she held his look, and there *was* a reassuring humour there behind the steely, penetrating gaze. Eleanor held the gaze for a moment, then smiled.

"I'm sure she will, er, Edward. I just hope she'll come up

to expectations. It's been a bit of a leap from her original ideas to all this, but she does seem determined, you're right there. Talented, well, let's see. You'll be the judge of that. Ah, Jo – sitting room, I think. Then you'll fetch your work?"

Freshly made cucumber sandwiches with just the right amount of black pepper and the iced lemonade at his elbow; Edward surveyed the self-portrait propped up on a makeshift easel. His eyes narrowed, a pensive look, then head on one side, he stepped forward and studied the lines carefully. He said nothing, but held out his hand for the sketch pad Jo was holding. He sat back in the chair, crossed his legs, took a sip of the lemonade, before turning the pages over, slowly; pausing at each one of the half-dozen or so sketches, or outline drawings. Jo sat silently in the chair by the window, holding her lips tightly together to stop herself from biting them. Her mother stood quietly by the door; half hoping David would come. The mantelpiece clocked ticked away; the faint hum of conversation, the little bursts of laughter that could be heard from the garden, and the annoying buzz of an intrusive fly were all background sounds to the otherwise suspensive stillness.

He looked up, placed the pad on the table beside him, and reached for a sandwich. "These are good."

Jo blinked. Did he mean the sketches, or the sandwiches?

"Is there anything else you want to show me?"

Eleanor spoke up. "The painting you did for your father, Jo? Do you want to show Edward that one?"

She'd all but forgotten it, stupidly. Still unsure of what his reaction would be, she moved to fetch it from upstairs. As she passed him, he put out a hand.

"I like what I see, Jo. If I may see the painting?" So it can't be too bad then, she thought, and almost ran up the stairs. The painting lay on her bed. Her, in the burgundy dress. She picked it up, carried it, open, carefully down and across the hall, just as her father came through the front door.

"Jo! Where're you going with that?"

"Mr Petersen's here, Pa. Looking at my work. In here." He followed her back into the sitting room, and Edward stood up.

Jo introduced him "Mr Petersen – my father."

"Edward, please, Mr Danielleson. Thank you for your welcome. Your wife makes some delectable sandwiches, and the lemonade is as good as I have ever tasted, especially on such a warm day. Your daughter has been exhibiting her work. This is another?" He took the sheet of paper from Jo, and moved across to lean it on the board balanced on the back and arms of the other chair before returning to his viewpoint. The burgundy-clad figure of the girl stood out and smiled at him, the evident warmth and love in the painting told of a meaning, whoever she had in mind when she had created this was a lucky person. His eyes began to prick. He would have been pleased to call this his own work.

Looking back to Jocelyn, his face expressionless, he asked the question. "Who were you thinking of when you did this, Jocelyn?"

"My father. He gave me the dress."

"Ah. I see. You're a very lucky man, Mr Danielleson. You have a daughter who can not only paint, but she can tell stories in her work. Mrs Danielleson, Eleanor, your girl has talent beyond her years. I'm proud to think I encouraged her."

Jocelyn saw in his smile the opening of vistas unknown but exciting. She looked at her mother, but Eleanor was looking at her husband. And David was holding his eyes on this Petersen who had confirmed the change of direction their lives, Jo's life, would take. Edward carried on, speaking to a girl who barely heard him.

"Strange, Jocelyn, that I did not appreciate your work at college. There was not the depth and expression in what I remember of it – not in the same way as this," he gestured at the painting, and his movement seemed like a caress, "or this," and he reached to lift the charcoal self-portrait back into view. "You have a yearning in here, and a vision of yourself. And these sketches. Your father, under these trees. A trifle rough, maybe, and the perspective not ideal, but the story is there, and you could expand on this, as well you can on this." He had picked up her pad and turned the pages. The evening light on the garden was really an outline, but he knew what she had wished to achieve. "Jo?" Her glance flicked back to him. She'd heard, but not heard. She was waiting for her parents' reaction. Edward suddenly appreciated the significance of his visit, a turning point. She was staring at him, but not seeing him, her mind contemplative, on a mental visit to her orchard scene. A yearning? A vision of herself? Then she flicked back into time.

"Thank you, you've been very kind." Jocelyn turned back to her bemused parents.

"So where do we go from here?" her father was asking, as Eleanor, almost absent mindedly, topped up Edward's lemonade glass.

"Thank *you!* Where do we go? Well, you have to decide. I deem she has talent; it needs to be encouraged, developed. I would like to offer to coach her further, but I believe there is a consideration of the History of Art degree? A good grounding, if rather a broad topic. There has to be some commonsense in all this. She has to live, unless she is going to depend on your good selves until she has a name, a reputation and a meaningful return from her work. Which will come, of that I am sure. But you will need to consider the options by yourselves." He paused. "Allow me to wander, if I may. I won't leave without saying goodbye. Thank you, Eleanor, David. Jocelyn, I mean what I say. You have talent, dear girl, and I'm honoured to have seen these examples. Now, I beg you excuse me. I will see myself out." He collected his hat and cane, and with a half bow and a smile at them all, left the room, and they heard the front door close behind him. Eleanor collapsed into the nearest chair, and David moved to put his arms around his daughter, giving her a gentle hug.

"He's right, Jo. That painting you've done for me *does* tell a story. I'm rather glad I bought you that dress. So it's art, then. So be it, my daughter. You have our support, doesn't she, Eleanor?"

Eleanor nodded. She was feeling drained, her emotions had risen and all but choked her. So much to consider, so much had been said. "Jo, dear, we'd best look after our guests. David, you'd better check on things. Felicity's due to come.

We've got an hour or so before we start on teas. All those sandwiches!" She shifted her mind onto the regular things to do. No more day-dreaming. She bustled out of the room, giving her daughter a pat on the arm as she went. David let his arms fall.

"We'll talk again, Jo, later, or perhaps tomorrow. You'd better tuck these pictures away safely, then go and see what your girlfriends are up to. I'll go back to the barbecue. Hope Betty's step-mum doesn't turn up, at least, not today. I don't know if I can cope!"

Jocelyn came back to earth. At least she was over that hurdle and her nerves were beginning to relax. At least old Petersen – Edward, how right, – had seen something of what she was trying, maybe subconsciously, to achieve. "That you can, Pa. She's decorative, we know, so there'll be others trailing after her. Anyway, Betty will be tagging along. I'll go and have words with Trish and Brendan." She reached up to him and pecked his cheek. "Love you, Pa. Like the painting says!" She laughed, briefly, picked up her handiwork, and vanished upstairs. David, left on his own, heaved a sigh. All this was only a prelude to her going off somewhere, and he'd miss her. He shrugged, and headed off towards the barn.

* * *

At the gate table, Trish and Brendan had welcomed Mrs Summers and watched her mingle with the growing numbers of villagers. It was half past one. Two more cars crossed the drive entrance looking for a space, then the low slung sports car with Felicity at the wheel turned in, avoided the 'No entry for cars' sign, and she had it parked before Trish could say 'Oi!' The broad-shouldered chap alongside her got out first and reached into the back to heave out a couple of those aluminium cases so beloved by photographers. Felicity waved at the two young people behind the table.

"Trish, isn't it? I'm Betty's mother. Is she about?" She had had her fair hair wrapped in a bandana but reached up to take it off and shake her curls. Brendan couldn't keep his eyes off her, with low cut sweater, short skirt, lovely legs, and those boobs! Trish caught the direction of his glance and kicked his shin.

"Keep your eyes off that cleavage, Brendan," she hissed, then in normal tone, as she moved forward, "The other side of the shrubbery, I think. I'll find her, if you like."

"That would be kind. And we need to speak to Jo's parents?" Her escort, case in each hand, was behind her, a pleasant open-faced sort of chap. As Trish was about to explain their possible whereabouts, she spotted Jo coming across from the house and waved at her.

"Jo!" she called. Jocelyn needed no further explanation. The dreaded Felicity had arrived. As she crossed the gravel, she mentally rehearsed her speech.

"Felicity!" Her voice was all smiles and cheer. "*How nice* to see you! Mother's in the house, my father's looking after the barbecue, and it might be as well to leave him to concentrate. It's *very* important! Can I take you into the house?"

"Yes, of course, that would be kind," repeating herself. Trish hovered. Should she fetch Betty or not? "If Betty could be told where I am?"

So Trish went off, Brendan helping himself to another eyeful as Jo took the shapely Felicity and her silent escort away. They were no sooner out of sight before *another* car pulled *into* the drive with a couple in it; he caught a glimpse of yet more curvy legs as the girl driver slid out and opened the door for the chap. Strange! Youngish bloke, too, looking quite smart, saying "thank you" to the girl, then she was back in the car and reversing out. The bloke was coming over.

"Afternoon! I'm looking for Mr and Mrs Danielleson?" An educated voice, bit of an accent there he didn't recognise. Decent enough chap. Tall, thick brown hair, tanned complexion, a newish scar below his hairline.

"Mrs Danielleson's in the house, but I think she's got people with her." Brendan nearly said 'Sir', because of the effect of this chap's manner. "Mr Danielleson will be over by the barn." He offered no other suggestion, but looked around for his girl. Trish would sort things. Yes, there she was, with Betty.

"Hang on a moment, one of the girls will take you to find him. Trish!" he called across.

Trish looked up at Brendan's call. Who was that dishy-looking bloke? Leaving Betty with yet another gardening guru, she went to find out. Her curious stare got results.

"Hello. I'm Nigel Haversed. I believe you know where Mr Danielleson is? He might not know me specifically, but I sort of fell across his path the other day. Can you show me?" He smiled at her, and she melted.

"Sure. Glad to. See you in a bit, Brendan." Brendan eyed the two walking off, this guy, what's his name, Haversed? Nigel? Yes, he looked like a Nigel. He shrugged, turning his attention to yet another latecomer.

* * *

"Mr Danielleson!" Trish spotted him sitting down with one of those W.I. ladies, the organiser one by the look of her. "I have a Mr – Haversham, wasn't it? - here to see you!"

"Haversed. Nigel, please. Haversham was out of *Great Expectations.*" Trish was treated to another smile, and she shivered. David looked up, excused himself to Mrs Blounce, pleased at the fortuitous interruption, got to his feet.

"Do I know you?"

"Well, last time you saw me I was being whisked away in a Lynx helicopter. I'm here to say a heartfelt thank you to you and, perhaps more specifically, to your daughter? Rumour has it she may have saved me from some far more serious consequences of a misjudged parachute drop. And I have an official commendation for you from the Base." He fished out a stiff envelope from his inside pocket.

Trish was all ears, Jo had never said? Helped this bloke out from a parachute drop? How ever did she get involved in all that?

"Good heavens! You're the chap in the tree! Good to see you – we thought you were still in hospital! Well, well, you'd

140

best come across to the house. Trish – Mrs Blounce wants to start serving up – can you round up the other two and start doing your waitressing act? I'll get Jo across in a minute. This way, Nigel, wasn't it?" Taking the young man's arm, he guided him back across the lawn. "Jo – Jocelyn – my daughter, will be pleased to see her acrobatics in the tree did no harm!"

David pushed open the kitchen door, to hear voices, the Felicity woman, another deeper man's voice, and then Eleanor's. The magazine feature; he'd forgotten all about it. This was becoming silly; with the tea party idea looming, Felicity to cope with and now this Nigel chap. Thank goodness Jo's friends were here to help, but he'd be glad when it was all over. Eleanor spun round as they entered the kitchen. She'd been poring over Felicity's sketch plan of the feature, with Jo at her side, happily agreeing with most of what had been suggested, apart from some minor deletions over the bits she knew weren't up to her standard. This photographer chap, Britten, as Felicity had called him, seemed to be quite with it; and if he'd been responsible for the photos in the copies of the magazine she just been looking at, then fine. Now David was back, thank goodness, she didn't have to go searching. But who was the handsome young man he'd got in tow?

"Eleanor – meet Nigel Haversed. Nigel - my wife. And this young lady first saw you upside down. Jocelyn, our only daughter. I'm sure she won't mind you calling her Jo."

As Nigel first shook hands with her Mums, then turned towards her, she felt all goosepimply, and sure she was blushing. This was the chap she'd cut out of the tree? He can't be more than twenty or so! His eyes, deep brown, like his hair, were gorgeous. He was smiling at her, and there was his hand. In a bit of a trance, she took it, firm, dry, warm, and held on perhaps a fraction too long?

"Jo. I've come to say thank you. For what you did may have saved my life, but certainly prevented me from being seriously hurt, from all accounts. Not that I knew too much about it after my helmet got knocked about as I crashed into the tree. At least you can see your efforts weren't in vain." He laughed, and it was a pleasant musical sort of laugh. Yes, she thought, yes, *he's nice.* I'm glad I struggled up that tree. He can't have been too badly hurt. Her colour was subsiding; at least she didn't feel quite so red. Her father was looking at her, quizzically; Eleanor noticed the effect he'd had on her girl, and Felicity, who had no idea about all of this, watched the by-play with interest. Britten – was that a surname – just looked out of the window, hoping he'd get what was needed before the light changed so he could get home.

"Jo?" Her Mums broke her reverie.

"Sorry!" She smiled, and shook her head to make those luscious auburn girls bounce. My, but she *was* a pretty girl, Nigel's thoughts were racing away. Crashing into that tree to find this girl? Jocelyn; like the name. Lovely shape, too. Freckled, well, so was Fergie.

"Look, you two, stop staring at each other. Jo, go and take him round the garden or something, but be back to change in an hour – no, half an hour. David, you take Britten on tour, and I'll chat some more with Felicity then join you. We can't not do our tea party thing, Felicity; I've too many scones and sandwiches made to waste. You'll see. May even be worth some photos!" Eleanor had to push them along.

* * *

Jo and Nigel made their way into the garden; before long he'd managed to persuade her to hold his hand, which she found she didn't mind; when Trish and Betty spotted her they both looked at each other in surprise. Jo, with a bloke? Where did he spring from, they wondered; she'd not said a word to them. Well, she'd have to tell!

* * *

Britten and David discovered common ground in a love for vintage Jaguar cars, which made the task of collecting enough background photos a lot easier. Eleanor and Felicity shared a few reminiscences and giggled a bit, especially when Eleanor explained how protective Jo had been over her father. Then

142

Betty found her stepmother and all three of them did another tour round, catching up with David and Britten so he could finish with the smiley smiley shots. But time was marching on. The Morris Dancers had appeared en mass, spending half an hour working themselves into a frenzy before calling it a day and escaping back to the village pub, which then left the coast clear for the little school choir to do their thing. The gaggle of people around the barbecue area seemed happy enough; the ladies were starting to clear up; a few had wandered off around the garden; time now to move into tea mode. Britten retreated to download his shots onto his laptop, and Felicity surprised her host and hostess by volunteering to help.

The stage was soon set with all these helpers to hand; tables, clothes, a couple of large umbrellas with frilly edges, and Eleanor began to look around for Jo. David had gone to change, so where was her daughter?

Jo had taken him up into the orchard; he was so easy to talk to, such a lively smile. In turn he saw the truly charming girl she was, no pretensions and a ready listener. She'd heard all about the ill-fated parachute drop, his love for action, his deep desire to become a doctor, about his home in Norfolk, his interest in the countryside; his passion for dancing. Dancing? Yes, dancing. Ballroom, Latin, not the nightclub hop about shaking your arms stuff. She should try it, she was told, she certainly had the figure for it, and was treated to a sideways glance. She blushed; changing the subject by explaining how her father was intending to convert the old shed to a studio for her.

"You paint?" He was curious.

"Well, sort of. I've started doing sketches, and a self-portrait of just me, then another in a new dress my Pa bought me, and now I *just* know I've got to do more. So I'm going to do a History of Art course and see what happens. I've got ideas of some paintings I'd like to do," she hesitated, going on to reveal to this comparative stranger who she felt she'd known for ages something of her concept of apples and trees and her and and...

"Jooeeee!" A call from the gate. Julie, sent to fetch her.

143

"Oh Lord. The tea party! Sorry, Nigel, I'll have to fly. Julie! Look after Nigel for me. Tell him what we're doing and bring him on down!" She ran, cleared the gate in a bound of flying skirts and lovely legs, and was gone. Nigel blinked. One moment she was deep in a philosophic explanation of some obviously profound work of potential art, the next a vision of athleticism. What a super girl he'd found!

Julie was regarding his amazement with a grave face. Jo had very decidedly made an impression.

"Nigel. As you've gathered, I'm Julie. One of Jo's college friends. Her mum and father are staging this Edwardian-style tea party for those who've stayed on after the village thing – off their own bat – and Jo's dressing up, well sort of, as an Edwardian girl to act as a hostess. Her father's already in his stripy blazer and cricket flannels; she'd gone missing and I find her with you. No one's supposed to be up here today. You're privileged, it seems. But we'd better get on back. I'm waitressing."

And very suitably and attractively dressed for the part, too, he thought, and wondered what Jo was going to look like. "Fine, Julie. I did rather gate crash, but I had to come and say thank you to Jo. She saved me from a nasty situation a while ago. Didn't she say?"

"No! What was that all about?" They were walking slowly back down the paddock.

"I did a parachute drop with the Terriers on the Plain, landing in a solid tree, caught some large branches and had my helmet knocked sideways, clouted me unconscious upside down and getting strangled by the cords. She climbed up and cut me free before I choked to death, luckily. Brave girl. I owe her."

Julie just didn't know, Jo hadn't said a word. She was dumbstruck. Jo – rescuing this guy? No wonder they'd struck up a friendship. Goodness! Jo couldn't have told anyone, else Betty or Trish would have said.

"I don't know whether I should have told you, Julie. If she hasn't said, perhaps she didn't want to play the heroine. P'raps you'd better not say; do you mind?" He was such a nice

144

sort of bloke, Julie just had to agree, pity though, 'cos it would make a good talking point.

"S'pose not. Are you all right now? I mean, you didn't break anything?"

"No, luckily. The Range guys got me down safely, and I spent a few days in the Medical Wing, but I think I've recovered from any concussion. Few bruises, though, which are a bit sore. I'll have to give up on the dancing for a wee while."

"Dancing?" She looked at him. A dancer? "You dance? What, professionally?"

He laughed at her. "No, nothing like that. Just for fun, relaxation. I'm on a Medical degree course at Edinburgh. Third year." By this time they were back to the lawn where the tables were all laid out, and already quite a few occupied. The other two girls were busy taking orders; in the same attractive waitress-style dresses. "Let me be a customer, Julie. I'll sit here. What's on offer?"

"Cucumber sandwiches, fresh scones, tea to your taste. All for a fiver a head. Proceeds to Jo's Mum's gardening fund."

"Fine. Whatever. I'll be happy here." He sat down at a vacant table to watch the happenings around him. Then Jo appeared; in her flowing white dress, her hair bunched with a flower, she was *beautiful.* He couldn't keep his eyes off her. She smiled across at him, but started chatting to the group at the first table, playing the hostess. Her father, dressed as Julie had described, was doing the same, and with the trays coming out with tea and sandwiches, he could have been in another world. It was *so* right, somehow...

SIX

The guests, villagers and friends, the curious, the inspired and the less inspired; whatever the motive for their visit; most expressed their thanks, some profound, some conventional, some matter of fact, as they drifted home. Gradually the garden began to draw breath and resume its tranquillity, as the W.I. team cleared up and went, Trish and her Brendan said their goodbyes to return to another round of customers of a different sort; Felicity and her Britten had feasted on the left-over sandwiches before he dragged her and Betty back to her car, anxious to get home to his family. She was more than pleased with her afternoon; the tea party theme was really going to make the feature. No one saw the going of Edward Petersen, despite his promise to say his farewells. He must have melted into the background and quietly slipped away. Only Nigel and Julie were left. She was a disappointed lady, not having seen hair nor hide of her expected escort; had hung on anticipating him at least to call and collect her. Nigel was in no hurry to get back to Larkhill, especially as Jo and her parents seemed to have accepted him as part of the scenery. He'd got stuck into the clearing up, shirt-sleeves rolled up and hands in the washing-up bowl.

"You don't need to do that, Nigel. We've got a dishwasher!" Eleanor caught him at the sink with a stack of plates and cups and saucers. Jo was at his elbow, doing some drying up. Julie was quietly putting the cups into the box for their return to the village hall.

"It's no bother, Mrs Danielleson. I rather like washing-up, sort of therapeutic. It's been a successful day?"

"I think so, Nigel. And *do* call me Eleanor, please. Jo, dear, you don't need to dry everything. Can you just nip round the garden and check we've no stray crockery lurking in the flowerbeds? Your father's just putting the barn to bed and then we'll have a de-brief. That's the expression isn't it, Nigel? Oh, and before you do, Jo, go and change, there's a dear. That dress needs looking after. It's a bit fragile." She gently took the cloth from her daughter and manoeuvred her towards the door. "You've been great, Jo. Thank you." She kissed her girl's cheek, and closed the door behind her. "How are you getting back to wherever, Nigel? Not that I'm anxious to get rid of you, especially if you're that domesticated."

Nigel chuckled. "Well, I must say I didn't *quite* expect to end the day like this, but it's been a treat, really it has. You have a lovely daughter, Eleanor. She's a fantastic girl. I couldn't have wished for a nicer rescuer." Then he reddened. "Oh, I'm sorry!" Should he have been quite so forthcoming?

"Sorry? What for? Telling us what we already know?" She laughed. "Get on with you. Jo's our only child, and we love her – and we won't see her come to any harm. She'll have to fly the nest some time, though." There was a sudden stillness. Why did she say that? Then David came in and broke the silence.

"All safe and sound. I've closed the gate. Seems everything's as it should be, apart from wear and tear on the grass. Julie – you still here, your lift not arrived? Where's Jo?"

"Upstairs, changing out of her party frock. You may have to run Julie home yourself. Hadn't you better get out of those flannels?"

"S'pose so. How are you getting back, Nigel?" The same question he hadn't answered.

"I call the Base and they send a car. Privileged – but really it's official business, a personal thank you mission. I did give you the letter, didn't I?"

"You did. I'll run you back, if you like, if I'm taking Julie home. Could do with a change of scenery. Whenever. Stay for supper. There's a few left-over sausages!"

Eleanor snorted. "You know what you can do with those! I was merely going to put the cheese and biscuits out, a bit of fruit. We can open a bottle. Nigel?"

"Sounds lovely, er, Eleanor. So long as I'm not outstaying my welcome. I really should thank you both for making me so much a part of things. I hadn't envisaged…"

"That's all right then." Eleanor cut him short. "Look, David, go and change. Find out what Jo's up to. I asked her to check the flowerbeds for stray crockery, just in case. We'll put things together and have it outside, okay?"

Julie was close to tears. Not how she'd envisaged the end of the day at all, but she'd have to make the best of it, for Jo's sake. She sniffed, and Eleanor put a comforting arm around her.

"Never mind, Julie. There must be some good reason. Thank you for all this. It's nice to have you around. You'll have supper with us, anyway."

David had wandered off upstairs. Giving a little tap, before pushing open Jo's bedroom door, he startled her. She was sitting, just in her underwear, furiously sketching away. She looked up and went bright red. "Pa!" Getting up, she turned her pad upside down on the bed. "I'm coming!" She shrugged into the dress she'd laid out, picked up her brush and attacked her hair. "Sorry!"

"What were you drawing?" He was curious. "Do you normally sketch half dressed?" She had been sitting so she could see herself in the mirror. Not *another* self-portrait? She put down the brush and came towards him, a mischievous look in her eyes.

"Shan't say, Pa. Not until it's finished. Don't let on, please."

He eyed her up and down. "Had a good day?"

Relieved, she nodded, and put an arm around him as they moved to go downstairs. "Lovely, despite the crowds. Such a lot has happened." She lowered her voice as they got towards the bottom of the stairs. "Nigel's nice, isn't he? Glad we rescued him."

David looked at her sideways. "Hmmm. Yes. He is. So was your Mr Petersen. Didn't see him go, though. He might have said goodbye. We'll have to talk again. And Mrs Summers? Did you speak with her?"

"Briefly. She asked about my Uni course. I said I was going for Art. That's okay, isn't it, Pa?"

"Seems so, Jo. Oh, and I had a word with our maintenance guy. He's coming to have a look at the shed on Monday evening." Under the large beech across the lawn Eleanor, Julie and Nigel were sitting by the old Victorian castiron table, a bottle and glasses with the fruit bowl evident. David squeezed Jo's hand as she withdrew her arm. "Don't be too enthusiastic, Jo. Take it steady."

Her glance back at him was a trifle puzzled, but they were too close for her to question him.

"This looks good. We deserve it." David pulled a seat to a position more to his liking, picked up his filled glass. "To us!" He nodded to Nigel. "Seeing as you might not be here if it wasn't for this young lady, you can be part of 'us'. Julie – you've been working hard, so you're 'us' as well. Eleanor – was it all worth it, darling?" He didn't always call her darling in public, so he must be in a good mood.

"I'm relieved it's all over. I've not done any figuring, but we took a fair amount on the teas. *And* our reputation hasn't been besmirched. Betty looked after the garden buffs very well, from all accounts. Mrs Blounce and her mob went off happy. Felicity got what she wanted – at least, from the professional point of view. Did she flaunt her knickers at you?" Eleanor was pulling his leg. David grinned.

"I saw enough, darling. She made sure of it, but there's no malice in her. Just her technique, I guess. Make sure she gets her own way." He raised his glass. "To us!"

They clinked glasses. Nigel had his own little speech.

"To Jocelyn. And her parents. My profound thanks, for everything. It's been a splendid day. May I call again, if I'm not presuming?"

How polite, Eleanor thought. How sweet! He's taken to Jo, that's for sure. Oh well, could be worse. Could have been that Tony bloke. She cast her eyes at Julie. The poor girl was feeling left out. Silly chap. Such a lovely girl, and he'd not even had the courtesy to ring.

"Nigel, any time. But you won't be here much longer, will

you? Did I hear you say your home is in Norfolk?"

"Yes, it is. My father's a parish priest near Fakenham. So I'm well used to houses like this – large and rambling. Very pleasant, though."

"Any other brothers or sisters?"

"An elder sister. Married, two years ago. She's gone abroad with her husband; he's farming in France. I think they're quite enjoying it out there, but my parents aren't too happy with her so far away, in their view. And me up in Edinburgh most of the time. They don't much care for my penchant for the army either, especially as I'm thinking of signing on as an army medic. Good pay, less hassle than the NHS. And a chance to travel about." He sipped his glass, reflectively. "I gather Jo is thinking of her own change of tack?" He'd far rather talk about her, or even Julie, than himself. Julie was a pleasant-looking girl, too. She'd lovely legs, under that short skirt. Stop it, he said to himself. He was out!

* * *

The conversation drifted on, and finally, as the evening sun was about to tuck itself behind the hill, David stood up. "Better get you two back, Nigel, Julie. Look, do you want me to ring your parents, let them know you're coming?" Julie just shook her head. She didn't want to go now, she was feeling more relaxed with two glasses of wine, but abruptly she uncrossed her legs and stood up as well. She'd changed her mind.

"Yes, sorry, perhaps I will let them know. Just in case. Can I use your landline? My mobile's gone flat."

"Jo will show you where." Eleanor began to gather the glasses and plates together. The light was going off the garden, and the air had a sudden chill. David went to get the Jaguar out of the garage, and Nigel tucked the chairs back under the table. The day was coming to its tired end.

* * *

Jo busied herself in the kitchen while Julie was on the phone. The murmur of her voice changed, a cry, and then suddenly, shockingly, "No! NOooooee!" The girl was in distress. Jo dropped the tea towel and ran.

Julie was on the hall chair, head back, tears streaming. The phone dangled on its cord. Wide, staring eyes turned to Jo. "It's not right! It's not true! Jo! Tell me it's not true!" Her voice high pitched, reaching a shout. "NO!" She slumped off the chair, legs splayed, skirt catching on the seat and pulling, an untidy heap sprawled in thighs and arms, head finally resting on the chair seat. "Jooooee. My mother. Accident." Her head slipped sideways, and Jo was cradling her in her arms. She'd fainted.

Then Eleanor was there; and Nigel; and Julie picked up by strong male arms.

"Where?"

"Upstairs, Nigel. Jo's room for now. First right. Jo – your father. Now!"

Jo was shattered. Julie's mum, in an accident? Numb, she went as she was directed, to find her father. He was just coming back indoors.

"Are they all set, Jo?" He was bright and chirpy, until he saw her face. "Goodness, girl, you've seen the resident ghost? Whatever's the matter?" Something had gone dramatically wrong, that he could tell, Jo suddenly in his arms, and crying.

"Julie's mum, I think, been in an accident. I'm not sure. She's hysterical, Pa, and Nigel's taken her upstairs with Mums."

"Okay, Jo. Look, go put the kettle on, then just sit down there. No argument. You *stay put,* understand? Make us some tea when the kettle's boiled. I'll find out what's happened." Gently, he disentangled her, kissed a distraught pair of eyes, and went into the hall. The dangling phone caught his eye, and he picked it up. No sound. He depressed the headset rest, listened. A dialling tone, so push last number redial. It was ringing. Then a voice.

"I'm sorry, I can't take any calls just now..."

David quickly interjected. "David Danielleson. We have

151

Julie here. We can look after her, but tell me what I need to know." As he listened to the haltingly told story, his face became grim.

"I'm *so sorry* to hear that. My deepest condolences. We'll keep Julie here tonight, if you like, and then please let us know when you'd like her back. We'll do anything to assist. Really. Thank you for telling me. You have our number?" He spelt it out, and replaced the receiver. He straightened out the hall chair and sat down. What an awful thing, he couldn't possibly imagine what he would have done if it had been Eleanor. Cupping his chin in his hands, felt the prick and pull of tears, Julie, poor, poor Julie. Then there was Nigel, coming back down the stairs.

"I'd better go, Mr Danielleson. I'll phone the Base, they'll send a car. You don't need to run me back, not under this state of affairs. I'm so, so sorry for Julie. Such a lovely girl, and to have this happen to her, whatever the circumstances. Such a shock. I would *never* have told her on the phone, never. She should have been at home. It'll take days for her to get over this. I've done trauma at the University and it's a real nasty thing. Anything else I can do, you will let me know?" The sincerity and depth of feeling in his voice was clear. He cared.

"Yes. Nigel, of course. Thank you for your support. You sure I can't run you back?"

"Positive. If I can use the phone?"

* * *

Leaving Nigel in the hall, he went to find Eleanor, sitting alongside a washed-out looking Julie, lying still on Jo's bed. Eleanor looked up and shook her head, fingers on her lips. Quietly she got up to pull David out of the room.

"She's in shock, David; we just need to keep her warm and quiet, then give her a cup of sweet tea. So Nigel says!" giving a little bit of an unsteady laugh. "He's a useful chap. Any more like him left in the tree?"

He couldn't join her in the humour, not having heard what had happened. "Julie's mum was involved in an car accident,

Eleanor. She didn't stand a chance. A rubbish skip lorry skidded, somewhere on the Warminster road. Hit her head on. Her husband's just about coping, but he's not thinking straight, only natural, I guess. I've said we'll keep Julie here tonight, and then perhaps we'll see what the morning will bring. Oh, Eleanor!" He couldn't help it, his eyes filled, and he had to turn away. Eleanor went cold. What an end to the day! Such a happy day, then this. Why? Why did these disasters happen, and wreck lives? She put arms around him, her head on his chest, and squeezed.

"I know, darling. We'll look after the girl. Where's Jo?"

He straightened up, and wiped his eyes. "In the kitchen. Making tea. I told her not to move. We'd better go to her. She'll need us just as much." They went back downstairs, hand in hand.

Nigel was in the kitchen, and holding Jo tight to him. She was crying, soundlessly, and her sobs shook her body.

"Cry, girl. Cry. Best thing." He looked up at her parents, and in his eyes they saw caring, and compassion. Then there were lights on the darkening driveway, and he carefully unfolded her arms.

"I must go, Jo. Your parents will look after you. I'll phone you in the morning," and as she lifted a tear-stained face he gave her a gentle kiss on the cheek. "I owe you my life, Jo. Bless you." He gave half a wave to David and Eleanor. "Thank you," he said, and was gone.

* * *

Eleanor poured them all a stiff mug of tea each, and sent Jo upstairs to Julie. "We'll move her into the guest room, David. She'll be better in there. Goodness knows if she'll sleep tonight, but there's not much else we can do. We can't drug her."

"Nope. What a mess. Poor girl." He knew he was repeating himself but the stark recall and overtones of the past were in his mind. Eleanor's mother had taken drugs, leaving her motherless and alone, to all intents and purposes. And now Julie was left with only a grey imitation of a father from all accounts.

Jo returned. "I think she's coming round. She's drunk the tea," she said, putting the empty mug on the sink, and picking up her own. "Yuck. Tea, at this time of night. Where will I sleep, Mums?"

"In your own bed, chump. Julie can have the guest room and borrow one of your nighties. Let's go and sort things. We'd all be better in bed. Come on. David, put the lights out."

* * *

Jo slept fitfully. She was a very tired little girl after all that had happened, but twice she came to the surface that night. Once, when she had a reoccurrence of the dream of the shadowy people in the orchard and one of them nightmaringly had Julie's face and she woke, then later on when she felt an undeniable need to go to the bathroom, and had to creep quietly across the landing. She'd peeped in on Julie, happy to see her sound asleep. Dawn, the early dawn of summer, brought her back to the surface yet again, and her mind flicked back into gear. Julie. Flinging bedclothes aside she tiptoed back to the guest room.

"Julie?" she whispered, "Are you awake?"

"Jo?" A dark haired head came off its pillow. "Oh, *Jo!*"

Jo, full hearted Jocelyn, slipped across to the bed, and reached for her friend. The two girls clung to each other, before Julie shook her hair and released an arm to brush stray fronds from her forehead.

"I'm going to have to be brave, aren't I? Oh, Jo, thank goodness I was here. I'm sorry I was such a freak last night. Really. It's not like me to go all girly and...," and the tears came again.

Jo got up from the bed to draw back the curtains, letting the clear light of early morning flood across the carpet and onto the tousled dark haired girl. "Right, Julie. The shower's next left. Breakfast in an hour. Take your time. Use what smelly stuff you like – it's all there. Leave you to it."

154

* * *

Eleanor had organised a good breakfast, cooked bacon and mushrooms and scrambled egg. David made a nice brew of coffee and the combined aromas couldn't help but lift the spirits. With Julie facing reality in a strangely determined way, the atmosphere was far less strained. She even managed a smile when Jo talked about the shorty skirts from yesterday. There was just a flutter of hearts when the phone rang. David took it on the fixed hall phone, and came back with the update from Julie's father.

"I'll run you back just before lunch, Julie. He seems to be speaking quite level-headedly. Okay?"

"I'll come with you, Julie," Jo was adamant, then the phone rang again and this time she skipped out to answer it. Eleanor's eyes met David's "Nigel" she mouthed. He raised his eyebrows.

Back after two minutes, she said "He wants to come over, Mums. I've said yes. Is that all right?"

"Of course, dear. You like him, don't you?"

"Uh huh. He's okay." She was uncharacteristically non-committal, and turned back to Julie.

"What do you think happened to your Robert, Julie? He should have let you know if he wasn't coming. Can't think too much about you." Then realising how callous that sounded, coloured up. "Oh. I'm sorry. I didn't mean it quite like that."

"I should think not, my girl. He probably couldn't get in touch if Julie's phone was dead." David took her to task, before tapping Julie's arm. "Let me look at your phone. Maybe we've a charger to fit." Anything to keep her from brooding. "How's Nigel getting here, did he say?"

"I think he's borrowing someone's car. His is at that Lyneham place, where the Hercules live. He shouldn't be long. Can he stay for lunch?" As if she needed to ask, thought Eleanor.

* * *

By the time Nigel arrived, they'd agreed to have an early

155

lunch, ensuring Julie at least would go home fed. As soon as he came in the drive, Jo was at the door. There was a smile, and a kiss on the cheek, a polite greeting to her parents, another embrace for Julie and then coffee all round. Jo took Julie and Nigel up to the orchard while Eleanor put a scratch lunch together. David busied himself in checking the garden and the barn again to stop himself from brooding. What a calamitous thing to happen to any girl. Such a pity.

* * *

In reflective solemn silence the trio, guided by Jo, crossed the paddock, long grass swishing under their feet. The robin's cheerful chirp seemed too insensitive, too intrusive. Jo tucked her arm under Julie's, and the sudden contact broke Julie's reserve.

She stopped, lifted her head and howled. Floods of tears, and she collapsed in a heap. Jo made to lift her, but Nigel shook his head, merely crouching alongside her, and stroked the long black hair, took a hand in his, exhorted "Cry, Julie, cry."

Jocelyn felt helpless, a bystander. She'd risked life and limb for Nigel, and now here he was, supporting one of her best friends in her tragic loss. Whose loss the greater? She was all mixed up, and walked on into the coolness of the orchard. The trees seem to enfold her; calmed her turbulent thoughts as she reached her seat on the log. She wiped misted eyes. Oh, Julie, Julie! Through the gate she came, Nigel at her side. Julie. Jo stood up, held out her hands.

Julie, red eyed, streaked with tears, took them. "Sorry, Jo."

"Julie, it's me who should be sorry. I'm not much help, am I?"

Julie just squeezed her friend's hands, and Jo could see more tears. She gently pushed her down onto the log, and put an arm around her. "Nigel?"

"Look, I'll leave you to it, don't worry; she'll be better for the crying. Got a hanky?"

That produced a wry smile. "Lend me yours?"

"Not much use. It's already soaked." Another smile. "Use your petticoat."

"How very old fashioned, Nigel!"

The repartee allowed Julie to wipe her eyes and begin to recover, "Jo doesn't believe in too many layers, Nigel," she said. "Perhaps I shouldn't say. Take her back with you. I'd like to be on my own for a while. You don't mind?"

"Of course not. If you're sure."

"I'm sure. Really. I've got to come to terms with this. And I've got my father to think of. I can't be a wimp. He'll be a bit of a dead loss, I'm afraid. Go on, you two." She stuck her legs out straight and stared at her knees.

Nigel took Jo's hand, and they turned away. Once through the gate and into the paddock, Nigel pulled Jo round to him. "You care, don't you, Jo?"

"She's my friend, Nigel. I know how I would feel if it had been my Mums. She'll be all right, won't she?"

"I think so. She seems tough enough, underneath. I just hope she's not dragged down again once she's home. Are *you* all right, Jo?"

She nodded. "Just hold me tight for a moment, Nigel; if you don't mind."

He had to laugh. "That's what Julie said. Mind; of course not, why should I? You're the nicest possible girl to hold, Jo. Too tempting by far." With his arms around her, she nestled beautifully into his shoulder and rested her head.

"I've never been held like this before, you know. Strange, but I feel as though I've known you for *ages*. You're privileged, Nigel. Still, I suppose I own you, having saved your life. That's what the Chinese, isn't it, or is it the Japanese believe? Okay, you can let me go," she added, coyly, "If you want to, that is."

"Hmmm." The peaceful surroundings and the subtle scent from this delectable armful were getting to him. "I think I better had. Else I'll have your father after me. What was that about an early lunch?" He spun her back towards the house.

Eleanor looked up at the pair curiously as they entered the kitchen. Hand in hand? "No Julie?"

"Left her on her own in the orchard, Mums. She'll be fine

when she gets back, I know. It's *so* peaceful up there. *You* know what effect the place has on people. So does Nigel, now." Her look at him told its own story. Oh dear! Eleanor did a private internal shrug. Well, it had to happen sooner or later, and he seemed to be a nice sort of a chap, and well, *all right!*

She changed the subject. "We've had a phone call while you were out. Your Mr Peterson. Edward. He wants to come and see us again. Apologised for slipping away, but said he couldn't stand Morris dancers. Seems he left with your Mrs Summers. There's nothing between them, is there?" Her face gave the game away.

"Mums! Really! Mrs Summers? Your guess, not mine!" Then the realisation of her Mums's comment hit her. "Wants to come and see us? Why? Do you think...," she broke off to explain to Nigel. "He's my Art lecturer from college. He's seen something of what I've painted, or sketched, rather, and maybe he's going to help me. Does Pa know?" She spoke back to her Mums. Where was he?

"Not yet. I've told Edward to phone tomorrow. Your father's still messing about out there somewhere. Go and find him, Jo. No, leave Nigel here." Her daughter gave her an old-fashioned look, but did as she was told.

Eleanor wasted no time. "Like my daughter, do you, Nigel? If so, just you ensure that you take great care of her. She's very precious. I don't want to think rescuing you from a tree was a bad idea. You don't mind me saying?" She busied herself putting plates round the table as she spoke.

It was a bit of a surprise, but he rallied. "I think she's a great girl. In every way. I wouldn't see her come to any harm, whatsoever. I'd love to become a real friend. If that's all right with you and Mr Danielleson."

"Fine. Now perhaps you'll put the cutlery round." Abruptly, she changed the subject "When do you go home? Or is it back to Edinburgh?"

"I really ought to go home tomorrow. Show my folks I'm still in one piece. But I think I'd like to come back, if I may, though probably it'll be at the army's expense so I don't know when."

"Well, let us know, Nigel. Now, are you tea or coffee or soft drink?"

* * *

Julie returned, sombre but dry eyed. Jo took her back upstairs for a quick wash; David got the Jaguar out once more, and after a quick bite to eat, she was ready to go home.

"I'll be all right, Jo, you don't need to come, I'll give you a ring tomorrow. Thank you all for being so good. Nigel -," and she gave him a kiss, "Jo's a great girl." David opened the car door for her, she swung herself and her long legs in, and they were gone.

"Well. I'd better be off, too. I've got to pick up my own car. Thanks, Mrs D. Jo - take care of yourself. Don't risk any more tree rescues. Best of luck with the painting. Let me know how it goes. Here's my address."

Eleanor tactfully turned her back. Jo got her goodbye kiss, saw him into the car and waved him out of the drive. There was a cloying silence after the car had gone; the garden seemed strangely empty. After all that joy, all that happiness, the pleasure *so many* people had felt that day, all gone. Her heart sort of shivered inside her. She kicked at the gravel, swung round and ran. Ran, through the garden, past the yews, across the paddock, into her refuge, and flung herself down onto the grass, rolling over and staring up at the now sullen sky through the branches. The light suited her mood. She tore at her blouse, her bra, anything to get rid of the pressure. She kicked her shoes off. And cried, cried for Julie, cried for an indescribably silly loss of an instant friend in Nigel. He'd been so nice. The trees whispered above her, moving insistently, forcefully, as the storm clouds rolled in. Why? Why, why, why? After she'd been *so* happy? Julie'd lost her mother. She'd thought she'd found someone who was going to be *different*. Now she'd lost him. And she was going to have to face up to changes. What did Peterson want?

With a sudden violent flash of lightning came an ominous roll of thunder. The trees stilled, a brief respite, then a few heavy drops of rain splattered through the branches, catching her bare breast and creating dark blotches on her skirt. Would she ever make an artist?

She rolled over again, wincing as the stiff grass caught at her tender skin, cushioning her head on her arms. The ground smelt of dampness now and the rawness of earth. The flimsy blouse had torn, leaving her shoulders bare. It was no good. It was all going wrong. Slowly, she pulled her knees up beneath her, like she was praying, to raise her head, fearfully. It was getting so strangely dark; then another immense flash lit up the trees, starkly, prefaced an almost immediate colossal bang. She jumped to her feet and tore back, back to the house. Tore into the kitchen, past a flabbergasted Eleanor, and crashed up to her room, flung herself onto the bed and hid her head under the pillow. She hated thunderstorms.

Eleanor put her cookbook down, having looked for inspiration for a nice Sunday supper for when David got back, it shouldn't be long now, as a wreck of a daughter flashed past, half naked. Silly girl! She'd best go and calm her down.

There was a heap under the bedclothes.

"Jo?"

The covers were flung back, and dishevelled hair emerged, then near naked Jocelyn. She really did look a mess. Nothing for it, then.

"Come and have a shower, Jo. We can't have this. You're supposed to be becoming a young lady. Young ladies *don't* go rushing around tearing their clothes off, or burying themselves in the undergrowth. Come on. I'll scrub your back if you like." Eleanor started to undress, and Jo watched her.

"Mums?"

"You need a bit of t.l.c. my girl. Then you'll dress to please your father. He needs a lift, after all the trauma. Right?"

* * *

So when David eventually returned Jo had come back to life, sitting demurely in the lounge with a drink, wearing *her dress* and feeling all glowey inside. The thunder had come and gone, leaving a nice steady and persistent rain. She felt entirely different. The drama diminished, her inner-self more at peace, and her Mums with a happy self-satisfied look, some semblance of normality had returned. David sensed that something had gone on, but couldn't put his finger on it. He'd returned in the only to be expected sombre mood, but correctly guessed he wasn't required to elaborate. It had actually been quite grim; he'd wished Julie didn't have to cope with the greyness and the sadness, but there was nothing to be done. Maybe later; but in the meanwhile there was Jo, beautiful Jo, looking lovely.

"You look a million dollars, Jo. You've recovered? Silly question. Course you have. Eleanor, you look a deal happier. What a day, eh? Not quite what we had in mind." He wrinkled his nose. "Do I smell supper?"

"Not exactly cordon bleu, dear, comfort food. Tagliatelli, home-brewed sauce and a few prawns. Bottle of red? Will that do? You get it, dear. I'm quite tired. I think we'll eat, then call it a day." She closed her eyes, ready for bed, tired, but not *that* tired.

Jo watched the body language. She couldn't complain, not with her recent experience. She was tired too, exhausted. She'd sleep, she knew.

SEVEN

Monday. David's day off. They'd overslept, unsurprisingly. Eleanor slipped quietly, silky smoothly, out of her nice warm bed, leaving David comfortably quiet and still fast asleep. With a distinctly fresher and more relaxed feeling now that the barbecue thing was all behind her, she went to the half-open window and breathed in the marvellously clean morning air. *Her* garden was greeting her, smiling up at her, freshly washed with last night's cleansing rain. With half turned head, keeping an eye on her husband, she pulled her nightdress over her head, allowing the coolness to pert up her breasts and bring goose pimples to her skin. He didn't stir, so she moved, quietly, to look for her daughter. Poor Jocelyn, up in the air and radiantly happy yesterday, then dropped into despair for her friend's loss, her own loss too, in finding a friend and then losing him! She'd need some comforting, and how to start? Last evening, taking her to herself and *loving* her was part of the comfort, but that was only a play on the body's feelings. Okay, it had worked to a degree, but it wasn't going to be the answer every time. Her daughter needed something more. She was metamorphosing into womanhood, a painful process that could go dramatically wrong at times. How often does one go back to the start line?

* * *

There she was, enviously beautiful spread of auburn hair across the pillow, regular breathing lifting the single sheet over such a lovely shape, and experienced a tinge of regret that she'd lose her, physically at least. Her gorgeous daughter

162

wouldn't always be sleeping in her single bed. Would she wake her, talk to her, or let her sleep herself through? Her thoughts were powerful, and Jo woke.

"Mums! Goodness! What's the time? Why are you starkers?" She sat up, wide eyed. "Heavens! Is it that bad? Did Pa kick you out? No, he wouldn't have, not you looking like that. Oh Mums! You look lovely!" Honestly, she *did* look lovely, all womanly and *nice!*

Eleanor smiled, that enigmatic, Mona Lisa smile. "Jo, darling, you're very complimentary. Did you sleep well?"

"Hmmm, think so. Can't remember. Gosh. It's Monday, isn't it?" Then the realisation of last evening's events focused. "Julie! Oh, *Mums!* What can we do?" She swung long legs out of the bed and stood up. She'd not bothered with a nightie either. Stepped over to her mother and hugged her. "Oh, *Mums!* I love you so!" She wasn't just saying it, either. She felt her heart swell up, and her eyes water.

"Silly girl!" Eleanor's voice, buried in Jo's auburn curls, was muffled, with emotion as well as hair. She brushed her girl's tresses to one side. "Let's get us dressed and have breakfast. Then we'll have a family conflab. I love you too, girl." She carefully disengaged herself. Her nipples were tender and crushed against Jo's breasts, soft as they were, had begun to feel sore. "Look pretty, my girl. I'll see you downstairs in a minute."

Left alone, Jocelyn padded across to her window, taking in the same welcome feelings of a garden refreshed. "*So lovely, Mums!*" she whispered to herself. Indeed, even after being trodden by all those people yesterday, the grass was still deep green, flowers flaunting beauty at her, shrubs moving in gentle applause in the light morning breeze. Above all, the sky was clear and that simple powder blue. Just a whisper, a trace, of white over the distant hill; giving scale to the horizon. She shivered. Best get something on, then, and sorting herself out that simple little rubbed light creamy cotton dress, she contemplated. If she wasn't going anywhere, could she do without? Would Mums mind? It had a tight neckline, and it wasn't too short. Okay, she'd try.

163

Eleanor had managed to get herself dressed before David finally woke, probably just as well, she thought, otherwise breakfast might have been postponed half an hour. The three of them sat down around the kitchen table to toast, tea; for David, coffee; and talked.

"I can't just ignore her, Pa. Julie's been a good friend. We've got to *do* something! Her father's a wimp. She'll be *so* miserable. I know her mother wasn't like you, Mums, but she was still *there!*"

David was buttering another piece of toast. "We can't interfere, Jo. Not unless we're asked. I said we'd do anything that was needed, in a polite sort of way. I know she was distressed, but then, so was her father. He'd lost a wife, you know, however distant their relationship. Perhaps we should leave it a day before ringing her? Do you think you need to have a word with Betty, or Trish? See if they have any ideas?"

Jo thought for a moment. Eleanor, pouring her second cup of tea, nodded. "Good idea, David. We need to thank them again for Saturday, anyway. And we need to find out if Felicity was happy with her visit. It's only polite. Before anyone else rings us?" But it was too late. The phone began to ring. David frowned, got up, and went into the hall.

"How do you feel now, Jo?" Eleanor took the opportunity.

"Okay, I think, Mums, thanks. I just need a bit of time, I guess. Pity Nigel had to go home. He was good, last night, wasn't he?" She could say it without a pause, convincing herself she could shrug him off?

Her mother eyed her up and down. "Hmm. Yes, he was. Like him, do you? Left your bra off, haven't you?" She shook her head. "You're a strange one. Giving all those boys the heave-ho that you see all the time, then going for a guy you met up a tree! Why no bra, Jo?"

"Too constrictive. Or I just feel nicer without being strapped up. I don't know really." She changed the subject. "Nigel's different, Mums. Not like the others. He wasn't pawing at me. And I liked his eyes. Oh, okay, we held hands, but...," she was interrupted, by her father coming back into the room.

"That was Edward Petersen. He's coming over in half an hour or so. Wants to discuss things with us. Seems to have taken a shine to you, Jo – or your work; I'm not sure which. He's all right, isn't he? I mean, not just an eye for a pretty figure?"

Jo had to smile, her father being protective, just like she'd been over Felicity. "Pa! As if! He's a college lecturer, for heaven's sake. Oh, well. So what if he has. He's an *artist!*" saying it like it was an excuse for stripping naked in front of him. Then she blushed; she'd got no bra on. She pushed her chair back, and stood up. "I'll just pop upstairs for a mo. Then I'll ring Betty."

While she'd gone, Eleanor quizzed David. "What do you think, David?" She didn't need to elaborate.

"I think he's straight. A character, yes, but genuinely interested in what our Jocelyn's trying to do." Then he asked the same question. "Why no bra?"

"You're too observant!" Eleanor reached over and patted his hand. "She's a feisty girl, Dave. Likes what she's got. Don't knock it!" and laughed, realising what she'd said. He looked puzzled for a brief moment, then grasped the pun and joined in as Jo re-emerged, and they both noticed her more orthodox presentation.

"Can I phone Betty?"

"Sure. Then we'll have a potter around the estate, shall we? Before Petersen comes?"

Betty answered the phone. "My mother's at the office, Jo. I'm on my own. How's things?"

Elaborating on the train of events, Jo got a sob from her friend. "Oh, poor, poor Julie! How's she going to manage? She'll have to look after her father now. What can *we* do?"

"I don't know, Bet. Not a lot, I suspect, apart from keeping in touch. My Mums wants to say 'thanks' for Saturday. You *were* a great help, really. Any idea what your step-mum got out of her visit?"

"Not yet. I'll let you know, if she doesn't get in touch direct. How's Nigel?"

Loaded question, thought Jo. "He's gone home, to Norfolk." She waited.

"Nice chap, Jo."

"Yes. Look, better go, I've got to phone Trish. Come over, any time, Bet. Thanks again."

* * *

When she managed, eventually, to reach Trish, there was a not dissimilar reaction. The two girls, not being poles apart in their views, had a mutually tear-jerking conversation that ended with Trish promising to go round to Julie's; she wasn't all that far away. "I'll tell Brendan, too. He's a great one for shoulders to cry on. Maybe we'll go round together." That's a splendid idea, Jo thought. About to put the phone down, she was minded to say about Petersen coming round, but it was too late, Trish had rung off. Another sudden thought; didn't Pa say he'd got someone coming to look over the orchard shed?

Back in the kitchen, she prompted him, "The studio, Pa?"

He smiled at her. "Mike will be on his way, Jo. It looks like a busy morning. Just as well you're not in the shop, Eleanor. If Petersen's coming, it'll dovetail in nicely. Haven't anything new to show him, Jo?"

No, she hadn't. What with the village 'do' and Sunday – black Sunday for Julie – there'd been no chance, let alone inspiration. Her Mums's portrait was still very much in mind, but overtaken by events. It was all getting a bit much. She sat down in the basket chair and closed her eyes.

"Jo?" Eleanor wasn't used to having her girl around on a Monday other than in college holidays; today was different. No college, never, ever again. Her girl wasn't fully herself, either, not after yesterday, well, the weekend, really. Nigel, Peterson, Julie's mother's death, all impacting on their lives.

There was a car on the drive. Peterson?

"Jo, dear. Are you with us? Peterson's here. Unless it's your father's guy?"

"I'll go." David, a smidgeon anxious that Jo seemed not to have heard his question, also felt Eleanor's unease. Closing the kitchen door behind him, he pondered on the effect all this was having on his daughter. School kid no longer, college behind her. He'd dressed her, feted her, encouraged her; now becoming a party to her eventually leaving home. Then it would just be him and Eleanor.

The car was Mike's. "Thanks for coming, Mike; care for a coffee or something first? We've got Jo's artist friend coming over – he can probably give us some idea on what light we need to achieve." He led the way back inside. Mike was an abrupt, no nonsense sort of guy, but extremely good at establishing what was what in the building trade. If he couldn't do it, he knew a man who could, and as cost effective as any. No short cuts either. A good solid job done always, which was why he worked for the company.

"Mike, meet Eleanor – my wife, Jo, here, she's the budding artist."

Shaking hands, taking his coffee mug, merely acknowledging them with a nod. Jo made her excuses, went upstairs and flung herself onto the unmade bed to stare up at the ceiling. The joy had gone out of the day, and she couldn't understand why. Her mind flew around, Pa buying her that lovely dress; the night out; running naked in the rain; rescuing Nigel. Her heart skipped a beat. Nigel. Oh Lord! Then there was the tea party thing. Her special dress for that was hanging up in front of her wardrobe.

Then… "Jo-ooh!" Her Mums was calling. "Mr Peterson's here!"

Slowly she sat up, took a deep breath and slid off the bed. She smoothed her hair down, shook the creases out of her dress and went back downstairs.

"Fair Jo – you're not yourself? No smile?" He was beaming at her, twinkling eyes, smart summer jacket, one of those linen things, Panama hat and cane in his hand; Eleanor making him a black tea.

She had to respond somehow, managing a wry grin. "Sorry, Mr Peterson. We're recovering from a bit of a sad thing. You remember Julie? Tall, dark haired girl? Her mother was killed in a car crash on Sunday," and after saying that she had to sit down again, collapsing into her chair.

"How tragic! Now I can understand. Such a *nice* girl. I am *truly* sorry to hear that." He took his tea from Eleanor. "Send her my commiserations. What else can one say? Heartbreaking. No way for anyone to lose a mother."

After a reflective silence, Jo looked up. "Pa gone up to the orchard?"

Eleanor nodded. Mike was not one for small talk; he and David had soon gone off to 'sus it out'. Petersen gave a little cough. This wasn't *quite* what he'd expected. Jo started at the sound and Eleanor came to the rescue.

"Perhaps, if you don't mind, Edward, Jo can show you what her father has in mind for her; we're thinking of creating a studio out of an old shed. He's up there now with a chap who knows what buildings are all about. Your advice may be extremely useful. Then we can maybe have a bite of lunch? Provided you have the time?"

He had. He certainly wanted to help, to guide Jocelyn and, specifically, to make her an offer, so he'd go along with whatever happened. With panama back in place, and swinging his cane, the pair went up towards the orchard. He slipped his arm through hers.

"Whatever the reason, Jocelyn, I am sad that you are sad. It bodes ill for your creativity if black moods prevail, does it not? Tell me, how best do you draw?" He glanced sideways at her, from under shaggy grey eyebrows. She stopped, and thought. How best? The self-portrait, the dress picture, the evening light over the garden, even the sketch of her father on that log, all done when she was feeling *something* inside her.

"I'm not sure. I have to be in a mood, I guess?"

He nodded. "Good, good. Now how the mood?"

Such cryptic questions. Was there a specific thing she could remember? She'd done the portrait half naked, the evening light just before she got into bed, and the dress she'd done with nothing underneath; but the sketch? It was her father, and she'd been fully dressed. No common denominator, just her desires? "Just happy, I suppose?"

"Hmmm. All right. Why happy?"

"You're teasing me!"

"I'm not, Jocelyn. I'm serious. It is *essential* to understand one's motives. You cannot draw, or paint, or sketch, unless you have the *right* motive. Some have financial reward as a motive. That will not produce *real art.*" His eyes were penetrating, serious. "You say you were happy, so consider why you were happy. Was it because you were warm or cold, hungry or well fed, alone or with a friend, inspired by light or dark? Consider the options, Jo, and we have a start point. Not that it has to be one factor, it may be two, it may be three, we may even find other aspects as we go on."

She stood, head in the air, looking at the sky. Bright, azure blue. Sunlight. She felt warm, and itchy. She longed to feel her shoulders free, but she couldn't, not unless she was alone. How could that alter things, anyway? She walked on, and Petersen followed, caught up and took her arm again.

"I'm serious, Jocelyn. There's something inside you to give you inspiration. You did not produce *inspired* work at college, but you have here. I want to find that inspiration, encourage and develop it for you, for lurking in the depths there's talent. Can I talk to you, Miss Danielleson?"

Surprised, she looked at him, this wonderfully bohemian sort of character who had gone out of his way to become interested in her, of all people. Why suddenly be so formal? Intriguing, and a shiver ran down her spine. She couldn't continue to hold his gaze, and had to drop her eyes. He took her hands in his; they were sort of rough, but strong and strangely comforting. Another shiver, and a strange feeling, almost like fear, certainly apprehension, ran through her, but she gave a sort of nod. He tightened his grip for an instant, and then released her.

"You're not concerned about *me?*" The last thing he wanted was for her to think he was at all predatory. This time she was able to shake her head; no, she was not in the least bit worried about *that*, not that she had any experience of how *men* tried to influence girls into unhealthy relationships, but sufficient feminine intuition to know that wasn't his motive, despite his banter and innuendo, which was just his way, no malice intended, and a latent giggle turned into bubbling sort of laugh, dispelling all tension between them. She had to smile at him, and his eyes were smiling back at her.

"Mr Petersen. What would you wish to talk to me about that elicits such a serious approach?" She would play along with him; this was going to be fun.

"My dear Miss Danielleson," he said, retrieving her hands. "I have a proposition for you."

She blinked. This was dodgy. "Er… I thought…"

The smile deepened. "A proposition that is strictly business, and how ever much my inclinations may lead me, I can reassure you that you have my word of honour that's the way it will remain, unless you inform me otherwise." So was he leaving the door ajar? "In return for becoming a poor artist's model, I will teach you all the techniques I know. Give you the best professional edge that I can instil, with your *best* achievements in mind, and provided you have your parents' blessing. If so, you and I must remain on the most formal of social relations. To prevent *any* misunderstandings, you understand, though I profess to some sadness in that, for you are the most delightful of creatures, my Jo, and I shall take great care that you remain so, so long as it is within my power." With that, he pulled her towards him, and very chastely, gave her a small kiss on her cheek. His little beard tickled her, and surprised as she was, she still found it within her to draw back and play the part.

"*Really*, Mr Peterson! Such a liberty to take on a poor defenceless maiden! I protest, sir, you quite take advantage! None the less, I shall seriously consider what benefits may construe from such an arrangement as you propose, and shall also consult with my guardians. Pray, do me the honour of accompanying me further." Then she giggled, quite spoiling the illusion of her pretence at being a Jane Austen girl. Her mind raced on, quite wondering what this was all going to mean. A model? A mental picture of having to drape herself in the nude over some seedy couch, like an eighteenth-century pretend Venus, or maybe lying in a pond all draped in pre-Raphaelite manner, or, boringly, just looking enigmatic so he could do another Mona Lisa. No, that wasn't his style, so what, what could he have in mind? She'd find out soon enough, if Mums and Pa thought it was okay, and then she'd at least have some professional slant on what *she* wanted to do.

They were walking on, a width apart now, and reached the orchard. Pa and Mike were deep in conversation, looking up at the shed roof. David broke off as they approached.

"Hi, Jo. Edward. This is what we thought might make a sort of studio for Jo. Mike's come up with the practical side of things, and though it looks quite simple, I would appreciate a professional's comment. Come along in."

While Mike continued to make some notes, David ducked into the doorway, Edward following. His first reaction was one of horror. It was dark, dirty, albeit it historic dirt, and with a not very high roof. He liked space, and sunlight, but as his eyes adjusted to the gloom, evidently the fabric was solid, and it had character. Jo, behind him, whispered in his ear. "I love this place – the old orchard and everything. The inspiration you asked about?" Oh, so maybe he was getting somewhere, but it couldn't be just the *place*? Her self-portrait couldn't have been done here. He turned back and they stepped outside again. That pile of old, old boxes, a few sticks of furniture, a broken chair and a relic of a table, all in a heap, having been thrown out of this shed. Fascinating stuff that must have been there for some time, judging by the state of things. They were all waiting on his observations.

"It's been here some time. Solid, though, has character; pity the roof's so low. Needs a lot more light. Faces the right way, I think. Yes, has potential."

"We'll take this wall out, replace it with glass shutters. Put a roof light in as well. Maybe retile, check the flooring, new stable door. Try and leave as many original timbers in as possible. Looks good." Mike's enthusiasm sounded quite encouraging. "I'll do some drawings for you. Okay if I stay up here for a bit and take measurements?"

"Sure, Mike. Just let me know what it's going to cost."

"I'll keep an eye on that, worry not, David. Someone I know will do the woodwork in keeping. Original oak. We'll have to put double glazed windows in, though, and maybe insulate the walls. At least we don't have to worry about planning, but we'd better keep on the right side of Building Regs. Leave it to me. Happy to do it. Okay?"

"Okay. Thanks a lot, Mike. We'd best be getting back, I don't want to usurp Mr Petersen's time. See you later?"

Leaving Mike to his tape measure and pencil in his teeth, David, Edward and Jo retreated back to the house. Eleanor had organised a nice little buffet-style lunch on the table below the big beech tree, and put out another big jug of her lemonade.

"Delightful. Thank you *so much!*" Edward took one of the cast-aluminium chairs and popping his hat and cane onto the grass beside him, reached without ceremony for a sandwich. Jo squatted on the grass, decorously adjusted her skirt to cover her knees, and waited. Eleanor passed her a plate, offered her the sandwiches. Jo took one, but being on tenterhooks couldn't bring herself to take a bite despite being prawn and mayonnaise, her favourite. David plumped for the only teak chair, and poured himself a glass of lemonade. After a brief pause Edward cleared his throat to give his verdict.

"You both know I think Jocelyn has talent. She does, however, need to refine her style and brushwork. I am confident that she will become an even more talented painter. Less so on the sketch work, but it has its place. I would like to coach her. In return, she would suit me well as a model – no, please do not misinterpret this requirement. Flattering though it may be, I am *not* an exponent of the reproduction of the female form in its, ahem, raw state. I am more an advocate of the use of figures in the landscape, and yes, I do appreciate the ladies in that respect. If she would like to accompany me on my jaunt into France to paint for a week, then I'll coach her. No costs involved – I would be pleased to cover all expenses. Her company, fulfilment of the role, would be reward itself." He reached for another sandwich. Jo took a deep breath. So that was what he had had in mind! France! Just with him?

Eleanor looked at her husband. Jo, off on her own with this Edward? David put his glass down.

"What does our daughter think?" His eyes first on his wife; she didn't look too unhappy, and so he glanced down at Jo. There was almost imperceptibly a nod, then an inspiration.

"Mr Petersen. Would you take *two* girls?"

He blinked. Two girls? Goodness, he'd not considered adding to the cost that much. Rapid re-assessment of logistics. Well, there were advantages, not least in the protection it would offer against any suggestion of impropriety. Two girls! Why not? The more the merrier!

"Who had you in mind, Miss Danielleson?" He was being true to his word, formality, albeit with humorous undertones.

"Julie. She'll need something to take her mind off things, and her father won't miss her. He didn't really know she existed. She's dark haired, too, so you'd have a choice. She doesn't eat very much either, so she'd be quite cheap to keep." Jo jumped up. "I could give her ring, if you like?"

"Hey, Jo, hold your horses. Mr Petersen doesn't need to be press ganged into this. He hasn't said when, either. Neither have we given our permission yet, though it seems you quite like the idea?" Her father reached out, held her arm. "You want to go?"

"I think so. If you'd let me. It's only a week, isn't it?"

Edward nodded, his craggy face all humour. "Auburn and black would certainly make a change from blonde and brunette. I don't mind at all, in fact it would be all the better. We're looking at the first week in August; the light would be about right. Which might mean that Julie has seen her mother's funeral over. I'll leave it with you. Your sandwiches are delicious, Eleanor," he said, picking another one off the tray, "And the lemonade is superb. Just one thing more, Miss Danielleson. Please *do* think about where your inspiration lies; it *is* important. And if you could expand the sketch of your father on that log – and even produce another piece of work for me to look at?" Already he was assuming a tutorial role. "Can I expect something by the beginning of next week?" He finished his sandwich. "I must go. I've taken up too much of your time, Eleanor, David. Thank you so very much for your hospitality. I'll give you a ring tomorrow, if I may. Miss

Danielleson." He picked up his panama, crushed it back onto his greying hair and collected his cane. "Good day to you all." A slight nod, a touch to his hat, and he was striding off across the lawn en route for the drive.

"Why so formal, Jo? I thought it was all 'Edward and Jo?'"

"It's his way of keeping his distance, Mums. He doesn't want to be seen as a sugar daddy. He's nice, isn't he? I know he likes me, but not *that* way. I feel quite safe with him. Can I go?"

Eleanor looked at her husband. "David? What do you think?"

"Well, if Jo's happy, then I've no objection, especially if Julie can go as well. An experience for the both of you, and while you're away, we'll get on with the studio. Mike won't want to waste any time; he's obviously keen on the idea, which is half the battle. Then your exam results will be in, and we can plan ahead. We need to have a holiday ourselves, Eleanor. I know we haven't planned anything seriously, but maybe you'd give it some thought?" Getting up, he touched his wife lightly on her shoulder. "Bit of a sudden change of direction, all this. I think I need to take a break. I'm going to do some maintenance on the car. That okay?"

"Mmm, of course, dear. What about you, Jo? What would you like to do?" Jo was in a brown study, miles away, thinking of sun and vivid landscapes, and what dresses she'd wear, and how Julie would take it. It all seemed too good to be true. "Jo?"

"Hmmm? Oh, sorry, Mums. I was thinking."

"So it seems. I asked you what you wanted to do. The day's too good to waste. Your father's gone off to tinker with the Jaguar." She paused; had a flash of inspiration. "You said you might do my portrait, Jo? I've not planned anything for this afternoon, so what about it? Your Mr Petersen said he wanted to see something new. How about it? Is the light right?" She was getting quite enthusiastic, and Jo made a decision. Inspiration, Edward had said. She'd always think of him as an Edward.

"Okay, Mums. Stay where you are. I'll go and fetch my things."

Running up to her room, she was thinking 'inspiration, inspiration'. Her Mums was inspiration all by her own, but what else? She scrabbled through desk drawers, looking for better pencils. Luckily a few larger sheets of cartridge paper were left and she pulled one out of its packing, smoothing it out. She picked up her board, still wondering about what Edward had meant by inspiration. Back in school – college – days, they'd had to do what they were told, and the only inspiration was in the mind.

Her Mums, her beloved Mums, was dozing. She sat opposite, clipped the paper to her board, and placed the pencils on the table. There was a gentle snore.

"Mums. Mumumms!"

"Oh. Sorry Jo. It's so nice and quiet. Didn't mean to fall asleep. How do you want me?"

"Just as you are, Mums, you're fine. Do you mind if I take my top off? I work better without a bra."

"Goodness, if you must, girl! So long as we're not disturbed, feel free. How long will this take? I need to go to the loo."

She had to laugh. Ever practical Mums! Five minutes later, and she was getting the outline and the form into place. As she sketched in features, she began to feel inspired. Inspired? Then it hit her; she was working half undressed. Was that her *inspiration*? She wasn't a naturist, as such, but thinking back, what she'd done, what she was wearing, always she'd taken something off. That self-portrait she'd done; she stripped off. The dress picture was different, but she hadn't had anything on underneath. How weird! She carried on, conscious her Mums was about to fall asleep again.

"Mumumms! Don't fall asleep, there's a dear. I need to get your eyes right. Another half hour?"

"Sorry, dear. This is very therapeutic. I feel a bit goose-pimply. Is it working?" She grinned. "Aren't you a bit goose-pimply as well, being half naked? I hope you won't always need to be half naked to paint! It might limit your opportunities, my darling!"

Jo pulled a face. She deftly added some shading to the side of her Mums's face, and changing her pencil, a few thicker lines to emphasise her hair. It was coming together. She wasn't feeling cold, just happy, and carried on. Silence fell, apart from an occasional clunk or tinkle from the garage, and the scratch of pencil on paper. Using her fingertip, she carefully rubbed the pencil lines to soften them over the familiar face on her paper. It was *definitely* her Mums, that subtle grin, the mischievous eyes, the soft and sensual mouth. She wasn't sure about the hair, maybe more wispy, darker. With the finer pencil in her mouth, she tried to get the emphasis right, shading away with that lovely smooth 6B. Yes!!

"That looks good!" She nearly jumped out of her skin, and the mouth held pencil fell away onto the grass. Her father had crept up behind her to steal a glance at the portrait.

"Pa! You could have made me spoil it!" She stood up, and her un-buttoned half-off blouse fell away. She stooped, picked it up and shrugged it back on. Blow the bra. "So what do you think? You recognise her?"

"Do I! I think it's great. I like the smile. Just her." David put an arm around her shoulders, gave her a kiss on her cheek. "Eleanor – have a look, dear," and taking the board from Jo's lap, turned it round. "Good, heh?"

Eleanor pushed her hair out of her eyes, and peered at it. She was facing the afternoon sun, and her eyes needed to adjust. Jo stretched, and swung her arms. Back to querying *inspiration*, I bet it's feeling free, she thought. At least this one worked; as her Mums looked at her handiwork it was evident she liked it; the grin was broadening.

"You sure got my mood, Jo. What were you thinking?"

"Oh, how much I loved you. And how nice it is to be able to work in the open air. And what I can do with – oh – but it's yours, Mums, what do *you* want to do with it? I might have to clean it up a bit."

"It looks fine as it is, Jo. As to what I want to do with it – well, I might like it in our bedroom, eh, David? Do one of your father as well, Jo, so we have a pair. And we've got you already. On paper I mean. Clever girl. Come and have a hug!"

176

Later that evening, Jo took herself off up the garden. Having been treated to wine with their evening meal she was feeling quite deliciously warmly happy, if a little light headed. On the old log, she sat and let the cooling air flow over her. The last notes from the resident blackbird rang like a trumpet voluntary over the whisper of the evening breeze through her apple trees, and the sun's reddening rays slanted through the leaves. Peace, she thought, perfect peace. She hitched her skirt up over her knees, and shrugged her blouse off her shoulders, but that was as far as she dare go. Why did she feel so nice when she did that, she wondered? The sunset glow deepened and even the long grass was tinged red. I still have to start on that idea of an orchard painting, she thought. After I get back from France, after the studio is finished. The studio – behind her. She spun round, lifting her legs over the log, her skirt flowing up her thighs as she moved, and gazed at the old shed. The door had been left open. She'd best close it, and got up, skirt falling back into place. She smoothed it down, and pulled her blouse back on.

"*Pity. You look nicer half dressed.*"

She started, looked around, alarmed. Where had that voice come from? The shed seemed on fire with the sunset, and the black void of the door was in stark contrast.

"*Undress, girl.*"

Who was there? She began to panic, but stayed still.

"*Be naked. Enjoy.*"

"No! Who are you? Where are you?" She spun round, but there was no one. In the shed? With apparent courage she didn't exactly feel, she walked steadily towards the open door, to see her long shadow climb the walls. The gloom of the interior also had the sunset tinge, and was empty. No one. Had she been imagining? She ran outside, round the shed, through the trees, round and round, hair-bobbing, skirt swinging, and stopped, breathless.

"I'm dreaming!" She spoke out loud. The orchard stayed quiet. Even the blackbird had given up. Her courage returned, and she sat down on the log again. She kept her skirt round her knees, hunched up, waiting to see what might happen. Nothing, absolutely nothing. Was she disappointed, deep inside? There was a mixture of emotion. The girl in her was scared, the woman, curious. *It must have been in her mind.* She thought back to the last time she'd half stripped off up here, but then she was still at college. Not now, she was about to go abroad with a *gentleman,* to be his companion, which sounded really Edwardian, but then Peterson would have made a good Edwardian. He should have worn that blazer. The clothes! That dream she'd had. It was weird. She shivered; it was getting cold, and almost dark. Back to the house, then. Her footsteps swished in the grass, but otherwise, silence. She wasn't afraid now, just curious.

"Mums?" Her mother wasn't in the kitchen.

"Here, darling. You've been a long time? Fall asleep, did you? Want another glass of wine?"

Her parents were in the sitting room, another bottle open. *They must be well sozzled*, she thought.

"Lovely. Yes please. I don't know about falling asleep, Mums, but I may have been dreaming."

She recounted her experiences, and added in something about her previous dream. "It's weird, Mums. Weird. I don't feel worried about it, just curious. Do you believe in ghosts, Pa? Do you think we've got a *presence* up there? Why were those old clothes there, anyway?" Flopping down in an armchair, she took the proffered glass, taking a deep sip. "That's nice."

"If we have, it's pretty benign. No one else has felt anything, as far as we know. *I* haven't. But then I'm not likely to want to go half dressed, perhaps our ghost likes naked women! Best go in your jeans next time, Jo. Time for bed, I think. See you tomorrow, girl." He hoisted himself out of his chair and went upstairs. Eleanor stayed.

"Sure it wasn't someone lurking, Jo? I wouldn't like to think we have a stalker. I'm not very happy about it."

"I ran around, Mums. If there *was* someone, they'd have to have been either well-hidden or a fast mover. The voice *might* have been in my head. Maybe it was wishful thinking. I still want to find out about the clothes." She emptied her glass in one swallow. "I'd best get to bed, too, Mums. Before I get too merry. Thanks for sitting. Love you!"

Left alone. Eleanor leant back in her chair and wondered. What was going to happen to her girl?

Jo hadn't mentioned Nigel since he'd left, despite an obvious liking for him. One moment she was still a schoolgirl, the next a sophisticated young lady; now she had shown this wonderful talent. Jo's portrait of her was looking down from its vantage point, leant up against the wall above the fireplace, with her eyes drawn in as reflective but smiley. If that was how Jo saw her, she wasn't unhappy. Quite impressed, actually. She emptied her glass of the dregs, put the light out, and went to find an appreciative husband.

EIGHT

Postman Reg caught a brief glimpse of his favourite girl as he walked up the drive the next morning. Jocelyn still up to her tricks, he mused, pretending not to see her as she streaked across the lawn. He wasn't sure if she had anything on or not, but he wasn't the sort of chap to ogle her even so.

He pushed the small bundle through the wide panelled door's letterbox. He'd wanted to say 'thank you' to one of the Daniellesons for hosting the village do last Saturday, but it didn't look as though either of her parents were about. Just as well, p'raps. Never mind, he'd catch them sooner or later.

The letters clattering through the door disturbed Eleanor, and she hopped out of bed for comfort's sake, before looking in on Jo. But she wasn't there, only ruffled sheets and a tangled heap of nightie on the floor. "Silly girl!" she mouthed to herself, picking up the slip of a thing and folding it onto the pillow, straightening out the sheets. They were still vaguely warm, so she hadn't been gone long. Padding back to her room and without disturbing a still somnolent David, she took the large comfortable towel bathrobe from the back of the door and headed off in search of her errant daughter. She didn't have to guess where she'd gone, and true enough, found her perched on the log, with only a pair of scanty pants on.

"Hi, Mums. Couldn't you sleep either?"

"You're a daft girl, Jo. Why *do* you have to play lady Godiva at this time of the morning? If someone sees you… and you'll catch your death. It's not very warm, is it?" Eleanor hugged the robe tight around her; aware her feet were damp from the dew.

"Don't fuss, Mums. You're only cold if you think it. I don't think cold, so I'm not, and I feel okay. I'm laying the ghost. If

I'm up here undressed it'll be satisfied and go away." She stood up, and to her mother's consternation, slipped her pants off, and danced, stark naked, round and round. "There!" she said, coming to a stop alongside her mother. "I won't do it again. Promise. Not ladylike!" and she laughed, picking up her underwear. "Better go back, I guess. Lend me some robe, Mums?"

Eleanor undid the belt, took her very cool feeling daughter under her arm, wrapping the robe around them both so they returned in a strange lopsided togetherness, giggling, to the warmth of the kitchen.

"Best have a shower, girl, before you wake your father. He's at work today, you know, and so am I this afternoon. What are you going to do?"

"Ring Nigel. Ask him when he's coming back to see us. Me. If he wants to. Make sure I'm happy with your portrait. Start fleshing out the sketch of Pa up on the Ranges. Wait for Mr Petersen's call." Jo turned reflective, with her Mums watching her. "You're all right with this, Mums? Me, changing my life, and all that?"

"Well, it's nice to think you want to keep in touch with Nigel, after last weekend. Perhaps he should be ringing you, but never mind. Maybe you ought to ring Julie as well, sound her out about your French trip. It'll be good for her, after this, so long as her father can cope." Then, more seriously; "Your father and I have to come to accept there'll be change; so long as you're happy, dear, then we are. Now go!"

* * *

After breakfast, and with her father back into the work-a-day world, Jo got on the phone. First Julie's number and luckily she answered. Jo got the feeling that all wasn't well, from the tone of her voice, but after she'd explained the reason for her call, apart from determining what arrangements had been made regarding the funeral, there was a change in tenor. "Go to France, with you, and Mr Petersen, Jo? When?"

"Couple of weeks. Just for a week, Julie, but it could be

fun. We simply act pretty, that's all. What do you think?"

Unhesitatingly. "Love to, Jo. Oh, thank you *so* much for thinking of me! Just what I need! Father will be pleased to be on his own; so don't worry about that side. I'll tell him later. Speak to you soon, Jo. Oh, *thanks again*, Jo, *Love you!*" Jocelyn felt a prick of tears and wiped her eyes. Poor Julie, without the same love from her parents as she had. Then, determinedly, she rang the Norfolk number, albeit with some trepidation and a wee flutter in her tummy.

"The Vicarage, how can I help?" came the answer. Oooh, how formal Nigel's father sounded!

"Jocelyn Danielleson. From Tinsfield. I wondered if Nigel was about?" She heard her voice quaver. There was a pause, and she gulped. "I just wondered how he was?" she added, unsure as to what else to say. Then back came a heart-warming reply.

"Jocelyn! *The Jocelyn?* My dear girl, how splendid you should ring! Nigel will be delighted, I'm sure. He's fine, my dear, just fine, and we owe you such a debt of gratitude for rescuing him from one of his silly capers. Just you hold on, now, and I'll go and fetch him. We're just finishing breakfast. Won't be a moment." Jo heaved a huge sigh of relief, then grinned to herself. "Breakfast? At nearly half past nine! Lucky for some!" Nigel's voice on the phone, "Jo, I was going to phone *you* today! Lovely to hear your voice. How are things with Julie? I'm glad to hear that... look, I've had the chance of doing another jump, this coming weekend. Pop's not very happy, but I can't just let the one mishap stop things. So can I pop in and see you all? It'll be either late Saturday or Sunday, whichever...? How's the artistry? Done anything since? How's the studio idea? I'll catch up with you later, then. Take care, bye."

He'd gone. But he was coming back, *this weekend!* She wasn't sure how she felt, excited or flattered, shiverery or just plain happy.

"Mums! Nigel's coming down next weekend! Can we have him stay or something? Just the one night?" She flew into the kitchen, catching her mother off balance. "He's going to do another parachute jump to make up for last time. Oh, *goody goody!*" She was jumping up and down, curls bouncing. Eleanor eyed her, this strange daughter of hers. Was this a schoolgirl crush manifesting itself, for if it was, it was a unique phenomenon! Jo had never been this enthusiastic over any boy, if ever!

Calmly, she considered the options. If he stayed, then yes, he could use the guest room, and no, they weren't doing anything special next weekend, not after the last one. He was a nice lad, and mature for his age. He'd also done a splendid job of calming Julie down. Jo was hopping from one foot to another, her face a picture, freckles all aglow. Oh, heavens, was she that taken with him already?

"Yes, my darling, he can stay. Provided you behave yourself," she grinned. "No running about in the nude, my girl. *And* no sketching with your bra off either! You have to behave like a young lady. Tell you what, though…" her mind was slipping into overdrive, "If it's Saturday night he's here, we'll have a dinner party, and you can wear your best frock. We can have one or two of your other friends, if you like?" That would take the pressure off a bit, she thought. What she'd cook was another matter, but she'd sort that soon enough. "What do you think?"

"Oh, *Mums!*" Jo beamed. "What a smashing idea! But I can't just invite the girls, can I? And Julie's got…" She was about to say 'no one', and remembered about Robert. Well, maybe. "Trish and Brendan? But Betty?"

"There's always Tony," said her mother, mischievously. "He'd make the party go with a swing!"

"Mother!" Jo stopped dancing about. "Don't be *silly!*"

"I'm not. You don't know. I have a shrewd idea it might just work. You wait and see. Get back to Nigel, and then sort out the others. It'll be fun!"

* * *

By midday Jo had it all in place. Eleanor watched and listened to her, seeing a different side to her daughter; very professional in all her arrangements, talking beautifully to her friends, and Eleanor was inwardly not only impressed, but proud. Saturday it was, Nigel's jump was at noon so he should be back, d.v, by teatime. Robert would bring Julie, Trish and Brendan would round up Betty, and though Tony had taken some convincing, Eleanor had been correct in her assumption he wouldn't pass up on a chance of mixing with the girls, itemised or not. Jo retreated to her room to sort out her drawings in preparation for Edward's next call, and titivate her last effort, her mother's portrait.

In this flurry of excitement, the morning's mail had been left unopened, but now Eleanor was taking ten minutes before putting a scratch lunch together for her and Jo, and catching her breath. She sorted idly through the little stack; apart from the couple of bills, the bank statement and what looked like David's payslip, there were three letters. The first a thank you from Mrs Blounce – only to be expected – the second a similar thing from one of their visitors who *'had been very impressed with the garden'*, the third she read cursorily, expecting it to be the same, then she sat up to read it more carefully.

"JO! Jo-ohh!" she called upstairs, "darling – spare a minute?" When Jo appeared, she handed her the letter, soundlessly. Jocelyn took it, curiously, and scanned it, then, like her mother, re-read the crabby writing out loud: *"It seems evident that you have stumbled on the collection of costumes previously used by the village Dramatic Club that was very successful in presenting out-door performances in the early thirties. I have happy, if now indistinct, recollections of some wonderful evenings on the 'old' Vicarage lawns. I had often wondered what happened to these; and as I had a hand in making some recognised the dress that your daughter wore so beautifully last Saturday. If it is at all possible, may I ask if, as a special favour, I can inspect what else you have found?"* Jo looked at her mother, letter in hand.

"Drama Club? Plays? On our lawns, Mums? Gracious me. Sixty – seventy years ago? And I thought that was a petticoat or something!" She dropped into the basket chair, and then bounced up again. "Mums! Come with me! Let's look at those shrubberies. I've just had a thought!" Taking her mother by the hand, she dragged her out onto the large lawn. The midday sun was now at full blast, and the heat hit them. Eleanor blinked at the sudden change in light, but Jo was staring at the shrubberies.

"Look. You've cut those back, but see, there, and there? Those paths, and the change in species; don't you see, a backdrop, entrances, and the way the lawn rises away? It's a *stage!* And if we look behind...," she pulled her mother along with her, through one of the gaps, into the patch they now used as a rose garden, "It's a sort of back-stage area. You can't see the lawn, now, can you? And you can get back to the house along here – it all works, Mums, doesn't it? 'Midsummer Night's Dream'? 'She Stoops to Conquer'?"

"So it does. Well, I never. I'd never have thought. Well, that explains the mystery. What price your dreams, then, Jo? Not quite as mysterious?" She led the way back to the kitchen, and scrutinised the letter again. "It's from old Mrs Parsons. She must be eighty at least – you remember her, the one with that purple straw hat with roses on it? With Mrs Pierce and Colonel Jones? Well, I never," she repeated. "We'll have to invite her back, Jo. I wonder what your father will make of all this. Oh well. Let's have a bite to eat. I've got to get a move on – I'm in the shop at one to let Susan off for her lunch. What do you fancy?"

* * *

Left alone that afternoon, Jo took her smaller sketch pad and started drawing out the garden layout with the stage concept in mind. She paced it out, got it more or less to scale, and then inspired by the drama of it all, grinning to herself at that thought, did a quick isometric thing with outline people to represent a performance, and the whole concept began to come alive. Then came another mad idea, and she tore upstairs, flung her old things off and slipped into the white dress that had restored those memories to the dear old lady. Back onto the lawn, and she pretended to play a part. Perhaps she should have a parasol? The little frilly umbrella from the hallway? She paraded back and forth, dreaming her dream, before another inspiration. Retreating to the shade of the beech, she repositioned a chair against the bole, moved the table so she could use it as a support, took up her pad, and with feet on the table, knees as a desk, frilly skirt tucked carefully out of the way, she drew herself as a nineteenth-century lady, parasol and all, against the backdrop of the garden. Fully engrossed in the way it was all coming together, she became oblivious to all but the picture she was creating.

Sometime later, "You make a lovely sight, Jo?" Jocelyn nearly fell off her chair, looking up into the sun couldn't quite make out – oh, yes, it was *Felicity*. What on earth was she doing here, and how, why, didn't she hear her come? She scrambled to her feet, shook her skirt out.

"Felicity! I didn't hear you come?"

"So it seems. Well, sorry to break into your quiet afternoon, Jo, but I did ring and left a message. I wondered if I could leave these – and just remind myself of a few details? Our feature on your mother's garden, and the tea party thing, you know? It's coming together very well." Then she said, reflectively, "I love that dress, Jo. Suits you. It's what you wore last Saturday, isn't it?"

Jocelyn wasn't too pleased at the interruption, destroying her concentration, but she had to be polite. "Yes, it is. I'm using it – or at least the idea – for a picture." Should she let on? Well, why not? "We had a letter today, from an old lady who remembered this," Jo waved a hand around, "as a stage setting in the thirties. She saw me in this dress, and I think she said she made it, way back, when there was a Drama Club in the village. It's a bit of a long story. It is nice, though. Makes me feel sort of, er, *sexy*."

Felicity smiled at her. "I wouldn't disagree, Jo. Shows your assets quite well. But this theatrical club thing sounds intriguing. May I see?" She held out a hand. A trifle reluctantly, Jo handed over her afternoon's sketches. Felicity studied them; the plan where Jo had very effectively shown the way it could have worked, and then the picture of the girl in the white dress with parasol. Her shading had been superb, the whiteness, the texture; the whole feel of it was right. Beautiful.

"Hmmm. I rather like this, Jo. Pity it's just a ten by twelve. Could you enlarge it, say, to something this big?" using her hands as a measure. "I'd love to have it in my office. It's so, *so* relaxing, somehow. I'd pay you for it."

"*Pay* me?"

"Yes. Of course, that's how artists make their living, Jo, or hadn't you realised? What's it worth? Two hundred?" And she wasn't joking either. It was good, very good, and she'd fallen in love with it, especially seeing Jocelyn actually *in* the dress, very *dishabille* and as she rightly said, it *was* sexy. She felt herself inwardly shiver. It's what a painting, or drawing in this case, should do. Exude emotion.

"*Two Hundred Pounds?* For this?" Jo's voice squeaked. "But it's only a sketch, and it just took me an hour, well, nearly two. Two hundred pounds!" She collapsed back on her chair.

"No, not for this, Jo, a larger one. If you want to do it, that is. I could have this one enlarged photographically, of course, but it wouldn't be the same. And you'd have to sign it. A Danielleson original. It might be worth thousands, later on."

"You're having me on. You don't *really* mean it."

"I wouldn't play games, Jo. No, I mean it. It's lovely, I think what you do is full of meaning, expression, and I'm asking a favour, Jo. If you want, name your price. I mean it." She pulled another chair round, and sat down, taking the picture and smoothing it out on the table, studying it again. Jo relapsed into silence, watching a blue tit hopping in the leaves above her, looking for caterpillars. A breeze stirred the bright green leaves, and the dappled light moved gently across the table. Felicity's gold hair flicked lightly across her forehead, and the fine bones of her face were gently shadowed. Her silk blouse, opened at her neck, revealed the soft curves of neckline rising to the swell of her breast.

"Stay still, Felicity. Just pass me that pad."

The tone of voice and the instruction sent shivers down her spine; she was in thrall, inspired by the subject and romance of the picture in front of her on the table. Jo concentrated, catching the fall of the light, the expression, and the depth of profile. Her subject daren't move, for she was captivated. This she had never anticipated, sitting for a portrait in an English garden in the height of summer, the last thing on her mind when she'd walked up the drive, leaving her car on the road for once. All she could hear, other than the rustle of leaves and the light chatter of birds, was the pencil on paper and Jo's steady breathing. A doze was not far away, and her body twitched.

"Right." Jo stretched, put her pencils down and turned the pad towards her subject. "That you?"

Felicity took the pad and held it at arm's length. There she was, a far away look in her eyes, a wistful expression, and her hair dancing. A lump came in her throat. It wasn't often she was moved by a picture, a photograph, a drawing; she'd seen so many; and it was her business to be critical, but technique aside, this girl had got something. She handed it back, got up and walked away, to hide the tear in her eye, stopped, turned and held out her arms.

"Jo. Jocelyn. How do you manage it? You've made me look far too pretty. It's, it's…" for once, she was lost for words.

"Magic?" Jo moved forward and was smiling. "Mr Peterson told me I seemed to capture what I thought about people. I don't know how, I just do it, but I have to be in the mood. He calls it inspiration. I was just in the right mood. Perhaps it was you offering me silly money for a doodle."

"No doodle, Jo. Don't underestimate yourself. And it's *not* silly money." She couldn't get through to her, seemingly. "Look. Let me borrow these. I'll show them to a friend of mine who knows a thing or two, see what he says. *Then* will you do a larger version of this?" She waved the sketch "I shall call it 'White dress on a Young Girl', unless you have another title?"

"I've never thought about titles, Felicity, I've just sketched and that's that. I think I'd rather call it 'Jocelyn in Summer time' or something. I don't know. Whatever. But as for borrowing them, sure, but not until after later this week; my Mr Petersen wants me to show him something new. You can have your picture after that. For free." She giggled. "Sorry, I'm still shell-shocked. You really mean you want to pay for a picture?"

"Sure. I'll be privileged to think I was your first purchaser, Jo. And I'll give you something for this," she looked at her portrait again. "It's worth it. I'm glad I came. Give these to your parents, Jo. I must go; I've overstayed my time. And you're a pretty and talented girl. See you."

Jocelyn watched her go, hips swinging, long legs, that lovely bobbing mass of blonde hair. Pretty? Her? Felicity, now; she was a dream, but she'd looked a bit sad, but then she'd no children of her own, and Betty would be a constant reminder. Shame, really, as she knew how much *she* meant to her parents. A sigh, as she gathered up the papers, Felicity's packet, and walked back to the house. The lawn was beginning to crunch under her feet; we need rain again, she thought. A waft of scent came from the border, as she brushed past the shrubs another scent from the conifers, and a subtle change in temperature, cooler in the sheltered spot.

Back in the kitchen, she placed her pictures, her pad and the packet carefully on the dresser and put the kettle on. It was nearly five o'clock, and Mums would be home soon. Maybe she should have invited Felicity to stay for tea. Should she change back into scruff clothes? No. She liked the feel of this dress, and she wanted to keep hold of the mood of the afternoon. It had been a good day. Falling into her basket chair, she relaxed, closed her eyes.

* * *

Eleanor swung her little car into the garage, heaved a huge sigh of relief, climbed out and edged alongside the vehicle, pulling a bag behind her. Why did David put so much clobber in here so she could hardly open the car door? Men! Always plenty of room where the Jaguar goes! It hadn't been too bad an afternoon, all things considered. Lots of nice things said about Saturday. Hope Jo's got the kettle on. Wonder what she managed to do? Jumbled thoughts, as she entered the kitchen to find the girl fast asleep in the chair, in *that* dress, all screwed up and rumpled! What on earth had she been doing? Noticing the sketches on the dresser, she picked them up. Well, well, well. Felicity! So she's been here! My, this is good – so's this! Lovely expression; she's a clever girl, my Jo. The packet was addressed to her. Sliding her fingers under the flap, she slid some photos out and a few sheets of double-spaced typewritten – well, word-processed then – text. The feature? Tea first. Yes, the kettle had boiled. Moving the teapot over and picking up the mugs, they clinked. The girl stirred.

"Mums!" She struggled to her feet, "Sorry, I fell asleep."

"So I see," Eleanor returned, wryly. "Had a busy afternoon, Jo? When did Felicity turn up, then? What persuaded her to sit for you? It's very good, even if a bit sort of sad."

"I draw what I see Mums, but more what I feel. She hasn't got a daughter of her own, oh, yes, I know there's Betty, but she's not *hers*. She liked that one – she wants to buy it."

"*Buy it?*"

"Mmm. Guess how much?"

"Ten, twenty pounds?" Eleanor stabbed at a figure, unthinkingly optimistic.

"Up a bit." Jo's eyes were sparkling.

"Fifty?"

"*Two hundred!* I know, it's silly money, but she was serious. Really. She wants me to do a larger one, thinks it may appreciate in value as people get to know what I do. It's scary, Mums. I didn't think I was that good. What's Mr Petersen going to say?"

Eleanor was, in a word, flabbergasted. Two Hundred Pounds! "Did you accept?"

"Uh huh. And she'll pay me for this as well. She wanted to take them to show to some 'friend' of hers for an appraisal, but I hung on to them for the time being. I'll show Mr Petersen. Tea, Mums?"

Almost on automatic, Eleanor made the tea, and poured out the two mugs. Two hundred pounds, maybe more, in just an afternoon. Goodness. "Don't spill tea on that dress." She picked up her bags and started to put away the few groceries she'd brought back. "What's your father going to say?"

She put the cornflour alongside the large mustard tin, moved the coffee to one side and put the custard powder in the space. "What's my portrait worth, then?" She spun round. "Oh, *Jo!*"

"Aren't you pleased, Mums?" Her mother's reaction wasn't quite what she expected, and felt a tinge of uncertainty. "Shouldn't I have said I'd sell?"

Eleanor took up her mug and leant against the cupboard. "You're still a girl, Jo, plenty of time yet. Don't rush at things. Oh, I don't know. Go and change before you spoil that dress. Your father'll be back in a minute." She turned her back on her daughter and fiddled with the packet of photos. Jocelyn went upstairs without a word, flung herself on her bed, and felt tears. Her afternoon's pleasure, and joy, had been diminished by her mother's lack of enthusiasm and she couldn't understand why. She tucked her head onto her folded arms under her, and wept.

Fifteen minutes later David returned and found his wife in a mood. He had to make his own tea, while Eleanor had started furiously to mix a cake.

"What's to do, my lover? Where's our favourite daughter?" She didn't answer, just pointed at the sketches. David picked them up, saw Felicity, loved it, then next he saw his daughter looking beautiful, in what must be her white dress. Jo was excelling herself.

"She did these today?"

"She did. And she's sold them."

"*Sold them?* To who?"

"Felicity. I don't agree with it, David. She's only a girl. Sketching, yes, going out to France with Edward, I don't mind, but I don't think she should be exposed to the likes of Felicity. Sorry, but I don't."

"Eleanor, my love, if Felicity wants to spend her money on Jo's sketches, then that's her choice, and if Jo wants to sell, that's her prerogative. I can't see a problem. Where is she?" All he got was a nod of a head towards the upstairs. He went. This wasn't like his Eleanor.

"Jo. Jo, dear." David sat on the edge of her bed stroking her shoulders; all he got was a sob. He ran his hands under her, eased her up, and held her. She nestled into his chest, and he let her cry. "There, there," as if she was just a small child suffering from tummy ache.

"Daddy. Why's Mums so horrible about my selling those sketches?"

'Daddy.' Oh dear, she *is* upset. David held her tight. He didn't quite understand, either. Perhaps she was jealous? Or cross because Jo was being her own person, taking decisions? Or was it Felicity? Whatever the reason, she shouldn't have upset her Jo.

"Darling, I don't know. She's not being horrible, just concerned." Hopefully, he thought. "Why don't you get yourself cleaned up – have a wash, change. Wear something nice. I'll talk to your Mums. I think those portraits are fabulous. How much did Felicity want to pay?"

"Two hundred, Pa. And more for the drawing of her, though I said she could have it for free. I didn't *want* to be paid, Pa. She volunteered. She was very sweet, and complimentary. I did her portrait 'cos she looked so – so *right.* And she wants a larger one of me in this dress," Jo pulled at the skirt, straightening it out over her legs. "That's what she'll pay for. So it's my first commission, Pa. What's wrong with that?" He could see she was still upset, so he resorted to stroking her curls, just like he used to years ago when things went wrong at school. Were they trying to make a woman out of a girl too quickly?

"Do you want to come down, Jo? I'd like you to, please, looking beautiful. There's my girl. I'll leave you to it." He patted her curls once more, was tempted to give her a kiss but decided perhaps not, and went downstairs to sort Eleanor out.

* * *

He didn't mince his words. "Don't pour cold water on the girl,

El. What she's done is fine, nothing wrong. Maybe she should have talked to us first, but so what. We trust her, don't we? So give her credit, dear. Smile at her; tell her she's done well. Otherwise we might destroy her confidence. No point in me buying her expensive dresses if you tear them up. Okay?" He looked straight at her.

Eleanor scowled at him. "Don't call me El!"

"I shall if you don't behave!"

She was trying not to grin, he could see. Her lips were twitching. He blew a kiss at her.

"I just don't want her to put money before her art, David. I don't want her *used*."

"I understand that, but without hurting her. You have hurt her, El. You'll have to make up for it. She's coming down. Be nice to her."

* * *

Jocelyn had taken pains. She'd had a quick shower, used the nice talcum powder, put on her best underwear, and taken care to make her bust fit properly into the bra. She hesitated over the burgundy dress, but her Pa had been very comforting, so it was for him. As she stepped into it she felt great. At least she didn't need tights; thank goodness. Finally, a tiny little drop of scent. She brushed her hair vigorously till it shone. Shoes? Yes, the court shoes with the higher heels. She spun round in front of the mirror, and liked what she saw. With a much more buoyant spring in her step, she headed back downstairs.

"Jo, darling! You look lovely. Oh my dear girl! I'm sorry if I hurt you. I never meant to, I promise. Those drawings – they're wonderfully good. You're a talented girl, Jo, and very pretty, and I'm very proud of you. Just…" David nudged her, and she shut up.

Felicity had told me I was talented, and pretty, Jo thought, advancing into the room, I'll get big headed. "Mums." She hugged her.

David was impressed; from a wet wimp to a gorgeous

chunk of feminity in half an hour. She'd worked hard. "That's better, Jo. More like my daughter. Though I like the white dress as well, that dress befits you." He added his arm to her shoulders, so they were all clasped together.

"Hey! I'm suffocating!" Jo struggled, and ducked out from the enveloping arms. "Is there any supper?" And they all burst into laughter.

NINE

The rest of the week went past in a blur, with all sorts of things happening. David took four of Jo's pieces of work to have them framed; the original charcoal self-portrait; the 'Girl in the Burgundy Dress', as he called the one she'd done for him; the portrait she'd done of Eleanor; and the rather special one of her in the white dress. When he'd shown them to the guy who did the local picture framing, he'd whistled.

"David! Your girl did these?" He picked up the one of her in the white dress. "Blimey! She's stunning, mate. Forgive me, but she is. Proud of her? I would be if she were mine. This is Eleanor, I can see that, but somehow she looks kind of special. How long did it take her?"

"Couple of hours, I think, Bert. You won't let anyone see these, will you? And can you do your best to let us have them back by Friday?"

He left; feeling rather chuffed, with a promise for them to be delivered back the following evening. It'd been quite difficult, choosing the frames and so on, but Bert knew what he was on about, so in the end he left it to him.

Mike arranged to come back to see the shed/studio again, and showed them all the plans he'd drawn. The good news was that the Buildings Inspector, who Mike knew very well, couldn't foresee any problems, as technically it was still an outhouse or garden shed.

Eleanor went round to see old Mrs Parsons, taking a few of the old clothes they'd rescued from the shed, and spent a very pleasant afternoon hearing all about the old village thirties drama club. The dear old soul had quite a twinkle in her eye as she relived the 'goings on', some quite spicy and some quite sad. The white dress which had so dramatically made its come back, albeit altered, had been worn by a rather flirtatious young 'slip of a girl' who had broken more than one heart. The stripey blazer had belonged to a dashing son of the Manor, who had lost his life in the War, and Eleanor was fairly sure she'd seen a tear in Mrs Parson's eye. She talked about a pink satin creation of hers as well, which they had yet to reveal. It was all very evocative stuff. As she got up to go, Mrs Parsons asked for a list of what they had found, so she could perhaps put some names to them, or something of the productions, then finally made her promise to send Jo round wearing the dress again so she could see it just one more time. Eleanor felt quite moved.

Then Felicity came back to spend some time with both Eleanor and David over the feature details, while Jo had taken herself off for an afternoon's stroll on the edge of the Plain. Eleanor had attempted to take Felicity to task over the matter of the sale of the sketches, but soon got put in her place.

"Eleanor, your girl is going to be – is – brilliant, and if I feel I want to risk a few pounds on ensuring I get in on the ground floor of her eventual popularity, then that's my problem. I don't think it will alter Jo in any way; she's your daughter and is as level headed as they come. I'm envious, Eleanor, I know I shouldn't be, because Betty is a super girl in her own right, but she's not *mine*. If I can help your girl find her feet – apart from what I know you can and will do – then it will be a pleasure, I can assure you." Eleanor had to give in, and David, who couldn't hang about, having pinched a couple of hours off to see Felicity, squeezed his wife's shoulders, in a gesture that virtually said 'told you so', before going and giving Felicity a cheek to cheek kiss before he left.

"I told him he had a talented daughter when I came before," she'd said after he had gone. "But I didn't know how talented. Anyway, must dash. Thank you ever so much, Eleanor."

Jocelyn had talked to Julie on the phone a couple of times over the last two days, and once she had come back into the kitchen and sobbed her heart out on her Mum's chest, overcome with the emotion of hearing Julie's evident distress.

The funeral was to be the next Monday; she'd promised to go and support her friend, though it wasn't something she was looking forward to. Eleanor, remembering that and other times when Jo had become all weepy, wondered about Felicity's comment about her being level headed. This girl of hers was all at sixes and sevens sometimes, a little girl at some times and a sophisticated worldly-wise woman at others; all very confusing for them, though, she mused, her husband seemed more able to cope with Jo's mood swings than she was – but then, he was a man. And what a man, she happily added to herself, becoming all gooey inside.

* * *

Bert arrived later that evening, in that strange dishevelled old sweater and cords he always seemed to wear. Eleanor wondered if he actually ever took them off. His little van wasn't much better, with its own camouflage of rust and dents. Definitely a local character, and apart from being a dab hand with the framing business, did all sorts of other little carpentry jobs around the village. David gave him a hand in with the newly-framed pictures, all wrapped up in what looked like old curtains, still with hooks in them.

Eleanor had to laugh at him. "Never heard of bubble wrap, Bert?"

He gave her an old-fashioned look. "Costs money, that stuff. You wouldn't want me putting my prices up, now would you?" He dumped the pictures on the kitchen table, but David was going to be more up-market, opening the door into the hall and beckoning them through.

"Let's see them in the right place, Bert. Bring them through here." He led the way, and Bert, Eleanor and Jo traipsed through, Bert with two, the girls with one each. "Reckon we should have a proper easel here, Jo, if we're going to be showing off. Let's have 'em," he said, clearing the vases off the sideboard so they could prop them up against the wall. Then as the fabric was removed, carefully, so as to avoid hooks, the 'Girl in the Burgundy Dress' was looking at them.

Bert had done a good job. The picture was set off in a pale green border, a dark frame with gold relief.

Seeing it in a different light, David couldn't help himself. "Jo." It was a bit of a croak, his stomach contracted with emotion. "It's lovely!" Then he couldn't say any more, just found her alongside him, arms around each other. Eleanor felt a pang of, what, jealousy? No, she told herself, just being happy at his evident love for *their* girl.

Bert stood back, eying his handiwork. "Not bad, even if I sezs it myself. Pictures good too. Pretty, ain't you, gal? I prefers this one, though," lifting the next largest up. There she was again, but in white, parasol in hand, staring at them with a precocious smile, the dress showing her lifting breasts, her narrow waist, and the fabric was alive. How she had quite managed that, she didn't know, Jo thought. And all in pencil!

"Forgive me, Miss Jocelyn, but I reckons you's too sexy by far. Just you watch out, now." He took it down, and put the portrait of Eleanor up. "Now, here's a good 'un. Reckon you's done your Mum proud. But," and he lifted the last one up, "You looks at this. See – eyes, cheekbones, bit of the chin, like, you's got the same faces. Mother and daughter, see? So I's done 'em the same." And he had, framing both in a subtle dark pink, light frame, the same size. "Shame this 'en's pencil, Should've bin charcoal, same as this'en." The vernacular made the Daniellesons all smile. Jo didn't disagree with him, though, but she hadn't thought they would be side by side.

"Well, I must be off. Bin a real pleasure, doing these. Any time, Miss Jo, I'll be honoured to frame your work," winking at her. "Whatever it is." She coloured up, because there was something in his eyes that seemed to know she loved to be free of fabric in doing her work. Then it hit her. Of course! That's what old Petersen meant! Inspiration – being half – or even totally – nude! Heavens! No, it couldn't be, it was so silly, childish, and not becoming. Confused, she turned to her father.

"Pa – what do we owe Bert for all this? I can pay, if Felicity's going to pay for this?"

"It's all settled, Jo. We'll see. Bert – have a drink before you go?"

"Bless you, but no. I've got another call to make – a cupboard door needs fixing at the Jones's place. It's bin a pleasure, just make 'ee sure I gets to do the next masterpiece!" And with that, he picked up his pile of old curtains and went.

* * *

"Jocelyn, why did you blush like that?" Eleanor was curious. Her girl had gone very quiet.

They had retreated from the dining room into the sitting room, a much cosier place, and Jo had insisted on bringing the 'White Dress' to stand on the piano. It was, in her eyes, the best she'd done, at least it had a value! She wasn't sure about doing another, larger one, but she'd give it a go. Her mother was waiting for an answer. How could she explain? Well, I'll just have to be grown up about it, she decided.

"Mr Petersen has asked me what I find as my inspiration, Mums. He reckons some of what I did in college was, well, rubbish, yet these seem to have a life of their own. He was trying to make me tell him what it was. When Bert winked at me, and that comment about 'whatever it was' he'd frame, it hit me. Rather embarrassingly. When I sketch, draw, whatever, the best ones are when I've got nothing round my shoulders, my arms free. Which means no bra, and so on." She tailed off, as her Mums grinned at her.

"So *that's it!* I can't say I'm surprised, but it might be a trifle difficult, Jo, to strip off every time you want to draw! You'll have to grow up, my girl." There was a lengthy silence, as mother and daughter eyed each other, Eleanor adamant she would have no more of this nonsense, but Jocelyn had a sneaking feeling she might struggle to achieve nice drawings if she wasn't in the right frame of mind.

Eventually she did a bit of a grin. "Yes, Mums," was all she said in a conciliatory voice, and went to make some coffee. Her father had beaten her to it, busy pouring hot water into a row of mugs.

"Bert was impressed, Jo. He did a good job on those,

though, didn't he? Why did he wink at you? I saw it. And you blushed!"

"Not you as well, Pa, Mums has just given me the third degree. Anyone would have thought the next would be me in the nude or something."

"Now there's a thought! You'd make a smashing picture, Jo, but I don't know that I'd appreciate seeing my own daughter in the buff on canvas!" He picked up two mugs, preparatory to carrying them through.

"Pa!" Jo, not sure whether to take him seriously or not, guessed her Mums would tell him all about her own thoughts on drawing without a bra, so didn't go back round that loop again. He just smiled. He was looking forward to hanging the 'Girl in the Burgundy Dress' over his desk.

* * *

A phone call from Nigel the following morning, could he come that evening? He'd leave his car with them, and transport would collect him at first light on Saturday. Two nights! Jocelyn looked at her mother, eyes aglow. Yes, of course he could, and help shift more of the things down from the shed/studio into the old barn. Another call, from Mr Petersen; he'd come over at lunchtime, if it were no bother. He'd be with Mrs Summers that morning, so it would fit in nicely. Had Miss Danielleson completed anything more? He was looking forward to meeting Julie – Miss Stuart – before he finalised the arrangements for France, would that be possible? Yes, Eleanor decided, if she went to fetch her and she was free, but as she had to be in the shop in the afternoon, could he come just a bit earlier?

Jo had a sneaking feeling that there *was* something going on between old Petersen and Mrs Summers, but daren't say anything to her mother. It would be good to see Julie again, and Nigel was coming. The day was looking good, although a few butterflies were struggling in her tummy over tomorrow night's party. In a fit of enthusiasm, she decided to have a stab at copying the 'White Dress' picture for Felicity. Having said as much to her mother, just about to spend an hour or so in the garden before going to fetch Julie, she was treated to an inquisitorial look, which said as good as 'without shedding clothes!' and she grinned. She'd try, but wasn't too sure. Her father, bless him, had been into town during a lunch break and spent a small fortune on more artist materials, far more than she'd asked him for, but he'd dismissed her effusive thanks with an airy gesture. He was just so pleased with the reactions he'd had when his newly-acquired picture had been put up, he'd even lashed out on a proper easel for her. So, sitting down in the dining room, where the light was just about right, she pinned a good sized chunk of the best cartridge paper on the board, and with the framed picture propped up on a chair, set to work. After some ten minutes or so, she was struggling. She abandoned it to make herself a drink, did a quick turn round the lawn, spying her mother weeding the rose beds, then went back indoors. She pulled her blouse open, wriggled out of her bra, re-fastening the bottom buttons as a sop to her mother's feelings. This time it was flowing, pencils flying, 2B, 4B, shading, rubber to soften the edges, back to the fine hard black to emphasise the lines on the dress edges, would she get the eyes right? It wasn't the same; different, she looked more grown up. Rubbing the dress lines out round her top, she lowered them a trifle, gave herself more of a bust, left the neckline loose; with a quick dash back to the eyes, suddenly the smile became quite coquettish. Felicity will like this, she thought, and shaded a little more on the shoulders. Wrapped up in the whole effect, she didn't hear her mother creep in.

"Jo? How's it going?"

Jocelyn nearly jabbed her pencil into the paper. "Mums! You startled me!" She sat back, put her pencil down. "It's not bad. Different, but I like it." Surreptitiously, she tried to fasten her blouse buttons, but her mother had seen the bra on the floor.

"Oh, Jo! Will you ever grow up? Ladies don't do this," she said, picking the bra up and handing it back to her daughter. "Put it back on, dear."

Jocelyn pulled a face. "It's no big deal, Mums. I did try,

really, but it didn't seem to work. This is okay, though." A sudden thought. "It'll be a bit cold in the studio, so perhaps I'll get used to wearing sweaters! With no bra on underneath!" she added, grinning.

"This is becoming silly, Jo. I shan't say another word. Let's have a look." She stood back and considered the newly-created masterpiece. "Hmm. It is different, but not all that much. Yes, I think it's okay. She'll pay for this?" 'She' was Felicity.

"I'm sure she will, Mums. You okay with that?"

"Yes dear. I'm 'okay' with it." She giggled, girlishly. "It – the picture, I mean – is a bit more than okay. We'll have to ask her if she wants it framed. Extra cost, of course!"

So Mums is coming round, thought Jo. Good-oh. "Shall I come with you?" Julie had to be collected, and quick, before old Petersen turned up.

"P'raps you'd better stay here, dear, in case he comes before we get back. Do you mind?"

Jocelyn could see the sense of that, so she was on her own for half an hour. In that time she'd tidied the new piece round the edges, added a bit more garden-type background, rounding things off quite well, and managed to nip upstairs to put a decent blouse on over a carefully re-fitted bra. She eyed her skirt, and decided to change that too. Then the gravel crunched, and had to quickly complete the re-adjustments before greeting a very dapper Mr Petersen. What had he done? Whatever it was, he looked an awful lot smarter, somehow.

"Come in, please. My mother's gone to fetch Julie, but she won't be long." She led the way into the dining room, where the newly-framed pictures, apart from the 'Girl in the Burgundy Dress', stood in a row on the sideboard. The two others, Felicity and the larger copy of the 'White Dress', she'd left on the easel.

"Hmm. Good framing. That's Bert's work, I warrant. Your mother – captured her spirit admirably. Yes, I like that, perhaps a bit more shading, more relief here? Yes, good. Now this one, really interesting, is this lady a friend?"

"Sort of. She's step-mum to Betty – you know, in my year at college?"

"Oh yes. Not an artist. Pleasant enough. You have a feeling for this lady?" He didn't expect an answer. "You have her solemn yet flirtaceous, quite deep. Good balance, perspective a tiny bit out, were you too close? A fraction jealous of her features?" He moved on, touched the framed 'White Dress'. "You wore this at the tea party. I like the parasol. You were in a good mood, Miss Danielleson. I have no criticism. It is superb. And another! Well, well, a copy! Now, this is something!" He had moved the portrait of Felicity to one side, to reveal the morning's work. "You've given yourself a different neckline. An older, more mature rendering, but," pausing, he inclined his head towards her, eyes twinkling, "Forgive me, rather more seductive. This would sell, my dear Miss Danielleson. There are those who would fall in love with you, as portrayed."

Jocelyn was not quite sure of her reactions. Was he being kind, critical, or just plain forthright?

"I – er – um – did that *to* sell. To this lady," she nudged the portrait of Felicity, and the springy paper curled and fell on the floor. Petersen picked it up and studied it again before putting it on the sideboard in its curled state.

"May I ask for what sum?" Not 'how much', Jo noticed.

"Two hundred."

"Hmm." Jocelyn waited, anxious. He smiled at her. "Not bad. I think under priced."

"*Under priced!*" She was taken aback. She thought he would have been dismissive.

"Yes, my dear girl. As I have said, seductive, well drawn, full of promise and yet aloof. I think perhaps a subject for consideration in the dreaded commercial world." She was looking at him, perplexed. "A limited edition print, Miss Danielleson. Signed, of course. I would suggest maybe at a figure of, say, thirty pounds a print?"

"You're joking!" This wasn't possible.

"I don't joke, Jocelyn. Not when it comes to matters like offering such good material to those who appreciate art – and maybe the seductive female form."

"Oh dear. I'm not sure my mother would agree. She

wasn't happy about me selling this."

"*Have* you sold it?"

"Well, sort of. Felicity – Betty's stepmother, offered. She did say I could name my price. I did that one while she was looking at it, in the garden. What do *you* think it's worth?"

"Maybe three, possibly four. But you must retain the rights to reproduction. Always do that, Jocelyn." She noticed he'd gone back to using her Christian name. Had she passed some sort of test?

"If you would like me to investigate the possibilities, I'll be pleased to do so, but maybe we'll mention the idea to your parents?" The whole concept of what lay ahead was beginning to swamp her, plus the uncertainty of how her mother would react, so she sat down, rather abruptly. Did she feel all right? She wasn't sure, and wished her mother would hurry up. Mr Petersen was concerned. She *was* looking rather pale, and the last thing he wanted was to find he had a swooning female on his hands. She was, after all, still technically a minor; at least he didn't think she'd got past her eighteenth birthday. Fortunately for both of them, Eleanor swooped into the drive just as he was considering trying to find a glass of water or something. He went to meet her.

"Why, hello. Sorry I've been so long. Traffic, you know. This is Julie, Mr Peterson. Where's Jo?"

"In your dining room, Mrs Danielleson, I'm not sure she's one hundred percent, and I feel I must shoulder some of the blame, for which I tender my profuse apologies".

Eleanor ran. Julie did a little cough; she seemed to have been forgotten.

"I'm sorry, my dear. I am very pleased to meet you on neutral ground, and please accept my condolences. It must be a great loss." In a very old-fashioned and cavalier manner, he lifted her hand and kissed it. "You're a charming sight, non the less, out of college uniform." It was true, she had made an effort to impress, long black hair tied back, an informal but well-cut skirt and blouse, long sleeved and full. She was no jeans girl, quite like Jo.

"Thank you, Mr Petersen. It's my father who's feeling the

brunt of our loss, I'm afraid. What's the matter with Jo – Jocelyn?"

"I'm not sure, Julie. Best wait and see. Shall we sit down, and I can explain what I've got in mind for our French expedition?"

* * *

Eleanor found Jo, as Petersen had described, not quite one hundred percent. She didn't bounce up from her chair, just sat, staring into space.

"Jo, my darling girl. What's the matter? Don't you feel well?" She put a hand on Jo's forehead, reassured by no feeling of sweatiness or undue heat. Jo reached up and took her mother's hand.

"Mums. Glad you're back." She made to get up, and Eleanor stood to one side. "Do you know what Mr Petersen has said?" Eleanor shook her head. "He thinks that the 'White Dress' is worth double, and that I ought to sell prints at thirty pounds each. Oh, Mums! I just can't believe it."

So that's what this is all about, the girl's in a state of shock, a nice sort of shock, but for someone who's only just started into the art world, very unexpected. Eleanor sat down herself, and pulling Jo onto her knee, had her curl up as though she was just a ten year old. The two of them stayed quiet for a moment before Eleanor had to move, Jo was quite slim, but she was still a weight. She kissed the top of her head, amongst all those bouncy curls, and whispered in her ear. "I love you, my darling girl, very much indeed. I think you're very clever, and I'm very pleased for you. Just remember that." In a normal tone, she added, "You won't get big headed, will you?"

Jo got up, smoothed herself down, tossed her curls and grinned. She was feeling better already.

"No, Mums, I won't. I'm just, well, gob-smacked. We'd better find the others."

The two, hand in hand, moved into the kitchen, finding Julie and Mr Petersen poring over a map he'd unfolded from his pocket. "Is – are you all right, Jocelyn?"

"Yes, I'm fine, thanks. Sorry if I gave you a fright. Your fault, telling me about how wonderful I am! Mums has told me not to believe you!" The mischievousness was back, and the twinkle in her eyes.

"My dear girl!" They were going to hear a lot of 'my dear girls' in the next few weeks. "I must emphasise I am not in the habit of misleading my students over their talents – or their lack of them as appropriate. If your sketches had been no good, I would have said so!" He sounded quite fierce, and Eleanor felt she had to make soothing noises.

"I'm sure Jo's pulling your leg, Edward. If her 'White Dress' is as good as that, we must thank old Mrs Parsons." Petersen raised his shaggy eyebrows. Old Mrs Parsons? Where did she come in to this, and who was she anyway? Eleanor explained, and it made the whole episode all the more intriguing.

* * *

By the time Julie had been taken into the other room to see what all the fuss was about, and some discussion had gone on about the rights and wrongs of having limited edition prints published, David was home, and Jo had to go through the whole saga again. Then Edward felt he must go, (for no lunch had been forthcoming) and having reassured Julie she was more than welcome to come with Jo on the trip to France, he left, on foot, leaving the three girls mentally exhausted. Tea was essential, before Julie was returned to her father. Jo was tempted to persuade her to stay overnight, but realising with Nigel's imminent arrival life would get far too complicated, her father had the job of taking her home. In the meantime, Jo was now getting quite wound up again, continually looking down the drive.

Eleanor eventually grabbed hold of her and sat her down. "Look, madam, if you get yourself into a tizz wozz over Nigel's appearance, you won't look at all pretty and demure, which is what young ladies are supposed to be when men friends call. Go and have a shower and change into something decent, before he gets here. Go on!" spanking the girl's behind as though she was a delinquent fifteen year old. Jo ran. She wasted no time in stripping off and charging through the shower, before twinkling back into her room, stark naked across the landing. She had such a vicarious thrill doing that, she waltzed back and through into the guest room, preening before the mirror, before she dashed back into her room again thinking she'd heard a car. Much more sedately, she re-dressed with considerable care, even to the extent of putting tights on, and chose the dark green shot silk dress she'd had for last Christmas. She'd save the burgundy one for tomorrow.

It had been her father returning, not Nigel. She heard him come upstairs as she was brushing her hair, and she called. "Pa! Do I look all right?"

He pushed open her door. "Hmm. What if I said no?" She frowned, laughed, picked up a scatter cushion and chucked it at him. He fielded it, but had the sense not to return the throw. "You look fabulous, my girl. When you make the effort. Shall I finish your hair for you?" He loved brushing her hair.

"That would be nice, Pa. Yes please." So as she sat on the stool in front of her dressing table, he stood behind her, running one hand through her curls and brushing with the other. It gave him goose pimples, and before he knew where he was, she was nearly asleep.

"Hoi, you two! What you doing up there? Jo – you have a guest!" Neither of them had heard the car, so engrossed they were in promoting each other's fancies. Jo jerked upright, and David reluctantly had to let her go. She was all for bounding downstairs, then remembered. She was a lady, not a school kid. Nigel stood at the foot of the stairs, and watched her.

"Hi Jo."

"Hello Nigel." There was an air of restrained awkwardness between them. Nigel held out his arms; Jo jumped the last three stairs into them and got a kiss. They were laughing at each other, and David, viewing the performance from above and Eleanor from the kitchen doorway, both knew she might well have found the man of her dreams.

* * *

They had supper, a relaxed meal of cold meats and salad and cheese and biscuits. David opened a bottle of nice wine, and afterwards they sat and talked companionably for ages, Nigel with Jo at his side, sharing the sofa. Nigel gave them a potted history of his life, Jo her school career; they discussed cars, and gardens; paintings and medical school; vicarages old and new, until it was way past a sensible bedtime. Then Jo was sent up stairs while Nigel held back and he and David talked about medical careers and the army. Then they too went upstairs, and the day came to a peaceful end.

TEN

Nigel slept well. It was a very comfortable bed, and he recalled that Julie had slept here the night after she had lost her mother in that tragic, futile accident. With the morning sun now streaming into the room, he should be up. He felt good, relaxed, and somehow, wonderfully happy. The thought that Jo, that lovely girl, had been sleeping not yards away, was even now maybe dressing, gave him the tingles. What a marvellous find she was, even though it was her who had really found him. The recollection of that day was not pleasant; he had to go through it all again. No mistakes today. There was a knock on the door. Jo's father. "Bathroom's free, Nigel, help yourself. Shower if you want, plenty of hot water."

Struggling up from the cosiness of the covers, he flung them off to cross to the window. Down on the lawn below, early morning dew long gone, there was his – *his?* – lovely lady, doing some exercises, in shorts and a camisole top. He tapped on the glass. She looked up, waved, blew him a kiss. Wonderful! He blew one back at her, and went for his shower.

* * *

Jo saw the sun-tanned Nigel, most of him, at the window, and couldn't believe her luck. How she had been in the right place at that moment – the wrong place for him, admittedly, but she'd managed to sort that – was really, really, really lucky. If Pa hadn't said yes to that walk, if they'd been half an hour later, or earlier, how different things would have turned out! She did a cartwheel, and another, and landed in a heap, just missing one of her Mum's precious shrubs.

"Hey! You'll do yourself a mischief! Come on in and help

me lay the table!" Her Mums was calling from the kitchen open door. *Lay the table!* Gosh, Nigel is honoured. Usually they just flung things onto the table and got on with it – but, oh no, guests make things formal! Scrambling back to her feet she rubbed her slightly bruised shin and limped to the door.

"Haven't hurt yourself, Jo?"

"Not really, Mums. Am I all right like this?" At least she was properly clad, underneath, her mother saw.

"You'll do. I thought we'd have breakfast out on the table, by the big tree. That all right? The things are all on that tray." Breakfast *al fresco!*

"Oh! Sounds good. Okay, I'll take it out. Where's Pa?"

"Still upstairs. He'll be down in a tick. Does Nigel drink coffee or tea? I've done some fresh orange juice, and dug the croissants out. Home-made apricot jam?"

"My, my. You must be happy with our houseguest, Mums. Coffee, I should think. He's not a tea type – at least I shouldn't think so, else I might not of liked him!" Her mother gave her a strange look. How does tea or coffee at breakfast influence your liking a person? Her Jocelyn!

* * *

Breakfasting under the big old beech was almost surreal; superb coffee, delicious apricot jam on those far too buttery croissants, David in a scruffy shirt and shorts with a floppy straw hat, Eleanor in a pinafore dress a bit too skimpy, Jo still in her shorts, and here he was, with a properly ironed shirt and summer slacks, looking far too elegant in comparison. He'd had a light 'good morning' kiss from both Jo *and* her mother. He must be acceptable!

"When do you have to be at the base, Nigel?" David eyed the last croissant and decided, reluctantly, he'd be told off if he pinched it when they had a guest. Manners said you never took the last one. He'd wait till they'd finished.

"Shortly, I'm afraid. Got to drive up to Larkhill, then transport over to Lyneham, I think the drops at thirteen hundred. Should be back by, say, sixteen hundred. Four o'clock, Mrs Danielleson."

"Nigel – please call me Eleanor – I know what sixteen hundred is! You will avoid trees this time, won't you? I'm not having my Jo standing by just in case!" She offered the coffee percolator to him, but he shook his head.

"I'm fine, – Eleanor. It's been a treat of a breakfast. Wonderful garden, this." He turned to Jo, and gave her a grin. "No, I don't think I want to end up in another tree either. There's only a few of us on this run, so there'll be plenty of space. It's a good day for it, light winds, good visibility. I'm quite looking forward to it. Get my card stamped! Don't forget to nudge me if I go on about it tonight – I'm looking forward to the dinner party, too. Well, best be off. Watch out for the Hercules around one, won't you?" He stood up, the light breeze ruffling his hair, and gripped Jo's shoulder. "Don't worry, Jo, I'll be okay – thinking of getting back in one piece!" He leant over and pecked her cheek. Eleanor watched, reliving her early courtship days with David. He caught her eye, and winked. Jo made to get up, reached for Nigel's hand, and squeezed. She couldn't trust herself to speak. She wobbled inside and this was a totally new experience. He gently disengaged himself.

"Don't get up, I've everything I need. Thanks again, see you later." He walked away, turned, waved, and was gone, past the end of the shrubbery; they heard the car start, the gravel crunch, and then silence. Eleanor got up, started to put the breakfast things onto the tray. She tipped the remaining croissant onto her husband's plate. "I saw you. Well done, manners maketh man. Go on, finish it up. Unless you want it, Jo?"

Jo shook her head, then changed her mind. "I'll share it with you, Pa. What shall we do for the rest of the morning? Unless you want some help, Mums, for tonight? What are we having?"

"Chicken, Coq au Vin, that is. Apple crumble, that sort of thing? I shan't need any help this morning. Maybe later on, veg peeling. No, you two do what you want." She picked up the tray and went back indoors.

"Well, young lady?" David added jam to the errant croissant, cut it in half, pushed the plate across to his daughter. "You are going to be a young lady, aren't you? Not a moonstruck teenager? You won't be silly over Nigel? No, don't get me wrong," seeing her start to bristle, which in itself was a good sign. "Hear me out. We – your mother and I – both like him, no worries, but I do want you to let things go their own pace. Don't rush your fences, Jo, take your time. If he *really* likes you, and from all the signs and portents it seems that way, then you won't lose him." Talking this way was a strange experience for him, and he wasn't sure if he was getting it right. "I know, I'm a pain, but I, we, don't want things to go wrong – for all the best reasons." He reached across and picked up his half croissant.

Jo pulled a face. So okay, Pa was concerned. Had she been too forward? It was entirely new to her too, a stirring interest in a representative of the opposite sex. She'd never felt quite the same over any other boy – young man, really. A proprietorial interest. She'd found him, even if it was up a tree, and he was – how could she describe him – nice? Betty, or maybe Trish, might say he was sexy, but that wasn't in her vocabulary for boys. Her Pa was munching through his half of croissant, and if she wasn't careful he'd pinch her bit too, so she ignored him for a few moments while she demolished her half, washing it down with the last dregs of coffee. She spluttered, coughed; a crumb had gone down the wrong way.

"Steady on, girl!" David stretched across to pat her on the back.

"I'm okay." Her voice squeaked. "Pa, I hear what you say. Don't worry, I know I like him, and he's fun, and very – is nice too simple a word?"

"Not at all."

"So it's a part of me growing into a woman, Pa. Or young lady. I think," she stopped, and had to cough again, "its better than messing about with some of those too touchy feely grab your tits erks from college." Then she realised what she'd said, seeing her father's face crease up. "Whoops. Sorry Pa, it just slipped out!"

212

He burst into hysterics. What an expression! "Okay, Jocelyn. You've made your point. Just don't use that phrase too often!" He had to reach for a hankerchief and mop his eyes, laughing like that made his eyes run. "Take those plates into your Mums, and then we'll go and sort out what's left up in the shed."

* * *

They spent a happy couple of hours shifting boxes, finally clearing everything out of the shed, soon to become a studio. The whole thing made sense now it had been seen as a forgotten cache of 'am-dram' effects and costumes. Anything of any apparent value was piled up for shipment down to the barn, the debris moved to a safe area for a bonfire once weather conditions were right. Jo's ghost and her weird dreams had finally been dispelled; she'd no further urge to either strip off or lay around gazing at the sky. The concept of a painting of trees as an expression of life was still with her, however, firmly locked away as a project to come. She was growing up.

Just as the dust was settling from their final sweep out, a call echoed up from the house.

"Jo-ohh. Davidddddd! It's – nearly – half – twelve! Any lunch-unch?"

David wiped his sweaty, dusty forehead and looked critically at his now scruffy daughter. She was as grubby as he was, and had torn her top. "You're a mess, girl. Let's go and clean up. Best listen for that Hercules, heh?"

She started, looked at her own watch. "You're right. I nearly forgot!"

David raised his eyebrows. "Forgot? Really?"

Jo laughed. "Yes, Pa. Forgot. Thanks for reminding me. But I don't think we'd miss a Herc, somehow."

"Hmm, that's true."

They'd started to make their way back towards the house, when Jo stopped. "Listen!" There was a distant hum, growing into that throbbing but unthreatening roar, a sound they both knew well. The Hercules, that big bear of a plane, the Maid of all Work for the R.A.F., was on its way. But rather than just a passing sound, usually fading again as the big aircraft veered into its run across the training grounds above and to the north of them, it kept on coming. Father and daughter stood rooted and Jo reached for her father's hand. The lumbering beast appeared above the trees and was directly on line for them, almost, seemingly, at rooftop. They ducked, instinctively, as it roared overhead, side door open, and a wave from the figures in the doorway.

"It's Nigel! Nigel! Pa, it's Nigel! He's..." The noise of the aircraft drowned her words, and then it was away, swinging round, headed in line for the drop zone, climbing as it went. "Oh, Pa!"

She started to jump up and down, trying to catch the last sight of the aircraft, but it had gone.

"Jocelyn, dear girl, stop dancing about like a dervish, and come and get some lunch. I know, he's clever, getting the pilot to risk a Court Marshal for jeopardising his craft or whatever. Your mother won't be pleased, you know she's got sensitive ears!" He was smiling at her enthusiasm, and if the truth were told, he was always very impressed by these lumbering giants, so it was a special treat to think one had flown over especially for his daughter.

* * *

After a scratch lunch and reconciliation with her mother after her less than impressed appreciation of Nigel's doings, Jo buckled down to vegetable preparation, whilst David went off to run the lawnmower quickly over the lawns, merely to keep them in trim. The afternoon dragged, waiting for Nigel's return. Every time a vehicle came within earshot she'd look out of the door, making her mother exasperated; ultimately she took the peeler away from her and banished her from the kitchen. Jo was told she was 'getting on her nerves' and that she should go and rake the gravel. Strangely, she did as she was told; it suited her mood and put her in a vantage point to welcome her – boyfriend – well yes, that's perhaps what he was. Finally, just before she'd got to the end of the main drive, he was back. She nearly flung the rake away to run and greet him, but as her Pa's little lecture leapt into mind, she did an inward grin and pretended not to see him, kept her head down, and carried on raking. He pulled up alongside her, so she had to stop.

"Hello, Nigel." She leant on the rake and kept a straight face.

"Aren't you pleased to see me back in one piece? What did you think about our flypast then?"

"Mums wasn't impressed. She's got weak eardrums. Pa loved it, though. He'll have a great time telling his mates. Want some tea? Say sorry to my mother." She stood back, and let him drive on and park by the garage. She sauntered off to put the rake away, trying hard not to show too much enthusiasm, but inwardly tremendously pleased to see him return safe and sound. Her father saw some of the by-play from the shadow of the shrubberies as he was tipping out the last of the grass cuttings, and smiled to himself. 'So long as she doesn't overdo it, she'll be fine,' went through his mind, closing the implement-shed door. The tea mugs were all lined up, there was even fruitcake, product of Eleanor's batch the day Felicity had called.

Nigel made his peace with Jo's mum, even gave her a kiss, and David had shaken his hand. "Your drop was all right, then?"

"Like a dream. Dead on target. Oops, better not say that. You know what I mean. And Captain Adams sends his regards, it's him you have to thank, if that's the word, for the over fly. He organised it, after what I told him. And, by the way, we weren't below the minimum height. Slightly above five hundred feet, or so I was told. So that's that. Qualified, and a bit of extra pay."

"Right. That's enough about Hercules and parachutes, Nigel. Dinner is at seven thirty; remember we have pretty and less pretty guests tonight. I want help laying the table, Jo, David; you sort the wine – *no beer*, please! Nigel, if you want to clear the bathroom so us girls can luxuriate in peace – then just watch the telly or something? Stay out of the way, and I don't mean that unkindly. Shoo!"

* * *

Eleanor was determined to ensure the party went according to plan. No, she corrected herself; it wasn't a *party*, not in that sense of the word. The table was set, and very elegant too, even if she said it herself; just as well there was plenty of space for the extra leaf. The main course was simmering away gently, and would be just right. She just hoped the youngsters would appreciate the efforts. She'd sent Jo up to shower, now it was her turn. David was keeping Nigel company in front of the television.

Upstairs, Jo, thinking 'be a lady, be a lady', was standing in the shower, letting lovely warm water cascade over her, living the day, seeing Nigel waving at her from the 'plane. Then she turned the water off, found her big fluffy towel, and her mother.

"Mums!" Her mother had found the bathroom door unlocked. "Sorry, was I too long?"

"No, dear, just that I'm a bit surprised to find the door unbolted. I know Nigel is a gentleman, but…" and she left the rest unsaid.

"He's downstairs, isn't he? Anyway…" then she twigged. Another lesson. To look after her reputation, and she supposed that also meant sacrificing her freedom of expression the way she was wont to do, chasing about in the altogether. Oh well. She'd just have to see how she got on with her sketching, and then she'd know. "Dry my back, Mums?" This was luxury indeed.

* * *

Now she was about to dress for dinner, conscious of a pull between wanting to present herself to the best advantage to impress Nigel, and not showing off in front of her college friends. It *had* to be the burgundy dress; it just had to be. Pa would expect it, and she felt absolutely super when wearing it. It was also a tights and best bra job, and a good old brush and maybe a ribbon in her hair. She pulled open her underwear drawer, to find a tissue wrapped package lying on the top. It hadn't been there yesterday. With a note. *From your father and mother. To our daughter, becoming a lovely lady. Much love.* Her eyes began to mist, and she had to rub them to see to open the paper. There was a beautiful silk slip, a bra and matching briefs, and a worn dark blue box. Slowly, ever so slowly, she sprung the catch, to reveal a jewelled hair clip, fashioned in a double leaf form, diamond chips and what seemed like rubies, no they couldn't be! It seemed to shine at her, and she went all soft inside. It must have cost a fortune! In a dream, she dressed, infinitely carefully, infinitely slowly, feeling the softness and gentle flow of the fabric over her skin. The dress dropped smoothly into place, and as she pulled the waistline round and zipped it up, she felt like a princess. Now for her hair. She went to the door, opened it just a fraction, peeped out, listening. Was her father upstairs?

"Pa! Are you up here?" No more than a loud whisper, "Pa – Mums?" She was rewarded by the sound of her parent's bedroom door opening, and her father looked out. "Help me with my hair?" He was doing his tie, but gestured 'just a minute', and she ducked back into cover.

When he knocked and came in, the first thing she did was give him a curtsey, before he took her in his arms. "Everything fit then?"

"Pa – beautifully. Thank you, thank you, *thank you!* This must of cost a fortune!"

"It's an heirloom, Jo. Your mother's, from her mother. Now it's yours, which you would have on your eighteenth anyway. Just a month early – but we thought it appropriate. Come on, let me brush your hair." He sat her down in front of the mirror and set to work on her auburn curls. Just as she was feeling those lovely waves of sensation down her back, all very soothing, he stopped, reaching down to pick up the hair piece and clip it into position, keeping the longer lengths in just the right place.

217

"I think you'll do. Then there's this." He fished out a small box from his pocket.

"Pa? Not *another* present?" She was becoming shell shocked with all this. It was a small bottle of Chanel. " Oh *Pa!*" She unscrewed the gold knob to dab the stopper lightly against her neck, on the back of her wrists. Her father watched in pride; she was behaving just like a proper grown up woman.

"You won't get carried away, will you, girl?" Calling her 'girl' was an endearment phrase she had come to love. She shook her head. Nothing was further from her mind. She was her father's daughter.

"Love you, Pa. I'll make you proud of me. Promise."

"Love you too. Now go and show your Mums. She's downstairs with Nigel. I won't be long."

* * *

A trifle nervously, Eleanor waited for Jo to emerge. Only after some careful discussions had she and David decided to let Jo have the heirloom hairpiece now, adding it to the lingerie set Eleanor had bought earlier as some recompense for treating her daughter unfairly over Felicity's offer. Nigel, totally unaware of what was in the air, was sitting comfortably relaxed and really rather happy after a successful day, when through the partially open door Jo appeared, with only eyes for her Mums. Managing to reach the middle of the room before her emotions got the better of her; an impressed Nigel watching her with a mixture of surprise and admiration, she stood still, and Eleanor saw a trickle of a tear. A schoolgirl tear from such an elegant lady, a contradiction in expression, before Jocelyn pulled her shoulders back, lifted her chin, and did a slow twirl; ignoring Nigel, looking only at her mother.

"Will I pass, Mums?" Her voice was squeaky. "Everything fits, Mums, and Pa did my hair specially, to show this wonderful gift – it's a lovely thing, and so *precious!*" The tear rolled.

"You look beautiful, Jo. Every inch our daughter. What do you think, Nigel? Is she presentable?"

Nigel was taken aback at the image she presented; who would have believed she'd climbed trees? He didn't expect to be asked, but rose as best he could to the challenge. "Very. Jocelyn, you look an absolute picture. I'd be very proud to be seen with you, really proud," and was rewarded by a soft smile and lowered eyes, and maybe she was blushing? Eleanor saw, and smiled herself. She'd been there, done that, a few years ago. The expense had been worth it; the surprise had worked.

* * *

Half an hour later, and they had a house full. Chatter, laughter, and a promise of a good evening's 'craic' as the Irish would say. Julie, brought by the previously unseen Robert, was looking understandably fragile, wearing a plain dark grey costume, with a nice dark red blouse; the first thing she did was to hug Jo, apologise for wearing a similar colour to Jo's dress, and introduce Robert. A quiet, saturnine featured tall lad, he seemed to be a very pleasant chap, with his attention firmly on his partner. Brendan, flamboyant in open shirt and necktie, was soon the life and soul of the party, and Trish looked very happy as she came in, clutching a bouquet of flowers given to Eleanor with a wry grin and a comment about 'coals to Newcastle'; nonetheless, Eleanor received them with a lovely smile for the girl. What she was a little unsure about was Trish's skirt, or almost lack of it – lovely thighs, yes, but far too showy for her taste, a stark comparison to Jo and Julie's elegance. Betty raised her eyebrows too, her escort Tony wasn't going to endear himself by constantly swivelling his eyes where they shouldn't go. Whatever their assorted dress, the group gelled, reliving college moments, exclaiming over Jo's sketches, Betty particularly impressed with the one of her step-mother; and the girls almost to a tee envious of Jo's exploits and the resultant Nigel. He, in turn, was quite taken with all Jo's friends, but was especially attentive to Julie, despite Robert's presence. Jo was firmly convinced that it was just concern for her state, not because she was the more attractive, and in a way, relieved Nigel didn't monopolise her; it would have so embarrassing.

Her father played things very low-key, going the rounds with the plates of canapés and the wine bottles. To everyone's credit they didn't guzzle; fortunately the evening was not becoming overblown. The Coq-au-Vin ready, seats were taken round the table, and quiet descended while the eating became far more serious. After the ultimate apple crumble, Trish, sitting alongside Brendan, put her spoon down and dragged him to his feet. Eyes swivelled, and Betty winked at Jo; she knew what Trish was about to say.

"Brendan should be doing this," she started. "But as you lot are *my* friends, he said I should. Just to say," beginning to blush. "We're engaged!" She didn't expect the spontaneous clapping.

"So that's why you're looking so happy, Trish!" Eleanor beamed at her. "Congratulations, you two, I'm very pleased for you. This deserves a toast – David – get those glasses filled up." Jocelyn went very quiet, not quite taking it in. Trish was only six months older than her – not yet nineteen. Engaged! She looked over towards Brendan, and wondered. Would he look after her, give her what she wanted – needed – for life? She sincerely hoped so, for both their sakes. Nigel caught her glance, rolled his eyes, and grinned, and that made her feel better. Continuing to look round, Julie didn't seem to be affected by the news, sitting quietly alongside Robert, a small smile available for anyone in general, as though she was in a trance. Betty had known, so it was no surprise for her. Tony wasn't a chap to much bother, but he liked Trish's legs. Eleanor was disappointed in him, thinking he might have been a bit more forthcoming, though yes, he'd had his arm round Betty a few times, there wasn't anything serious going on. Maybe for the best, for whereas Betty did have a companion for the evening, evidently she'd no real affection for the poor lad; in retrospect Eleanor was now quite glad Jo had given him the cold shoulder those weeks ago. This party was very revealing on the psychology front; she could imagine the discussions she and David would have later that night.

David played toastmaster. "Here's to Trish and Brendan. Our congratulations, and best wishes."

Glasses were raised "To Trish and Brendan!" an unexpected addition to the evening, surely, but nice.

Some surprise then, when Nigel took the plunge. "I'd like to toast Jocelyn. To my rescuer, lifesaver, and the loveliest of girls. May all her sketches be as clever as these," he said, waving his glass at the gallery propped on the sideboard. Various replies, from 'Here! Here' from Robert, to 'Yeh' from Tony. The nicest thing he could have done this evening, thought David. He added his own caveat 'My daughter – the very best'. Eleanor managed to catch Jo's hand and give it a squeeze. Her girl could be going into blush mode, unsurprisingly, but was she? It could have gone on, but Jo had the last call.

"My toast is to my Mums and Dad. The best parents out." Eleanor was surprised, and when she met Jo's eyes, they were clear and thoughtful. Last week she would have dropped her gaze and definitely blushed, but not now, her poise was still as good as when she'd first come downstairs, once those initial tears – probably sheer joy – had dried. She was learning, taking the attention on board without worrying, and still fresh. Predictably different reactions to Jocelyn's toast, but generally it was 'thanks for the evening', and really, truly, it had gone well. Then it was the good byes, Betty and Tony away in his car to the prospect of a dubious finale to their evening, Trish and Brendan departing for further nocturnal adventures no doubt; but Julie hung back while Robert waited patiently.

"Jo – you looked stunning tonight. Will you be with me on Monday?" The girl's voice was low and sad.

Jocelyn felt a tug at her emotions. "Of course, Julie." Nigel was at her shoulder. "I'd like to come too, Julie, if I may, but...."

Eleanor was listening, "Nigel – you're welcome to stay on, that's not a problem. We'll be pleased, won't we, David?"

"Sure."

Julie buried her head in Robert's chest: he put an arm round her for one brief moment before she came up for air. "Thank you, Eleanor, Mr Danielleson. It's been a nice evening. You're very kind. Monday then. Two thirty."

* * *

Eleanor set to, and the others joined in to clear the debris, loading the dishwasher and straightening out the furniture. It didn't take long. They collapsed in various heaps in the sitting room.

"More coffee, anyone?" Heads shook.

"I'm going up," Jo bounced back up out of her chair. "Before I fall asleep. Is that all right?"

She did the rounds, a peck on the cheek for Nigel, her father, and two for her Mums. "Thank you again, for this, Mums." She touched the hairpiece. "I didn't know. It's been lovely to feel it."

Nigel watched her go, seeing her form, her movement, her poise, knowing he was loving the girl in the best possible way, not just for her shape, but for her as a person.

Jocelyn out of the room, he was on his own. Her mother's eyes were on him. "Did you enjoy the evening, Nigel? Not quite a teenager's rave up, was it?"

Grinning, he had to admit it was pleasantly old fashioned, just what he would have expected if his parents had organised a similar do. Luckily he didn't subscribe to the hopping about waving your arms and pretending you were 'dancing' in an atmosphere of environmentally suspect noise and migraine inducing flashing lights regime, and said so. And Jo's friends weren't out of that cult either, with the possible exception of Tony, and maybe Trish and Brendan. Julie had said something about her interest in 'proper' dancing; with similar interests it had provided a means of getting her out of the dumps for a while.

"You dance?" David was intrigued.

"Mmmm, yes, ballroom, Latin mainly. Love the movement. Good relief from the old studying regime, so I'm in the Med. School Dance Team." Another grin. "We call ourselves the Flying Doctors, though it's not strictly accurate."

"Well now, another side to your activities, what with parachute jumping and all. Hmmm." David got to his feet. "I'm for bed. We'll have to find you something strenuous to do, to use up all this energy."

Nigel took the hint, and stood up. "Thanks very much for putting up with me. It's been a nice evening. What time should I appear in the morning?"

"Oh, half eight. It's Sunday, relaxing day – maybe morning anyway – perhaps gardening in the afternoon. We'll see. Goodnight."

* * *

Eleanor had a quick peep into Jo's room to ensure she was asleep, happy to see a curled up somnambulant girl, tousled hair spread over her pillow, quiet and slow breathing, all the signs of a peaceful mind. Now she could relax and mentally tick another box in her list of how 'to make Jo into a lady'. David, already stretched out and nearly at the nodding off phase, just managed to raise an interrogative eyebrow.

"Aye, she's asleep. Another hurdle. Thanks for being tolerant of the motley. Tell you what – I'd like to go to church in the morning, with Jo and Nigel – I'm sure he'd come; after all, his father is a Rector. It would be nice to go as a family, wouldn't it?"

"Sure we won't make the locals believe Jo's got a boyfriend?"

"So what? It's about right, isn't it? Nigel likes her – that much is obvious, and I know she likes him. So?"

"Fine. Let's see what the morning brings. I'm about bushed. Night, night."

* * *

Rain on the window brought Jocelyn back to the land of the living. She hadn't moved, not an iota, the sleep of the just, wasn't that the expression? Pleasurable, just to stretch, wriggle her toes, flex her shoulders, before a gymnastic leap out of the bed, scattering the duvet onto the floor. The panes were streaked with rivulets of wet, and the skyline grey, grey, grey. Good for the grass, but it wasn't going to allow much out-door stuff today. Shower next, then, before the rest. About to do her normal semi-naked run to the bathroom, she recalled her Mum's advice. The bathrobe then, and true, it was a cosy thing to use, and once in the bathroom, she used the lock on the door for the first time ever. Secure and confident, revelling in her consequent nakedness and showering was a good boost to her self-esteem. It would have been a bonus to have someone rub her dry, it was hard work on your own, and she giggled, wondering what her Mum's – and Pa, come to that, would think if Nigel had that honour. Well, maybe sometime, not now. Back to her room, still no sound of any companionable wakefulness. Dress, but in what? What were they going to do on a wet Sunday morning? Just a plain skirt and jersey top, it wasn't all that warm with all this wet. Down to the kitchen, get the kettle on, grab some orange juice. Glass in hand, she wandered into the dining room and saw her picture line-up. There must be something else to do, to keep her hand and eye in trim. Nigel? Would he? Not done a male picture, so that *would* be a challenge. Noises upstairs, would that be him, or parents? Go see? Ummm. Maybe not.

She wandered into the soaked garden, glass still in hand. Large drops from the trees and shrubs, splashing onto pathways and gravel, beautiful smell to the air now, a great sense of relief to all her Mums's precious plants. The herbaceous border, as she slowly meandered towards the big tree, had plants sagging with the wet, heads down. Bit like Julie, she thought, her head was a bit down last night; plants always perked up in the sun, so maybe France would lift her spirits. That's going to be fun, and goodness knows what's going to happen. When will Petersen tell us what's planned? I'll ring him tomorrow, before we go off to the funeral. Time for breakfast, I'm *hungry!* Back indoors then, now with wet feet.

"Jocelyn! What on earth are you doing out there; it's soaking! Aren't you cold?" Eleanor, in housecoat and slippers, very Coronation Street, Jo thought, was rummaging around for cereal packets.

"Not at all, Mums. Fresh, yes, but lovely fresh. Is Nigel up yet? I thought I might have a go at sketching him; what'd you think?"

Eleanor snorted. "So long as you don't sell him!"

"Mums! You're not still harping on about that! Thanks for reminding me – I've finished the copy for Felicity. Can I give her a ring?"

"After breakfast. Your father and I thought we might all go to church this morning. What'cha think?" A smile, and a sideways glance at her daughter. "Show Nigel we're a God fearing lot?"

Church going wasn't too high on her agenda, Sundays were for being on her own, walking, helping with the garden, oh, all sorts of other things. Sitting still and looking pretty for an hour, making polite conversation, repeating traditional sentences, singing sometimes weird, sometimes familiar hymns; not a recipe for her ideal morning. But today, well, it could be fun, with Nigel to show off.

"Okay. What do I wear?"

Goodness me, thought Jo's mother, she'd agreed. "Best dress, my girl, best dress. I'll make no suggestions – you wear what you think right. Now, you go and drag your father down. Go on."

* * *

Nigel met her on the stairs. She had no compunction about offering up her face to be kissed, just a friendly 'good morning' peck.

"You're a cool customer this morning. Slept well?"

"Like a top. You?"

"Hmmm. Dreamt of you." He was grinning at her.

"You never!"

"Well, I had to try and impress. You wouldn't like it if I said

I dreamt of Julie, now would you? Actually, I can't remember much. The beds comfortable, and it *was* a tiring evening, with all that chat. Enjoyable though. What's to do this morning?"

"We're all going to church. That all right? Not too boring? Now mind out the way, I've got to go and drag my father out of bed. He won't come down stairs unless I do. Mum's in the kitchen. I'll be back in a mo." She pushed past him, dodging another kiss. Nigel laughed at her, and went on down to greet the day with Eleanor.

* * *

Jocelyn trod softly into her parents' room, managing to get within a couple of feet of the bed before she was ambushed and found herself on the floor, smothered in duvet, wrestling to come up for air, a father sitting on top of her.

"Rotter! You were waiting for me!" She found a gap and stuck a head out. "Get off me! I'm supposed to be a lady, Pa, and ladies don't get rumpled by their dads!" Not that she really minded; this was all part of a familiar father-daughter happy relationship that had become instinctively traditional. However… "Mums said we're off to church this morning? Your idea, Pa, or hers?"

"Hers, I think. I don't mind. P'raps I'm being egotistical. I feel like showing off with the prettiest daughter in the village." He eased himself off the now quiescent lump beneath the duvet, conscious he wasn't adequately dressed. She was on her back and waved an equally indecent leg at him.

"Pa- really! I'm not looking." Rolling over, her nose rubbing the carpet, she waited until she was sure he would have grabbed his dressing gown, then scrambled to her feet. "Only in the village, Pa? Not the entire county?" She giggled, watching him combing his dishevelled hair. She loved her father, he was so, so *natural*, not at all stuffy, she'd not swop him for the world.

"I don't know all the girls in the county, Jo, just the local girls, but I'm working on it." To get himself out of a possible hole, changing the subject slightly, he queried what she would wear. He had a shrewd idea, but let her say.

"I wondered if I should wear the White Dress, Pa," thinking of old Mrs Parson's request, the capital emphasis coming as a direct result of Felicity's pecuniary interest in her sketching. She'd feel right, and knew both her parents would be happy with her choice.

"Good idea, Jo. Now hop it, let me get dressed. Tell your mother I'll be down in five."

* * *

She'd change after breakfast. Plenty of time, they could walk to the church and still be there before the eleven o'clock service. She loved hearing the bells, regular churchgoer or no. Nigel had gone to stretch his legs round the garden; her Mums was just about to brew the coffee. Sunday breakfast always was an opportunity for a relaxed and happy time. Plumped down in the basket chair, legs tucked under her, cogitating, there came a sudden awareness that this pleasant routine might be coming to an end and her mood changed.

"Mums?"

"Hmm? What's up?" Eleanor's antennae twitched.

"What will you and Pa do when I'm not here?"

What a question! Not that she'd even considered it for a number of reasons. She sort of dreaded not having Jo around, being on her own when David was at work, not having a daughter to look after; and had put the thought of having to worry over what her girl was doing, how she was behaving, at the back of her mind. Maybe this idea of all going to church was symbolic; a statement, an affirmation of being a family, albeit a small one; her mind, and strangely, her body did a twitch at the hollow in her over the irreparable loss of her unfulfilled potential. Would that she could have had another Jo, given her a sister, or a brother. She gripped the table edge to hold back her tears, bit her lips, forced herself to face her girl with a smile.

"Carry on as normal, I guess. Think of you." Then her stomach churned, and she flew out of the room, met David on the stairs, and he caught her, held her.

"Eleanor?" She pulled at him; trying to get past, go to their bedroom, to redeem herself. "What's up?" Mutely, she shook her head, put a foot on the next step, and he let her go, following. In the refuge of their room, she let her tears flow, and they sat on the edge of the bed, his arm tucked round her, her head on his shoulder.

"Scared, David. Scared of letting Jo go, losing her. She's just a *girl*, Dave."

"Eleanor. She's *our* girl. She's our *Jo!* She's tough, resourceful, clever, and knows what's what. We have a lot to be thankful for. Think, El, would you swop her for Trish, or Betty, or poor Julie?"

She shook her head, and swallowed.

"We can't keep her under wraps for ever, El. I thought we'd agreed to give her all the chances to put on ladylike airs - get her tuned to becoming a woman. You told her what's what in the feminine line, didn't you? Showed her how to enjoy her feelings?" They hadn't talked about that side in detail, but each knew what the other meant. And he'd purposely gone out to add to her wardrobe, and there was more in mind. The studio concept was to give her a feel for a place of her own, and they'd have monitored how she reacted to organising the place. He stroked her thigh, and she sniffed.

"Don't, Dave." Not that she wouldn't have responded to him, but now was not the time. His arm's grip slackened, and she stood up. "Go and pretend, Dave. I'll give myself a wash and be down."

He nodded. There would be more, later.

* * *

Jocelyn, perturbed but wise enough not to follow, had sort of got her answer, not the way she'd anticipated, and felt cross with herself. Another small move up the learning curve; one's Mums was also subject to emotional turns. Sorry, sorry, *sorry,* Mums, she said to herself, felt her feelings leap, picked herself up and was going to look for Nigel, when her father appeared.

"Jo! What a girl you are! No..." he stopped her protestations; "Don't worry, girl, your Mums will be fine but we'll have to have a discussion later – meanwhile, keep your cool, okay?"

Keeping her cool, well that's an up-to-date Pa. "I'm sorry, Pa, I wasn't thinking. I didn't expect..."

"Enough. Go and get Nigel in for breakfast. Just be normal, eh?"

She nodded, mutely, and went. Nigel she found staring up at the barn roof.

"Jo! Sorry, am I holding up breakfast?"

"Nope. Not really, but I think we'd better go in. What's with the roof?"

"Oh, nothing, really, just fascinated with the tiling. Has a pattern to it – see, sort of zig-zag?"

"Hmm – never thought about it, Nigel. S'pose I ought to have noticed if I have an artist's eye. Not that buildings are my thing, I'm better with people, I think," mischievously, she caught his hand and tugged him round. "You know you're a candidate, don't you?"

He laughed and bent to kiss her, but she dodged him, and ran off. "Beat you to breakfast!"

His eyes followed her flying skirts and wayward curls bouncing as she raced away. One moment a staid young lady, the next a wayward minx. But what a delight! Never a dull moment.

* * *

Breakfast was a Sunday delight, though he thought his hostess was a touch subdued. David kept the conversation going, with Jo's interjections, all about the estate and how they had brought it back from wilderness. Discussions over the garden aspect brought Eleanor back to life, and she became more animated. Time was moving on, though, and suddenly Jo leapt to her feet.

"Goodness! It's gone ten! I'd better go get changed. Back in a tick."

"How longs a tick?" Nigel tried to keep the atmosphere light. There still seemed to be some undertones he couldn't quite fathom. David smiled. Eleanor got to her feet.

"As long as it takes, Nigel. I'd better change as well. You're all right as you are."

* * *

Upstairs, she looked in on Jocelyn. The girl had the dress over her head, struggling a bit, so a helping hand was no bad thing. Between the two of them, they got it right.

"Tights, Jo, please. Otherwise you're fine. Sight for sore eyes. Good job you've got Nigel to act as escort, keep the rabble at bay. Sorry I bleeped a bit this morning, Jo. I'll miss you, girl." She took up the hairbrush and started to brush the auburn curls into place.

"Mums. Love you. Always will." Standing still, watching her mother in the mirror, seeing herself, standing almost as tall. She knew she was growing up fast, college and school days seemed aeons away. "I owe you, Mums. You're the best."

Eleanor put the brush down, gently caressed her daughter's breast, and gave her a soft kiss on her neck. "Love you too, Jo. I'd better change. Wait for me?" Going back into her bedroom, she stripped off her simple lightweight floral, and reached for her pale green two-piece costume. Jocelyn had followed, nodded at her, acknowledging the choice.

"Tights, Mum?" Eleanor laughed. "And that lovely little hat?" Her mother nodded.

* * *

Before the two re-appeared, David had found his jacket and Nigel his best sweater. He was cross with himself not having brought his suit, but then he hadn't been primed, not that he would have expected to be. This was still uncertain ground. Then Jo emerged, and looked everything she should be, and her mother, superbly elegant, had a lovely poise. David gave them an approving look.

"Right, folks? Let's go stun them all!"

* * *

Arriving at the church, a relatively small stone towered building nestling into the wooded side of the valley, the little party had welcoming smiles from others joining the motley. David and Eleanor had a favourite pew, half way down the aisle, and by the time they all took their places there must have been some thirty-odd souls present. The single bell tolled the minutes, then the small choir processed, and the Rector intoned "Lift up your eyes unto the Lord."

"From whence shall come our help and salvation."

* * *

Nigel was on familiar territory, joining in the responses with gusto. Both Eleanor and David had good voices, and Jocelyn's quality soprano moulded well, so the Rector was extremely pleased and consequently his sermon came over with a better feeling than most had ever anticipated. Then the final responses, the blessing, the choir recessed, and the service was over. Emerging into sunlight, into the gathering of celebrant villagers, Nigel had the benefit of some curiosity, Jo mixed glances of delight and maybe even envy – while Eleanor and David were swept along on a variety of topics including remembrance of the good day of the village barbecue, the word that had gone round of the re-discovery of the vintage Dramatic Club's effects and the compliments on the appearance of their daughter. Mrs Parsons couldn't help feeling Jo's dress, overcome with her recollections. Eleanor's alterations hadn't upset her, quite the contrary, it was lovely to see her creation worn again, after all these years. The fabric must have been good to stay in such condition. Jocelyn was feeling the strain of so much attention, being the centre of attraction, but Nigel was there, her Mums was there, and her Pa was smiling at her. She squared her shoulders, grew an inch, and took it all in her stride. When the Rector shook her hand, as he had everyone's, it was to tell her it was *so nice* to see beautiful young ladies in his congregation; then it was time to go home. David had a sudden urge to suggest they all went to the pub for a pre-prandial drink, but thought better of it; Eleanor wouldn't appreciate a spoilt Sunday lunch.

* * *

As they strolled along the footpath, Nigel longed to take Jo's hand, show her he was proud to be seen with her, but Eleanor had other ideas, and he found himself talking to David, mundanely, about how Tinsfield Church differed from his father's, while Eleanor slowed Jo down to widen the hearing gap.

"Well?"

Jocelyn, young lady Jocelyn, was pleased with herself, and her smile was seraphic. "Nice service, Mums. The Rector was quite thought provoking, wasn't he?" And she meant it. She got a poke in her midriff for her pains. "Hey! What's that for?"

Eleanor gave up. "Well done, girl. You pleased old Mrs Parsons. She'll talk of nothing else. Did you see the looks Miss Thompson gave you? At least there weren't any ogling boys about." True, no one she could have flirted with, even if she'd wanted to. Perhaps the dance club thing that Julie went to might allow her that chance, just to see if she could cope. Another time. A cloud on her mind, thinking of Julie. She had a funeral to go to tomorrow. Arm round her mother, she mentioned it. Eleanor gave her a squeeze.

"You'll be fine, Jo. Nigel will look after you."

"You like him, Mums?"

"Yes, dear, I do."

* * *

Back home, Jocelyn slipped back upstairs, took off her show-off dress, would have happily divested her bra and gone back down in light sweater and shorty skirt, but daren't. Instead she got back into her light floral thing, picked up her sketch pad and a few pencils, and found Nigel downstairs.

"Come on, you. I'm going to add you to my collection. Back to the barn. You can look at the roof tiles again while I try and find some inspiration. How long to lunch, Mums?"

"Half an hour. You'll never do him justice in that time!"

"Wait and see." She grabbed his hand and pulled him outside. "You don't mind?"

"Not sure. Depends." He would tease her. "I charge for modelling."

"Yeah, yeah. I'll give you a kiss or something – that do?"

"Promises. So long as I don't get a cricked neck"

* * *

She got him propped up on an old table and a chair, used another scruffy table poised on its side as an impromptu easel, and set to work. There was subtle difference in her approach, for one he was a male and she'd only drawn girls – well, women, then, - and she daren't free her shoulders of those irritating straps for another. So the lines were more rigid, but somehow more intense, and after five minutes of juggling her stance, it came together. She dropped a pencil, broke the point, and swore.

"Jo!" Nigel was surprised rather than shocked. He was used to expletives in his army circle, but not from shapely females. "Makes you feel better?"

She scowled at him. "Keep quiet and stay still, will you? Otherwise I shan't pay you!"

"Sorry, ma'am." He tried to stop himself from grinning too much, as she resumed her concentration. Her head went on one side, then another, her expression went grim and then she frowned.

"I don't know. Well, maybe. Hang on. Push your hair back a bit, will you?"

Nigel did as he was told, tried to catch a look at her out of the corner of his eye.

"Hold your hand there, no, up a bit. That's it. Freeze!"

"Hurry up, Jo. I'll get cramp!"

"Shut up. Don't whinge. Nearly done." There was a shout from the house. *"Lunch!"*

Nigel was about to move, but got a warning 'heh! from his mentor. It took her another three minutes to satisfy herself she'd got it right before she'd let him go. He massaged his arm, and rubbed his neck.

"You're a hard girl to please. Hope it's all worth it. Let's have a look," he reached for the pad, but she snatched it away, held it close to her chest.

"Got to titivate. Later. Don't be impatient. Want to eat? Roast lamb? Peas and new potatoes?"

She was distracting him; she didn't want to reveal what she'd done, not just yet. "Pa will have opened a bottle. Look, Nigel. I like you, I like you a lot, but I've got a long way to go before I can think too seriously about men friends. Don't mind, do you?" Whatever had made her come out with that statement at this time she couldn't possibly imagine and it had just suddenly slipped out. Maybe the concentration on his features, sketching in the details, had crystallised her thoughts. He was nice, *very nice*, and of all the boys – men – she'd known he certainly had sparked something in her, much much more than any of the lads who had ogled her at college, those who would have been too keen to look at her knickers, her cleavage, and had tried to touch her. He'd not given any of *those* sort of signals to her, but subtle things, the caring sort of token gestures; he'd held her hand, given her those little kisses; she'd felt comfortable with that, even conscious of some sort of internal glow. But sketching him, taking in the detail of his expression, the look in his eyes, the set of his mouth, it alarmed her. There was more there than she could cope with, at least just now. With a toss of her head, she ran off.

Nigel blinked. One moment she was all flirtatious, then solemn and directive, then she'd flung this at him and gone. Just when he thought he had the measure of her, and liking everything he'd seen, happy with her, looking forward to lots more time in her company, suddenly the pond wasn't ripples, it was bloody great waves. And he'd got lunch to deal with.

He rubbed his neck again; it had gone stiff down one side. Maybe the stress of having this vibrant young girl around, being so close to her, with no hurdles to cross with her parents; they obviously approved of him. So now what? As he walked slowly back to the house, and back into her aura, he supposed he'd just have to behave as though she'd said nothing, just take it as a sort of mission statement.

* * *

Eleanor nearly dropped the joint. Just as she was taking the dish out of the oven, Jo flung into the kitchen, pad clutched to her front, and rushed off up stairs. David, relaxing with the Sunday paper in the sitting room, heard her bounding up the stairs. Nothing new, she often did. Folding the paper, he levered himself out of his chair and ambled back to Eleanor.

"All organised? Shall I grab a bottle?"

"Yep. I've put a red over there," with a nodded head towards the Aga. "Oh, there you are." Nigel appeared at the door. "Survived the ordeal?"

He nodded, keeping his expression neutral. "Jo seems to think she needs to 'titivate' – her expression – and I haven't been allowed to peep."

Eleanor grinned at him, well aware of her daughter's mixed up emotions over her drawings, high drama rubbing alongside tentative innocence. "She's very sensitive to ambience, Nigel, and mood. If it isn't right for her, it won't come right on paper. I daren't tell you what works best for her."

He raised his eyebrows, hoping she'd relent and reveal what it was, but she just shook her head. She wasn't going to split, not when it meant explaining that her daughter liked taking her bra off, no way.

The cork popped with a satisfactory 'fllopp', and David was ushering him into the dining room.

"Sunday lunch – best part of the day. Hungry?"

"Hmmm. Very much like home. It's certainly been a very traditional day. I really should say how grateful I am for all

your generous hospitality – taking me into your family life."
So very inadequate, saying things this formally, but how else?
"It's not every day I have my portrait – er, sketched. Hope
she'd got it right – for her, I mean."

"Sit there, Nigel?" David indicated a seat. "She'll say, have
no fear. And we're pleased to have you, worry not. It's good
for Jocelyn, having a different male around. She – fortunately
– is very choosy about any male acquaintances. Not like some
we could say about. Think yourself privileged, even though
we had to pull you out of a tree!"

"Don't remind me! I shan't live it down."

* * *

During lunch, Jocelyn kept her conversational input low key
without being churlish, her thoughts about her attempt to
keep Nigel at just the right distance churning around. Casting
surreptitious glances at him, she didn't think he'd gone off
her; by the time lunch was over she felt sufficiently reassured
to respond to the question over her sketch of him to go and
fetch it down from her room.

Her Mums followed her upstairs, while David and Nigel
tackled the washing up.

"Jo, aren't you being just a little stand-offish? I know you;
you've said or done something you're not sure about. What
happened out there? You came tearing back indoors, and
hardly smiled at the poor boy at all? He didn't make a pass at
you, did he?"

Jo flipped the cover off her pad, and tore the sheet
carefully from the edge binding. "No, Mums, he didn't make a
'pass' at me. I don't think he's that type. I – silly, I suppose -
just said I didn't want a serious boyfriend, or words to that
effect. Out of the blue, Mums. Now I hate myself. Look. What
do you think?" She held the drawing out in front of her.

Her mother considered it gravely. There was seriousness
about the lad's expression, yet still a twinkle in his eyes.
Certainly more dramatic, lines stiffer and the aspect wholly –
well – *masculine* – at least that was her reaction. She couldn't

help having a bit of a leg-pull at her daughter's expense. "I take it you took your bra off?"

"*Mums!* As if! – You're poking fun at me, aren't you? You won't let me forget, will you! No, I *didn't*. What do you think, then? Is it up to the mark?"

"Well, I'm not a critic, darling, and I'm new to all this, but I'd say you've still got a feeling for him. It comes out in the drawing. I can see it, I wonder if he will."

"Shan't show it to him then." She put it back on the bed.

"Don't be silly, Jo. He'll wonder if you don't. Oh, grow up, girl. One moment you're all serious and behaving like a proper lady, the next a silly schoolgirl. I can't help you all the time, and you've got an awful lot better lately, but you do flip every now and again. Bring it downstairs, there's a good girl." Drat, she thought, I'm treating her like a kid again.

"Okay, Mums. Hear what you say. It's not finished, you know. I'll give it some background, then I might go over it with charcoal." She ignored the schoolgirl jibe; she didn't mind. She had an idea in the back of her mind and it made her feel all shivery in anticipation. She was going to get her own back, to satisfy her inner self, the bit that was becoming increasingly urgent and uncomfortable as the days went by. Once her mother had left her, she flicked her skirt up and removed her pants. She was going to be daring and devilish, if she couldn't run around without a bra, she'd dispense with the other bit. Picking up the sketch she hesitated, just for a second, then determinedly went on downstairs. At least her skirt was long enough. She found them all in the sitting room, Pa still immersed in his paper, Nigel had found a book, and her Mums was flicking through seed catalogues. They all looked up at her, and she nearly panicked. Her hesitation was taken as good manners, not a wish to flaunt her talent.

"Darling?" Her father had dumped his paper on the floor, stood up. "Do you want the easel?"

It wasn't going to be that much of a demonstration; there needn't be too much by-play.

"It's no big deal, Pa, what I'm showing you isn't in need of a theatre – it's just me and my need to express myself, me

being me. I like doing what I do, in the way *I want to do it*."
Advancing into the room, and very conscious of her daring,
she carefully stayed upright holding the sketch in front of her.
"Is it what you thought?"

Nigel sensed that her nerves were on edge; he was good at
determining people's mental attitudes, something that would
stand him in very good stead in his chosen career. He smiled
up at her, willing her to smile back, to re-create that empathy
between them. He took in the overall effect first, the way in
which she'd got him staring up at the barn, just those few
expressive lines outlining the building and its roof, then how
she'd managed to capture a bit of his seriousness, as well as
something of a grin. Clever, she was clever. "Hmmm. Not bad
for an amateur!" His smile turned into a broad grin.

She nearly hit him. "Shall I tear it up, then?" and made as
if to shred the paper in two. His grin turned to alarm, and
Eleanor put her hands to her mouth.

"No! Jo! No! He's only joking!" The last thing she wanted
was any despoliation. "Let *me* see!"

She managed to take the paper from Jo's clutch and
breathed a sigh of relief. She wasn't to know Jo would never
have torn her first portrait of Nigel into shreds, at least, not at
this moment. She studied it, carefully, as though she hadn't
seen it before, but now she was looking for those telltale signs
of her girl's expressed emotions. There was *something* there,
but she wasn't quite sure. "David?" She handed it over. He
took it and held it at arm's length.

"Perhaps a bit more of the barn, Jo?" He, too, was grinning
at her, pulling her leg. "No, girl, only joking. It's not bad. For
an amateur!"

Jo stamped her feet "You lot! I'm going back to my room to
finish it. Give me a shout when it's time for tea!" She took it
back and flounced out.

"The sooner you get her studio done, the better, David.
The girl's just starting on something great, you know, despite
her antics." Eleanor's eyes hadn't missed a thing. She knew,
and there wasn't much she could do about it, either, apart
from hope that the growing up process, getting her out of

schoolgirl into woman – hopefully, lady – wouldn't get too complicated.

* * *

Back in her room, the door firmly closed, Jo stripped completely, and shivered. Catching a glimpse of her total self in the cheval mirror, she froze for a moment in a sort of pose. Then pulled her knickers back on, threw her bathrobe over her shoulders, tied the cord round her middle, put the sketch back onto her board and started to concentrate. The late afternoon light was softer, reflected rather than harshly direct, and mellowed her mood. Time passed, the shadows moved round, as she carefully, lovingly, freely, worked on, until the picture gave her the satisfaction she craved.

"Jo-oh!" A cry from downstairs. "Tea!"

"Right-oh!" She gave a loud reply, not wishing anyone to come up and see her state of *dishabille*. She redressed, properly, completely, enjoying the feeling of warmth after her cold concentration, brushed her hair, got the right level of bounce back into her curls, and returned to meet her critics. This time she did use the easel, using the clips to eliminate the natural rolling so her audience could all see what she'd done.

Nigel felt his eyes watering as he saw the difference. Even though he was looking at himself, he could see life and expression, an expression showing a feeling that he knew he had but thought he'd kept to himself. He couldn't trust himself to speak, not just yet. Jocelyn's father was evidently equally impressed, whereas Eleanor had taken Jo's hand and put an arm round her, given her a light kiss on her cheek.

"It's beautiful, darling." Then she whispered into her girl's ear, softly. "Let me guess…"

Jo didn't let her finish, just nodded. It was a secret thing, between mother and daughter.

239

ELEVEN

Monday. A grey, cold, Monday. It had rained, adding dampness to the air. Nigel had slept well, though he had dreamt couldn't for the life of him remember about what. It took a few moments to get his mind into gear. Where he was, what he was doing, what there was to do? Monday, yes, after Sunday. What a Sunday! Distantly there were sounds of the household moving about. Jo's father would be going back to work, if selling cars was work. He'd promised to accompany Jo to Julie's mother's funeral this afternoon, which was why he was still here, not back home and possibly studying. However much he felt for Jocelyn and his vested interest mixed with the high regard for Julie, he wasn't relishing the prospect, though on reflection, it would be a good, no *useful*, experience. After all, if he was to be a doctor, he'd often be dealing with other's personal loss.

A tap on the door – "Nigel! It's Jo. Are you awake?"

He wasn't sure how to react, not being used to wake up calls from pretty girls, mostly being tipped out of bed by his fellow student lodgers. "I'm awake." The best he could do.

"Fine. The bathrooms free, if you want a shower, help yourself. I'm off out for half an hour. See you at breakfast." All this heard through the door, so he was spared any difficulty over social conventions, and then silence, so she must have gone. Rolling out of bed, he picked up his borrowed bathrobe and headed for the shower. It smelt pleasant, seductively even, from previous occupants, and still damp and drippy. Better than the one at home, thought he, revelling in the luxury for longer than he really should have before using the extra fluffy towel. Dressing in casual gear, light sweater, at the same time considering the rig he'd be in for the afternoon; same as yesterday morning, there was no choice; not ideal, but it would have to do.

Eleanor greeted him politely, offered him a cooked breakfast, so he settled for scrambled egg. No sign of Jocelyn.

"She's gone for a bit of a jog round, Nigel," she reading his thoughts. "Nothing serious, I assure you, but she's always the one for slight masochistic tendencies. I won't tell you what she's done some early mornings, rain or no rain, but leave it your imagination. There. That should keep you going." A big plateful, three eggs on two slices of toast. "Coffee?"

He nodded. This was splendid-looking egg, far better than the rubbery stuff the university dining room called scrambled. Eleanor sat down facing him, with her mug of coffee.

"Tell me why you want to be a doctor. Does it tally with the part time soldiering?"

He had a moment to consider while finishing his mouthful. "Not sure, really. I think I'm good with people. I liked biology and was quite good at chemistry, I had a reasonable grasp of Latin – coming from my father – I suppose it was better than following him into the Church. Pays well," grinning at her. "Not that that was the consideration. Hearts of hearts I don't think I could do anything else. Sort of vocation, I guess. If that doesn't sound too trite. As far as the army side is concerned, I like the adventure bit, and army doctors are well thought of in the trade. So maybe I'll go down that route, and the Terriers will help. And it landed me a lovely breakfast!"

Eleanor laughed. "You've made quite an impression on my Jo, Nigel. Landing on top of her, well, sort of. What do you think to her artistry?"

He had scarcely managed another mouthful "She's very talented, Eleanor." He still didn't feel quite at home calling her by her Christian name. "How long has she been drawing?"

"Not long, not like this. You saw the one of her in charcoal? That was her first proper one, and now she's just taken off. It's made a bit of a mess with her – our – plans for university. She wants to do a History of Art course now, so we'll have to wait for exam results before she starts applying for places. You know about her going to France?"

241

He nodded. She went on. "It'll be the first time she's been away from home without us. She's been rather molly-coddled, I'm afraid, we haven't even taught her to drive. Do you think we should have? She's never asked."

She was asking him? Molly-coddled! What an expression. He'd been left to get on with things, but he knew he'd not unduly worried his parents, which was what came of having a decent family home and so on. "She doesn't strike me as being 'molly-coddled'. As far as driving, well, I suppose we take driving for granted. I learnt in an old banger going round and round a local farmer's field, with a few other lads from the village. We wrecked the car and destroyed a gate I seem to remember. My father wasn't too impressed, but it taught me to take care. I should think Jo would make a good driver; won't take long to teach her. Good eye and hand co-ordination, being an artist."

"Hmmm." Eleanor got up and rinsed her mug out. "Sorry, Nigel, I should have left you to finish your breakfast – it'll be cold. More coffee?" Evidently she'd heard all she needed to hear. Nigel had enjoyed his plateful, despite it getting cold. Weekends with the Terriers made one appreciate one's food in almost any state. He moved his mug so she could top it up. "I suppose you'll want to get home tomorrow?" Now, was that a question or a suggestion? "You don't have to, Nigel, you're welcome to stay, but I don't know what my girl has in mind. She'll be thinking of France, she and Julie."

"That's very kind of you, Eleanor, but I don't want to overstay my welcome. You've been more than good to me. I mustn't lose track of my need to keep on studying, but I think I'd love to come back another time, if it's appropriate. There'll be more opportunities for training on the Range." He stood up and pushed his chair back to the table. Eleanor noticed. He had been well brought up, and she wanted him to be good for Jocelyn.

"You'll be welcome, Nigel," she repeated. "You may even get your portrait done again!" That made them both laugh, just as Jocelyn returned, looking quite flushed. In her shorts and T-shirt, wet legs and muddy trainers, messed up hair, she looked more the schoolgirl, less the lady. Eleanor reacted.

"Shower, you, and quick, if you want any breakfast. And come down decent."

Jo didn't need too much bidding, she was hot and sweaty and no sight for Nigel. She vanished upstairs with just a wave for him.

* * *

"She doesn't spend ages texting her friends on her mobile, she doesn't go out clubbing, she doesn't use make-up other than under protest, she doesn't want to spend money on clothes, she's hardly ever been out with a boy, come to that, she positively discouraged them. She's spent ages mooning about in the orchard, she reads, she does help a lot in the garden, she loves going out for long walks with her father – and both of us sometimes – so the epitome of a model daughter, and she worries me, Nigel. Then she goes out almost…" Eleanor stopped, very suddenly. No, she wasn't going to tell on her. "She goes out on her own like this morning, comes back looking like a fifteen year old. I want her to grow up, and yet I don't. Is this daft, Nigel? Will she manage on her own?" Why was she unloading this on the poor boy? But it seemed all right, and he was listening. The shower was running upstairs, so she couldn't have heard the outburst. "You won't say, will you?"

"She's the apple of your eye, isn't she?"

Eleanor nodded. That was very true. Jocelyn was the most precious possession. Possession?

Was that how she felt? This talking with Nigel was opening up a whole new set of imponderables. Apple of her eye? Yes. Jocelyn, her apple girl. Still on the tree.

"Nigel. I've taken up too much of your time. What do you want to do this morning? What's left of it?"

"Eleanor – please, I'm flattered with your confidences. She's going to be fine, I'm sure; from what little I've known about her. She wouldn't have rescued a wayward soldier boy otherwise. She could have made a mess of things, but she didn't. She could have gone off with some guy with loose morals, but she wouldn't, would she? She's not that sort of a girl. I like being with her, she's intelligent and quite fun and – forgive me – easy on the eye." Was that going too far? Taken by surprise, he found himself being hugged, and that was when Jo reappeared.

"Mums! What *are* you doing! You wait till I tell Pa!" She giggled, recalling her concern over Felicity. What parents got up to when left to their own devices! "What's Nigel done to deserve that?"

Eleanor went red. Her impulsiveness was getting her into trouble. There wasn't anything that she really could say, but Nigel came to the rescue. "I told her you were lovely to look at." Which was very true, in every respect. He gave her such a charming smile she couldn't be cross, or even put out. Eleanor scuttled out into the garden, diplomatically leaving them alone. Jocelyn wasn't too sure how to react, but Nigel seized the initiative and the moment, reached for her, delightful girl that she was, freshly showered, that lightweight floral full summer dress floating round her; he reached for the Apple girl, and she found she could melt into an embrace, and she also found that being properly kissed was a most pleasurable feeling.

When she came up for air, shaking her curls away from her forehead, Nigel didn't want to let her go. "I mean it, Jo. You look a picture. I couldn't help myself. Don't mind, do you?" For two pins he'd kiss her again, but there was a slight frown on her adorably freckled face.

"Mind, Nigel? Why should I mind?" She wanted to go on about how nice it was, this new experience of being kissed like she'd never been kissed before, but her tongue couldn't get round the words. It was all too new. How was she supposed to react? Should she leap back into his arms, throw herself at him, or pretend to be affronted, put him in his place, should she encourage him, or behave ladylike and keep him at arm's length? Trish would have taken all that was on offer, well, up to a point. She knew Brendan had had to be stopped from going too far, Trish had said. That wouldn't be Nigel, she was sure, and anyway… but her tummy was giving her funny signals. He was holding onto one hand, pulling her back towards him, this time she kissed him, lightly, the lady in her coming first.

"Thanks for the compliment, Nigel. New experience for me, being kissed so early in the morning!" She spun round, letting her skirt twirl, and he glimpsed lovely legs, almost all her length. Then she laughed, and ran.

Her mother was crouched down, looking critically at her herbaceous border, passing the time and contemplating whether she'd done right talking so forthrightedly to Nigel. She saw her girl's shadow appear, felt a light touch on her shoulder.

"Mums. Nigel's just kissed me. Rather well." Her voice was sparkling, but also quavered.

Eleanor carefully stood up. Getting up quickly made her go giddy sometimes, and her knees weren't what they used to be. "I thought he might. Enjoy?"

"Hmmm, yesssss. What should I do, Mums?"

"Do? What do you want to do? Kiss him back, wait for more, or kick him in the – on the shins? I can't tell you what to do, my Jo. If you like him, then play it cool and careful, if you don't, keep him at more than arm's length. My guess is you like him, and I'm happy that you like him. Just don't get carried away, Jo." Holding her daughter on her shoulders, looking into sparkling eyes, seeing a slightly flushed face, it brought back those lovely times she'd been courted by David – and steered clear of others following a different route. At least Jo had avoided becoming the target of other predatory males – so far.

"Remember all I told you, my Jo?"

"That day we had a lovely sexy shower together?" Jo remembered, and all the wonderful, wonderful feelings she'd experienced. "That was beautiful, Mums. I've never felt that feeling since, though."

Her mother breathed an inward sigh of relief, though a trifle disappointed for her at the same time. She had thought that Jo might have experimented and found joy in her own body, dangerous though it could be. How could she help her girl forward, along the path to delightful passion, without risking her virginity? How much should a mother do? Jocelyn, her Jo, was the only girl she had, the only girl she'd *ever* have. She *mustn't* get it wrong. At least there'd be a breathing space; Nigel was going home tomorrow. In the meantime there was a solemn afternoon ahead. That should cool things rather. She hugged her daughter, held her close, whispered 'I love you' into her ear, and then let her go.

"Where's your boy now, Jo?"

"He's not my…" then she giggled. The schoolgirl still in her, she blushed, aware that nothing would be the same any more. "Nigel – I left him in the house."

"You didn't Jo – he's coming over!"

Having tactfully decided not to chase her into the garden, he'd gone and had another long look at Jo's growing collection of portraits. The one she'd done of him – well, he loved it, rather Narcissus like, and he hoped she'd let him take it home to show his parents. Then he missed her, and went to find her.

* * *

Eleanor made them a scratch lunch, before sending Jocelyn upstairs to change into a more sombre outfit and giving Nigel the job of emptying the kitchen rubbish bucket into the big Wheelie bin before finishing the washing-up to earn his keep. When Jo returned in a strange admixture of grey college skirt and a dark blue sweater – at least she had black shoes – Nigel popped upstairs to clean himself up, deciding his service outfit was as good as any and came down in khaki trousers and army-style sweater over collar and dark tie.

Eleanor pursed her lips, viewed the couple with narrowed eyes, then nodded. "You'll do. You're only friends, after all. Give my love to Julie. Tell her she's welcome here any time, won't you? Hope that father of hers looks after her. Don't overstay, Jo. We'll eat out tonight – so be back in good time." Eating out was a sudden inspiration, she'd have to work fast after the two had gone, not only to ensure there was a table

246

somewhere, but that David would go along with the idea.

* * *

With Jocelyn in the passenger seat, Nigel felt very conscious of his responsibility as a driver. Normally quite fast and just a little furious, not taking risks but not hanging about either, this afternoon he drove sedately, following her directions carefully, but still getting to Julie's village chapel in good time. To just a few curious stares, they slid into the last but one row from the back, and sat silent. About five minutes before the service was due to start, a red-faced elderly man scurried down the centre aisle, put out two trestles and plonked himself in front of the sideways facing organ consol to begin playing. A few more people arrived, and then Trish and Brendan, seeing Jo and Nigel, joined them. Jocelyn, getting emotionally wound up, calmed down with Trish next to her. The organist stopped, and as the minister began intoning the verses, a sombre procession made a difficult entry with the coffin, manoeuvring around the corners. Julie, alongside her father, was in a dark grey costume, albeit with her dark red blouse. Five others, two men and three women, followed on. They must be sisters, or brothers, thought Jo, with spouses? She reached for Nigel's hand, feeling tears welling up. Poor Julie! The service was short, just two hymns and a reading, a brief address from the minister chap, a prayer, and the bearers were back, lifting the coffin high to avoid the pew ends, the family behind, and it was over. Julie's father's face was impassive; hers streaked with tears but she caught Jo's eye and managed a bit of a smile. Jo couldn't help it, she sobbed, and felt Nigel's hand squeeze hers. Trish didn't look too happy, either. With the cortege gone, off to the crematorium, Jo managed to wipe her tears away and with a few deep breaths, got herself back on an even keel. Nigel hadn't let go of her hand, not once, until she needed to get her hanky out. The minister had issued the congregation with an invitation from the Stuart family to go back to the house, a normal sort of procedure Jo knew, and felt she had to go. Nigel concurred; he'd have been surprised if she

247

hadn't. Trish and Brendan ducked out – they were on the early shift at the pub – but it was good to have seen them.

* * *

Back at Julie's house, with a next-door neighbour playing host pending the return from the crem, they accepted the glass of sherry and helped themselves to the sandwiches piled up. No one Jo knew, not even from the church, but then, she'd only known Julie at college. Feeling out on a limb, she was incredibly grateful for Nigel's presence; with much more of an aptitude for ad hoc conversation, he managed to keep the chat rolling, kept bringing her into the forum, not that it was crowded. Beginning to feel more at ease and gathering confidence, she was introduced to a grey-haired, serious looking man and his very attractive mature wife. They turned out to be both local councillors, and on Jo's college Board of Governors. With no axe to grind, Nigel asked questions about college standards and prospective exam results, to be subjected to a diatribe on how good it was, what splendid products the college turned out.

He couldn't resist it. "Like Jocelyn here? And of course, Julie, the late Mrs Stuart's daughter. Lovely girls, aren't they?" and turned to the lady. "Mrs Reynolds – Do you think the college should attempt to address the problem of adolescence?"

Mrs Reynolds deferred to her husband, as she always did when the question seemed a bit obtuse. He raised his eyebrows. A rather interesting question, though with wider implications, he thought. The red-haired girl accompanying his questioner was certainly an attractive youngster, despite her freckles. He bounced the question on.

"Young lady – what would you have us do? Is there room for non-curricular education in the art of life?" Without meaning to, he'd hit the nail on the head. The art of life. Jocelyn liked the phrase, and her recently-acquired confidence didn't let her down. A month ago and she wouldn't have dared, but with Nigel by her side, well, she managed a reply.

248

"It's very important, Mr Reynolds. Having good qualifications is all very well, but you need to stand proud in society, to be able to exhibit all the requisite social graces. I'm sure future employers look for fully rounded people, not just clever – well, paper clever – ones. My Mu... mother is doing her best to explain life's problems to me, and I'm very grateful to her, but not everyone has a special mother like mine. Poor Julie's just lost hers and her father may not be able to fill the role, so maybe college should look at ways of encouraging social manners and things, and explain what pitfalls there are out there. Mrs Summers is aware, I think, but maybe the pressures on the system are too great?" She paused for breath, and suddenly became conscious her audience had expanded and were *really* listening. Her heart skipped a beat; maybe she'd gone too far. Unseen, Nigel's hand found hers and squeezed. Mrs Reynolds was smiling at her, and her husband looked very thoughtful.

"Well now. Your escort's question has been answered, it seems. What you say is very true, but we tend to sweep it under the carpet. How would you deal with it, young man?" His question went to Nigel.

Nigel had an inspiration. "College dances for one. Get everyone to dress properly, to try and impress the opposite sex, and maybe stage a Dinner, so they could learn how to hold a knife and fork," thinking of Sandhurst. "Hold fashion shows? Have a hobbies exhibition? All sorts of things where you build on a college comraderie?" This was not what he'd expected at a funeral tea. Where was Julie?

"I hear what you say. Food for thought, eh, Marjorie?" His wife nodded, mentally making a note to talk to this Jocelyn's mother. Then Julie and her father and his sister and brother-in -law were back, and Julie went straight to Jo, and hugged her. The little group broke up, and the moment had passed.

* * *

Nigel stood alone, watching the melee and decided it was time they went. "Jo?" He raised his eyebrows at her, and she knew.

The telepathy was working. She was mouthing at him, something he couldn't make out, so he shook his head. She detached herself from the group and pulled him to one side. "It's Julie, Nigel. I'm bothered. Her father's spaced out, he doesn't know she exists. I think we ought to get her out. Now. I'd like to bring her home. What do you think?"

"You sure it's right?" They were like two conspirators.

"Uh huh. She'll come. Look, use my phone, have words with Mums, while I get her a bag packed. Ten minutes?" She went back to Julie, and the two of them left the room.

Nigel moved outside with Jo's phone, and called. "Eleanor? It's Nigel. No, nothing amiss, not with us. It's Julie; Jo's concerned about her, wants to bring her home. I think she wants me to get the all clear while she gets Julie's bag organised. Yes, I think she's right. Sure? Okay, we'll be back within the hour. Bye."

Eleanor put the phone down, slowly, thoughtfully. Well, this made Nigel's rescue of the Julie girl a double. Picking the phone up again, she dialled the restaurant and reluctantly cancelled their dinner reservation.

* * *

Julie was suffering from delayed shock, Nigel thought, concerned for her, and blessed Jo's instinct and commonsense. They put her in the car, her bag in the back. Jo sat with her, and Nigel drove quickly back. They had left her father with his sister, and no worries there. It was mid-evening and the day had improved, weather wise. Clouds had dispersed and the low sun caught the tree line, edging the shrubs with gold. Getting out of Nigel's little car, Jo was happy to be home; the evening air smelt wonderful, cleansed by the early morning rain. She could feel the garden's relief. Julie stood and looked about her, as though she'd never been there; Nigel got her bag out and went into the house. The two girls linked arms, and walked away up the path.

* * *

Up in the orchard, Jo's haven, they sat, side by side, and Julie on her hands. Her mind was racing, running events over and over and over again, and coming back to the dead stop of her mother's death and her father treating her as though she had ceased to exist. The isolation, the coldness and the impasse had got to her and she knew nothing about the way out. Only Jocelyn, alongside her, showed warmth and comfort. Nigel, of course, but he was Jo's. Jo's mum, yes, and she wished, oh how she wished, she was hers – but then she'd loved *her* mother, and now she'd lost her. Jo was quiet, just letting Julie come to terms. The girl looked across the orchard, and up to the darkening sky, and started to shake.

"No, Jo. NO NO NooH. Why, WHY?" She shouted. "I loved my mother! *I loved her!* Why did she kill herself?"

Jocelyn started, seized Julie's arm. "No Julie, she *didn't kill herself!* It was an accident, an accident! Don't blame yourself. We have to deal with life, not death. *Live*, Julie! *Live!*" She stood up, moved behind the log and massaged Julie's shoulders, running her hands over and eventually under her breasts.

Julie reached up and stopped a hand. "Thanks, Jo. Thank you for caring, but I'm cold. Cold. I don't think I'll ever be warm."

"Yes you will. Let's go in, Julie." Simply said, but all that was needed.

* * *

Eleanor had a simple supper organised, and despite it being technically summer and out of season for soup, had intuitively got some tomato on the go. The grey and drained wimp of a dark haired girl was seated, plied with hot soup and tempting spiced chicken rolls with fruit to follow. The men retired to the sitting room, tempted by a particular programme on the television, so Eleanor and Jocelyn looked after her on their own. Eleanor had made up the foldaway guest bed in Jo's room, and didn't waste any time in getting their guest horizontal. Once her two girls were settled, then she could relax. What a day! She cleared things away, looked in on the boys. David was dozing, nothing unusual but very anti-social.

"Psst – Nigel!" she whispered. "I'm going to bed. Don't disturb the girls. See you in the morning." He nodded back at her. David would come to when the television programme ended.

Once in bed, she stretched out, allowing all muscles to relax, her mind to sag. This was the moment she'd either drift off to sleep, or thoughts would appear like wisps of cloud, and congregate to annoy her peace.

This night had brought Julie and her troubles, and her future without a mother. Let tomorrow sort things she kept repeating. Let tomorrow sort things. Let tomorrow...

David crept up half an hour later and managed to slide in without waking her.

* * *

Jo spent a very wakeful night. Every time she rolled over, she woke. Each time she checked Julie was asleep, and when dawn brought glimmers of steely lightness into the room, she couldn't bear it any longer. A tentative whisper.

"Juulleee?"

"Morning, Jo."

"Sleep well?"

"Yes, I did. This bed's astonishingly comfortable. I was tired, of course. Did you?"

Jo was not being truthful. "Yes, thanks. Are you warm enough?"

"Hmmm, at the moment. When do we get up?"

"When you like. Hungry?"

"Not sure. Maybe. I feel a lot better than yesterday."

"I'm sure you do. Want to share for a while? Plenty of room." The concept of sharing her bed surprised her; she'd made the offer without thinking, probably still wanting to make Julie feel loved. It was easy to move the covers back and beckon the girl up from her floor level mattress.

Two girls, entwined, soft, sensuously and sleepy; the sight

greeted Eleanor when she peeped in an hour and a half later and surprised her. Ooops, she said to herself. Well, better the one than the other, and I hope they know what they're doing. She backed out, silently closed the door. Two eighteen year olds? Hmmm. Shook her head and went on down to get breakfast.

* * *

She didn't burden David with explanations, just got him a proper bacon and egg plateful, and saw him off. Nigel was next down, looking a trifle subdued. "Morning, Nigel. Sleep okay? Bacon etcetera? Girls still asleep?" She poured him a coffee while asking.

"Good morning, Eleanor. Slept sort of all right. If it's all the same, I'll pass on a cooked breakfast this morning. Bowl of cornflakes, maybe some toast, thanks. No sound from their room. It's good of you to take Julie in. I feel for her, being landed with only an abstract father. She seems a very nice girl."

Eleanor wondered, looking at his expression, how nice she actually did seem to him. In less than twenty-four hours, life suddenly had become complicated.

* * *

Jocelyn arrived downstairs all wrapped up in her bathrobe, looking still decidedly sleepy, most unusually. She gave Nigel a 'good morning' and a peck on his cheek before collecting her mug of coffee and returning upstairs with a 'Back in a tick' comment. Her mother wondered; was life ever going to be the same? The upstairs shower started to run.

"When do you have to be away, Nigel?"

"Half ten. Plenty of time, I suppose, but I'd like to have time on my side. Can I say how much I've enjoyed my stay? You've all been very kind to me. Do you think I might invite Jo up to Norfolk some time later in the summer – and Julie, of course, if she's still with you?"

253

"I don't see why not. Sure you want two girls? Julie might not want to be tied to Jo's life all the time." Subtle hint? Well, mothers sometimes had to try. "Don't forget you're welcome any time. I'll just go and see how they're getting on."

* * *

The bathroom door was bolted. Well, that was something. She tapped, loudly, to overcome the noise of the shower. It stopped, and a second later Jo unbolted the door, peered out.

"Oh. Mums. Sorry, are we being too long?"

"No, not really. It's just that Nigel will need to be away shortly, and maybe you should be about? How's Julie?"

Jo opened the door to let her mother in. Julie, starkers, was drying her long black hair, looking lovely and glowing, decidedly different from yesterday. Obviously they had showered together.

"How are you this morning, Julie? Slept all right on the 'put-you-up'?" She picked up the other bathrobe and draped it over the girl's shoulders. "Don't get cold. You can have the guest room tonight. What would you like for breakfast? Go and get dressed, Jo."

* * *

She managed to get them under way, breakfasting while Nigel finished packing his bag and clearing his room. It seemed so strange, seeing him off, making sure he hadn't left anything; he had kisses and hugs from all three, getting him to promise to ring when he got home, wishing him a safe journey. The sound of the engine exhaust dying away left the Old Vicarage feeling somehow empty and hollow. Eleanor was strangely grateful, then, of Julie's presence, distracting Jo's attention from that emptiness.

Nothing was said until they were all back indoors, instinctively going into the larger front room, where Jo's portrait gallery still leant up against the wall on the sideboard. Then "What are..." and "Should we..." and "Perhaps you

254

might…" all came in chorus, and spontaneously they burst out laughing. Eleanor put an arm around each girl. "What a pair you make! Look, you two, I'm in the shop this afternoon. Any ideas what you want to do? You could always go on weed patrol. Jo?"

Jocelyn wasn't sure Julie was a gardening girl, and someone who didn't know a dandelion from a dahlia was a liability. "Julie?"

"Not exactly my scene, but I'm willing to learn. I'm no Betty, so you may have to keep an eye on me if we do. Whatever, Jo; I'm just pleased to be here." With a tiny little shrug, as though she had had a moment's reflection on her strange situation, she looked all round, taking in the calm and contentment of her surroundings, contrasting this garden with what she'd left behind; and from the last time she'd been here, amongst all the razzle and rant of the village barbecue day. Jocelyn and her mother had become her props; guardians against her depression, Jo particularly this morning, stroking her, comforting her, giving her some intense physical pleasures she'd never experienced before; stroking her, soothing her, opening new thresholds in that blissful hour after dawn. Then that sublime feeling of total relaxation and slumber, before another intoxication under the cascading warmth of water, which moved her on towards the completion of transformation from dullness to butterfly beauty. She felt an urge to dance, to express her body's delight, and disengaging herself, started to move, slowly at first, the opening sequence of a ballet score she'd mastered as a younger girl, then into the stronger, wilder routine of a choreography for accompaniment she'd learnt for 'Carmina Burana', moves that sent her skirt twirling and hair flying. She crashed against the table, and stopped.

"Ouch!" She lifted her hem, inspected a reddened patch on her thigh. "That'll teach me. Sorry, folks." Her eyes were shining; incredibly she felt ten times better this morning. The past was receding, under the influence of place and emotion.

Jo was quick off the mark, smoothing her hand over the on-coming bruise, getting a tingle from her feel against the

255

girl's petal smooth skin. She'd crouched down, sensing the hurt, turned her gaze into Julie's, meeting eyes of sudden want. "Oh, *Julie!* I didn't know you could move like that! She's good, isn't she, Mums?" Deep within her, strange things were happening. The common feel of day-to-day activities were fading greyly away; in their place an excitement, a *frisson* of an uncertain future in the company of another girl. She didn't know what was going on, but it was *nice!*

Eleanor saw what was happening, and with the wisdom of maturity, elected not to interfere, not just yet. It was all part of growing up, and shouldn't be driven away into secrecy, divisive or malicious subterfuge. No harm would be done, not at present. "Hmm, she is – Julie – do you want some Savlon on that?" Jo had continued to stroke, gently, then let Julie's skirt drop, reluctantly.

Julie recovered. "Don't think so, Eleanor, Jo's got a magic touch; it doesn't hurt anymore, thanks. I should have danced outside! Still could, I suppose; I feel in the mood, though it's not the same on grass with no music!"

Her musical little laugh made Jocelyn's shoulders tingle, and there was *that urge!* She looked at the clock; it was only half eleven. Nigel had been gone an hour, and she hadn't missed him. That wasn't fair on him, he really had been very good towards her, and there was a pang of conscience. "Nigel would have loved seeing you dance, Julie." She paused. "I hope he's all right." Then the plunge. "Julie, would you pose for me? I'd love to draw you in dance mode. Would you mind? I think you've turned me on, as they say. Outside, on the lawn, in front of the border? It's still sunny. Would that be all right, Mums? Better than weeding!"

Eleanor had to laugh; at the same time relieved Jo had wittingly mentioned Nigel. Maybe the evidence of a sudden girly pash for Julie wasn't as strong as she thought. If Jo's feelings were that strong, maybe a drawing session would help. "Seems like a good idea. I' m sure the weeds won't mind! Julie?"

"Oh *yes! I'd love it!*" This dress wouldn't be right, though. It was a simple, full skirted, plain cotton thing, right for messing about in, but not to be *drawn* in. "What should I wear?

I didn't bring much. My dance dresses are at home. This is far too plain!"

"I'll lend you one," said Eleanor. "You're not that different a size and shape." True, they were much of a same height, and Julie hadn't got that much of a bigger bust, unlike her daughter's. "One of my earlier evening dresses might do. Let's go and look – no Jo, you stay here. Let it be a surprise, or a challenge." She was going to get the girl on her own.

* * *

They had fun sorting through Eleanor's wardrobe, with a couple of try-ons before that pale green, lightly patterned very full skirted one she'd had for a celebratory ball about five years ago caught Julie's imagination. It wasn't too long, and would flare beautifully, lightweight, low but not too low a neckline, with no sleeves, it had been designed for a shoulder wrap, but not necessary in this case. She slipped into it, like a glove.

"Perfect, Julie. You look lovely. *Really* lovely. Before we go down, just a word. I've noticed Jo's quite taken with you, and I don't mean this at all unkindly, Julie, but there's a limit to girly friendships, and I know from past experience, it's lovely, but you won't get carried away, will you?" Had she overcooked it? Julie coloured up, and Eleanor saw her shrink. "Now, now, my girl – I'm not cross, not at all, far from it, really, I'm happy for you both. But you don't mind if I ask for common sense? Please? I shan't get cross if you – well – keep things in bounds. Ask me if you're unsure, Julie. Jocelyn would. Now, let's see you perform, you lovely girl. Do a twirl. Show me your knickers!" She laughed, and after a moment's hesitation, so did Julie, and did her twirl, not quite reaching the dress's full potential for flirtatious movement, but Eleanor was sure Jo could capture something of the girl's spirit.

* * *

Out on the grass, in the gentle light of cloud wisp filtered sun,

Jo had set up her new easel, and took on a professional air. While she'd been on her own, she'd done a circuit of the flower beds, put her thoughts in order, and daringly, in keeping with her *inspiration* had shed her bra, tucking it carefully out of sight in her knicker elastic, despite it feeling a bit strange, but at least her shoulders were free which was all that mattered when she drew. When Julie emerged, she felt quite envious; her friend was looking rather gorgeous, borrowed dress or not. She could just about recall her mother wearing it to some do or other – but then she never threw hardly anything out.

"Okay, Julie, love. Go dance. Be an inhibit. Do your thing, I'll tell you when to stop – see if you can freeze!" This was going to be quite exciting.

"An 'inhibit'! Whatever sort of a word is that, Jo? I really need some music."

"I'll ask Mums for the kitchen disc player. Practise, girl, practise!" and she went in search of the portable radio thing; to come back five minutes later with the gadget playing the strains of some lively dance music she couldn't readily identify, but then, she wasn't a music person. It was okay for Julie, though, gyrating happily in bare feet on the grass, the dress swirling about, showing legs, bouncing boobs with hair following suit.

Jo watched for a few minutes; called "Freeze!" just as the music was about to expire and laughed as Julie nearly fell over. "Can you hold that angle? I've got to imagine the dress swirl, but I think I've got the idea. Hi, Mums, come to see the fun?"

Eleanor, creeping out and seeing the girl cavorting, was glad that they didn't have any onlookers, unless someone was hiding in the hedge. "Looks painful, Julie, are you all right with that bruise? Can I do anything, Jo?"

"Hold the dress out a bit? And up – so I can see a bit more leg? That's it." She drew, quickly, lightly, outlining the figure, then the dress; lines showing the flower-bed position, a flourish for the tree, swopped pencils, shaded in the bobbing hair – and got a rush of pleasure over the feel it had.

258

Changing pencils again, she went for detail on Julie's face, capturing bright and flirty eyes; her curves, shading again to give her the proper cleavage, around to catch the fullness of her bottom and the length of thigh and leg, out to keep the dress folds right with the swirl, underskirt just showing, and then those really lovely shaped lower legs. Then Julie fell over, with Eleanor tumbling on top of her; nearly pulling the skirt off her instead of just letting go. Jo laughed, she had to; but at the same time cross she'd still got to get that right arm position. Her laughter was infectious; within seconds they were all in hysterics.

"Sorry girls, but I need to finish the arms. Can you just get that bit back, Julie? You can stand upright if I can get the angles correct."

Julie scrambled to her feet, helped up by Eleanor. "Like this?"

"Bit more to your right; now up? Bend the elbow – hand with fingers pointing, hmmm, bit more stretch – no, don't fall over. Right. See what I can do." She got some shape to it, and then frowned. Not quite right. "Lean forward a bit. Mums, can you hold her – round the waist or something – yep – now lean. Thaaat's better. Hold it!" Feeling like a film director, she sketched more lines in and it all came good. She stood back, critically; added a few more strokes, a trifle more shading, took another comparative look, and said, very magnanimously, "That'll do. Take a break!"

Julie relaxed, but gave her friend a look that was clearly 'about time too' in meaning. Eleanor stepped back to catch a glimpse at Jo's handiwork, but her daughter was having none of it, standing in front of the easel.

"No, wait till I've finished, Mums, please. I'd like to carry on with it upstairs, after lunch. I haven't got my studio yet, so the bedroom will have to do."

"What about Julie, then, what's she going to do this afternoon?"

"Oh, I'll be fine, Eleanor, thanks. I can always go for a walk."

"Come with me to the shop, if you like. If you fancy being a shop girl for a change?"

Julie thought, briefly. "Hmmm. Yes, I think I might, if you don't feel I'd get in the way. I'd better change, methinks. Thanks for the loan, Eleanor. Let's hope it's all worthwhile!" glancing at Jo, who pulled a face.

"Course it'll be worthwhile!" Taking the paper off the easel board she let it spring back into a roll, collapsed the easel, and carried them off. Julie looked at Eleanor, and they giggled, like conspirators. The earlier serious behavioural talk had been diminished, even if neither had forgotten the import.

Lunch, usual salad and cold things, was fine; a glass or two of lemonade, a slice of home-made cake round the kitchen table and Eleanor took Julie off to do her afternoon stint.

"Back just after five, Jo, have the kettle on. Have a good afternoon."

Jo retreated upstairs, where she watched the car out of the drive before she took her dress off. She couldn't help it; her inspiration was what she felt was appropriate; to have room to flex and no one would be upset. It was nothing to do with being a schoolgirl or a lady; it was just her and the way she worked.

Time passed. The sun moved round; the shadows changed, and she angled the easel to suit. An annoying blowfly arrived and was going to make her cross unless she got rid of it, so that's what she did. It died, unmercifully.

After a bit she felt hot and thirsty, so padded downstairs and got another glass of lemonade, nearly emptying the jug; a visit to the bathroom following inevitably.

Still feeling warm and sticky despite the already wide open windows, she took a shower, and felt heaps better, especially after not drying off completely so the evaporating damp helped pull her temperature down before she partially re-dressed.

Back at her easel, she got the background sorted in detail, then concentrated on Julie's figure; such a strange feeling, drawing a person who had become so close. With Felicity, it had been easy, someone for whom she had no specific feelings. Her Mums, well she was her mother! For Julie, now, that was different. Not like Nigel even, for he came into a different league, and she wondered how he was getting on. He'd be home by now. She reflected on the chances of seeing him again soon, a friend she'd miss; but there was Julie, smiling at her from the paper, and she was a *special* friend. It was all but finished. She peered at the bedside clock for the time. Just gone four. She'd take a rest. Lying back on the bed, stared at the ceiling and contemplated. How things had changed since the end of the college year! New challenges, new friends, different feelings, and how! And she was going to France with Julie!

* * *

Eleanor and Julie had had a hilarious afternoon, with some nice chat and leg pulls from customers, like the dear old chap who wanted to know if Julie was for sale, or hire; neither girl could take offence because he had such a lovely smile and a twinkle in his eye. Someone else who Eleanor didn't know thought Julie her daughter, which made them both grin at each other. Finally, a stack of tins suddenly collapsed so they spent a quarter of an hour on hands and knees retrieving strays from all the place. Once they'd closed the door and cashed up, Eleanor heaved her usual large sigh of relief and collapsed onto the only chair in the shop.

"I wouldn't like to be here full time, Julie. I only do it to keep in contact with people, and to help out, I suppose. Nice to have you here, helped to pass the time. Well, we'd best get home and see how our artist is getting on."

Julie cast an eye round the shelves, nodding her head. "Yes, s'pose it could get a bit boring, but an experience for me. Better than being till girl at a supermarket, which is what some students do." The idea caused her to reflect on what was ahead; university and more years of studying, and it wasn't a happy thought. "I envy Jo, with her talent. Shouldn't really, but I can't think of anything like that."

Eleanor pursed her lips, wondering how best to respond. Everyone was expected to go to university nowadays as a matter of course; in her view that made the whole concept of a 'degree' rather valueless, for if everyone had letters behind their name it was pointless. One might just as well *be* a till girl! "What is it you're doing?" she asked.

"Well, it was Business Economics. If I get the results, and a place; but it's not certain. Mother – well, she thought it would give me the widest choice of careers. I've really got no clear idea. There was a possibility of retail trade management, heaven help us." Without much thought, she spun round, taking in the whole surroundings and gave a brittle laugh "Running a shop! I'm not too sure about that!"

She was a graceful girl, no doubt about that, being the willowy type. Eleanor eyed her up and down. "You should be a model, Julie. You move well, and you're not bad looking! Probably better money, too. Hey – look at the time. We'd best get out of here, before we get late night shoppers!"

* * *

Jocelyn's father got home first, a trifle surprised to find the place seemingly deserted, even the door was open, though that wasn't unusual. No Jo? He called; got no reply. It had been a sticky sort of a day, and annoyingly he'd had a couple of customers who smoked incessantly, so his clothes reeked. How folks could live in that aura he knew not – certainly he fancied a shower, a change, then life might be better. Upstairs, of course, he discovered a somnolent Jo, half dressed, or more accurately, half undressed, looking decidedly dishevelled, skirt ruffled up under her; if he didn't know better, he could have assumed she'd had an afternoon of passion. Well, that'd happen sooner or later, not much doubt over that, but if he'd anything to do with it, not until he was happy with her prospective lover. And she was certainly lovely to look at, bless her. Torn between letting her sleep and waking her, but apprehensive how she'd react if she woke and found him staring at her semi-nudity, he took the simpler line, and tiptoed away. The noise of the shower might rouse her, unless Eleanor got home. Mind you, what she'd make of Jo's state heaven only knows. She was always telling him about the girl's strange habit of going about under-dressed.

The shower did wake her; at first she focused on what time it was, then who was in the shower, and finally why she felt cold. Oh lord, it must be Pa – and he would have seen me all messed up!

She sat up, swung legs off the bed, brushed her hair back, stood up, felt unsteady, sat down again, waited a moment and got up again. The shower stopped; she was tempted. "I'll have another shower, then!" And with no more thought, she headed for the bathroom to bump into a towel girt father.

"Hi Pa. Finished with the bathroom?"

"Hi, Jo," he replied, solemnly. "Hot, are we?" He had to look, but it didn't seem to worry her, in fact, she hopped out of her skirt while he stood there.

"Fling that in my room, Pa, shan't be long," she said, turning her back and closing the door on him. He'd dressed and got himself downstairs again before the shower stopped, simultaneous with Eleanor and Julie's return. They seemed to be in good spirits, happily; Eleanor swinging straight back into action to organise a large pot of tea and some leftover fruitcake.

"Julie's doing a Jocelyn, David," she said, pouring out. "The afternoon's shop duty may have put her off Business Economics and a career in retailing. I thought she'd be better off as a model. She can dance well, we know that, and she's shapely enough. The idea seems to have found favour!"

David looked across the room at the dark haired girl, sitting prettily with legs folded sideways in classic fashion. "Well now. Are you asking me to comment? It's bad enough finding one's own daughter half dressed in the afternoon without precipitating me into appraising another ravishing chunk of femininity!"

His wife pretended not to hear the bit about Jo's state of *dishabille*. She'd mention it to the girl again later, if she didn't forget, but she liked his description of Julie. "That's good enough, David. Not that the word 'chunk' may be accurate. Do you want to be a chunk, Julie? You don't look like a chunk to me. Nor a hunk, either. Sprig, to use a garden term?" After a brief thought, she gave that away, too. "Shapely piece? That doesn't ring true."

Julie interjected "I don't mind 'chunk," not in that context. Do you think I'm – er – *sexy* enough? Robert hasn't called me since the dinner, you know. I think he's found someone else. Maybe I wasn't sexy enough for him," not that she had been too concerned; her mother's death and now staying here with Jo, let alone the age difference, all conspired to put him to the back of her mind.

"You don't have to be *sexy*, Julie. I suppose it helps, I don't know. But hey, this is getting a bit steamy." He was interrupted by the phone ringing, starting to rise out of his chair, but as it stopped, relaxed back again. The sound of Jo's voice in the hall followed, and from the tenor of the conversation, from what they could hear, it suggested Nigel, making the promised "I'm back home" call. It was all of ten minutes before Jocelyn appeared, making up for her earlier mis-presentation by wearing the burgundy dress, just to please her father. With face aglow, Nigel's call had evidently improved her humour, and she was looking her best.

"Hellllloooo! That's better! Are we going somewhere?"

"Not that I'm aware of, Pa, but I felt like it." She turned to her mother. "I have to look ladylike some of the time!" Eleanor looked critically at her. Yes, everything seemed to be in place.

"What's that, then?" The roll of paper in Jo's other hand was behind her back. "Let's see!"

Jo unrolled it carefully, doing her best to be dramatic. It was a good drawing, she knew; it had given her nice vibes and finished when she was feeling just right. Holding it in front of her, there was Julie, caught in flowing dance, a leg half up, her arms above her head, the dress swirl almost alive, and a beautiful expression, full of life and joy. In pencil, too, but her shading gave the picture three dimensions.

"Wow! That's a good one, Jo. Watcha fink, Julie?" David was impressed, despite becoming used to his daughter's talents.

Julie blinked, felt her eyes misting, for there was the essence of how she had felt, alive, and happy in her newly-discovered depths of friendship with Jocelyn, captured by the self-same girl; an expression of their mutual feelings. She could only half smile and nod her head. Eleanor saw, intuitively felt how Julie had reacted; realising there may well be problems ahead, for now she'd got not just had one girl emerging into womanhood, but two, and possibly in girly puppy love with each other.

* * *

Later that night, after a happy evening playing Scrabble, of all things, and making sure Julie was comfortably ensconced in the guest room vacated by Nigel, Eleanor and David had a bedtime conference.

He described his earlier confrontation with Jo; Eleanor filled him in about the afternoon with Julie, and then voiced her fears about the girls' infatuation with each other to her husband, who hadn't realised the implications. Once she'd explained, the situation became clearer, though it left him somewhat unhappy and a trifle concerned. With the French trip ahead, there wasn't much they could do, other than hope the girls' close friendship didn't develop into anything unnatural. "It's a pity Nigel went when he did," was his principle comment. Eleanor wryly suggested he tried to make Julie fall in love with him, and got thumped for her pains, starting a mini-wrestling match with inevitable consequences.

TWELVE

The phone rang twice that Tuesday morning. The first was Julie's father, surprisingly, checking that she was all right, and announcing that he was going to Yorkshire with his sister, Julie's Aunt Sarah, for at least a fortnight, and hoped she didn't mind. He'd be in touch before she went to France, but in case he forgot, hoped she had a nice time, and to send him a postcard. Then half an hour later Mr Petersen rang to ask if he could come over and go through the arrangements for France. That gave much more of a focus to the morning, making Eleanor a lot happier. She'd almost dreaded having to invent something for the girls to do, but after mid-morning coffee the two disappeared upstairs and she heard laughter, giggling more like; it seemed like two steps back into schoolgirlitis. What they were up to was anybody's guess, so she took herself out into the fresh feeling garden – it had been a good shower of rain overnight – and pottered, dead-heading, secateurs in hand, trimming here and there.

Upstairs, Jo was drawing again, but the subject was a new one, or rather, not a new subject – Julie – but a new approach. With the idea of Julie's modelling in mind, and not being into photography she'd suggested another study – *life study* – or 'in the nud' as Julie had said, giggling. Going along with the concept, she'd stripped off, and they'd experimented with sundry poses on her bed, laughing as naked limbs moved into all sorts of provocative positions, until sense prevailed. There she was, folded legs under her, one hand on an ankle, the other behind her head, holding out some strands of well-brushed hair, the rest draped to cross one breast. Actually, Jo thought, it *was* an artistic pose, not at all suggestive, something she didn't think she'd ever look to do. She set to work, quickly,

266

to get it done before Mr Petersen was due. For a complete change she used red crayon, and loved it.

Julie watched her every move, enraptured, felt goose pimples but not from cold. Her nerves tingled, and the tiny soft dark hairs on her arms were standing on end. Jo shook her curls away from her forehead, brushed it with one hand, and caught Julie's look.

"Nearly done, love. Bear with me." She giggled. "Bare – get it?"

"I'm getting pins and needles. I'll have to move, Jo."

Jo gave up. Maybe she'd got all she needed. "Okay Julie."

Julie stretched, one long shapely leg after another, massaging her thighs.

"Can I get dressed now?"

Jo grinned at her. "If you insist. I've got you here!" and she lifted the paper on its board. "I rather liked doing this. Gave me nice tingles. P'raps another pose, another day, Julie, please?"

Julie smiled back. "Gave me more than tingles, Jo. You're very good for me. I sure am glad I came here. Every cloud has its silver lining, and this is it." She couldn't bring herself to explain out loud, it was so *special,* so getting off the bed she whispered in Jocelyn's ear.

Jo's face started to flush up. "Go and take a cold shower, Julie. There's a time and a place, and this isn't it. Go on – I mean it!" She flung the towel robe at her friend, and pushed her towards the door.

"You know what to do – take your time. You can use my shower gel. I'll see you downstairs."

Julie did as she was told; feeling the way she did it might prove an effective antidote. Jo rolled the paper and tucked it away in a drawer. It might not be the drawing to exhibit, not yet, she'd have to let it simmer for a while, then titivate when she was on her own. That would be something to look forward to; a pleasure in store. With a wry smile, she wondered what Nigel might say when she showed him, as show him she would, no doubt over that, not that she'd either ask or tell Julie. She wasn't going to let on what Nigel had said on the phone, either. Something she'd discuss with her mother in due course, meanwhile she kept it to herself, inwardly very, very, happy. She felt love for Julie, intense and very womanly as it was, but she had a totally different feeling for Nigel now and she wasn't about to spoil it by allowing Julie's pash to get out of control. Just as well they were sleeping in different rooms. What possessed her to invite her into her bed yesterday morning she didn't know; perhaps she just felt sorry for her. That's what comes of having such caring parents, she supposed, it rubbed off on you.

Downstairs she found her mother putting a lunch together. It seemed Mr Petersen would be in luck this time, she recalled he went without last time he came. Salmon salad indeed!

"What have you two been up to then, Jo? Lots of giggles coming from up there! Not doing anything you shouldn't? Julie's behaving herself?"

"Of course! I'll tell you later, Mums. Oh, and don't get the wrong impression about us – I know what you've been thinking, at least I think I do. Nothing more than what you explained about – showed me. Poor Julie didn't have quite such an open-minded mother; and as she wasn't aware, I passed on what I knew. Hope that was within bounds?"

Eleanor flung her arms around her daughter. There was much more to this girl than she gave her credit for; looking after a waif and stray in a way over and beyond the call of duty, but nothing untoward.

"Thank heavens!"

"Hey, Mums, Steady on! You didn't…,' Jo struggled out of her embrace, but held onto her hands. "Oh well, so what if you did, shows you care for me, doesn't it, not that I don't know – listen," she cocked an ear. "That sounds like footsteps. I bet he's walked in from Mrs Summers' place. He fancies her, you know!" There, she'd admitted it at long last.

That was a bit of a surprise; eyebrows lifted as Eleanor took the comment on board, but realised her daughter knew the man from her college days and she didn't. So what? An artist, with old-fashioned tendencies, always correct, always polite; so why shouldn't he have an understanding with the college Principal. She nodded. "Fine. Good taste, then?"

"Humph. Matter of opinion. I'll see him in." She got to open the door before the knock. "Good afternoon, Mr Petersen! How are you?" Formality was always his order of the day.

"My greetings, dear girl. I'm fine, positively fine. I trust you and your dear mother are equally well?" He doffed his traditional panama, mopped his brow with the large colourful hankerchief he always kept in the top pocket of his lightweight summer jacket. Cord trousers today, Jo noticed and a leather document folder under his arm.

"We're both well, thank you. Do come in. You'd like some lunch?" She stood to one side, allowing him access ahead of her.

"No, dear girl, after *you.*"

So she allowed him the privilege of treating her like a lady.

Eleanor listened to the by-play with interest; Jocelyn, 'dear girl', behaving so impeccably, Mr Petersen, also behaving impeccably. How would they get on for the week? He took her hand, gave a little bow, and she was flattered. He didn't change.

"Your offer of lunch is gratefully accepted, dear lady. Do I understand Miss Julie is with you? So we will be a foursome. How pleasant!"

* * *

Indeed it was; light conversation, slight banter, trifles of innuendo, a smattering of Petersen humour and the three girls revelling in the attention. Then he unzipped the case to produce papers, and handed out a sheet to each. "Down to business. This is what I propose...' It became a military-style briefing which immediately Jocelyn thought would have done Nigel credit. Nigel! Her heart did a little skip. She wished he were coming with them. Departure would be this coming Saturday, leaving Tinsfield at half past eight. He'd collect them, they would be driving down to Portsmouth and taking the ferry across to Cherbourg; he had accommodation booked in the form of a gîte; after that each day would be taken as it came; it was all weather dependant, the return ferry was booked for the Friday, so they should be back late Friday evening.

Eleanor paid great attention to the whole proceeding, watching Petersen's expression; she scrutinised the details of the accommodation carefully, but there was nothing to cause alarm. He emphasised that the girls' mobile phones should work perfectly well in the area, and then he surprised them all.

"I have one other piece of information to impart," his eyes twinkling. "I've arranged," he gave a small cough, "for a chaperon," the pause evidently for effect. "You may know the lady who has consented to accompany us." Another pause. "Mrs Summers. I trust you will have no objections?"

"Mrs Summers!" the two girls chorused. Eleanor swallowed her smile, after what Jo had said earlier maybe it wasn't all that surprising. How would they take to that?

"Perhaps I might ask for your confidence in the further intelligence I can impart. The dear lady in question and I have reached an *understanding*. So it will be a very pleasant interlude." He leant back, and reached for his glass. Eleanor's lemonade production would have to increase.

Julie and Jo exchanged glances, and both tried hard to contain their surprise. Neither was quite sure how this would impact on the enjoyment of the week, but there wasn't much they could do about it. At least there wouldn't be a problem over any 'improper' insinuations.

Jocelyn spoke for them both, given she was the instigator of all this. "We must offer you our congratulations, Mr Petersen. We're very pleased for you. She's a very lucky lady. Of course we will be thrilled to have her company, though maybe we should be extra grateful to you for taking us along, under the circumstances."

He beamed at them. "Not at all. I shall be overwhelmed with delectable ladies. Except, of course, you two will have to earn your keep. I shall expect to have some model models but we will have some *wonderful* pictures to bring home, and not all mine either, Miss Danielleson, for I fully expect some to be your work. Now, I have taken up far too much of your time. I can be reached at Mrs Summers' most of the time – do please feel you can telephone at any time if you have the slightest query." About to get up from his chair, he remembered another point. "Miss Danielleson. I took the liberty of asking a contact of mine about the prospect of publishing prints of your 'White Dress' drawing. She was quite interested, I am pleased to report, though naturally it depends on her scrutinising the work. Is there any chance I might be allowed to let her have sight of the drawing?"

Jocelyn looked at her mother. She nodded; it seemed a sensible move. Jo got up and went to find her first sketch of this composition; the larger copy was awaiting collection by Felicity. On impulse, she also nipped upstairs to find the first one she'd done of Julie; but ignored the temptation to reveal the nude study. Mr Petersen scrutinised this latest offering, totally unaware of the delights he would be shown in due course, looked at the drawing, then at a too-demure Julie.

"This shows very effective representation of movement, and quite full of life in its true sense. I like the way you've caught the dress, Jocelyn. Did you have some difficulties with the arms? I see some impressions!" He smiled at Jo. Without waiting for a reply, he went on. "Anything else new, dear girl? Have you extended your repertoire?" Julie perked up, and despite Jo's frown and a shaken head, she let the secret out.

"We did a beautiful thing this morning, didn't we, Jo?" The wonderful feelings that the modelling session had given her were fresh in her mind. "Didn't you finish it?"

Jocelyn became cross. It was her work, it wasn't finished, and she wasn't ready to show it to anyone. However, she couldn't ignore her friend's input. "We did. Julie's modelling for me, I'm trying life studies, but I'm not ready to demonstrate, not yet. I did one of Nigel – *not* a life study, Mums," seeing her mother's consternation. "A portrait, but I let him take it home. So that's it, really."

Mr Petersen was satisfied. "Life studies, Jocelyn, sell well, needless to say. Don't prostitute your art for quick returns, though. I want to take you into the world of oils and landscapes, while we are in France. My instinct is that you have more potential, as yet unexploited. Let us see what materialises. Now I really must take my leave."

* * *

When he had gone, panama at a jaunty angle, briefcase and the de-framed precious sketch of the 'White Dress' in a roll under his arm, Eleanor had her say. "You've been drawing Julie *naked?* Is that right, Jo, do you think? Was it your idea or hers?" Her glance took in both girls. Jo wasn't fazed at all, and Julie, with a bit of a blush and a seductive smile, spoke up.

"I wanted her to, she agreed. I think we both enjoyed it, and I don't mind her doing more. I'm really quite happy about it, Eleanor. Please don't be cross, or upset. It's very *beautiful*."

Slightly appeased, Eleanor patted her daughter on her arm. "All right dear. I look forward to seeing it in due course, if you'll let me. Had I better see it before you show it to your father?"

Julie's blush deepened. She hadn't thought that far ahead, though now she had, it was inevitable.

Eleanor changed the subject. "What do you think about Mrs Summers, then? You were right, Jo. At least there'll be some comfort in that for me. Not that I don't trust him, or you two, but it does make me feel happier about you going off like that."

Jocelyn, in her heart of hearts, was quite relieved herself; Julie wasn't worried either way, she had been quite confident in her companion's acceptance of any risk to their reputation. Eleanor knew David would be better pleased as well. "Let's send her a note of congratulations, Jo?"

Jocelyn was appalled. "You can't do that, Mums! He said they'd reached an *understanding*, not an engagement, and I thought it was still a secret. He only told us because she'd be coming on the trip!"

"Oh, yes, I suppose you're right. Still, it's very lovely for them both. He's such a nice man, and she's probably quite a lonely person. Right, now you've got your joining instructions, we can rest easy. What ideas have you for keeping you and Julie busy for the next few days? I've something up my sleeve if you haven't." A pity neither girl was able to drive, for then they could have gone off by themselves, but Jo had never really been bothered about driving, and maybe, Eleanor thought, Julie hadn't been encouraged. Perhaps she should organise lessons for her daughter; she'd discuss this with David. In the meantime, she had them under her feet. Silence, while the two girls thought. Jocelyn was no longer in the mood to draw, so that was out, at least for today. Julie wouldn't have said no to modelling again, but that being up to Jo, she wasn't going to say. If she'd been at home, she may have just curled up with a book and a disc, or maybe gone onto the Internet and surfed around. As far as she knew, the Daniellesons didn't have a computer, which put paid to anything like that. Jo would have gone for a walk along the Range boundary, but didn't see Julie as a serious walker.

"Okay, girls. Your time is up!" With something of a mischievous grin, she picked up a spiral-bound notepad and a couple of pencils, moved to the door and beckoned them outside.

"No, Mums, we're not raking that gravel again!" Jocelyn was concerned.

"Don't worry. It's not that. Come on, round to the barn." She led the way. Opening the large creaking doors wide, she explained: "You've been through this lot already, Jo, but I want to do the job properly." She used an elegant leg to point at the stack of boxes moved down from the old shed. "These costumes – they need sorting out, cataloguing and then folding up. I'd like to give a copy of the list to old Mrs Parsons – she's going to try and recall what productions they staged here. I've an idea we might resurrect the stage."

"Mums! Oh, what fun! The garden would need to be changed round a bit, wouldn't it?"

"Maybe. We'd get a lot of interest, I think, and you're right, it would be fun. So this is the first stage. Is that all right with you, Julie?"

The girl hadn't quite understood what this was all about, so Jo explained. Julie became intrigued, especially as she'd seen the white dress, both worn and drawn. "You mean they actually did plays here? Ages ago?"

"Uh huh. I had some weird dreams up in the orchard, where I found the costumes. I thought they were something left from an old house, maybe earlier than our house, but Mrs Parsons recognised what I wore. Good, isn't it?"

"And the others are in here?" Julie started to probe into the top box. "Goodness!" She pulled the first item out. It was the pink satin dress; lots of fabric, stitched meticulously around the bust and the waistline. She shook it out, and measured it up against herself.

Eleanor detected the change in Julie's demeanour. From being a politely bored guest, she'd become intrigued and alive. "Made for you! It looks as though it would fit."

"Put in on, Julie! Go on, put it on!" Jocelyn was keen for her to get the same experience as she'd had, those weeks ago. She might never say she'd not been the same since, but wearing the white dress had certainly changed her life – it inspired the drawing that she had completed the day Felicity had turned up; the copy that had been sold to her, and now Mr Petersen might get prints done. So, Julie, my girl, she thought, I'll get you into that dress even if I have to rip that other plain thing off! Certainly what she'd put on after the model session didn't do anything for her. Eleanor was much of the same mind. She took the satin from her, shook it out, examined the seams critically, no tears, no damage she could see, and sniffing it, found no nasty surprises. Julie wasn't sure. If she was going to try this on, surely better in the privacy of her room?

"Here, Julie. Get that thing off. There's no one about – you've got your knickers on – Come on, it's proper sexy!" Jo reached across and unzipped the back of the dull grey striped cotton. The dress all but fell off her; so Julie was forced into stepping out of the heap, and let Eleanor offer the satin over her head. The fabric fell sheer and clung, immediately moulding itself to her figure. The waistline was quite high and the skirt full and pleated on the sides; the panelled front was plain apart from the stitch lines. The side had no zip, just old-fashioned, fabric covered buttons, and Eleanor carefully pulled the waistline together and fastened them up. Julie looked sideways down at herself, shook the fullness out, and then hitched the bust into place. Not as well endowed as Jo, the cut was actually about right for her, and the neckline, low certainly, wasn't too low, the rise of her breasts just visible. Shaking her hair, brushing it straight with her right hand, she felt comfortable in, and was enjoying, the dress. Her shoulders went back, her chin lifted. Jocelyn glanced quizzically at her mother. Eleanor gently nodded, happy with the surprise revelation. Julie *was* a model!

"Jo?" Her mother's expression was asking the question.

"Okay. Back in a moment. Oh, and Julie?"

"Yes?" She was still titivating the fit.

"Er – can you do something with those knickers? I can see the pantyline, and the fabric clings too well over your bottom. Can you stand being a model again?"

"You said…"

"Yes, I know I did, but this is something different. Mums – if she sort of sits on some of those boxes, feet up, hand on her hip, that sort of thing?"

Eleanor caught the drift. "Right, yes. Not quite what I had in mind, but if you think it's worth the effort?"

"I do. Julie – pants off, please. I'm going to fetch my kit." She sped off, and Julie wriggled under the satin and did as she was told. Eleanor moved a box, ensured the two on top of each other were solid, put one of the old decrepit chairs as a foot rest, helped Julie up, and draped the skirt to show a lot of lower leg, suggested she held her knees wider so the material dropped in, and by the time she'd done the arranging, Jocelyn was back, lugging her easel and a box of watercolours, which was all she had in colour apart from crayons. She'd found she only had one large sheet of paper left, so she'd better get it right.

"Mums – that's a lovely pose. Are you happy up there, Julie? Can you stay put for half an hour?"

"I'll try. I feel okay at the moment. It's a lovely dress. I feel quite at home in it – and it's warm, just as well, there's a drafty place up here!" They all laughed and Jo picked up the pale blue scrap, offered it back to her friend.

"Want to shove it between if it's that bad?" Julie shook her head, waved it away.

Eleanor frowned then. Girlish humour was all very well, but there was no point in emphasising Julie's coverless crotch. "Jo!"

"All right Mums. Are you staying?"

"I am that. I've not seen you work from this side of the easel. Aren't you going to take your top off?" She was teasing her daughter, hoping that she'd not rise to the query.

"Not at the moment, Mums. Now, quiet please. Julie! Can you look over there, at the right-hand doorpost? Yes, that's fine." She started with deft, rapid outlines, light and precise. Seeing the girl in the pink satin, shadowed darker, folds and sweeps of the fabric catching the sunlight from the barn door, perched on the old boxes, the deeper shadows of the barn interior behind, contrasting with the pale face and the dark tresses of her hair cascading down, it fired her imagination, and she worked well. As soon as the bones of the picture were in place, she switched to the watercolours, hoping the paper wasn't too dry. Eleanor was mesmerised, seeing the sweep of colour flow onto the paper as the dress began to appear, then the greys and browns, adding depth to the picture. Not too solid, leaving the eye to complete the imagination. Jo added deeper shades to her pink, creating the dress's folds. Then, while the major areas were drying a fraction, she detailed Julie's expression, her arms and hands, then her legs, imagined her shoeless despite the presence of her old pumps.

"I wish I could catch this as a photo, Mums, make the titivating a lot easier afterwards. What do you think?" Standing back, she surveyed it critically. "Julie? Are you okay up there?"

"So far, dear Jo! I'm watching a spider in the door frame."

Jo turned and looked. True, there was a web. Too fiddly to get that in. She picked up her soft black pencil, gave the point a rub to sharpen it and added outlines to the colour- washed areas. All of a sudden, it worked, and Eleanor couldn't help patting her daughter on the back.

"Steady, Mums. Don't knock me." She was picking up the curve of Julie's thigh under the fabric with subtle, gentle strokes, and where her tummy dipped into her lap. "See?" She moved up and accentuated the bust line, an extra shadow where the dress left the gap over her modest cleavage. Then the neckline and detail of strands of hair went in, a touch on the eyebrows, another on her nose, a bit more on her lips. "I think – yes, maybe. Mums?"

"Very, very, nice, Jo dear. Captured the moment. Now I've seen what you can do, I'm proud of you even more. Julie! Down you get. Before you fall asleep up there!"

"Fat chance! You aren't going to want me to model any more of these things, are you? We'll be here ages!" With great care, she stepped down, avoiding treading on the dress's hem and shook herself. The dress shimmered, as with the shine on her hair, as if it had taken on new life now warmed with the woman's body. The tiny hairs on Jocelyn's arms tingled as she absorbed the titillation of the moment; the sun through the barn door catching the sheen on the satin against the backdrop of the dust motes, shadowed over the ancient planking. Something of the aura of the past, with Julie as the centre figure, gripped them all. Jo's painting had caught the essence of the event, frozen yet mobile; her incomprehensible talent for capturing mood and meaning had worked its magic once again.

Eleanor shivered, for an indefinable reason, with a strange sense of déjà vu. Jocelyn picked up her easel; picture firmly clipped, the rest of her paints, nodded at Julie, and ran off back to the house. She too, had a weird feeling, very akin to the atmospheric effect she'd experienced up in the orchard that time she'd fallen asleep up there, and she didn't know quite how to cope with it, running off was an attempt to break the spell. Julie stood, frozen for a three breaths spell, then quickly, fumble fingered, undid the waistline buttons, reached for the hem, pulled the dress over her head oblivious of the absence of her underwear.

The scene clicked back into focus, Eleanor's momentary trance evaporated, as her first thought was to get the girl decent. "Here, get back into this." Picking up Julie's simple grey dress, she helped her back into it, found the pale blue scrap and with a wry smile, saw it back into place. Their eyes met, and nothing more was said.

Jo returned, mind back into the present, painting safely weighted down on her dressing table to dry, to find her mother and Julie halfway through emptying the first box, the satin dress carefully folded on one side, other items segregated into male and female costumes. They were laughing over the strange design of some of the 'nether garments' as Eleanor described them.

"Here, Jo, take the pad, will you. I'll dictate – you list. Julie – carry on delving."

Jocelyn, seeing item after item emerge, remembered how she'd done the same thing. Now at least it was making more sense, though the threads of unknown circumstances were still tangled around. Would their list and Mrs Parson's memory unravel them? They worked on, as the sun moved round and eventually put them into shade.

"Enough! We'll call it a day. Your father will be home soon, so let's go make some tea. Well done, girls. Good job jobbed." She was pleased with them, and especially with the strange artistic interlude that had left them all with ingrained memories. "Don't say anything to your father, Jo, about the 'Satin Dress' painting, just show it to him when you're satisfied with its finish. As a surprise. See what he says?"

Jocelyn, a trifle surprised, thought for a minute before concurring. "Okay Mums." There was the other study of Julie to finish as well. She sure was going to be busy; oh for her studio! She was longing to become more involved with her feelings; working with Julie was great, with the rapport between them and no inhibitions, she knew lovely things would happen; still that tingle down the nape of her neck. A gnawing doubt over the enthusiasm for France was creeping insidiously into mind, which wouldn't do; wouldn't do at all, not after everyone had been so adaptive to her inclinations.

Dear Pa, sorting out the studio idea, Mums just going along with it, but mainly good old Mr Petersen, encouraging her – she couldn't let him down. This all trickling through her mind as the three of them walked companionably back to the house.

Eleanor, casting a sideways glance at her daughter, could sense some uncertainties in the way her expression had gone into more of a frown. "Penny for them?"

That brought Jocelyn back into frame, and the corners of her mouth twitched. "Worth more than that." There were other things to think of. Nigel, for one, though he wasn't a *thing*. "This time next week we'll be in France. Hope the weather's going to be good."

"I'm sure it will be, darling. You'll come back with a suntan!"

"With these freckles, Mums? I'll be more like a lobster. All right for you, Julie – you look as though you take a lovely tan. Do you think it'll be a bathing costume job, or long peasant dresses?" She had visions of some of the Corots she'd seen. As they got back into the kitchen, the query gave Eleanor one quick burst of concern that she tried hard to push away. Surely Petersen wouldn't take advantage of her girls? Her *girls* – well, yes, Julie was becoming more like another daughter, wouldn't that have been great?

"Long peasant dresses I hope. I don't want any attempts at a *faux* 'Bathing party'!" which made Jocelyn giggle, while Julie looked perplexed. Eleanor explained, and that made the girl look worried.

"Posing for Jo's one thing, doing something for old Petersen's another!"

"Oh, come on, Julie, he's an *artist*. Artists don't look at girls like *that*." Jo's emphasis begged some questions, best left unanswered, Eleanor thought.

"Let's get the kettle on. David will be back soon. Then maybe we'll have an *al fresco* supper later. That an idea?" Anything to divert this topic of conversation, which could develop into all sorts of second thoughts if they weren't careful; and anyway, Mrs Summers would be with them, so it was surely going to be fine.

Tea brewed, and her father back home, it was as much as Jocelyn could do to prevent herself from showing him the two new pictures, the red crayon study of Julie in her nothings and then the more seductive – seductive? – one in the pink satin. Her mother guessed what was running through her daughter's mind, catching her eye she shook her head gently. Jo returned a wry smile, and then Julie blew it. With an obvious attempt to stay involved, she asked a simple question.

"Will you have to ask a gallery to exhibit the watercolours, Jo, if you're thinking of making some money from them? Will I get commission?" She was actually feeling rather pleased with her day's work, it had given her a strange, a sort of different, feeling she'd never had before, and wondered what sort of feelings these super thin models got when showing off skimpy things on a cat walk that no one in their right mind would wear.

David homed in on the commission question. "You been modelling, Julie?"

"Yes…"

"David – shall we eat outside this evening – it's still quite warm, and I've got cold chicken and we can have a chilled Chablis if you like?" Eleanor tried to intercept, while Jo didn't quite know whether to come clean or duck. Her father wasn't going to be put off, this sounded far too intriguing.

"Chicken and Chablis sounds fantastic, darling. What has Jo done of Julie, then?"

It wasn't going to go away. "If you promise not to stare, Pa, and if Julie doesn't mind, I'll fetch them." David looked at their guest girl, and she'd dropped her gaze to her lap, might even be blushing. She gave a little shrug, as if it was of no consequence, and Jo pushed her chair back and ran upstairs.

"That was a bit naughty, David. Jo likes to finish these things and show them off all in good time." Eleanor was a mite cross, but then, as Julie had provoked the query; she had to stand the consequences. Jo returned, and solemnly held up the red crayon one up against her chest. Her father was getting accustomed to these impromptu exhibitions, but not used to the extent of his daughter's talent. Julie, shown with an astonishing combination of beauty and mystique, and such an expression! The girl herself sneaked another glimpse, seeing herself like that produced a funny sensation running down her spine, then found she became actually quite proud of herself; Jo had made her look rather mysteriously beautiful, and not at all cheap or tawdry, unlike some of those dreadful newspaper pictures that exploited girl's bodies.

Eleanor, in her turn, seeing something of the emotion that had produced this, reached across and touched Jo's forearm.

"Don't let Felicity see this one, Jo. I don't think we want to see Julie being sold, she's too beautiful – isn't she, David?"

"Have you finished it, Jo?"

"Not really."

"Ummm. Well, when you have, we'll have to get Ben to do some more framing. I agree with your mother. She's not going anywhere. Julie – you don't mind if we keep you special?" There was humour in his voice as well as a hint of pride.

The feelings that she'd experienced overcame her self-consciousness, and she sat straight and proud of her body. "The other one, Jo? That's special, too."

And so the pink 'Satin Dress' was exhibited as well, and David was sure he'd seen something like it before. Frowning, giving Jo some misgivings before he smiled. Of course, those watercolours of Spanish girls that had become collector's items. Well, sort of. This was much, much, nicer and this time Jo had captured a sort of wistfulness in her face, but the contours of the subject's body, dress, were very well done.

"What I can't understand, my darling daughter, is how you've managed to get so good so soon. No disrespects," he added quickly. "I'm just so happy to be so impressed. Problem is, can you keep it up? Will anything you do *not* be as good?"

"Only if I don't feel happy with what I'm doing. Then it might be a bit dreadful. Actually, I rather like using the watercolours. Sort of relaxing, you know, gentle and soothing. Which one do *you* prefer, Pa, or shouldn't I ask? Let me guess – Julie in red crayon!"

Visions of his earlier reactions to Felicity came to mind as she said it, mischievously. She was right, of course, but by now Julie didn't mind; after all, if she was going to go down the 'model' route she must get used to the idea of using her assets. How odd it seemed; last week she'd have run a mile or screamed her head off if anyone had as much as suggested she'd show what she had; this evening, if Jo had wanted her to, she'd cheerfully have gone back to buff conditions. Perhaps it was all part of the process of getting away from adolescence, which so much figured in adult minds when talking about teenagers.

She moved another notch forward. "I don't mind – I think Jo's shown me rather well, and I've promised her I'll model anytime. Now I've had a chance to think about things."

"Okay girls, David, that's enough. Otherwise this could get all a bit intense – Jo, please go and put 'Miss Julie in red crayon' and 'Satin Dress' back upstairs. Then we'll have supper. David – a bottle of Chablis, please."

* * *

Later, after the girls had been persuaded to disappear off to their respective beds, Eleanor and David took a familiar stroll up to the orchard, with the remnants of the Chablis, not unaware that Jo may have seen them go from the vantage point of her bedroom window. The evening air had become sultry, almost velvety in its feel, not a breath of wind, and the late scents of the garden floated up, adding their own heady subtlety. Eleanor had her hand slipped into David's, giving him little squeezes as they walked.

"You're a bit of a rogue, you know."

A sideways glance at her, drinking her in, all the nice womanly aspects that made him supremely happy she was his wife. "How's that, my darling?"

"Poor Julie, having you staring at her body!" She swung their clasped hands to thump his thigh. "You could have made her all embarrassed – and she is our guest. Jo did rather show all her assets up, didn't she?" They had reached the orchard gate, and David picked his wife up, sweeping her round and sitting her on the top rail.

"So what if she did? My guess is that Julie has suddenly become quite proud of herself, which in its own way won't do her any harm, will it? We've got two girls here, fresh out of school, or college, whatever, and about to be shoved into the real world. If we can knock a few corners off, make them aware of life, then all the better. In two weeks – three at most, and I reckon we've achieved a lot. Okay, Nigel and Julie's poor mother have had something to do with it, and our Petersen chap, maybe Felicity, but it all helps. I don't think we have done so badly. I'm just amazed at what our Jo's doing. Those drawings of Julie; so true to her as a girl, as a person. The expressions, the way she's got the proportions so right. It's incredible, it really is. Goodness knows what a week with Petersen is going to do. You know we'll get most of the work done on the studio conversion done while she's away? Our Mike has it all organised – so with a bit of luck she'll come back to a surprise. Birthday present, eh?"

Eleanor bent down, not quite falling off her perch, and gave her husband a kiss on his nose. "I love you, David Danielleson! Do you love me more than your daughter?"

He laughed, and made to pull her off the gate, so she fell into his arms. "Without you, my lovely woman, I wouldn't have a daughter to pander over. You're not jealous, are you?"

"Nope. Just happy." They stood for a moment, hugged together. "Julie? How has she fitted in so well?"

"Our Jocelyn, I guess. Seems to have developed a soft spot for her; maybe 'cos she felt sorry for her. It comes out in the drawings, rather. What about Nigel? Will he figure in future, d'you think?"

"Not sure, David. Maybe. Jo's gone a bit quiet on that front, but with Julie about it keeps her from fretting over him." She shivered. "I'm getting cold. Let's go back."

"Sure?" He explored, feeling for her.

She took hold of stray hands quite firmly. "Quite sure, randy. There *are* better places, provided *les girls* have gone to sleep!"

Jocelyn wasn't asleep. Her mind was far too active, trying to work out all sorts of reasons why she was able to draw like she did, wondering about what Julie was going to do, and how Nigel was going to find them in France. The thought of meeting up with him again was rather exciting, especially as it was a bit of a secret. She heard her parents coming up the stairs, a few whispers, before other noises, which suggested some happy goings-on. She smiled inwardly and cosied up under the duvet. One day, one day...

THIRTEEN

The remaining days of that week flew by. Eleanor sacrificed some of her precious gardening time, and took the girls out on some 'educational visits', a heavy diet of museums, art galleries, and at least two National Trust houses, together with the obligatory teas. On one afternoon they arranged to call on Mrs Parsons, primarily to hand over the list they had compiled of the vintage drama costumes, with Jocelyn, persuaded after some reluctance, showing the watercolour of Julie looking so beautiful and pensive in the pink satin dress. That had opened the floodgates of reminiscences, culminating in another very 'nice' afternoon tea and Eleanor hinting that she'd thought of rejuvenating the open-air drama idea. She couldn't have given the old lady a better present; promises of searches for the early programmes and names of some of the Drama Club members who may still be around were made, and Eleanor and her two girls retreated home that day full of virtuous feelings.

While she spent her obligatory afternoons in the shop the girls made up for her generosity of time by weeding, lawn mowing, and Julie, much to her surprise, found she liked raking the gravel once she mastered the sweeping action, leaving trails of patterned lines behind her. The two girls, working together, living together, became closer to each other than ever before during the week, though happily neither felt the need to become physically entwined anymore, not after that first day after the funeral. The trauma in the dark haired girl had worked itself out; she had almost returned to her confident self. But there was another hurdle waiting; a problem she'd pushed to the back of her mind.

David insisted on taking them out to the Italian restaurant

on the Friday, although Jocelyn wondered if she should wear a different dress, as she'd already been there in the 'Burgundy' one. It didn't seem to matter in the end; it probably meant the waiter remembered them from last time, as he was very polite and attentive. "He fancies you!" hissed Julie at an opportune moment, and got a kick from Jo under the table.

"More likely you," she replied. "You've got the dark hair the Italians love."

"Girls! Behave! You're supposed to be young ladies!" Eleanor's remonstration was tempered with a broad smile for she thought the waiter was quite dishy herself. David stayed above the girly chitchat as his only concern was ensuring they had a happy evening. Tomorrow his girls – for he had become quite used to Julie being part of things – would be launching themselves on an unfamiliar experience; he and Eleanor would be on their own and he had that sneaking feeling he'd miss the company. The other thought that was niggling away at the back of his mind was Jo's exam results; these were due in by the end of August and there some decisions to be made. One part of him wanted his girl to stay at home, the other for her to get some marketable qualification behind her. A lot would depend on this forthcoming week; how this chap Petersen would report back on her.

"David – you're looking rather pensive. What *are* you thinking about?" They'd reached the coffee stage and he was stirring his sugar round and round. Jocelyn seemed to be mesmerised by his actions. Julie stopped eyeing the waiter and focused in on the table. All three girls waited for his reply, poised for reaction.

With a bit of a wry smile, pulling his spoon out of the cup and clinking it back on the saucer, he had to own up about his concerns. "I didn't want to spoil the evening by talking over mundane topics like exam results and what happens next, that's what. Maybe the wine's making me feel maudlin. Sorry."

"No, Pa, nothing to say sorry about!" Jocelyn was perky still, partially due to her wine intake, partially her increased confidence in her own ability during the last ten days. Felicity had rung just that very day to say how much the copied 'White Dress' drawing had been admired by most, if not all, the visitors to her little office in the publishers. Evidently she was very proud of her purchase; and Jo's newly-established bank account had swollen by the three hundred that had been the final agreed price. And there was still the question of the prints that Edward Petersen was seeking to promote, an uncertain quantity but one that could boost her finances still further. Felicity, accepting that Jo had the right to have prints published, had even been good enough to offer to give them a plug in the magazine if it was the right thing to do. So life was being quite kind to her. "I'm not all that bothered, really."

"You might not be, but I don't want you to miss out, dear. And what's Julie going to do?"

Julie didn't know; that was her problem. The original concept of her university course, as designed largely by her mother, had been all but wrecked by her decease and, probably more importantly, by her new yen for becoming a model. She had the common sense to know posing for artists wasn't going to be the answer, but it had given her an inkling of what it was all about, and it felt good. She did have worries about her father's reaction, and said so.

"Well, if he's at all concerned, that must tell you he cares for you, Julie, surely?"

"That's it. I don't know that he will care. It's as if I don't exist half the time, I mean, he was quite pleased in a funny sort of way that you offered to look after me. I guess he'd pay the bills for Uni without looking at them." Her expression lightened. "Do you think he'd pay a modelling school bill without knowing?"

A laugh from David; a lip-tugging grimace from Eleanor, and a giggle from Jocelyn brought Julie to her senses. "I'm going to have to discuss it with him, aren't I?"

David did a sage nodding exercise. "Reckon you will, but not until after the French week. And maybe we ought to explore what is involved, like what it *would* cost, how you get accepted, where courses are run, how long they last, what job opportunities exist afterwards – you know, all the boring stuff."

"Ask Felicity, Pa. She'll know, I'm sure," was Jocelyn's contribution.

"You're right! Julie, I'm pretty positive we'll crack it, but are you happy to let me do some legwork while you're away?" The girl nodded, close to tears. Jo's, dear Jo's, parents were being *so* good to her, and her life was once more full of colour and brightness and so three-dimensional. True, when her mother looked after her, she had felt secure, and motivated, and she knew she used to cope. Then her world had fallen apart and she'd nearly got a fit of depression before all this had happened. Now it was going to be like being back on the start line again. "Can I use Jo's drawing of you – the red crayon one?" David wanted to ensure she would have no reservations. "Maybe the pink 'Satin Dress' one as well – I like that one just as much."

Julie nodded again. If it was going to work then she owed Jo a lot. And Jo winked at her, her smile full of confidence. With her father on the job, it was bound to work. He'd bought her this dress, and it all started from there. Of course it would work; it had to. "Ought we to go, Pa. I think our friend is getting restless?" True, the waiter was hovering. David stood up, and went to pay the bill. It had been a good evening, and well worth the money.

"You are a lucky man, Sir, with the three lovely ladies. That dark haired one – she is a model, no?" He was genuinely complimentary, not merely flattering, David was sure.

"She could well be, my friend. Thank you for looking after us so well. It's been a very pleasant evening." He added a good tip to the bill, unusually for him, but it seemed a good omen.

* * *

Saturday morning – *the* morning – Jocelyn had had a restless night, ideas of what lay ahead intermingling with where the way forward lay amongst all this, her and her drawing; Julie and her possibilities as a model. She climbed out from under her tangled covers and bagged the first call on the shower.

Then dressed, carefully, ensuring she had a good blouse and tidy skirt. The battles she'd had with her bra top were receding, so much so she didn't give fastening those silly behind back clips another thought. Only a few weeks ago she would have given up and flung the thing back on the chair to go unsupported rather than mess about. A lightweight sweater top, and a furious couple of minutes hair brushing, and she preened in front of her mirror. "Next time you see me, Miranda mirror, I'll be as brown as brown. Probably all over!" She giggled; then went to rouse Julie.

Downstairs, Eleanor finalised the breakfast things. Day of departure then, and it wasn't something she was looking forward to. She'd supervised the packing of the girls' cases, well, case and duffle bag thing for Julie, fussing a bit over how many pairs of clean knickers they should take, until Jocelyn had, quite intelligently, said she thought French girls wore them (sometimes, she added, giggling), so they could always buy more. She had a discussion with David over the use of the mobile phone, and he agreed that Jo should take it with her; he'd organise a replacement. They'd never gone over the top on gadgets but a phone as an emergency thing had seemed like common sense, and at least Jo could phone home if it were needed, which was a relief.

"David! Are the girls coming down?" He wasn't looking forward to their departure any more than his wife was, but had to put on a brave face.

"Any moment now. I rather think Jo's organising Julie a bit too much, but there we go. That's our girl. How's things?" An arm around her shoulders, another little kiss. She leant her head on his.

"Don't know. What'll we do?"

"When they've gone? What would you like to do? Garden, shop, trip out, whatever?"

"Orchard, Dave. Just to reflect a bit. Do you mind?"

"Nope. Mike'll start on the conversion on Monday. He *may* come this afternoon. Hey, we'll have to watch the time. Girls!" He put his head round the kitchen door and shouted up the stairs.

Breakfast – merely cereals and toast, but a good brew of coffee – over, and the bags were in the kitchen all ready. This was the time she feared the worst, thought Eleanor. The hanging about; she couldn't ever imagine herself going on an air flight if it meant even ten minutes waiting about. She hated it. Then there was a car in the drive, and what a car, in a beautiful polished maroon. She'd never seen Mr Petersen's car, he'd walked before. Come to mention it, said Jo, neither have I, so they were all quite pleasantly surprised, David impressed even, when the old Bentley crunched its wide tyres up the newly raked gravel.

"Good morning all! Ready for the fray?" Petersen leant out of the wound-down window. "Do you like my chariot? I call her Hermione, didn't think Hermes was quite right, but the old girl has his wings. Hence Hermione. Plenty of room and all the clobber goes in the tonneau." He climbed out, and watched David as he walked round the car.

"This is a spectacular machine, Edward. Have you had it long? It must be what, forty years?"

"Thereabouts. My fathers; a hand-me-down. Wouldn't have anything else; bit heavy on the juice, though, so she only comes out on special jaunts like this. At least I don't contribute any more to HMG on the road fund side. Ready girls? We've a ferry to catch." Opening the heavy lid to the boot – *tonneau, please* – he heaved the two bags into a corner of the cavern, not even full with his cases and the miscellany of painting kit. "Mrs Summers awaits. We'll make our adieu." He turned specifically to Eleanor, picked up a limp hand and gave her the formal salutation. "I promise to return the young ladies in pristine health; I assure you they will have the best attention. Thank you for the loan of their company. We'll give you a call once we're installed." The rear door was opened, the girls given hugs and kisses from both, they slid onto grey vintage leather, settled themselves down, and the big old car rumbled away.

* * *

David reached for Eleanor's hand, as she stood stock-still in the middle of the drive; hearing the last vestige of exhaust noise die away. He saw she was biting her lip, wasn't sure if it wasn't a moist eye, she'd never before been separated from her girl before, not for this projected period of time.

"They'll be fine. All part of growing up. Another coffee?"

She shook her head, soundlessly, but followed him into the kitchen and started busying herself clearing away the breakfast things. He left her to it, picked up the Saturday paper, brought up from the village by Reg as a favour, and vanished into the sitting room, only to see a new drawing propped up on the mantelpiece – a small one, but evocative, of him, sitting on that log up on the Plain. She'd completed it from the essence of her sketch, done some colour wash and detailed in crayon, an admixture of media that seemed to suit it well. He picked it up, looked carefully at the minutiae of the lines, and how exquisitely careful she'd been with his figure. He turned it over, and on the back, an inscription. *'For my Pa, the best, with all my love, Your Jocelyn, your Jo.'* She must have crept in with this before breakfast, the devious little madam. He didn't know whether to laugh or cry, but he felt something in his eye.

"Eleanor!" He moved back towards the kitchen. "You know about this?"

"About what, darling?" She met him, wiping hands on a tea towel. "What is it?" She took the little drawing from him. "Oh, how lovely!" She looked at him, at his eyes watering, and suddenly, inevitably, burst into tears.

"Hey, El. You'll have me crying as well!" He rescued the paper, held it out of harms way. "I think we're going to have to organise a contract with Ben. All these drawings she's doing. Let's get them done while she's away." He smoothed the tears away with a gentle hand, gave her his large white hankerchief so she could blow her nose.

"Sorry. It's just that…"

"I know. Come on, my girl. Have you done?" She nodded. "Then we'll go round the garden."

* * *

All her favourite flowers were smiling. The shrubs, gently moving in the morning breeze, gave an impression of waving at her, and the grass was soft under their feet. She kicked off her pumps and walked barefoot. Above, through the upper branches of the old beech a single aircraft trail, and just a few white fluffy edged clouds. She caught sight of a daring thistle amongst the phlox that Betty had so admired, and ejected it. Betty!

"David, do you think Felicity would allow Betty to come over?"

He turned his attention back to her from his scrutiny of the upper branches of the beech. He didn't want to think there was an incipient problem. "Betty? I don't know. Maybe, why?"

"Oh, just a sudden thought. She's so keen on the garden, and Jo seemed to ignore her after the garden party. Perhaps she might like to spend a day with us, help look at the changes we may have to work out if we put the dramatics back." Her fingers were at her chin, a sure sign she was cogitating.

He smiled. "You want another girl about – to keep you company. I know you. All right, I'll phone Felicity. We need to find out when we'll see ourselves in print. Back in a while."

Maybe Dave was right. Betty to be a stand-in? She strolled on, reached the paddock, and leant on the fence to survey the orchard beyond. The near-noonday sunlight was shimmering on the canopy of the apple trees, giving emphasis to the dark green shade below, just the sparse gaps shedding spears of light onto the rough grass. Jocelyn had hardly been up here since Julie's first night with them. What had changed? She opened the gate, crossed the paddock, aware she'd left her shoes off, trod carefully to avoid the stony patches. Under the old apples there was that palpable air of tranquillity, the relaxing feel unsurpassed by even the nicest bits of the garden below. Standing alone, taking deep breaths, there was no difficulty in understanding Jo's fascination with the place. She used to just lie on her back, over there, didn't she? Eleanor moved, with an unconscious motivation, to the place, and crouched down, feeling the grass. Her daughter lay here, just staring at the trees above, sometimes for half an hour or more.

What did she achieve? Carefully, smoothing her ample skirt beneath her, she stretched out in the same place, as near she could imagine, cupping the back of her head on her hands, to see if there was anything that would connect. The branches above, still moving gently, had a calming effect, and the warmth and the quiet lulled her, to the point where she must have dozed off.

…There were people moving about, figments of her imagination, the old shed seemed to be newer, there was a small child running over the grass, a basket full of apples freshly picked, then a handsome young man was offering her a hand, to pull her up from the grass, he looked ever so much like Nigel; a young woman appeared behind him, in a lovely white dress, so like her daughter…

She woke up, startled, and the images evaporated amongst the trees.

"Eleanor! Whatever are you doing down there?" David stood over her, offering her his hand to help her up. "Doing a Jocelyn, are we? Did you doze off?"

She lifted her head to squint up at him. Moving her arms, she found she'd got pins and needles, and started to rub the circulation back before taking a proffered hand and being hoisted to her feet.

"Weird, David. I just wanted to see what Jo saw in lying stretched out here, next thing I knew you were talking to me, but I must have had a sort of dream – with Nigel, and Jo, and the old shed being a new shed, then some apple baskets, and a…" she broke off. "Oh Lord, there was a young child as well! Have I been staring at the future or the past? I wonder if Jo had these – hallucinations. Weird," she repeated. "Best go and get some lunch, I think. It's late. Did you reach Felicity?"

"I did. The magazine we're in gets published in two weeks time, but she's letting us have a proof copy. Betty would love to come over – I spoke to her and got the impression she's a bit miffed that Jo hadn't talked to her, so I explained about Julie and that seemed to put things right. So, tomorrow, you've got a girl back, if only for the day. Felicity will bring her over about tenish, then I had an idea we'd invite her for supper, which went down well as hubby will have gone back to his workaday science research pad. Was that okay?"

"Well, provided we can dream up something sophisticated. I guess she'd appreciate a bit more than cheese and biscuits!"

"Likely. We could do one of those pasta things, you know, smoked salmon and prawns and so on? Sundried tomatoes, and a good bottle of Chianti?" He must have had a flirty chat with the woman, thought Eleanor. Not to worry, it'll take his mind off missing Jo. A little chirp of a tremor went down her spine, thinking of how they were getting on. They'd just about be at Cherbourg by now.

* * *

In fact, they had already docked, having completed the four hour crossing from Poole, a last minute change from the earlier idea of going from Portsmouth, and were sitting in the car waiting their turn to drive off the ferry. Amongst those who cast admiring glances at the car, there were also those who envied the driver his companions, unsurprisingly, for both girls and Mrs Summers – Dylys, the girls found out she was christened – had spent a fair amount of the journey across on the upper decks with the fresh breeze playing with their skirts and hair, while Edward had taken his own little sketch pad and sat unobtrusively on the boat deck drawing cartoons of passengers to amuse himself and pass the time. It had been a pleasant crossing, fortunately, despite the haze impinging on the view of other vessels and the approaching French coast.

Easing the big Bentley onto the quayside, Edward had no problem with the French officialdom, being the character he was and with such an *auto* no one wanted to be a problem. Jocelyn, not being a driver, had no concerns whether they were on the right or left, but they knew Dylys didn't much care for being on the outside seat and not having a steering wheel in front of her. Edward knew his way, he'd been here many times afore, and they were out of the port before they'd had a chance to take note that *this was France!* Edward took them through the old town, the flower-filled market square, did a detour up the hilltop fort so the girls could look down on the busy port below, and then on to the Musée Thomas-Henry so Jo could get an idea about Millet's portraits.

* * *

Saturday afternoon was a strange one for Eleanor. David retreated to the garage to complete a routine service on the Jaguar, leaving her on her own, for the first time for ages. No daughter to find jobs for, to share jokes with, to tease or comfort. Half-heartedly she got out her little fork and commenced loosening the soil in the long border, really just to make it look better, rather than for any productive reason. Every now and again she'd cast a glance back at the distant line of trees where the orchard was, and wonder about what she'd dreamt – if it was a dream, or a just a figment of imagination. She recalled Jo's talk of something similar. The place was casting a spell on them, but there was no malice or dread in the occurrences, nothing Tolkienish about them. Halfway through the afternoon Mike arrived in a beaten up Toyota pick-up truck, and David met him on the drive. In the back he had a collection of tools and a fold-up workbench. There was a consultation about getting closer to the old shed with the wheels, and one idea was going up the lane, and then making a gap in the hedge to drive across the orchard. Eleanor had wandered across by now and being privy to this conversation, promptly applied her veto on the idea.

"Definitely not. We're not having anyone drive across the orchard, Mike. Let's ask Derek if we can cross his field. The shed's just on the boundary, so we can make a gap there if you like. I'll phone him, he likes me." With a raised eyebrow at this statement, David concurred. Mike wasn't bothered so long as he didn't have to haul things across the paddock from here. Eleanor went, to return quarter of an hour later, looking a little flushed.

"He's a card, that one. If you ever leave me for Felicity I know where I can go. He says yes, but I owe him. So just watch it, David!! Out of the drive, Mike, next turn to the left, up the little track, the field gate should just be on a latch, then keep to the hedge line, he says. Top of the field, that's where the shed is."

"I'll come with you, Mike. Open the gates. See you up there, Eleanor?"

"No, I don't think so. I've had my fill of the orchard today, thanks. I'll have tea on the go at half four."

* * *

They were back before the deadline; it had been so easy. Mike had even offered to haul back some of the accumulated rubbish to lessen the amount they had to burn, so the back of his Toyota resembled a scrap dealer's truck. At least he stayed long enough to swallow a large mug of tea, then typically, just raised one hand in farewell and went, the parting shot "See y'Monday" all that was needed to reassure David and Eleanor all would go according to plan. Going back into the kitchen, having seen him off, realisation hit them. No girls.

"I wonder if she'll ring." Eleanor's wistful query echoed David's unspoken thought. They looked at each other, half in concern, and half in comedy.

"What are you going to do, El? She's only been gone ten hours!"

"Paint. That's what I'll do, paint."

"*Paint?*" The incredulous tone of his voice made her giggle. "*What* are you going to paint?"

She took him by the hand and tugged him into the hall. "See? *I did those!* If your daughter can draw, I can paint. Somewhere I've still got some brushes. The oils may have dried up by now, but we can remedy that. I'm going to give it a go, Dave."

"Do you know, I'd just about forgotten those, El., to my chagrin. I'm sorry, my darling. Where are your brushes and things?"

"Probably in the attic with the old books and Jo's early toys. You don't have to go and look, Dave, we can do that another day. I've had enough. Early night."

296

"It's not seven o'clock, El."

"Don't call me El."

"Sorry. You call me Dave. I love you, Eleanor, What next, then?"

"Silly question. I'm going to get a shower."

"No supper?"

"Bring the wine bottle, maybe some cheese and biscuits. And the phone."

"Sure?"

"Very. Lock the doors."

David selected a smooth red, put the water biscuits, the butter and some of Eleanor's favourite Jarlsberg on a tray, and put it on the hall table. The shower started to run; he'd leave her to it for half an hour while he watched a programme he'd earmarked on the television. It would take her that long to work her way through wash, hair wash, dry and powder and all the rest. The programme was reasonably interesting, so the half hour easily went; he doused the lights, picked up the tray, and climbed the stairs. The shower had been off some time. The lights in the bedroom were only just on the dimmer; despite the late summer evening daylight was still good enough to see by. His Eleanor was a curled shape under the bed covers, a spread of damp hair on the pillow, and a gentle regular lift and fall in time with heavy breathing. She was asleep, bless her. Oh well. He crept back downstairs, turned the television on again, settling himself down in front of an old James Bond film. Some time later, an hour or two, he woke up, fuzzy and with a bit of a head; the phone was ringing. Somehow he managed to stagger out to the hall, picked up the base phone.

"Pa? It's Jo!"

"Hiya, girl. Are you all right? Safe and sound?"

"Yes, and yes. We're fine, Pa. We're in this lovely old farmhouse, up in the hills above Etretat, on the Normandy coast. It's a super place, Pa. We've just had a lovely meal, Dylys is a *super* cook. I can see why Edward is keen on her. Can I speak to Mums?"

"Not without waking her up, Jo, dear. She's collapsed in a

heap, gone to bed. We've got a busy day tomorrow – 'cos your Mums is missing her girl I've had to find a substitute. Betty's coming for the day and we've invited Felicity for supper."

"Oh. Oh well. Give her my love, won't you Pa, and keep those beady eyes off Felicity's you know whats. I'll call you Monday evening if you're busy tomorrow. Love you Pa, Night, night." The phone went dead. David pulled a face. Two lost brownie points. Betty coming for the day without Jo's prior approval, and her Mums not available! Hope it won't spoil her day tomorrow. He went quietly back upstairs and found his wife awake and waiting for him.

"Was that Jo?"

"Yes, my darling. Sorry, I thought you still asleep. She sends her love, she's fine, eaten well, and seems cheerful; she'll phone in again on Monday. Do you want some supper now?"

"Don't think so, not now. Come to bed, my darling, I need a cuddle."

* * *

Jocelyn closed her phone up, and reflected on what Pa had said. Mums was missing her girl! As for finding a substitute, there wasn't anything wrong in having Betty over, actually she was a bit conscious stricken she hadn't got in touch with her before they'd left. Good old Mums, making up for her. Felicity, she'd been *so* helpful she deserved a supper at the least, so all in all it was good to think they'd got on with things. Was she missing them? No, not really, not at the moment. Julie was here, and Mrs Summers – Dylys – was a real bundle of fun now they'd got over the 'former pupil/college Head of Year' bit. She was tired though; it had been a long, long day. Edward had been the life and soul of the trip; she couldn't fault him for his attention and his concern for them all. After that tour round Cherbourg they'd high tailed it for Etretat, reaching their little gîte – a farmhouse on the western side of the town – well before dark, but it was pretty late and rather black now. She rejoined the others, settled into those cosy settees in the raftered family room, with just oil lamps for light. *So atmospheric!*

"All well at the family *maison, ma chérie?"* Edward looked up from behind his copy of 'Le Monde', picked up in Cherbourg. Obviously he adopted the 'when in Rome, etc.' principle; it was highly likely both Julie and her were going to be a good deal more proficient in French by the end of this week than they'd bargained for. Jocelyn did her best.

"*Mais oui, er, tout bien, merci."* Then she bust into giggles. "I'm not very good at French I'm afraid. It seems so strange, leaving Wiltshire just this morning, and now we're here." Glancing around, there was Julie, asleep, Dylys with her head in a paperback and only Edward really taking any notice.

"Have no worries, dear Jocelyn. It will all fall into place, I assure you, but may I suggest you two young ladies should retire? We will breakfast – *le petite dejeuner* – at half eight. I have in mind a brief tour of familiarisation, and then, dependant on the light, perchance, our first *construction*. So..."

She took the hint. "Julieeee." She gently held the girl's shoulder, and the dark haired girl stirred.

"Wa – oh, sorry, was I... yes, oh. S'pose we'd best get to bed!" She struggled up out of the depths of the soft cushions. "Good night, Edward, Dylys."

"Sleep well, girls," Dylys smiled up from her chair. Edward nodded at them and resumed his reading. Tomorrow would be a good day; he could feel it in his bones.

* * *

The two girls were sharing a room, at the top of the outdoor staircase, under the wide eaves of the tiled extension to the main building. Atmospheric certainly, seen by the light of the small wattage lamp. Two mattresses on wooden frames and plenty of duvet covers, but it wasn't cold. Neither girl was in a chatty mood, both were far too tired. Julie merely peeled off her clothes, stretched once, dropped her lengthy nightdress over her head, collapsed onto her bed and was out like the proverbial light. Jocelyn took a moment, sitting on the edge of her bed, to allow her brain to return to idle mode. She took her time to undress, trying hard not to think. One self-portrait, that's all it was, as a schoolgirl, and here she was, in France, first time away from home without her Mums, or Pa, and she didn't feel at all concerned, it was all *so right* somehow. She glanced at Julie, now fast asleep, and loved her; then she thought of Nigel, and that was even better. About to slip her own nightie on, she very nearly didn't bother, but the thought of an uncertain duvet cover ensured she did. Somehow, she had to get that light out and find her bed again without barking her shins.

* * *

Edward Petersen put his paper down, relaxing into his seat. It all felt very right, with the soft glow from the oil lamps and the characteristic scent of the old timbers added to the comfort of the informality around, nothing modern, nothing too tidy, just peace and history all mixed up, like a glorious palette of oils. Dylys caught his glance, returned her knowing smile, picked up the worn handwoven bookmark and put it carefully into her place.

"Happy, Edward dear? You look very much at home."

"Aye, you see me as I am. There is much compensation for crossing the Channel. The French way of life can have much to recommend it, dear lady. Would you appreciate a nightcap? Cognac, perhaps, or Calvados?"

"Calvados would be nice. But Edward, these girls; I know we've discussed Jocelyn's potential, and so on, but what about Julie? I knew her in college as a well-rounded, mature sort of a girl with quite some potential, but now I'm not as sure. What's your thought?" On holiday they may have been, moving their own relationship a step further into the bargain, but once a teacher, the future of young people in their care was always a matter of concern. Dylys had known the pair for three years; Edward probably a little longer, and despite having no formal need to consider that future, neither would have dismissed their interest. Edward found his precious Calvados bottle and poured out two not ungenerous measures.

He handed Dylys her glass and toasted her. "Your health,

dear lady. May our sojourn be suitably satisfactory and sensible to all aspects!" His smile broadened, the nearest thing to what could be described as a fully blown grin. "An assessment? You feel this an appropriate time?"

"Yes, Edward," Dylys sipped appreciatively. "Just so that we know how we handle things. I want to think these two lovely girls turn out to be a credit to the College – but especially to us. Let's just see what we can do for them, eh?"

"Julie – her mother, an academician, tragically, very tragically, killed as the result of a road traffic accident. Her father, unfortunately, is remote from the girl, so she has had the proverbial carpet removed. She is intelligent, thoughtful, and, I believe soft hearted. She's nicely proportioned and moves with considerable grace. Apart from that, she can't draw."

Dylys chuckled. "Trust you, Edward, but well done; now, Jocelyn?"

"Jocelyn. Ah, our Jo. Lovely girl, draws like an angel, full of life, has a deeper side to her, and an uncanny instinct for her sitter's feelings that she can get onto paper. Blessed with parents who dote on her without spoiling her. She has a lovely bohemian sort of touch, you know. She'll go far, that one. Roberta is going to publish prints of one of her drawings, subject to parental consent; she's already sold and there will be more to follow. Dylys, my dear lady, I am privileged to have had some small part to play in her development," and the nearest thing to a laugh, "I gave her the first charcoal sticks!"

She raised an eyebrow at him. "Is she naturally talented, or was it your superb tuition? And should she abandon her almost certain place at university – Reading, no less, or change to that easiest of generalities, a 'History of Art' degree at another redbrick? She also has an almost sisterly care for Julie – I've seen them together – who may well forego her Business Economics place for something a good deal less stressful. Not that I blame her, I despise these money raising 'products' we're forced to sell to gullible students to make ends meet, but don't you dare quote me!"

Edward snorted. "Most of these new-fangled courses are

'products' as you call them. I've no time for them, nor the administration that believes all our children should spend more money than sense on paper I wouldn't use for the outside privy. 'History of Art', you say; yes, yes, good if all you want to know is which museum exhibits which Goya. Better than Business Economics though. Top up?" He waved his glass towards the bottle.

"Thank you, dear Edward. You'll have to buy another!"

"No better place, Dylys, no better place. These girls – apart from giving them a nice introduction to the delights of '*la belle France*', and thus ensuring they are adequately fed and watered – should be given every opportunity to express themselves, so perchance we can offer guidance *once* we know their inclinations. And I will most definitely paint to show them at their very best – the weather should hold good, and I have an *Inspiration!* But now – dear lady…'

Dylys smiled at him. Such a gentleman, but once he was '*inspired*' he certainly was an artist. She started to feel her baser instincts beginning to glow. "Lead on, dear Edward."

FOURTEEN

Jo was the first to stir. The light was different, totally different. Golden, not grey, or even light green. A deep breath; seeing the shaft of sunlight through the shutter shine across the bare floorboards and slant onto the peeling distempered wall, to be reflected onto the multicoloured quilts over their beds.

"Julie?" Her dark hair strewed over the unbleached grey cotton pillow was about all Jo could see of her. "Juuulleeee?" Her covers were moving with her gentle breathing. Jocelyn pushed her quilt away, put toes to the floor and instantly recalled how her father played doggo tricks. "Julie! First day in France, love. Time to get up," and was rewarded by the girl rolling over, in imminent danger of tipping herself off the low mattress, but at least awake.

"What sort of time is it, Jo? It's a bit bright, isn't it? Have we overslept?" Struggling to sit up, she rubbed her eyes. "Not a bad bed, really. I don't know why I thought French beds were hard, but I slept like the proverbial. You?"

Jo brushed her hair back off her forehead. "Not bad. Jolly hungry now. D'you think we should get dressed?"

"Might as well. Race you!"

Jocelyn rolled back on the bed and hooted. "Like schoolgirls in the dorm! Really, Julie, be your age! We don't really know what's planned yet anyway. I say we wait and see. Tell you what, sleepyhead; I'll get my hand in. You stay put, sit like you're just waking up and I'll do something quick, do you mind? If I can find my pad."

"You're not serious! Me, looking like this! You're mad."

Jo scrabbled in her bag and found the part-used pad she'd stuffed in at the last moment; at least she had the pencils handy. "It's all a bit sexy, Julie, sure you don't mind?"

"If I'm thinking of being a model, I'll have to get used to it. This okay?" With an adroit wriggle she slipped a nightdress strap off her shoulder and hitched the quilt thing round her legs, messed up her hair and yawned.

"Fantastic! If I can…" Julie froze, and Jo sketched furiously. The thing she really liked was how the light fell on her subject, the dust motes accentuating the rays from the shutters. Rather like a Dutch Old Master, she thought, beginning to emphasis the rounder curves. Working fast, she had most of what she needed in place before there was a tap on the rickety door, and Dylys appeared, neatly dressed in slacks and sweater, not a hair out of place.

"Morning girls! Julie, what do you look like! Jocelyn, you're not drawing her *again?* And before breakfast! Come *on* girls! Edward's brewing coffee. Five minutes?"

"What should we wear, Dylys? What're we doing?" The last few lines did enough to satisfy her and her nod to Julie allowed the girl to stand up and stretch. "Not that we've got too much choice."

"Don't know, to be perfectly honest. Just anything; we'll plan the day over coffee." She left them to it, and within five minutes both were down for croissants and the freshly brewed coffee. Edward was in fine form.

"Top of the morning to you both! I trust you slept well? First night *en Francais?* Nice light this morning. I suggest we see what the beach has to offer. You know the cliffs here are celebrated? I claim rights to the first assignment, dear Miss Danielleson, after which we'll set you a task to see if your brushwork will pass muster. Pass the croissants, Dylys."

"Your protégé has already started her day, Edward," Dylys handed over the basket via the girls so at least they had something to be going on with before Edward polished off the rest. "Our Julie's already earning her keep." Her look towards Jo was a smiley one; she was beginning to really take to the girl, well, both of them, actually.

"In what manner, may I ask?" Edward raised his bushy eyebrows interrogatively. "A bedroom farce?" This Jocelyn was a continuous surprise. "A privileged glance, *si vous plais mam'selle?*"

Jo had sort of anticipated his enquiry; at least she wanted to show she was still on the ball and had her pad tucked behind her, bringing it out now with a flourish. "*Julie, ma chérie, en déshabille en chambre! Voilà!*" and handed it on via Dylys to Edward. Then she wasn't so sure about things, because he frowned, holding it out at arm's length.

"*Dishabille! Très déshabille! Vous, non,*" he looked directly at Julie, who promptly started to blush. "*Tu es charmant, charmant absolument! Mais, c'est trop petit.* In other words, my dear Jocelyn, it's too small." The frown vanished in favour of a beaming smile, and he handed it back. "Your task for the day. Repeat, please, *in oils!*"

"But I've never used oil paints!"

"*Exactament!* That's what this week is all about, my girl. You can experiment. You have the subject, the *inspiration,* and the light. Excellent! More coffee?"

She couldn't argue. She took a refill on autopilot, mind racing. Oils? "What about a canvas and so on? Are you going to stand over me, all day? What are Dylys and Julie going to do? What happens if I mess it all up?"

Now Dylys was smiling, knowing Edward's mind. "You won't *mess* it up, Jo. You'll be on your own so you can sort out your mistakes – *if* you make any – in private."

"But..."

"But nothing. I shall take the fair Julie away, with my excellent and punctilious chaperon, request her to er, um, shed a few clothes, and we'll see what she looks like on the beach with this admirable light on the water. You may stay here and try and emulate a Dutchman. See?"

Jo was not at all sure, but with breakfast things tidied away, Edward dug his blank canvases out of the car's cavernous boot, together with a brand new set of oils and brushes. With due ceremony, a slight bow and an Edwardian grin, he presented the box to Jocelyn, together with a newly-stretched canvas.

"These are for you, my dear. My contribution to your education – or rather, your *continuing* education." Dylys coughed, gently. "Ahem, yes, *our* contribution. I have rather erred, sadly, in not bringing two easels, so we'll have to improvise. One thing; have you a smock? Oils have an uncanny knack of going everywhere, and I mean, everywhere."

"I'll find something that doesn't matter. But all this…" she knew something of the cost of oil paints. "It's extremely kind of you!"

"Ah, yes, vested interest, d'see. You do well, then as *my* pupil, *I get the credit!* Now, if we are going to have a good day, best get started. Julie, my other lovely girl, are you prepared to carry on in modelling role, and, if so, have you a slip or something that you don't mind getting damp and sandy? Or should we forage for something in the market?" Now things were getting underway, he was becoming quite animated. "Dylys?"

"Something light and cottony – is that what you had in mind? We'll pick something up in the market, I'm sure. So long as you have a decent…" A knowing look at Julie elicited the coy smile.

She nodded. "I think so," she said, and added, "This is quite exciting. Poor Jo – you'll be stuck indoors and I'll be out on the beach!"

"Her turn will come," Edward was getting anxious. "Best be going, got to get a good spot."

He hustled his two ladies out to the car, and Jocelyn was on her own.

At the back of the farmhouse she discovered an attempt at a type of lean-to pergola, with old cast iron chairs and a elemental table home-made from rough hewn planks. She rummaged around and found a flimsy old door that would lean up against the table and form an easel of sorts, managing to hold the canvas in place on the cross member. Then she opened up the box, and stared at the rows of tubes.

Such wonderful names! Burnt Sienna, Carmine Red, Umber… The brushes weren't very flexible, nothing like her watercolour ones. And then there was the little bottle of turps and the pristine palette. A strange feeling, mixed up between awe and nerves, gave her spine the heebie-jeebies, and she remembered the comment about the smock. Had she got anything suitable? She'd said she had, but what?

In her room, she flung the contents of her bags onto the rumpled quilt, and turned them over. Nothing really, apart from an old sweater and that long cotton skirt. Well, they'd have to do. Off with the blouse and the better skirt, and into the scruff kit. No. *Not the* sweater. It was getting warm, too warm, and she went one step further. At least bare skin was washable.

How does one start? Pencil? Try. She sketched an outline, gently at first, getting the feel, then bolder, soft, soft pencil. The outline grew, eye flicking from sketch to canvas, adding detail, before she brought herself up sharply. This wasn't a *sketch* on canvas, it was just a guide. Instinct told her what to squeeze out onto the palette, how to hold it. A pensive selection of a brush, then away she went, starting with the quilt covered bed; that didn't matter so much. Then Julie, in the lightest of pinks, whites, a dash of yellow, whoops – not that bit. She went to her bottle of turps and a little finger in the cloth, carefully, tentatively, smudged and wiped. Botheration! A harder rub, a bit of drier cloth; there, that was better. She tried again, finding the oil spread a bit too readily on the turps dampened patch, and learnt, quickly. Her penchant for detail wasn't doing her any good in this medium, and so another notch up the learning curve; try more informality. Those brush strokes looked a bit ragged. Perhaps another brush. There, that was better. She painted on, beginning to revel in this splodgy medium.

Gradually, the morning wore on, the light was moving round, and she felt peckish. Goodness! Was that the time? Taking a step or two back, viewing her progress critically, nearly falling over a chair, and conscious that oils *did get* places they shouldn't, she sat down on the errant chair and wiped her front. Perhaps turps on tits wasn't a good idea, though, and she giggled at her pun. Maybe there were some biscuits or something in that corridor place Dylys was using as a store cupboard, and her thoughts took her on some exploration.

Three shelves and a couple of tins later she discovered a

roll of ginger snaps; took three then another one for luck. Munching reflectively, she went back outside, and the heat of the early afternoon hit her after the cool of the house, despite not having anything on top. Oh well, in for a penny, or was it a centime – no, cent now they were in Euros – she giggled again and stepped out of her skirt. Julie's seductive pose she'd created seemed to beckon her on, and there were funny stirrings somewhere inside. She flexed her tummy muscles in an effort to dispel them, and picked up the flatter brush to carry on with the rest of the background. Time seemed to fly by, and the ginger biscuits hadn't gone very far. How long till they got back? At least there was something fairly presentable to show for her efforts, though goodness knows what Edward would make of it. Had she used too much paint? The tubes looked rather the worse for wear and there was still a lot – too much – paint on the palette, but at least she'd cottoned on to the way the colours ran and mixed on the board. It really was quite addictive. Head on one side, she took another contemplative look. Hmmm, not sure…

…that sounded like the car! Heavens, she wasn't presentable – far from it – and oil paint everywhere, on her arms, her tummy, and still dabs on her front, so she couldn't dive back into her skirt and sweater – it was far too hot anyway, and she longed for an old coat. Too late anyway!

"Hiya! Jocelyn?" Julie's voice, sounding cheerful. "Out the back?"

"Yep. Where's Edward? – and Dylys?"

"Dylys stopped off to get some more supplies; Edward's getting the paintings out the car, why?"

Julie emerged into the space, and saw. "Oh. I see! Starkers, are we? Hang on, I'll fetch something." She vanished, to be heard rummaging upstairs. She came back with an old, rather long, blouse cum shirt thing and threw it at her friend. "Try that; it's past its sell by date anyway."

Shrugged into it and buttoned up the front, it reached to just below her pants, giving her a very Brigitte Bardot look. Edward appeared, clutching a canvas; took no notice of Jo's state of undress, merely propped the canvas on another chair and went back to presumably fetch another.

Julie studying Jocelyn's efforts; remarked "Bit sort of, er, smudgy, isn't it?" She stood back from it, frowning. "At least I don't look too revealing. Have a look at that one," she said, pointing with a toe.

Jocelyn already had, seeing Julie in a long diaphanous white flowing thing, carelessly belted, standing back to viewer, staring out at the sea and the cliffs beyond. The way in which Edward had caught the essence of the water, the flow of the dress and the girl's feminity was amazing; left her own efforts drab by comparison.

"Well, girl?" Edward was back with his second frame. "Had a good day?" His eyes met hers, and twinkled. "Bit warm, was it?" The next chair was pressed into service, and this time she saw the promenade, the colour of plants and paintwork, the people and the two girls in the foreground, Dylys and Julie, obviously, hand in hand, again with backs to the viewer, but just turning, as though they were saying farewell. She liked it, the expression of warmth, the cosmopolitan mix, the image of curiosity of why the girls were looking back, and could see how the brush strokes gave the picture its life.

"I think I've wasted my time, Edward, seeing these. They're lovely."

Viewing her efforts and wrinkling his cheeks, Edward pursed his lips. "Mmmm."

"I'm sorry. Rather messed up a canvas, haven't I?"

"Not sure, Jocelyn. This *is* a first attempt, and has much more to commend it than maybe I might have expected. Let it dry overnight and we'll see what tomorrow brings. Perhaps you'd best not let Dylys see your costume, eh?" She had been dismissed, and Julie followed her upstairs.

"He's very discreet, isn't he?" Julie whispered. "I felt quite comfortable with him, you know. Dylys had to chase off some loutish types who whistled at me, but otherwise I've enjoyed my day."

"So have I, I suppose, but I'm better with pencils – and watercolours. I'm not sure oil's my thing." She slipped out of the coverall and reached for something to wipe the oil marks off.

"Here, let me," Julie found her nail varnish remover and began to do a far better job; this brought the girls into close proximity, and unexpectedly as their eyes met; Julie blushed, and Jocelyn felt those tummy twinges again. "Oh, Jo! I *do* so enjoy being with you. Hold me?"

There was something, Jocelyn could feel the static charge between them, and it bothered her. Nevertheless, she put her arms around her friend, and hugged. She felt Julie's lips on her shoulder, and a tingle went down her spine. "I'd best get dressed, Julie. Dylys'll be back. We need to eat."

The kiss repeated, Julie drew back, gave a coy seductive sort of smile, and left Jocelyn alone.

"Phew!" she thought, "steameeee!" and quickly made herself presentable. "I'd better watch myself. I know, I'll ring Nigel. Then Mums." Which she did.

* * *

At the Old Vicarage, Eleanor was finishing putting the meal together for the supper party, finding it a wee bit difficult adjusting to not catering for Jo, when the phone rang. Her heart did a bounce with instinctive knowledge it was Jo. "David!" She yelled; he was still outside with Betty. "Maybe it's Jo!"

And it was. "My *darling!* Are you all right? What's the weather like? Are you being fed proper? How's Julie? What are…"

"Hey, Mums! Steady on! A question at a time! Course I'm all right. I'm fine, so's Julie. Yes, Dylys is looking after us – (hope it's a nice supper, she thought) – it's been rather warm, and I've done my first oil painting – well, sort of, Edward made me do a copy of a sketch I did of Julie. It's a bit sort of murky, though. He's done a wonderful sexy thing – well, maybe not *sexy* sexy, but very er, feminine, of Julie, by the sea, and a great one of the promenade, bit sort of Cézanne-ish, I think. Or is it Millais? I don't know, but it's nice. He's going over my painting with me tomorrow," she drew a breath, to go on at a pace. "Mums. I rang Nigel. He's coming over; I think he said the day after tomorrow, for a couple of days. He says he misses me. And he wants me to go and spend a week with him in Norfolk before the new term starts? What d'you think, Mums?" There was an abrupt silence. Eleanor had a quick think. Jocelyn's exam results were due in a couple of weeks; they had still to agree what she should do; there was the studio to consider, and Felicity's offer to advertise Jo's prints, was Nigel a complication or an asset?

"Can I talk things over with your father, Jocelyn? This isn't a bit too sudden, is it? I mean, he's only known..."

"*Mum!*" Jo's voice almost squeaked. "You're being very Mumsish! Let me speak to Pa!"

"You can't dear, he's still outside. Look, I'll ask him to ring you back. We've got Betty here, remember, and Felicity's due here any moment, for supper. That all right?"

Eleanor could sense her daughter's frustration, imagined she heard a sigh. "Oh, all right. Give Betty my love, and regards to Felicity. Keep an eye on Pa if *she's* around. Love you, Mums."

The phone went dead.

Eleanor had to smile, her daughter, telling her about Felicity! Within minutes, David and Betty returned to the house, having been up to the orchard for a last look at the old structure before the work started in earnest tomorrow morning. Eleanor sent Betty off to clean up, and gave David the low down on Jo's call.

"So what do *you* think? If Nigel's going to France there's not a lot we can do – but Jo going to Norfolk for a *week!* Heaven knows what she'll get up to!"

David was much more matter of fact about the whole issue. "For one," he said, "Nigel's father is the local Rector, for another, we *know* the lad; and we both have confidence in *our* daughter, don't we? She is about to become eighteen, anyway, and legally her own person, so what's the problem?"

Eleanor collapsed into the kitchen chair Jo normally used, and David sensed she was near tears.

"Look, dear, we have to get used to it. She can't be tied to our – your – apron strings forever. Let's talk with Nigel – or his parents – if you're that bothered. Come on, El!"

"Don't call me El!" She rubbed her forehead. "Let me think it over." And totally forgot she'd told Jo she'd ask him to call her.

David patted her shoulder, and heard Felicity's car. "I'll meet her."

"Jo told me to keep an eye on you and *her*."

He laughed. "She would! Don't fret yourself. She may be decorative, but you're *my* girl," and with that he went out again. Betty came back in the kitchen; she'd been tactful and waited.

* * *

Felicity, as ever, was all beams and smiles, but tonight was dressed in a less casual manner. "Best frock, tonight, David. Like it?"

Certainly she looked ravishing, and he said so, rewarded with a kiss for his compliment. "I've brought you these. Advance copies. Hot off the press. Hope you approve. Has my Betty been a good girl?"

"Of course. Kept Eleanor's mind off her missing daughter, but there's an element of fragility in her. Jo's got an admirer about, and Eleanor's not happy. Doesn't want to lose her affections to another."

"Ah. Hmmm. That lad Nigel?" She raised an elegant eyebrow. David nodded. "Then there's not a lot wrong, is there? If my judgement's anything to go by, and I've seen a few prospects in my time, he's a good 'un. Not many like *him* about. She's a lucky girl. Just hope my Betty manages to catch one as caring."

"Reassuring words, Felicity. Thanks. Bend Eleanor's ear some time, eh?"

She nodded in her turn. "Sure. Now lead on. The prospect of your wife's cooking has made me hungry. Have a bottle," she leant back into her open car and collected the three copies of the next month's magazine and the bottle of wine. "By the way. You know those prints? I think we need to up the numbers; there's lots of interest. Your Jo's going to be a wealthy girl if she keeps this up."

* * *

Supper was convivial, quite low key, but both Eleanor and David enjoyed Felicity's company; she had a great way of sparkling the conversation along, including Betty at every opportunity. Only Eleanor remained restrained, still worrying about Jocelyn, wondering what she was doing, how Nigel would fit in. She took the problem to bed with her, despite Felicity's parting shot about how lucky Jo was to have found a lad like Nigel. David could only put a comforting arm around her, allowing her to drift asleep, hoping she'd not wake too early. It had been a tiring day, but enjoyable enough. What was Jo doing now, he wondered, would she be asleep? He pictured her in his mind's eye, whispering "I love my girls" to himself before he, too, let sleep overtake him.

* * *

Jocelyn stirred, pulled her knees up to her chest, pushed an arm under her pillow and cosied up to her dreams. Nigel! Hugging Julie was okay, but not the same. Would Mums say she could go to Norfolk? Pa was okay, but he hadn't phoned her back, so Mums can't have asked him. Oh well. Would she have a studio when she went home? That apple painting; she must get on with it when the studio was ready. Felicity – how was she behaving, and were her prints selling? What about her exam results – what should she do? What should she do? The whole paraphernalia of mixed up thoughts went round and round, and rou… She slept.

* * *

Was it today when Nigel might appear, or tomorrow; she couldn't for the life of her remember now what it was he'd said, 'cos she'd been so upskittled by the thought he was coming specially to see *her!* Jocelyn's tummy contracted at the thought, hoping against hope that she would be able to convince him she was still the light of his life, unwittingly more as a direct result of having Julie around; for lurking in the back of her mind was that niggling jealous little nonsense over him showing too much concern for her dark-haired friend. Why she should be so bothered when boys had never figured in her life before to the same extent puzzled her – but then, he was the guy she'd rescued from the tree and the residual proprietorial interest must mean something, and she wasn't having Julie hijack him. Time to get up, anyway.

No sunlight this morning? Carefully negotiating the worn floorboards and their threat of splinters she padded across to the door and eased it open, trying to avoid the squeak of the rusty hinges that might wake Julie up; she wanted time on her own. The early morning sky was a veiled wreath of lacy mist – a prelude to another scorcher then. Down below her the bare earth and bits of scrubby vegetation were a backdrop to the old cart and that pile of useless looking timber, then the rickety fence, the rough track, and further on, the denser tree cover before the land dropped away to the deep grey blue of the sea. Three deep lungfuls of fresh morning air, with subtle hints of something botanical, couldn't be lemons or olives surely – she wasn't sure quite what grew round here – but it wasn't the same as *her* orchard, and got a twinge of homesickness. How was she going to get on with the review of her painting later on? Looking out over the landscape set out below her, she could see what sort of inspiration it had been for some of those names that echoed through the art classes; why Edward had settled on spending some of the summer break down here; but I'm not going to be a landscape painter, that's for sure; the emphatic thought cornered her mind. Yesterday's episode, interesting though it had been, left a funny sort of taste. Taste? Well, it was a bit more than a feeling. A sort of restlessness drove her down the stairs to get closer to the trees, the nearest to her orchard that she was going to get, but wandering around didn't inspire her. Until she heard what Edward had to say about her efforts, it was not going to be a fully decided thing. Back to dress, then, flitting around the scenery in her nightdress wasn't going to enthuse the natives.

* * *

Nigel, exasperated by the tedium of getting into London, wondered what he was doing. He'd promised the girl he'd go and see her in France, had mixed feelings about the whole idea, taken the plunge, seen it as an adventure, but the novelty was rapidly wearing off. The die was cast, however, past the point of no return, etc., etc. Sitting in the coffee shop at Waterloo prior to launching himself onto Eurostar, all the pros and cons got well and truly chewed, at the same time as the indifferent croissant. Jocelyn, Julie, both lovely girls, so the bottom line, the nub of it, was the buzz he'd get from their reaction. The tannoy jolted him into movement; boarding was starting for his train. At least the forward journey would be better; couldn't be much worse. Change in Paris, Cherbourg by early afternoon, d.v. Maybe he'd hire a car – hang the expense; it would reduce the hassle.

* * *

Morning at the Old Vicarage wasn't quite like a normal morning, because today the work was starting on the studio, therefore David scrambled out of bed without ceremony to ensure he was about before anyone turned up. Eleanor woke to relive last night's supper party, and Jo's request about Norfolk, so the memory of her failure to get David to call her back hit her like a big damp sponge. Her daughter wouldn't forgive her for that if she didn't do something, and she too, shot out of bed, falling over her nightdress hem and ending up in a heap on the floor, just missing cracking her head on the dressing table.

David heard the crash from downstairs and bounded back to ascertain the damage. Eleanor was still sitting on the floor, rubbing her elbow. "What *are* you doing?" He helped her up.

"Fell over my hem. David, phone Jo. I forgot to ask you,

last night. Speak to her about Nigel and Norfolk. Tell her she can go, anything, but I don't want to lose her!" Her arms were round him, and the warmth and softness of her pliant barely clad body was having its effect.

He hugged her, kissed her, and contained his feelings as best he could. "Okay, okay. You won't lose her. I'll phone her now, before the day gets going. Best get dressed, my darling, before I *undress* you. Breakfast?" She nodded, aware she wouldn't really have minded being *undressed,* as he called it, but sadly it was Monday morning.

He wasn't very confident that Jocelyn would have her phone charged up, let alone on at this hour of the morning, but no harm in trying. It rang the usual length of time before that banal voice told him what was so blindingly obvious – so he tried again, and, bingo, she answered!

"Pa? How did I guess it was you? How's Mums?"

"Apologetic, Jo. And a bit bruised."

"Why, Pa? Did you thump her for not telling you to ring?"

He laughed. "No, of course not; she fell over her nightie getting out of bed in a hurry to tell me to ring you because she forgot in the melee of the supper party last night. I gather you want to accept Nigel's invite to Norfolk?"

"Hmm, yes, I think so. He's supposed to be coming here tomorrow, I'll know better after that. But it might be nice. Could I?"

"Jo, you're as near eighteen as damn it, so you can make up your own mind, but thanks for asking, and of course you can go. Your Mums misses you though, and diving off again too soon after the French trip might upset her a bit. She'll probably get over it. What's the weather like over there?"

"Dry, and getting warmer by the minute, Pa. Thanks. Thanks for being *so* like you. Please give Mums a kiss for me, tell her I'll always love her... love you too. Must dash, coffee and croissants await. Speak to you tomorrow? Byeeeee."

Difficult, severing the ties that had grown and strengthened so much over the past few weeks and months, David had to admit to himself. He would miss his beautiful daughter as much as Eleanor, probably more in some ways, but if she was going to be her own person, then that's what was going to have to happen. Then he reconsidered, going slowly back upstairs; it wasn't so much as *severing* the ties as strengthening them still further, because if she was going to do her own thing she'd need as much if not more support, maybe more morally than physically. Maybe having her away from home was doing them all good; making them appreciate the relationship they had. In a better frame of mind he met Eleanor on the landing, and damn near swept her off her feet, as his love for her suddenly burst through him.

"Hey, hey, David, watch it, you'll have me on the floor again! What's come over you? How's our Jo?" She found herself near suffocated as he smothered her with kisses before dropping her back on her feet.

"She's fine. And I love you, silly girl!"

"So it seems!" she replied, with bruised lips But she was loads happier, inside and out. "You said yes?"

"I said yes. She needs her space, my darling, and she'll love us the better for it. Come on, I'm starving and it's a work day, remember."

* * *

The first thing Jo had done when she'd crept back into the *chambre* – occasionally trying French words – was to reach for her phone, and happily her father's call came in as soon as she'd switched it back on. Even after that brief conversation her day brightened up considerably, and with the smell of breakfast wafting up from below she couldn't wait to get started. Climbing into her newly borrowed shabby shirt thing and those denim shorts Mums had insisted she brought and now was glad she had, the next thing was rousing the sleeping Julie. Easy, she thought, grinned, and heaved the quilt off her. Woken like that, Julie wasn't impressed, and tugged her wayward nightdress back over random naked limbs.

"I'll have you for that!"

"Promises, promises! It's breakfast time! I'm off down. See you in a minute?"

"Hmmph!"

* * *

With another delightful continental breakfast behind them Dylys was commissioned to take Julie into the town for the morning so Jocelyn wouldn't be distracted whilst she had her painting criticised. They'd gone, and Jo wasn't feeling too happy at the prospect of her time with Edward and yesterday's effort, but it was a grin and bear it exercise. He'd not been terribly forthcoming at breakfast, though still pleasant and desperately polite; Jo assumed he was biding his time. Now it was crunch time.

"On my easel, Miss Danielleson – please, and if you would be so good as to explain what was in your mind, then, and now. No, not there, let us have some good light, across here, I think."

The canvas propped up, Edward folded his arms, put his head slightly to one side and waited. Jo reviewed her work, very unsettled; to do something she'd not done for ages; she bit her nails.

"I'm not sure I can. I do what my instincts tell me at the time, but I can't explain why."

She looked upset, so Edward eased off; let her relax by talking her through her choice of colours, her brushwork, and the way the paints should build and flow. With a sure hand, he added white and pale primrose to Jo's interpretation, an emphasis of light grey to the folds of the bed linen, finally some brighter yellow just to accentuate the sunlight, and stood back.

"See? You can always add, dear Jocelyn, but *never* subtract! Thickness works as well as brushstrokes to give you lift and depth. Look, here and here. Now come away from the canvas, look *beyond* the technicality and do you *enjoy* what you see?"

Standing back from her handiwork, as amended, it

suddenly came to life; she gulped and saw, not her friend Julie but a young girl freshly aroused from sleep. She had painted that?

Edward had his eyes on her expression and smiled. "You see? Different medium, but the same talent, Jo, putting soul into your subject." Raising a hand to silence her just as she was going to explain what she'd thought, "No, don't tell me. How you obtain your inspiration is *your* secret. Now, we need to start again. Choose a subject."

Jo was still staring at her first oil painting, watching Julie's enigmatic smile and the hint of seductiveness coming to life out of the canvas, and her mind went back to the dreams she'd had in the orchard, the strange effect that lay on her like a cloak, a mantle, a white dress, giving her a prickling sensation down the rib of her spine. If this was what happened to her after she'd created something like this, what was it going to do in the eyes and brains of other beholders?

"Jo?"

Edward's attitude to creations like hers must be different, it had to be, otherwise he would have surely seen the depth of wanting, the need for loving by the girl on the bed. That's what Jo had felt, the *wanting* in her Julie, the Julie who had lost her mother, and her connection with the realness of life. Jo knew now what was drawing them together; invisible threads of a need for a soak in human passion, call it love or sensuality, her still untried girlish emotions weren't able to complete an understandable definition.

"Jo. You're not in a trance, dear girl? It is good, you know, your painting. You have the makings of a style of your own, and I take my hat off to you."

The mention of the hat brought him back into focus, and Julie's painted eyes withdrew into the canvas. "Trance? Possibly. I... Julie's mother's death, sorry, it hit me, just then, how much she's lost. Sorry," she repeated herself, and tried to think what he'd asked, had said. "You really mean it, about this being good? You're not just being kind, are you?" She came back to the easel, and Edward watched her, recalling that fateful visit she had made to his little office next to the art room and announced she wanted to paint.

"Do you imagine, dear girl, I would say anything I did not mean? I have said your painting is good, and that is what I meant. However, in order to convince me that this not just a mere flash in the pan, a lucky chance, I want you to choose a subject, and this time I'll stand over you, guide your brushwork, which is to some all important." He'd captured her attention, as he went on. "Personally, I feel an artist should be free to use what actions suit the creation, the mood, but, and this is where we must regretfully accede to the *cognoscenti,* to be shown in some galleries one must adhere to certain accepted principles. Like using commas in the correct place in an essay, y'know." Jocelyn pulled a face, and Edward chuckled at her. "Perhaps unfair comparison, my dear girl, please accept my apologies, just had to make the point. Now, a subject?"

Silence, as she tried to think. It was as bad as studying a menu card, running through all the infinite possibilities, endeavouring to persuade brain and tummy to agree and then having to re-think because the starters clashed with the main course and it was too expensive anyway. Everything she'd done so far had been on a whim, an instinctive 'yes!' gutsy feeling, not considered, never analysed, she'd just got on with it, and it happened. Edward sensed her dilemma and uncertainty, inwardly smiling to himself as he'd been there too, a long time ago. When you had to paint for a living the discipline soon came on board, as it would for this young slip of a girl.

"Leave it with you for a short while, Miss Danielleson, Jocelyn. If it helps, try a sketch or two. When I return, we'll have another coffee. I have a passion for a certain delicacy from the *patisserie,* so I'll just take a stroll down to the village. Twenty minutes?" Without waiting for a reply, he picked up his Malacca cane and the room came in on her as his footsteps diminished on the stony path towards the village. She collapsed onto the old sofa thing, swung her legs up and studied her knees, not that they would give her inspiration. So far, everything she'd done had been of people, herself, her Mums, Felicity, Pa – bless him – even Nigel, and Julie, of course, dear lovely Julie. Never landscapes, or 'still life'; she could never see the sense of painting inanimate objects; cameras did the job far better. Landscapes? The image of the evening sky at home she'd rushed upstairs to capture that evening, and never finished. That was a watercolour job, never oils. How about the farmhouse itself? At least that would be a sort of 'look, this is where we've been' type of thing, and if it were simple, even in Van Gogh style? She tried to picture it in her mind's eye, closing her eyes to the room and Julie staring from her painted bed. Other images flicked into fuzzy focus, a bit like a slideshow, and the warmth, the comfort of the *chaise* and her early morning combined to gently drift her into sleep.

* * *

Nigel had found the connection down to Cherbourg remarkably easy, so his humour began to return, as well as heightening his anticipation of seeing the girls. No problem in hiring a little Renault either, though trying to understand Gallic directions to the gîte rather taxed his French. He wondered what might be on offer for lunch; he was starving, so perhaps it would be as well to take something up with him, in case. He'd see what was available in the next village, get some bread and maybe cheese, a bottle or two. Gosh, it was warm. He wound the window right down, and concentrated on this left-hand drive stuff. Just as well there wasn't anything like the traffic density of the UK – whoops, mind that scruffy old Citroen, looked like it was being driven by a ninety year old. Right, left into the market square, the guy had said; the farm track was off the right-hand corner – droit, that was right, wasn't it? He remembered 'Le Rive Gauche', so it must be right. Oh, and that looked like a bread shop...

* * *

She was having silly dreams again; in her subconscious mind she knew she shouldn't be sleeping like this, but images kept flitting in and out, all mixed up like a bag of salad, shaggy and stalky with red bits and white and green, dissolving into apples and trees and grass and... she woke, abruptly. There had been a noise, she was sure, and in getting up, all but fell off the sofa – *chaise* – with pins and needles in her lower arms where she'd had them behind her head. "Silly Girl," she said, out loud.

"Not in my eyes."

"Nigel! You horror! Oh, *Nigel!*" She couldn't believe it – but here he was, and she flung herself at him, almost jumping into his arms like Baby in *'Dirty Dancing'*.

"Hey, hey – you'll have me over!" He caught her, just, and swung her round. "Glad to see me then?"

"What do you think? Where did you spring from? How did you manage to find us – me?"

She was back on her feet and hoping he'd kiss her. Instead he was just holding her hands, but at least he was looking into her eyes. "I wasn't sure if was today or tomorrow you said. I'd forgotten once I'd put the phone down. Was that very bad of me?"

He kissed his fingers, planted them on her lips. "I'll forgive you. I found someone in the baker's place in the village. Your Mr Petersen. So we've brought the supplies. Fresh bread, cheese, olives, some apricot things that look far too fattening, and a couple more bottles of the local brew. Fancy lunch?"

"Edward? Oh! That's cheating!" She was behaving like a schoolgirl and she knew it, but then she was only seventeen, not a sophisticated uni girl he'd probably got tucked away up in Edinburgh. She let go of him and turned away. "Where is he?"

"Here, my dear girl. Just putting the wine in the cool. Your Nigel certainly came at an opportune moment. All we needed was to see the other two, but my guess is they'll be lunching out. So we'll go it alone, methinks." This Nigel was another side to the equation, and he still had to come to terms with the extension of his house party. Yes, Jocelyn had asked, and in reality there wouldn't be a problem in giving him the conservatory to sleep in, given he'd brought his sleeping bag, and his willingness to pay for the expenditure at the *patisserie* was commendable, but no guesses as to what impact he would have on the young ladies. This week was supposed to be a serious painting master class; no room for idle flirtatious dalliances. "Nigel, dear chap; if I can crave forbearance for another hour, maybe an hour and a half, while I go through Miss Danielleson's next task? Then we'll lunch? Perhaps you might find your bearings – the locale?"

Nigel retrieved his rucksack and grinned. "Leave you in peace, then, Jo. Where do I go?"

Jo recovered her *sang froid*, realising she'd probably jumped to conclusions far too soon, but ached for a bit more *togetherness* or something, exactly what, now she wasn't quite sure. Back home, he'd almost become *the boyfriend* and all sorts of assumptions had been made. Okay, then, she'd play cool, let him make the running. "Through there," she said, waved a hand, watched him push the screen door open and turned back to Edward. "Can we use the farmhouse as a subject? House and trees, try and catch the character of the place?"

* * *

By the end of the day she'd made a passable job of the farmhouse, the trees and the hills, though it was difficult to tell whether it was France or Italy. Edward had been quite good, really, not too pushy or clinging; she'd half expected him to be peering over her shoulder most of the time, but, no, he was very punctilious and at no time did she feel he was ogling her. He really was a gentleman. Nigel, despite her worries, had been more than just politely interested in her project, though he too kept his attentions low key. When the other two came back in the middle of the afternoon Edward switched his attention largely to putting Julie onto the old cart and sketching an outline ready for tomorrow. Dylys had found an large iconic floppy straw hat from somewhere, and with getting her into a flouncy floral skirt that happily Julie had fancied and bought for a very few Euros that morning she looked every inch a svelte young French countrified *mam'selle*. When Jo looked up to see her friend ensconced in the cart, she also saw Nigel's wrapt attention as the skirt wasn't quite as full as it should have been to cover the yawning gap between her knees.

Frowning, she whistled at him. "Hey, Nigel! Stop gazing where you shouldn't!"

Edward came to the rescue, tactfully suggesting he might like to be included in the composition. "If you lean on the side of the cart, Nigel, and Julie, if you look as though you're having a proposal or something?" Nigel grinned. Julie was certainly nice to look at, but he'd only been admiring the view that was on offer, no more. He did as he was asked, and Edward was pleased; his painting would tell a story.

* * *

Their evening meal was *al fresco,* with chilled white wine; the setting, the banter and the conviviality engraved as a moment Jo felt she'd not erase from her mind for some long time; with Nigel at her elbow, Julie happy and Dylys and Edward so at ease with each other; nice, really nice. At a suitable moment she excused herself and wandered off up the slope above the farmhouse to phone home.

"Hi, Pa. It's Jo! How's things?"

"Hello, darling girl. It's good to hear you. 'Things' are fine. And with you?"

"Yep. Nigel's turned up – I've been doing an oil painting of the farmhouse where we're staying, and Edward thinks it's not bad. Did one of Julie yesterday, but it's a bit sexy. How's Mums? Wasn't it this week work was starting on the studio? Did you have a good time with Felicity?" She'd hardly paused for breath. "It's still very warm. But I'm okay, drinking quite a bit. Haven't been anywhere yet, been confined to barracks. Might get out with Nigel – he's hired a car."

Her father's voice came over as if he was laughing. "Your Mums misses her daughter, but otherwise okay, thanks. She's keeping an eye on me while you're away, so that I don't get into mischief with Felicity. And the studio – well, it's a bit of a wreck at the moment, but no doubt it will start to look better once the demolition bit's done. I look forward to seeing the painting then, if it's a sexy one. Give my regards to Edward. I trust he's behaving?"

"Oh, yes, Pa. He had the opportunity of peering down my front all day today while he was explaining things on brushwork and how much oil to use and stuff, but he never did. I had to tell Nigel off for squinting up Julie's skirt while she was posing – but Edward got him into his composition instead. I had to laugh – but I suppose I can't blame him. She's very pretty, and…" Jo broke off; nearly said she loved her, but she didn't want it to be a declaration.

"You're the pretty one, Jo. Just make sure you keep young Nigel on a leash, now, you understand?"

"Uh huh. He won't – I mean…" She wasn't sure if she knew exactly what she meant. As she had been talking, the sun had begun to disappear behind the hill above them, the reddish glow creeping across the rough ground giving the buildings below her a surreal colour. "Oh, Pa, the light's fantastic, the sun's catching the trees like fire. Look, I'd better go. Talk to you tomorrow, maybe. Love you. Byeee."

* * *

She'd gone. David put the phone down, thoughtfully. He'd never have believed she'd have been speaking like that, so full of confidence and self-assurance, what, a month ago? And keeping a Nigel in check?

"Eleanor?" She was still in the garden, taking a last walk round before they called it a day. She looked up as he came to join her.

"Hmmm?"

"I love you."

"Hoh hum. I loves you too, but what's brought this on?" and put a friendly arm around him as he stooped to kiss her neck. David laughed. His Eleanor hovered somewhere between matter of factness and utter faith in their togetherness.

"Our Jo. She rang."

"Why didn't you say?"

"Sorry. You were out here."

"You could have shouted?"

"Her phone time, darling. She's fine, seems to be enjoying things. Nigel's arrived; she's keeping him in order, I think. Asked after you, the studio, and Felicity, in that order. I think she's growing up."

He stared over at the dimming line of the apple trees. "At least we'll have her studio done. Birthday present. Shall we go in?"

Eleanor's arm tightened round his waist, and whispered in his ear. She got another kiss in return, and happily knew that was only for starters.

FIFTEEN

The rest of the week just zipped by, as Jocelyn began to really enjoy messing about with her now familiar palette, confident in her growing ability to gauge brush strokes and depths of colour. Edward was *really* encouragingly nice about her attempts, too, so her happiness flowed round her like an invisible aura. She missed her Mums though, and when Nigel left after staying an extra night she had a weepy time for a while. Julie was such a consolation the evening after Nigel went, cuddling up with her on the bed for a while, making all sorts of funny inroads into her emotions. Nothing had been said between them about his visit; Julie's tacit acceptance he was *her* bloke had kept the lid on any potential rivalry. Not that Nigel didn't keep looking at her, Jo knew, but then he was a bloke and that's what blokes did, wasn't it, look at all the girls' curves. As she lay on her bed and pondered, shouldn't she have been a little less careful about her deportment and given him more of an eyeful? Time on my side, she thought. If I'm going to Norfolk who knows what might happen – even in a Vicarage, a real live Vicarage, not a redundant one like home. He hadn't firmed up the proposal though, so it was still in the air. Home! They'd be back tomorrow. Had it been all that successful, this week away? Certainly Edward seemed to be pleased; he'd taken more to Julie as being part of his several paintings, leaving her to get on with hers, and Dylys had been *so* pleasant she could only assume her week had been a happy one for her, too. As for Julie herself, well, it was nice to see her smile so much.

"Jo!" A shout from downstairs; supper must be ready. Rolling off her bed, she slipped her skirt back on, tucked her feet back into her shoes and trotted down the stairs. It was going to be their last proper meal; Dylys would be going to impress.

Edward was into reflective mode. "Dear girls! Are you glad to be going home tomorrow – or would you rather we had made this a longer stay? Speaking purely selfishly I believe it would be good to have had another day or two, but the weather change suggests a return. I gather it may be a trifle thundery tomorrow." He'd been reading his daily 'Le Monde' "Your feelings?"

Julie, having left Jocelyn alone with her thoughts earlier, had mixed feelings. On the one side she was concerned, strangely, for leaving her father on his own, absence having indubitably made her heart grow fonder; on the other, the return would mean facing up to challenges she'd ignored whilst immersed in this wonderful, strange week with Jo, Edward and Dylys. She'd enjoyed herself, and said so. Jocelyn nodded. "I have, immensely. It's been great, despite my amateur attempts at oils."

"Not so amateurish, my dear Jo, not so. You may be better with the crayons and the pencils, but the spirit is there for you, and with practice, you'll create some nice things, provided your inspiration stays with you." His eyes were twinkling, as if he'd guessed her secret. "That's the other thing," looking at Dylys, as if for inspiration. She nodded, gently, encouraging him. "Don't lose your innocence, Jo. You're still, forgive me, a teenager; fresh out of school. I know we've treated you both as young ladies in your own right, quite correctly so, but it's only been a month since our relationship was a trifle different, was it not? A considerable amount of your charm is that innocence, dare I say *naivety*, which reflects in what you do. Lose that, and you might diminish that lovely fresh finish you give to your work. You will lose it in time, inevitably, but by then your inspiration may come from other quarters – eh, Dylys?" To the girls' immense surprise, Dylys blushed, almost simpered. Her eyes widened, caught the air of mischievousness in Edward's look, and just had to smile. Yes, they'd been lovers, and so what? If it had been his *inspiration*, it had certainly improved her feeling for life. What could she say?

She tried. "Relationships, Jo, Julie, sometimes can work miracles in people. Edward and I, well, you'll have guessed, have a special relationship, one we never knew would work as well as it has – and, it has to be said, owes a little to you two. If you hadn't started sketching, Jo, Edward may not have invited you on this expedition, and if Julie hadn't been included, he may not have been quite so forward in asking me to act as chaperon – and..." she stopped, uncertain, strangely out of character, unwilling to forgo her 'Head of College Year' role talking intimate things with two former pupils.

Edward had no such inhibitions, and finished it for her. "We ended up in the same bed. Right, you two, just one thing more, from your elders and betters. *Don't*, I repeat, *don't* sacrifice your innocence by rushing into bad relationships. You've too much to lose. Now," he changed tone, "I suggest an early night, we'll pack first thing tomorrow. Thank you, both, for your charming and unmissable addition to my week's indulgence, and our joint thanks to our irreplaceable *Chatelaine. Bon soir!*"

They were dismissed. Back up in their eyrie of a room, tucked under the eaves, Jocelyn seemed preoccupied to her other room mate, and Julie tried to find out why. At first Jo just shrugged when asked what was in her mind, then as Julie wasn't going to give up and get herself in bed, risked voicing her fears about Nigel, and what was he going to do.

"What do you mean, what is he going to do, Jo? I think he's smashing, I really do. I just wish I'd been able to drag him out of that tree!"

"Oh, Julie, *grow up!* Smashing! Really, you sound like Betty! I..." She didn't want to explain to her friend what she felt about Nigel, in fact, she didn't really know herself, but when Edward had talked of staying innocent, she knew exactly what he meant, and she was a mite scared over both his intentions and her reactions. Time to go back to her Mums and have some frank discussions, or even Pa, come to that.

"I'm going to sleep, Julie. Time will tell. Night, night." She settled herself down and Julie had to be content.

Work had proceeded apace with the shed conversion to studio. Even David was impressed with Mike's commitment to the task, with early starts and working right through until the encroaching autumnal evenings put a stop to things. He'd even toyed with the idea of cabling up the studio to provide power, but both length of cable and cost involved put the kibosh on that concept, at least for the time being. When the glass, specially ordered to size, arrived and was fitted, the transformation was near completion. Out of his own store of materials, Mike unearthed enough genuine oak planks to put down a better floor, and the place had a new stable type door. Finally, and with Eleanor brought in as consultant, they decided to paint the wall opposite the new windows a light shade of creamy white to improve the light. Eleanor also installed, unbidden, an old piece of carpet out of the attic, seen when ferreting for her oil paints, and had bought a super stool she'd wouldn't have minded putting in the kitchen for herself.

Finally, they moved a table up there; Mike suddenly had an inspiration about shelving and sorted that overnight; David spent another mint of money on artist's materials, and the job was done.

"Just such a marvellous thing, David!" Eleanor was proud of him. "And Mike, what would we have done without you? Jo'll be in her element, I know she will. Thank you, both. Shall we have an opening ceremony?"

"We'll just give her the key, Eleanor, as a birthday present. Do we have a party?"

"Don't see why not, but not like that post-college dinner. Bit more grown up?"

"Felicity?"

"Trust you! Might know you'd think of her! But yes, she and Betty, maybe old Mrs Parsons?"

"Mike, you'll come, of course. Then there'll be Julie. What about Jo's other friends? Trish?"

"I don't know, maybe. Certainly Edward and Mrs

Summers; I should think that'll do. Don't want to overwhelm the girl."

"Nigel?"

"Hmmm. Maybe Jo'll have her own ideas. When's she going to Norfolk?"

"Did she say it might be the last week in August or first week September? It's got to be before he goes back to Edinburgh. If it's the last week in the month then he could come and take her back with him?"

"Okay. I'll try and remember to ring him. Take it on my own head. Mind you, he's been to France with her so we don't really know how things stand, do we?"

"Nope, but no doubt you'll find out."

Mike had had enough of this, pushed his chair back from the kitchen table where they'd gravitated post completion. "Right. I'll be off. Glad it's worked out. Happy to help. Your daughter's a fine girl. Let me know." And he'd gone, saying more than at most times.

Then the phone rang. David took the call in the hall.

* * *

Packing up the gîte was a trifle sombre, an end of term feeling but with no celebrations. A last look round and a slight lump in the throat, before Jo settled herself into the Bentley's cushions. Julie pale faced as though she too was sad at the end of the stay. Dylys saw their unhappiness, but there was nothing she could do, apart from giving them little hugs before they got into the car. Edward, humming to himself, was looking forward to showing his collection of a good eight 'not bad' paintings to his dealer friend. The first one, Julie in her lightweight flimsy cotton dress on the beach, he'd keep. She was far too nice to sell, and he caught himself bemoaning that he hadn't managed to get Jo to pose for him, but then, he could always buy one of the prints that were being run off at this very time. Time to go, then, and he eased the big car back down the stony road.

331

Once on board the ferry, the girls were off up to the top deck to watch the ship slip her moorings and ease away from the berth. They were fascinated at the way such a massive vessel could inch its way round, before the wake started to cream behind them and the land began to diminish into the skyline.

Edward and Dylys remained in the forward saloon, taking advantage of the large armchairs and the ever-ready supply of coffee and French croissants. After a while, as the vessel ploughed on into the freshening wind and the waves began to get icing top crests, the girls simultaneously said, "Let's go below," and ran for the stair head.

Julie was never quite sure how it happened, then or later, but Jo reached the top of the stairs first, and somehow her feet just went from under her. In horror, total and spine chilling horror, she watched Jocelyn tumble a whole flight of steel steps, in a flailing of arms and jean clad legs, crash against the railing, to go disastrously still in a contorted heap on the steel plating of the mid-stairs landing. She screamed, but her screams went away with the wind. She inched her own way down, and knelt over her friend. Jo had gone white, starkly contrasting with a swelling bruise on her arm, and her eyelids were fluttering, but worst of all was the way that leg seemed twisted, and there was more blood beginning to seep through her jeans. Suddenly, there were people, and white uniformed crew, and a girl with a 'paramedic' fluorescent jacket, and Jo was being lifted, ever so carefully, to be carried down the stairwell, and she felt her own head spinning, put her hand out, nearly blacked out...

* * *

Julie came to in the same cabin as Jo. The girl medic was taking Jo's pulse; her male assistant was cutting away at Jo's jeans, revealing the raw bruising and misshapen calf. Obviously the ship's Medical Centre, so they were safe, but Jo? It was a croak, but it got attention, "Ow is shhe?"

The Paramedic girl turned, and there had to be a vestige of a smile. "Hello, you. Are you back with us?"

"How's Jo?" She managed it this time.

"She's a Jo, is she? Not too good, to be perfectly honest. We're getting a helicopter in to fly her off. This leg needs setting, and I'm not happy with her blood pressure. She's still unconscious. Are you related, or just a friend? Has she anyone else on board?"

Julie gave the girl a description of Edward and Dylys, explained the association, and promptly fainted once more. By the time she came round again, Dylys was holding her hand, and Edward was giving the Medical Centre steward details of David and Eleanor's address and phone number. Still Jo lay inert, and Julie started to cry.

Dylys, tears misting in her own eyes, could only squeeze her hand. Nothing could be said or done that would alter the situation, Jocelyn had badly hurt herself and there were two very caring and loving people whose lives were going to take a severe shock, and she was going to have to tell them. She felt the ship heel as it prepared to take the helicopter on board, streaming itself against the wind. She'd go with Jo, let Edward bring Julie back. Just as well the wind hadn't freshened any more. She was not looking forward to this, but it had to be done.

* * *

Less than an hour, and Jocelyn was in Portsmouth Hospital, undergoing surgery to repair a shattered leg. Dylys was allowed to use the Orthopaedic Registrar's secretary's phone to break the news.

"David. It's Dylys, Mrs Summers. There's no way of telling you other than plainly. Jocelyn's had an accident on board the ferry, she fell down a companionway and broke a leg, she's been airlifted to Portsmouth, which is where I am, and she's in theatre now. She's not in any danger, but I can't tell you any more until after the Orthopaedic surgeon's done his best for her. I am most dreadfully sorry to have to tell you this, but there's no other way." She realised she was repeating herself. "Edward's bringing Julie back with the car, but he'll come here first. I'll stay with her until you get down here. You will come, won't you?"

David felt his body go cold, and his legs were trembling. Jo, his beloved Jo, in hospital, how was he going to tell Eleanor?

"David?"

"Yes. You have a phone number?" Practicalities were one way of coping. "Which ward?"

"I don't know yet, but Reception will tell you. How long will you take?"

He thought. About an hour, hour and a half. Oh, Jo! And how much he had been looking forward to her return, to showing her the studio, seeing what she had done in France. Anger welled up, and then as quickly dissipated. "I'll be there as soon as practicable. Thank you for letting us know."

The phone was back on its cradle, and he had to face Eleanor. Somehow she knew it was bad news, he could see it in her face.

"It's Jo, isn't it? David, what's happened?"

"She fell, on the ferry. She's been airlifted to Portsmouth..." He could scarce get the words out, and knew he was going to lose control. He sat down, head in hands, and Eleanor moved to hold him, feeling her own tears. "Our Jo, in theatre, damaged leg, God knows what else. Oh, Eleanor!"

"Let's get Mike to drive you down. He'll do it, I know he will." Miraculously, she stayed in control, and sent her prayers winging on to her daughter.

* * *

Mike simply said, "Yes, of course, no problem, five minutes" and was accurate to the second. His car didn't look much, but as a garage employee he'd had it well tuned. An hour and twenty minutes, and a good steady drive. "I'll stay put while you see what's what, give the girl my love." David had to raise a bit of a smile, that was so unlike Mike, giving anyone his love.

Dylys met him, and unsurprisingly, hugged him. "She's conscious, David, and well out of any danger. They've been able to do the reduction by manipulation; she's rather well strapped, but no long-term damage, as far as we know. She'll be here a day or three, though. This way." She led him through the maze of corridors, up two floors, and into the ward, tactfully staying behind as he crossed to her bedside. The mass of auburn hair spread over the pillow was stark contrast to the wan face; the bedclothes stretched over a cradle protecting her limbs and with the drip dangling from its stand it was a sight he did not wish on anyone.

"Jo. My darling, daarling Jo! Oh, what *have* you done to yourself?"

She opened her eyes to give a vestige of a grin. "Sorry Pa. I might be good at trees but not much use at ship stairways. My own fault, not looking where I was going, I guess. How's Mums?"

"Not happy, Jo. But how are *you* feeling?"

"Bit groggy. At least I'm still here. Poor Julie, she flaked out. Just as well I didn't break an arm or wrist or something. At least I can still draw." There was silence between them, as David reached for her hand, squeezed, and felt his tears coming. "Pa!"

He shook his head, as if to say Silly girl, wiped his eyes with his other hand. "You know your studio's finished?"

There was no reply. "Jo?" Her grip was relaxing. Alarm caused him to panic, called out "Nurse!"

A young-looking girl hurried over, checked her pulse and then just smiled at him. "She's only sleeping. Natural reaction, poor girl. She's been through a lot. Let her rest. She'll be heaps better in the morning, promise. We'll take good care of her, don't worry. Go and have a word with the Staff Nurse – she's the one in the maroon."

With more reassurance from the senior, there really wasn't any more he could do, other than reassure the Staff Nurse he'd be back in the morning, and please would she tell Jo when she woke. He rejoined Dylys. Edward was off the ferry and at this moment on his way to collect her; no need to wait. They'd take

Julie back to her father's home and phone when all was in place. David found Mike almost asleep in his car; explained the situation, and was driven home.

* * *

It was well and truly dark by the time they got back to Tinsfield. Eleanor was doing some needlework in the sitting room all wrapped up in her big woolly comfort sweater, with Jo's first portrait on the mantelpiece, looking down at her. Mike didn't stay, merely grunted "Any time, glad to help," and drove away.

"David?" She stood up, and he folded her, sweater and all, in his arms, buried his head in her hair, kissed her neck, held her tight.

"She's okay. Battered, bruised, but still our Jocelyn. We'll go and see her tomorrow. She made a joke about coping with trees better than stairways, then fell asleep on me. Let's go to bed, darling; I'm bushed."

* * *

Morning saw them back at Jo's bedside, the girl in better colour, though evidently still groggy and in some pain. Eleanor's self-control stayed in place until she saw her girl in that state, then it gave way, and it was David's turn to try and be strong. The morning shift of nursing staff were just as caring; the Ward Sister had welcomed them in despite it being outside conventional visiting hours. She took David to one side. "The Consultant has already done his rounds, he's pleased young Jocelyn's taking things so well, but concerned over the way the fracture occurred. We do have to warn you your daughter may end up with a permanent limp, due to some probable shortening that might occur. Too early to judge matters properly, but it's only right you should know. We haven't said anything to her – best left until we can x-ray her again. I'm so very sorry, she's a lovely girl." Her luminous dark brown eyes had genuine sympathy. It was

336

very evident how much the injured girl meant to them both.

* * *

Four days later Jo was allowed home, complete with crutches and a larger plaster foot to help her move when she felt able. Initially, rest as much as possible, she was told, but not to stay in one position, and come back for a check on progress in three weeks. The plaster would stay on for about six to seven weeks, and she was warned it would be several months before she would regain full mobility. The question of whether she would have any lasting scars remained open, as did the matter of a limp.

Within hours of her returning home she had a procession of visitors. Felicity and Betty, with the first, specially framed, copy of the run of fifty prints from her 'White Dress' sketch and the news that the magazine would run a half-page article on her work if she agreed; Trish, with the news that she and Brendan had a date for a wedding next year; then Edward and Dylys, bringing her oil paintings from France and a big bouquet of lovely flowers, including large white lilies and some strange orange ones that smelt absolutely gorgeouss. Later, Julie came up by taxi. She and Jo embraced like two long lost lovers, with Julie streaming tears; still in her mind the dreadful slow motion picture of Jo's tumble and the forlorn heap of body and limbs lying on that steel stairway. How many times had she gone through that scenario and wished she'd controlled Jo's enthusiasm?

"How has Nigel reacted?" she asked when she'd regained her composure.

"I've not spoken to him." Jocelyn didn't really want to be drawn, unsure of what had happened since he'd left them at Etretat. He'd gone off without much of a real goodbye, although they'd had a pleasant enough time together, he'd never really been all that affectionate. No more had been said about her going to Norfolk, and it wasn't for her to have pressed the matter.

Julie was surprised, sure in her own mind nothing had

happened to lessen his interest in her friend. "Hadn't you better let him know we're back safe and..." then stopped, flushed red, aware she'd really been a bit crass. "Sorry, Jo, didn't think. Well, he ought to be told. Hasn't your father – oh – well I don't suppose it's his job either. Oh, heck. I'm not doing very well, am I?"

Jocelyn had to smile, despite thinking she knew what really was in Julie's mind; two girls, one bloke. Who did he prefer? Red head or raven tressed? Peeved he hadn't been in touch, well, more than peeved, a little hurt if the truth was told. She pushed it to the back of her mind, and got Julie on a different tack. "Exam results tomorrow – or is it the day after? What are you going to do, Julie?"

"Go on with what my mother had planned, Jo, at least for the time being. It's not fair on my father to do otherwise. If I do some modelling work when I can, then all well and good, but I don't think I could make a career of showing myself, somehow. Peeling my clothes off for some leering photographer ain't going to be my scene. Dressing up – or down – for a *real* artist like our Edward, now that's different. Didn't you like that one of me on the beach?"

Jo remembered. It had been something, and that was the day she'd been doing another one of Julie, that *dishabille* thing of her on the bed. It was in the other room, and she wished she could have just nipped out and fetched it, but she couldn't. She had to sort of hop and lurch like an old-fashioned pirate. "In the other room, Julie. Edward brought my oils up this morning. Be a dear and fetch it. It would take me at least quarter of an hour!" She laughed, a trifle cynically.

Julie went, found, and returned. "You know, this isn't half bad. I didn't know I was as – er – well, you know what I mean!"

"Fetching? Sexy? Ravishing? Or just plain sleepy head crawling out of her pit?"

Julie's turn to laugh. "What are you going to do with it? Can I have it if you don't want it?"

Jocelyn considered. No, she didn't want to just give it away, not even to Julie, not yet anyway.

Maybe later. "I'll see." She went back to the exam results. Curiously, she wasn't the slightest bit bothered about what the outcome would be. If she passed, well, she had to make a decision; if she didn't, then the decision had been taken for her. "So you'll go to uni?"

"Uh huh."

"Oh."

"You?"

"Don't really know." There was silence between them. "You'll stay for lunch?"

"If that's all right?"

"Course it is. Mums will stretch the home-made pizza and salad, no probs. You won't have seen my new studio yet either. Pa's had to go back to work after he brought me home, but he's promised to come back this afternoon some time, early, so he can help me go and look to see what they've done. It was meant to be a birthday present, but tumbling down those stupid steps messed up the plans. I don't know quite what's going on; Mums and Pa have gone all secretive. Scary." She'd asked about her birthday party, but all she'd got was a "Wait and see, darling, let's get you properly mobile first." She didn't think that was fair, especially if it meant waiting six weeks until she got the plaster off.

* * *

David got home just before three, by which time Jo had decided she'd try and do some sketching again; with a bit of a struggle she managed to persuade Julie to stretch out on a garden bench with a book, and set to work. Again she blessed her lucky stars she hadn't seriously injured either arm or hand, apart from that still painful and beautifully coloured bruise.

"Hi, Pa! See, I'm back at work!"

"That's good. Can you manage to hold things okay? Hello Julie! No, don't move if you're posed. You look pretty. How's your father?"

"He's not too bad, thank you. Just a bit moodier than before." She didn't want to talk about him, apologising instead for not looking after Jocelyn as well as she could have. If only they hadn't run to get to that stair head…

"No, no Julie, don't fret, what's done is done. How much more, Jo? Then we'll show you the studio."

"How am I going to get up there, Pa? I'm not much good at hopping over rough ground yet," refusing to say how painful it was just getting around the house, and she still didn't know how she was going to get up and downstairs.

"Ah, well, you may not like it, but I've borrowed a wheelchair."

Jocelyn, sitting on a garden chair with her leg stuck out in front of her like a frozen footballer, very suddenly and not unsurprisingly, burst into tears. A wheelchair! And she used to *run* up to the orchard, remembered that time she'd done so completely naked in the rain, and here she was, like some old crippled arthritic eighty year old, dependant on her parents to *wheel* her about! It just wasn't fair!

David had half expected this, but he couldn't see any other way round the problem. He knew how hard it was going to be for her, largely because he felt that gut-wrenching spasm of emotion every time he thought about her accident, let alone seeing her like this. He could see Julie was getting upset as well, and before long the three of them would all be sobbing their hearts out if he wasn't careful. He patted her on the shoulder and spun round on his heel to fetch the thing from the drive. Eleanor popped her head out of the kitchen with an interrogative expression. He shook his head, and she frowned. She liked it no more than any of them, but someone had to be pragmatic about things, and followed at a discreet distance.

Julie, abandoning her pose, was kneeling at Jo's side, her head in her lap, just stroking her uninjured thigh. Both David and Eleanor could see how close the girls had become, and Eleanor decided there and then she'd see if she couldn't get Julie's father to lend his daughter back to them while Jo convalesced. She went back indoors.

"Come on, dear, let's see how we get on."

Jocelyn steeled herself, for with Julie's very evident concern she just had to get herself back into the running.

Running, ha! David put the wheelchair parallel to the bench she was on, and with a wee bit of a lift from her father, she moved across, rested her plastered foot on the extension bit, and the party made its way across the grass towards the paddock and the orchard beyond. It wasn't easy, neither for David pushing or Jo feeling every bump, but they made it, Julie trailing behind, and David paused at the gate so Jo could take it in. Brand new door, the picture windows shining, all the woodwork a nice new fetching shade of trendy blue, and a name plate on the side.

"You did all this? In a week! Oh, *Pa!*" It was almost a squeak.

"I'm just sorry we didn't think about the step height. We'll have to get Mike to fix a ramp and a rail so you can get in and out. At least the stable door's wide. Can you hop, or shall I carry…?"

Jo was already lifting herself out of the chair. "No jolly fear! Much as I love you Pa, this is *me!*" She nearly tripped, but with Julie quick to take an arm, then a hand, the two girls went into the completely refurbished old shed. Not a shed any longer, but a haven for Jocelyn and her developing talent. The high stool, and an armchair, a table – just a small one – an easel, the back wall all sort of white, with a soft board for pinning things on, the set of open shelves with some mysterious boxes, a wonderfully cosy feeling rug, and looking out through the large picture windows, there was her orchard, now in full glory with a bumper crop of fruit. She sat, carefully, still awkwardly, on the stool, and David saw tears glisten on his precious daughter's cheek. Her head turned towards him, and he raised his eyebrows.

"Oh, *yes, Pa!*"

"It's your birthday present. That and something else that may have to wait until you're fully mobile. Till then, this will have to do. Like it?"

"It's lovely. And it *feels* right. What do you think, Julie?" The dark haired girl was in her own emotional state, wishing, oh, how she was wishing, that she had a father like Jo's.

"It's nice, Jo, really nice. You're a lucky girl!"Her voice

cracked, and Jo understood. They were becoming even closer after the accident.

"You'll still be my model, Julie, if you want…"

"Of course, any time, oh, *anytime,* Jo. Whatever you want…"

David felt superfluous and quietly moved to the door. "I'll see how your Mums is getting on. You'll manage, between you?"

"Okay, Pa. I can't really say how much all this means. It's just a super idea," wishing she could have leapt up and hugged him, but she was stuck. "We'll manage. See you later!"

* * *

Eleanor had found Julie's father at home, and in a reasonable state of mind. She'd not only been tactful but also clever, persuading him it was Jocelyn who needed the support, and could his Julie stay for a while to help her around? Yes, he would be pleased if she was of use, and if she wished to stay, then that would be fine. He'd got used to managing on his own, anyway, so no bother. David came back in at that point, and Eleanor gave him the thumbs up sign. "She can stay, if she wants to. Now, how about Nigel? You've rung him?"

"Just about to. Want to eavesdrop?" She had to grit her teeth on this one, but it had to be done. It was going to be their trump card. "Oh, hi!" It sounded like his father. "Eleanor Davidson. Jocelyn's mother. Is Nigel at home? He's not? Oh! When will he be back? Oh, right. Yes, well, he won't know, she's had an accident. Well, yes and no. Tripped on a staircase on the ferry coming home, broke a leg, rather badly. Yes, she's home, but not very mobile. I think she's a bit down because she hasn't heard from him, so I thought…" David could hear something of what was being said. Eleanor was frowning, and then smiled. "*Oh!* Dear me. These young people! Well, maybe, if you were able to relay something of what I've said? You're very kind. No, *thank you!* Yes. Yes, I will. Goodbye."

* * *

"Apparently he felt a bit out of place in France, and Jo mustn't have given a good impression, so he told his father he didn't want to push himself on her, and went off on some wild expedition somewhere – he did say, but I didn't fully grasp it – he's back tonight. So we'll just have to wait and see. His father was very concerned about our girl. Which reminds me – you left her up there?"

"Sure, with Julie. They'll be all right. Julie seems much attached."

"Hmmm. Yes. Best go and see, David, please."

He might have guessed; Julie was back in her model role and he had to avert his eyes and cough.

Jo appeared completely unconcerned; her model almost equally so; though she did reach for her dress and draped it over her front.

"Hi Pa! Just christening the place and, well, it sort of just happened this way. Sorry, didn't expect you back so soon. I can carry on another time, Julie won't mind, will you?" The subject shook her head. Jo's father was all right, bit like Edward, really.

"Well, it's time you were in bed, young lady. We've had a word with your father, Julie, if you want to stay, he's happy. From our point of view you'd be a great help – what do you say?"

"Fine, Mr Danielleson, save me the taxi back, and I much prefer your guest room bed anyway! Hope I don't embarrass you, like this," and as she leant down to pick up the rest of her clothes David was treated to a fuller view of her assets.

He had to brush it aside. "I don't mind if you don't."

"That's all right then," Julie replied, unselfconsciously proceeding to dress properly.

Looking over Jo's shoulder as she was shading in some contours David found her representation very artistic, not at all suggestive.

"Do you like what you see, Pa?"

"Hmmm, I do, but I couldn't say otherwise. You're a very presentable girl, Julie, with or without. Hope you don't get too wrapped up in all this, though. Come on, Jo, finish off and let's get you back."

* * *

Halfway through their evening meal, the phone rang. David looked at Eleanor, raised eyebrows. "I wonder. S'cuse me a moment," went into the hall, picked up the mobile and walked out of earshot. "Danielleson?" Yes, it was Nigel. "Very good of you to call back. How was your expedition?" Nigel didn't want to be drawn, at least not now; he only wanted to talk to Jo. "Well, I'd like her to tell you, if that's all right. I'm using our hand-held thing, so I'll pass it on to her. She can't move quite so easily. One moment." He returned to the table. "Jo – Nigel, for you." His girl started, looked surprised, and blushed, staring down at her plate. "Come on then, don't keep him waiting!" He offered her the phone, but she shook her head. David frowned, waved the phone at her again. He covered the microphone and whispered to her, "He's very upset about your accident. Be nice to him."

Jocelyn looked at Julie, as if to seek advice. Julie nodded, mouthed, "Go on!" so she took the phone. "Hi, Nigel," She couldn't get up and run into the hall so she could speak in private, whereupon the whole stupidity of her situation hit her. The tears came and with it the sob which would not have escaped her caller. He was doing the talking, and the muffled words must have been thoughtful, for she was crying and smiling at the same time. Julie, let alone her father and mother, felt for her. Then she passed the phone to her Mums.

"Nigel, good of you to call." A pause. "Yes, we'd love you to. Of course you can. No problem. Don't worry, we are. Yes, she is to us. See you tomorrow then. Bye." Handing the phone back to David, she leant back in her chair. "He says you're a very precious girl, Jo. Doesn't that mean something?"

Jocelyn nodded, wiped her eyes with the back of her hand, and sniffed. She pushed at the table, scraped her chair back, and struggled to get up. Julie rose to help her, but Jo shook her head. "I've got to manage. *I've got to!*" She felt for her crutch and hobbled out of the room. Her parents watched, aware they could only do so much, and Julie subsided back into her chair.

"If Nigel's coming, I'll go back home, it'll be best." Very

344

mixed feelings ran through her, though she knew her loyalty was with Jo, not her own wishes.

Eleanor reached across the table, and placed a hand on Julie's. "You're a very understanding girl, Julie, and a caring one, we can see that. Whatever you think best. You don't have to, though. We can still find space. Nigel can always go into the barn – or the studio!" That made them all giggle a bit, and the tension ebbed away.

* * *

Nigel put the phone down, and went to find his father. They talked at length, and afterwards he felt a lot clearer in his mind. Then he went and packed a case, made a couple more phone calls, kissed his mother and went out to the car. He'd manage the hundred miles or so to the hotel before it shut down for the night. He'd been stupid, not trusting himself as he should have done. Well, he wouldn't make the same mistake again, running out on the girl without acknowledging his emotions.

* * *

Jocelyn made it to the foot of the stairs, and assessed the problem. Grasping the banister rail firmly, she tucked the hated crutch under her good arm, and took the first step, dragging her plaster leg behind. Now what? She couldn't do another step, 'cos there was nothing to push with. Then it came to her, and she sat down, carefully, hitching herself on her bottom, step by step, nearly losing her crutch back down the stairs. It took a little while, but she made it to the top, and the sense of achievement was out of all proportion to reality; for the first time that day she felt she was winning. Well, not strictly true, for doing that study of Julie in the buff was a nice one; and she wondered whether she dare show Nigel when he came tomorrow. Suddenly, she was happy again. "Mums!" she called, out loud.

Eleanor heard the cry, and leapt to her feet. Jo! *What had she done?* Out in the hall, and looked up, to see a grinning girl perched on the top of the stairs. "Jo! How on earth did you manage to get up there? Silly girl, you could have damaged yourself!"

"I had to try. It's easy! I miss my shower though. You may have to give me a hand in the morning. I'm going to bed. No! I'll manage!" Eleanor had started to climb towards her.

"If you're sure?"

"I'm sure. Night night."

"I'll come and tuck you up, later."

"Oh, all right."

* * *

Julie had popped in and given her a goodnight kiss. "I'll not stay if Nigel's coming, Jo. Let you two get on with things. No, really. Don't worry, I shan't be far away. Sleep well." Jo wasn't surprised in a way, but a trifle disappointed.

Then her Mums came in, straightened out the bed covers around her, kissed her forehead. "Good to have you back home, my darling. How're you feeling now?"

"All mixed up, Mums. Happy and unhappy. Cross, I guess. *Bloody* cross! What should I do about uni, Mums? What's Nigel going to say? What does Pa think?"

Eleanor laughed. "Questions, questions! Let's cross one bridge at a time, shall we? You're not going anywhere until you're fully mobile, and I mean, *mobile.*" She took the plunge, knowing it had to be said sooner or later. "We don't know whether you'll be quite the same once the plaster's off and you can walk properly again. Broken bones don't always heal the same, you know. If you will go crashing about you can't expect *not* to have some after effects. At least it was only one leg." She ran a hand over the length of the plaster under the covers. "You can't roll about with this lump, can you?"

Jo was frowning now, and the frown was in her voice. "Not walk properly? What do you mean, Mums? I'm going to leap frog that orchard gate again, you know!"

"Well, it's something to aim at, I suppose. One day at a time, heh? Goodnight, my darling. Sleep tight." Without waiting for any more queries, she walked out and shut the door, holding back on her tears. Jocelyn lay still, staring at the ceiling. Not walk properly! Of course she would. The memories of that tumble were dim; purposely she shut them out of her mind, thinking hard about her orchard studio and what she was going to do. Blow the rest; she was going to paint, draw, and sketch, whatever. She'd show them. At least now she could start on her mural.

SIXTEEN

She was feeling a little depressed now Julie had returned home after just the one night. Her father, too, had returned to work, and her mother had all but ignored her this morning. At least Nigel was going to turn up sometime, though he hadn't rung to say when. The day was colder, too, grey skies matching her mood. Coming down stairs had been painful, inching down on her bottom, step by step, having churlishly declined any offer of help. Her thoughts went on to what was happening at the college. Exam results day, lists of names posted on the boards, milling hopefuls pushing and jostling to see who had got what. If you didn't turn up, you got a letter in the post. Her Pa had offered to drive her over, but she couldn't see the point. Even Julie had said she was going to wait for her letter. She didn't even feel like finishing that thing she'd started of Julie yesterday, and had started to read one of her Mums's light romantic novels, but after a dozen pages she thought it was soppy and it got flung onto the settee.

She hobbled to the window and stared out at the prospect of rain. "Why did I bloody well go and tumble down those bloody stairs?" She hadn't realised she'd said it out loud.

"What did you say, dear?" Eleanor heard the voice and left her pastry board to see what Jo was doing.

"Sorry, Mums. I was swearing at myself. I can't even wear a decent dress with this thing." She'd made do with an old school dress, short though it was, still easier to struggle into, especially as she could button it up the front. "My plaster's itching like hell and I can't scratch."

"I know, dear. I broke an arm once when I fell off a gate. At least you can feel things. I'd worry if you didn't. Can I get you a coffee or something?" She eyed the novel, lying in a heap on the cushion. "Don't you appreciate a bit of romance?"

Jo snorted. "Not my scene, Mums. Sorry, but I'm getting fed up. And look at the weather!"

The greyness of the day had predictably given way to a steady light drizzle. "I can't even get up to the studio. When do you think Nigel will get here? He's not rung, has he?"

Eleanor eyed her daughter. "When he does, you'd better be in a more welcoming frame of mind; and you'd best realise you've still got a few weeks of all this. At the moment I reckon he'd turn tail and head back home, for you're no picture. Cheer up, my girl. Could have been a lot, lot worse." Helping Jo with a strip wash that morning she'd mentally winced at the bruising that was coming out. Jo must have bounced from step to metal step before coming to that bone-crunching stop, and how she didn't manage to break both arms and the other leg she couldn't imagine. "Now, what about that coffee. And I've got some interesting new chocolate biscuits I made last week. Join me?"

Eleanor had just settled down with her daughter on the settee with two mugs of steaming coffee and a plateful of her biscuits when the noise of a car interrupted companionable silence; the gravel scrunched, to be followed by the thud of a car door. A knock on the front door, so it wouldn't be Nigel, surely he'd just walk in? Eleanor went to investigate. Jo listened.

"Edward! How nice to see you, do come in, Jo and I were just having coffee. You'll join us?"

Jocelyn immediately became conscious of just how short her dress skirt was, but it was too late.

"Good morrow, my dear Jocelyn! How is the wounded soldier today? I cannot possible tell you how inexpressibly sad I am at the way our little expedition ended, you know." He'd actually said as much yesterday when he and Dylys had called, but that was yesterday, and time didn't mean that much to him, she knew. At least he wasn't staring at her. He had an envelope in his proffered hand. "Your results, my dear girl. Least I could do, deliver the news in person. Not bad, not bad at all." His eyes still had that familiar twinkle. Eleanor had fetched another mug, and he took it with a slight bow. Jocelyn reached out, then somehow just couldn't open it and passed it on to her Mums.

"Mums, you open it. Just tell me." She closed her eyes, and waited. Eleanor looked at Edward, who winked. She slid the single sheet out.

"Lord! Straight 'A's, isn't that what they say? Jocelyn, my dearest girl, you've got A's everywhere!"

"She couldn't have done better, Mrs D. Which represents a slight problem on the decision-making, methinks? Excellent biscuits, these. May I?" He took another one, and without an invitation, sat down.

Eleanor subsided back alongside her daughter and hugged her. "Did you think you'd get this high?"

Jo still had her eyes tight shut. This she could not believe. Straight 'A's? Her? She'd given herself two 'B's and a 'C'. Then she remembered her father's present to her, her beautiful burgundy dress, and she felt more tears. It was her Pa, giving her the confidence, and she'd ridden the crest of his wave.

"Mums! Look after Edward; I'm going upstairs for a minute."

"Sure you can manage?" Eleanor knew she would, but quite why she wanted to struggle up those stairs she wasn't sure, though no way would she ask.

"I'll manage." She heaved herself off the settee, glad the dress slid back to cover her decently.

* * *

Upstairs, she unbuttoned the old thing and dumped it on the bed. Opened the wardrobe door, lifted the burgundy dress out, propped herself against the wall, wriggled her way into it, and had to wriggle even more to get the zip done up and the dress pulled back round, but it was worth it. Wrong bra and so on, but she couldn't face going through that; and having a plaster leg sort of spoilt the effect, but just the feel of it, the magic of the memory of the purchase, the times she'd worn it, and just, oh, the *niceness* of what her Pa – and her Mums – had done. She bethought of the scent and put a small dab of Chanel on her earlobes. *Now she was ready to meet Nigel.* But, she couldn't do a bottom shimmy downstairs in this, *no way!*

She had to abandon her principles, and hopped to the head of the stairs. She made her call sound as happy as she could. "Mummumms?"

Eleanor heard. "Excuse me a moment." She went into the hall, saw an apparition, a burgundy clad apparition. "Jo? What *are* you doing in that dress?"

"Shhh – *Mums!* I'm celebrating, and I want Nigel to see me looking pretty. Can you help me downstairs?"

Eleanor's heart swelled up for her girl. Making an effort, responding. "Of course, darling."

Before she gave Jo her supporting arm, she fetched her hairbrush to brush out those auburn curls. Then the twosome descended the stairs in almost regal fashion.

* * *

"My goodness, what an amazing transformation! My dearest girl, you look sublime! This cannot be in my honour, I feel sure – but if it were, then I would be overcome. Magnificent!" Edward did a little bow. "Charming. Utterly, utterly charming! Would all my pupils respond in such a manner to their successes! Quite made my day! However, regretfully I feel I must press on – I have another part of my mission to accomplish," he patted his pocket. "Our mutual friend, Miss Julie. Another success – in confidence, of course. You have both done well. May I call again?"

Eleanor shook her head, but her face told a different story. "Of course. Any time, Edward. You're more than welcome, any time. I can't thank you enough for all you've done for Jo."

"Despite the misadventure on the ferry?"

"That can't be laid at your door, Edward. Just a bit of teenage over enthusiasm. She'll grow up."

"I think she already has. Jocelyn is a well-possessed young lady, Eleanor. Just you keep her working, she's talented. Now, my adieus. Thank you the coffee and the delightful biscuits."

He was gone, the subdued rumble of his precious Bentley fading into the quiet patter of the persistent rain.

* * *

"Well, my girl. A phone call to your father, I think. Then some lunch?"

"I haven't much of an appetite, Mums, I've eaten too many biscuits. I'd love to talk to Pa, but not on the phone, Mums. It'll wait till teatime, when he gets home. He'll see me in this dress, then." She felt very grown up all of a sudden, and well able to behave like the lady when Nigel appeared.

He'd made good time from the overnight stop, even taking the journey leisurely and thinking over what he was going to say. What he did not expect was a Jocelyn looking a million dollars, an odd million dollars with a stiff white leg, but a girl he now knew he loved. Loved. She'd saved his life, or as near as damn it, and what a way to meet a girl. How could he tell her, fresh out of college, he'd love to make her his wife, in fullness of time? Then he wanted to *hold* her, feel her close to him, and just not let go. Trite, wasn't it, saying you'd smother the girl with kisses, but if you didn't love someone like Jo... How she had jumped into his arms from those stairs that time before – and now she couldn't jump to save her life, well, that's as the expression went. Eleanor made herself scarce, and Nigel wrapped his arms round his Jo, breathed in the scent of her, felt the warmth of her, the touch of her fingers on his cheek, and the meeting of lips on lips.

"Why didn't you ring?"

"I wasn't sure you wanted me to."

"Silly boy. I've missed you."

"I've missed you, too. I didn't know how much until your mother rang. Oh, Jo!" He wanted to tell her he loved her, but wasn't sure what her reaction would be, and he didn't want to lose her. His hands slipped down to hold her arms, so he could study her reaction. Eyes met eyes.

She nodded, ever so gently. "I think," she said carefully, slowly, "I've fallen in love with you, or someone very much like you. Which is a bit silly, really, because I haven't been in love with anyone before so I don't know much about what it feels like, but if it feels like what I'm feeling, then it's quite a nice feeling, Nigel, and I don't want it to go away, or stop, and I've been waiting for something like this to happen but I didn't know when it would happen or what it was going to be like, but I wish I hadn't broken my leg to find out. That's why you came, isn't it, because I broke my leg and you felt sorry for me because I rescued you from not having a broken leg?" Then she couldn't say any more because her mouth being kissed. "Oh."

Nigel told her.

"Oh."

"Your broken leg has nothing to do with this, it's you I love, not your plaster. As your doctor, I'm going to ensure it mends as good as new. If you want me to be your doctor."

"I want you to be my Nigel, doctor. You are my Nigel, aren't you?"

He nodded, gravely. "I think so. Are you my Jocelyn, my Jo?"

"Yes." The two of them stood, in the middle of the room, staring at each other, holding hands.

And simultaneously giggled. "Well then," Nigel was smiling broadly, a real Cheshire cat smile. "Now that we have that quite clear, how about some lunch?"

* * *

Eleanor may not have been visible, but she was well within earshot. Very mixed feelings, but on the whole, happy ones. What David was going to say about all this remained to be heard. She bustled back into the room, as though she'd been miles away. "Lunch, you two? Made up your differences, have you? Nigel, you know she's still a minor till the end of the month?" She grinned at his startled expression, and playfully thumped his arm. "Don't look so surprised. I know she's an older, wiser, and at the moment, sadder girl, but she's also my only daughter, and I love her dearly, so if you don't look after her interests as well as me – or her father – you'd better look out! So just watch it!"

Nigel grinned in his turn. "I've just told your daughter I love her. She's a mite careless in what she does every now and again, it seems, so maybe I might be able to help look after her? If you will let me?" He was happy within himself, not regretting his decision. He'd marry her, if she'd have him, but not yet. They had time, and a long way to go, hopefully together. His father – and he had a lot of faith in his father – had met his mother when they were both still teenagers, and their 'engagement' had lasted three years, and neither of them had had a moment's doubt, so he had been told just yesterday. He'd had his blessing, but on the understanding that he was sincere, straight, and didn't prejudge any relationship. He knew what he meant, and promised. It might be difficult in the modern climate, but at least he thought he knew his Jo would be of similar mind.

Eleanor had already made up her mind about Nigel and Jo, soon after that fateful parachute drop in fact, when she'd seen them walking round the garden together. Strange how this garden of theirs had an influence on people. A touch of magic? She almost knew this would happen, but the broken leg hadn't been part of the equation. "Oh, I'll let you, Nigel. You can start by helping me get the lunch, while madam sits down and takes the weight off the remaining leg she's got. Then you can take her up to the new studio out of my way. She's got to earn her keep, mind, so no canoodling just because you've got her on her own! Her father's home just after five. Okay? And, Jo, I think, maybe, you'd better change into something less vulnerable? You can always dress up again later. If Nigel promises to be the gentleman, he'll help." My, she thought, I'm going loopy. Practically thrusting the girl into his arms. Oh well, no doubt she'll respond to my trusting nature.

Nigel was the perfect gentleman. He helped her up the stairs, out of her dress, into that crazy old one, laughed at the length, avoided the very obvious temptations, and they came back downstairs quite slowly, but very much together.

Later on, after he'd taken her across the garden, the paddock and into the new studio, he sat her down on her stool and apologised to her for the way he'd almost run off after the three days in France.

"I wasn't sure where I stood with you, Jo. There was Julie, and let's face it, you two love each other in a different way, then you were so wrapped up in the painting, I just felt, er, well, sort of in the way. I didn't want to push you, or make you think I was just after, well..." and he got a trifle tongue-tied, not quite sure of how candid he ought to be. "Do you understand what I'm trying to say?"

Jocelyn, with a newfound inner strength, nodded. "You didn't want me to think you were just trying to get into my knickers?" She blushed as she said it, knowing full well she'd been more than knickerless in this very spot.

Nigel didn't quite know where to put himself; he didn't know whether to laugh or look affronted.

Jo poked him with her crutch. "Go on, tell me! Then I'll tell you something." She felt very safe with him.

"Okay. Coming straight out of college, Jo, where so many spotty teenagers can't think beyond the end of their...' To give her credit, she blushed again. "So I guess we're a bit above average?"

"Yep. I can't tell you how many blokes have tried ogling their way into one place or another, Nigel, but I haven't cared for any of it. I have my own little quirks, and Mums knows all about me and my inspirations. I guess it's only fair to tell you – warn you – in case. It's just me, and nothing sinister or deviant. Just nice." Perched on the stool, she could just swing one leg, and longed for the time she'd swing both again.

"So? Go on. This sounds rather mysterious."

"I run about starkers, or used to, sometimes in the pouring rain. And I draw best when I haven't got a bra on. Silly, isn't it? I've been up here without a stitch. Doesn't half make you feel good, 'specially if you get rained on!" She laughed, and he loved her laugh. "I've this thing about a sort of mural, based on the orchard here, with apple trees and me, and life, you know, all the stages, childhood and growing up, and..." she was blushing again, she could feel herself going all hot. "...Getting married and having babies and finally dying to be buried in the orchard to be turned into apples again." She paused, stared into the depths of the orchard, conscious that the trees could be listening; it was such a magic place.

"I used to lie on my back, over there, and just let the sky talk to me. I've had dreams, Nigel, and so has Mums when she fell asleep in the same place. Spooky. I think the trees gave me the power to draw as I do. Mums calls me her 'Apple girl'. Apple of her eye, she said. You know I nearly didn't happen? It was touch and go, me or Mums when I was born. Pa said save us both, even if it meant no more babies. So here I am, the one and only. I feel very sad sometimes, not just because I have no brothers or sisters, but 'cos Mums hasn't anyone else. That's why I'm loved the way I am, Nigel, and I'm a very, very lucky girl. That's why Mums is so protective, in a funny sort of way. Pa loves me loads, in a different way. He gave me the burgundy dress, you know, and that was in the exam week, and I felt so proud and so I sailed through those silly exam questions in a sort of dream, and got straight 'A's in all three papers, so I can go to university and get a degree. Should I do that, Nigel, or should I just become a weirdy artist, who draws while wearing nothing but her pants, and sometimes not those either?"

Nigel was drinking her in, all of her, her bouncy, curly, long auburn hair, her freckles, the fullness of her figure and the shapely curve of the leg she was still swinging. She was a lovely, lovely girl, as well as being a beautiful person. He was so, so lucky. "I love you, Jocelyn Danielleson, you know that? And not just because you'll run about in the nude, or draw while half undressed, but because you are different, and lovely, and fun, and honest about life, and caring, and thoughtful, and responsive. And probably loads of other things I'm looking forward to finding out. Can I kiss you, you wonderful weirdo?"

She frowned at him. "I'm not a weirdo! I said weirdee.

Different. No, you can't. Not unless you promise never to tell anyone anything about what I've just said. Privileged information, Nigel. And you're too flattering by half. And don't think that seeing me half dressed at any time gives you rights above your station. I stay intacto, get it?"

She sounded quite fierce, bless her. "Jocelyn, you shouldn't need to say things like that, you know, but I respect your right to do so. I promise you I won't try and take advantage of you, if I can help it, but you could get me quite passionate if you tried!"

She laughed at him and his serious face. "That's all right then. I might, just might try sometime. When I feel the need. Then it'll be lucky old you, won't it?" She laughed again. "Did you say you wanted to kiss me? Can't think why!"

He took courage in both hands, stood behind her, cupped her breasts, and kissed her neck. She froze, never having been held like that ever before. A very strange sensation, not unpleasant, ran like a tingle of electricity round her tummy and the small of her back, and she felt her nipples move. She nearly said don't, but couldn't get the word out. His fingers lightly, very lightly, caressed her and the sensation intensified. So this was what the girls at college meant. Her breathing slowed and deepened, the instinctive reaction, and this was all new feelings. "Nigel. Oh, Nigel! Is this taking advantage of me?"

She wasn't sure whether she should stop him, or enjoy the feeling more. It was rather like that time when her Mums had shown – stroked her in the shower, just that once. Then he took his hands away and she felt a tinge of disappointment, a loss.

"I think we'd best go back to the house, Jo. Forgive me, but you're a temptation. Nice?"

What should she say? Yes, it was nice. It might even have been nicer if he'd carried on, but this was all new and disturbing. A non descript "Hmmm," then, and she made to slide off her stool, so he picked her up and carried her in his arms to the open door, set her down outside, then put an arm around her shoulder.

"Shall we hop together?" He was pulling her leg now, and

she poked him in the ribs.

"Not funny. You just wait. I'm vulnerable and you're taking advantage. Behave!"

* * *

David was home, and shook hands. "Nice to see you back, Nigel. Good journey?"

Jocelyn was pulled out of the sitting room by her mother, and the kitchen door shut behind her. "Stay here, young lady. Nigel's on his own. Your father needs to get an understanding."

Jo pulled a face, but there wasn't anything she could do about it, Mums had spoken.

Nigel saw her go, and inwardly winced. "Yes, thanks. Quite a trek, so I split the journey and overnighted near Bedford. I'm very pleased to see Jocelyn in such good spirits."

"Probably due to your presence. She wasn't as perky this morning, I can tell you. Eleanor tells me you've made her a happy girl?" Euphemism for explaining his feelings?

"I think I love your daughter, Mr Danielleson."

"Only think?"

Nigel swallowed. This was all very strange and peculiar, and smacked of Victoriana. David appreciated the lad's dilemma, and much as though he didn't really want to reach this hurdle quite so soon, if it was what made Jo happy, and Nigel was as decent a chap as he'd come across, then so be it.

"You really love her, don't you?"

"I do."

"When did you come to that conclusion?"

"First time I came here, to your garden party. She's a great girl."

"We know. She's all we have, Nigel. If she's happy with you, then we're happy for her, and you, but you realise what principles we have?"

"I believe so. I had a long chat with my father before I came down. Both my parents are very supportive, and are longing to meet Jocelyn. I'm just sorry I – we – got the wrong

358

impression of each other's feelings in France. Sorted now. Have I – we – your blessing?" How very like his father he thought he sounded.

David took a deep breath. Were he – and Eleanor – going to lose the delight of their life so soon?

"Yes, Nigel, you have. Eleanor and I both thought something like this might happen, though the speed has taken us a bit by surprise. You won't rush things, will you?"

"I don't know either of us want that. Just to get to know each other, have fun, do what we need to do, enjoy life, make sure we are doing the right thing?"

* * *

David nodded, perceptive to the mood of the moment. Nigel's ambitions, his interests, background, and his relative self-assurance – given he was still studying – all combined to give him confidence regarding the young man's intentions. Quite how Jo had so taken to him without any expressed qualms was a mystery, given she'd always been so defensive over all other approaches she'd had from a number of other boys, but then, that was what was so encouraging. "You'll be spending a lot of time apart, methinks. Does that bother you?"

Nigel hadn't really given it that much consideration. Just getting this far was an achievement in itself, reaching an 'understanding' that seemed so old fashioned nowadays, when so many of his peers simply took a girl's favours and let the rest take care of itself. Of course he'd had several flirtatious affairs, notably with a very delightful blonde back at home, but she'd been less than intelligent and he'd soon gone off her, especially as she suffered from b.o.; and admittedly he'd taken shameful advantage of a very sexy thing at Edinburgh, but she'd never had anything other than a penchant for different men in her bed, and that had been that. Now he was having a head-to-head with a prospective father-in-law, knowing full well this was a commitment which would influence his behavioural patterns and give his associates at college all sorts of reasons to make fun of him. So be it; Jocelyn was a girl in a million and he felt great about everything. He pulled a face, the realisation and commonsense of what David had said struck home and blighted his euphoria slightly. "I'd be wrong if I said no. I'm not sure how I'll manage, but to quote the hackneyed phrase *absence makes the heart, etc.*" He had a thought. "Would she be allowed to come to Edinburgh and see what I get up to at college?"

"Not in her present state she won't. I'm not sure, Nigel, let's take things as they come. What about the Norfolk trip? She was a trifle disappointed that didn't come off, you know."

"So were my parents. It'll happen. As soon as she's properly mobile and you can spare her."

* * *

He stayed for another day and a night, before all the pressures of an imminent return to another year's studies pushed him into a return home. It was now late August, and barely a week before he must be back to Edinburgh. Jocelyn's eighteenth birthday was the first week in September, and he just had return for that, come what may. He and Jo had gone off to see Julie late the previous day, to see how she was faring and to let her know how things stood. Jo had been a bit nervous of Julie's reaction, fully aware of not only their closeness, but the submerged feelings that her friend had for Nigel as well. After all, he had been a very caring person when she was at her most vulnerable. Jo needn't have worried; for in the meantime Julie's old flame had reappeared, probably, as she said, 'cos he missed his best dancing partner. Her comment brought out another momentary twinge of disappointment, wondering about the feel of being twirled around the dance floor by her Nigel. It will come, she comforted herself, it'll come, sooner or later.

But now it was another goodbye. First thing yesterday morning they'd gone up to the studio, and very carefully she'd sketched him sitting on her log, with the thick shock of dark hair, the prominent cheekbones and slightly kinked nose. With a half turned 'look at me' pose, she'd got his eyes completely right, loved what she'd done; it would be a constant reminder. Now he was going. Their goodbyes were breath crushingly tight hugs, and full kisses. Why hadn't she felt like this before? He'd written on her plaster cast, something she'd have with her until they cut it off – only another five weeks to go. 'Silly girl, I love you!' in large letters, but where really *only* she could see it. Her Mums had raised eyebrows after she was shown, and she'd blushed, but he'd been very good. Only once more had he held her where she tingled, but he'd winked at her then and there was no repetition of those feelings she'd had the first time. Now his little car had gone, and there was a hole in her life.

* * *

Later on in the sultry afternoon following his departure, and having mooched as best she could in hopping mode round the garden a couple of times, totally alone with her Mums away at the shop, she helped herself to a large glass of her Mums's lemonade and plonked herself down under the big old beech tree.

Heavy thunderclouds were building, and the blackbirds were in full voice with their rain song. Some of the late flowering shrubs were scenting well, as they did before the threat of rain; the peace and quiet and the truly all enveloping serenity of the garden soothed the little ache of missing Nigel.

Letting her mind wander she tried to analyse the way everything had happened since leaving, well, just before actually leaving college; her sudden explosion into the artistic mode, her developing friendship with Julie, the garden party, the dresses, the trip to France, her prints and Felicity's involvement, that fateful walk up onto the Plain and *Nigel!* So much, so much, so too too much. And now she had to cope with this *bloody* plaster! With two hands she lifted the errant limb onto the table in front of her chair, and leant back, looked up into the tree and watched the mother blue tit scavenging for caterpillars. A distant mutter of thunder heralded the approaching storm, but it was still miles away; often storms missed them, crouching as they did under the lea of the Plain.

What was she going to do now she had the exam results? Go to university, do that English degree, change it into a History of Art course if they'd let her, or mess about with her own artistic whims and see what happened? Would she marry Nigel if he asked her – there was every indication he would from the way they felt about each other, she'd really no doubt about that, so the long stop was she'd simply become a doctor's wife. Another roll of thunder, a bit nearer. A doctor's wife – her! She laughed to herself. A month ago and she'd never have believed anyone who might have suggested that's how she'd end up. The beech tree rustled all its leaves at once, the tits had vanished, and there was a sudden stillness. The first large, slow patter of heavy raindrops hit the garden, and brought a perceptive chill. "Indoors," she said out loud. "And before I get soaked." She hoinked her leg down, pushed to stand up, reached for her crutch and started back across the lawn. She'd covered the first twenty yards or so before there was the most almighty flash and instantaneous explosion in her ears, felt her whole body frizzle and tingle and she fell over, sprawling, not able to see with the dazzle from the lightning strike. Then came a rending sort of crashing noise, the ground heaved beneath her, and she screamed, not comprehending that the beech had lost nearly a third of its upper branches to bury her in a cascade of twigs and leaves, the intensified rain soaking her almost instantaneously. She was on her front and in sudden desperate pain from her leg, an arm twisted beneath her, legs akimbo, dazed and shocked. The branches of the beech were piled and twisted around her, she couldn't move, and she was terrified, tried to scream for help, but couldn't. She lay there, feeling herself slipping, slipping down, down into a deep velvet muzzy pit of darkness.

* * *

Eleanor heard the approaching storm and shivered. She hated thunderstorms, and would often go and shut herself in the downstairs loo where there was no window. The shop clock said ten to five. Good enough for me, she said to herself, no one will venture out now; I'm going home. There was an almighty big flash and a bang; the shop lights went off, flickered on, went off again and stayed off. "I'm definitely going home," she firmly said out loud. She locked up, not forgetting the alarm despite the power loss, and scurried out to her little car; that short journey pretty well soaked her, but the trip home wouldn't take long; she could have a shower and maybe tempt Jo into having a mutual back massage before David came home. He had said he might be a bit later, having to cope with the quarterly sales meeting, but maybe the storm would drive him home earlier? The garage doors were still open, and she shot straight in. The rain had lessened a little, but still persistent, so she kept her head down as she went across to the kitchen door, and didn't notice the change in the skyline.

"Jo? Jo-oh! Where are you, dear?" No reply; strange, she wouldn't be up in the studio, surely.

Perhaps she'd get David to organise a phone line or something. "Jocelyn! Are you upstairs?" Still nothing.

She went upstairs, shaking her wet hair; at least she'd get out of her wet dress. "So where are you dear?" out loud, but more of a question to herself. No, not in her room; she went to the window, and saw – saw a tangled mass of branches across her beloved garden, and – her heart leapt into her mouth – a bent leg and a white length of *plaster!* "Oh. OH! Jocelyn!" She tore downstairs, flung open the door, and ran, tears streaming. "Jo! Jo! Oh Jo! *Oh you silly, silly girl,*" said on her knees, pushing branches out of the way, crawling into the tangle, sweeping leaves aside, ruining her dress, scraping her legs and nearly getting a twig in her eye. Her girl was still breathing, and as Eleanor stroked her cheek, she opened her eyes.

"Mums! I'm soaked and my leg's *hurting!*"

"Soaked? Is that all? How are you hurt? Oh *Jocelyn!* Whatever possessed you to be out in this storm! You might have been killed!" She was cross and crazy with relief all at the same time. "Let's get you inside. Can you move?"

Jo tried unbending her arm, and it hurt. "Ouch!" She moved her good leg, half rolled over as best she could, lifting a knee and grimacing as fresh needles of pain stabbed at her thigh. Eleanor held her shoulders and heaved, to try and pull her clear, out of the debris, the injured limb dragging behind.

"It *hurts*, Mums. Have I damaged it again?" The nausea of the shock was making her feel faint again, her colour had all but gone and the pasty whiteness worried her mother. Should she continue to move her or call an ambulance? "I can't, Mums, I can't, it *hurts*!" That decided her.

"Sorry, my love, I'm going to call your father. Wait here, I'll get a rug."

Jocelyn managed a thin smile. "I'm not going anywhere."

Eleanor, reluctantly but of necessity, left her and ran for the house. She pushed the phone memory button for the garage; luckily David was just on the point of leaving. "Eleanor? Whatever...?"

"It's Jo. Our big beech got hit by lightning. She was underneath it, well, not directly, but she's been hurt again. Get home, David, *get home!*" Her voice squeaked at him. "I'm going to ring for an ambulance."

He heard her deep breathing, then it disconnected. He ran for the car.

* * *

When he arrived home, it was hard on the heels of the ambulance, already reversed in the drive with doors open. His heart pounding, he ran and nearly collided with the paramedics and the stretcher.

Eleanor, looking completely distraught, flung herself at him. "Dave, Dave, she may have lost the setting of her leg! You go with her; I'll follow in my car."

"Are you sure, wouldn't be better..."

"I'll be all right; if I know you're with her. Just go!"

In the ambulance, Jocelyn was strapped in, both legs together. The girl paramedic made reassuring noises, but they were away under twin-tones, and David's eyes watered. He reached and held a sweaty hand.

"Jo. You'll be fine. At least you weren't underneath. You're alive, and that's all that matters. I'll be here with you, Mums is coming."

Jocelyn could only manage a wan smile, but at least he felt her grip. The paramedic girl was checking her pulse, wiping her forehead; nothing else seemed to be of concern, he had to try and relax. Getting all stewed up wouldn't help, but he cursed not doing anything about his suspicions over the beech's upper branches. There was one hell of a mess to have to clear away.

* * *

At A&E Jo was whisked straight into theatre, and he could only sit and wait. Eleanor arrived within half an hour, and the two of them sat as close as they could get, waiting, saying nothing, but inwardly praying.

In due course, the Orthopaedic Registrar came out to see them. He wasn't smiling, but then maybe he never did. He sat down alongside them.

"Your daughter's fine, in no danger. You'll be able to see her shortly, after she's come round. We've had a good look at her, but it's not the best news. Falling as she obviously did, she's undone all the healing that was taking place, so the bone moved and as this amounts to a failed manipulatory setting, I've had to plate and pin it this time, which means she's going to have a scar and it's going to be a much longer job. We weren't sure whether the first break would cause some small limb displacement; now I'm almost certain that will be the case. I'm sorry, but at least she'll still have full movement, albeit with a slight limp. She's a brave girl, though. She'll pull through. I'll ask a nurse to bring you along in a while." He patted Eleanor's arm, and rose. "I gather she's an artist. At least she still has both hands. I'll keep a special eye on her progress."

As he went off up the corridor, Eleanor buried her head in David's jacket. "Our Jo, our beautiful girl; with a limp and a scar. What have we done, David, for this to happen?" Her sobs were interspersed with sniffs and deep gulps of breath. He could only squeeze her to him, and pat her shoulders. The picture of her bounding about, in those beautiful dresses, the imagery of her being half naked in the orchard, the way she'd clambered about up in that oak tree, and here she was, strapped and pinned and likely always to have a scar both physically and mentally. It was not real.

* * *

In a side bay of the ward, she was just an auburn haired head under the covers lifted on a frame as though she was an Egyptian mummy. Again, a rerun of the first time, she had a drip and now a drain as well.

"Jo. Darling? We're here!"

A slight turn of the head, a faint smile. "Sorry, Mummy, Pa. I'm a bit of a liability, aren't I?"

She eased a hand out from under the covers. "Don't tell Nigel."

"Why not, Jo?"

"Don't want him rushing down here; he's got his studying to do. He would come for my birthday weekend anyway."

"If that's what you want. What do we do if he rings?"

"Tell him I'll call him back. I can do that from here. You can tell Julie, though; I'd love to see her."

Eleanor looked meaningfully at David. He nodded, it wouldn't do any harm.

"All right dear. Now, how are you feeling? Has the pain gone away? You know they've had to open you up and pin your bone together?"

Jo didn't know; she hadn't been back from theatre all that long. Her eyes opened wide and she looked dreadful. "Nooooh! What does that mean, Mummy?"

Being called 'mummy' was a sure sign of her daughter's fragility, and David wasn't sure Eleanor should have broken the news to her so soon. "Well, it should mean that the bone is stronger, that it will mend better, but you won't be running about quite so soon." She wasn't going to mention anything about permanent limps.

Jocelyn wasn't at all sure she liked the sound of that. Her leg ached, certainly, but there was no stabbing pain any more. She changed the subject. "What you going to do about the tree, Daddy?"

"Not sure yet, sweetheart. Have to look at what's left, I guess. Looks as though we have some more firewood though. Pity, really, she was a nice tree."

"She? A tree is a she? Don't chop it down, Pa. Please. It wasn't *her* fault I was underneath it. The blue tits love it."

At that point a nurse appeared through the curtain across the annex. "I'm sorry, Mr and Mrs Danielleson, I think your daughter ought to have some rest now. She's been through rather a lot. Please do come back when you like tomorrow. We'll take great care of her, don't you worry."

So they had to leave her, all alone with her hurt and her thoughts, and drive slowly home.

* * *

An early night was no great comfort to either of them, just snuggled up and quiet. Sleep was an intermittent dweller that night, and dawn a grateful release. Eleanor heard David's deep sighs as he surveyed the wreckage; his expressed comment one of deep annoyance at not trusting his instinct. "I should have had those top branches taken out, you know, El. It's my fault."

"David, you couldn't have known that the storm would hit us like that, or that Jo would be underneath it. You can't blame yourself!"

"Well, I do. I've a good mind to clear the whole damned thing."

"No, NO! Jo said not, David; just do what's needed to tidy it up. It would spoil the garden, anyway, with no big tree."

"Not so big now. We'll see. I'll get Mike to give me a hand. Best get started. I'm taking the day off."

* * *

367

Mike grunted down the phone. "Sure. Be right over. Caught your lass, did it? Poor do, then. How's she be?"

"Poorly," David easily fell into Mike's abrupt vernacular. "Not going to be the same girl. We're a bit perch drunk."

"Ay. 'Nuff to make anyone do that. Bringing my big saw. See you." His expression, a version of 'falling off one's perch' brought back memories of the merriment caused when first heard, and felt a bit better with someone else coming to help. Eleanor did a big breakfast for them all after the first hour, by which time the loose stuff had been shifted and the extent of the damage exposed. A great jagged spear of torn timber jutted up from one of the three main stems where it had torn away. Examination of the fallen pieces showed where rain water had penetrated into an earlier branch's demise, starting a rot which had weakened that stem.

"Should ha' come down afore," was Mike's only comment.

"Don't tell me. I know. My fault. What do you think of the rest?"

"Looks sound enough. Leaves grow well, better un this un." True, the fallen branches didn't have anything like the same density or size of leaf. "Trim the stem, p'raps seal 'er. Keep an eye. Give 'er a chance."

So he wasn't the only one to give the beech a feminine gender. "Fine. Let's do it."

By the end of the day, apart from the fresh creamy orange scar on the bole and the rather messy lawn, it was tidy. A mound of bonfire material was waiting to dry out, and a much more useable pile of embryonic firewood stacked behind the garden tool shed.

"Missus gone hospital?"

There had been no tea break; a sure sign Eleanor wasn't there. She'd gone without either of them aware, and though David was sorry he wouldn't see Jo that day, Eleanor being with her some of the time wasn't so bad; he'd desperately wanted to get the tree tidied before she came home.

"Ay. My thanks, Mike."

"No problem. Give the girl the best. Sad do, could ha' bin worse."

* * *

Eleanor was late back, but with supper in a bag, fish and chips from the out-of-town chippery, an acceptable substitute for home cooking after a hard day's work.

"I don't know, David," was her response to his query. "The staff nurse says she's recovering well, anaesthetics coming out. She's been sick, but only to be expected. They won't be plastering her leg until the wound has healed, so she's still got that sort of cage contraption; leg on a support thing, and she can't move much. I think she's getting rather down. Not at all perky, not like the first time. She'll be there a while yet."

"Have you rung Julie?"

"No, I haven't. I'll do it now."

* * *

Julie was shocked and quite distressed when she heard the news. "When can I visit?" The thought that her friend and love had taken one step forward but now at least two steps back was horrifying to her. "Does Nigel know?" and surprised that he was not to know, but in a strange way, pleased. She said she'd go tomorrow, if that was all right.

* * *

Jocelyn lay still but could not rest. Her mind was swinging around like a flag on a pole in a hurricane; reliving the sudden way her life had been tipped on its side like the beech's branches. Why her? Just when she was getting herself sorted. All the nice things of the summer distorted and miscoloured like the bad bruise she'd had, and now couldn't see. How long would it be before she got home? Would she start university at the beginning of term? Pa was going to have to organise things for her. The vacillation of thought swung English, Art, English, Art, and what good art would do, anyway. If it hadn't been for her pash for drawing she'd still be intact, without that silly ferry trip. A sharp searing jolt of pain hit her, and she gulped air and nearly choked. A passing nurse heard and came over, said it was

*normal as nerves woke up. A good sign, she said! Damn all this, this
'You're doing fine stuff'. She felt rotten, and cross, and wanted to go
home and read a good book, dance in the rain in her nothings and
have her Mums scrub her all over in the shower and give her nice
feelings. Instead she was stuck here with this bloody knackered leg
and all because she'd drawn some portraits. Bugger it. The nurse
came back with a glass. She swigged it back, whatever it was, within
minutes felt as though she was being pulled up to the ceiling, before
her body switched off and she fell asleep.*

* * *

"Keep an eye on that one," the night staff nurse was told.
"She's heading into a depressive state, poor girl. Needs some
t.l.c and there's not much chance of that stuck in a cage. Let's
hope she heals well. I'm off, going for my own bit of t.l.c, well
t. and l., not so much of the care. He's a bit rough at times!"
The night staff nurse laughed, but checked Jocelyn carefully
when her colleague had gone. This one was pretty and having
a bent leg wouldn't please anyone.

* * *

Julie took a taxi into town. She couldn't ask her father to drive
her, and he needed the car anyway. She loathed hospitals, the
smell, the long corridors with anonymous doors and prosaic
notices, the robotic mop-pushers and the stony faced porters.
Jo was on the third floor, and the lift was large, slow, and had
stiff doors that rattled. She'd brought her a book, knowing
they didn't allow visitors to bring flowers in case of
contamination. Jocelyn seemed asleep, and she queried it with
a nurse.

"Just in a doze. A visitor will do her good, provided you
stay light hearted. She may be a bit moody."

Julie was surprised; the Jo she knew wasn't moody,
always smiling."'Jo! Jo, dear, it's Julie!"

Jocelyn struggled to lift her head, and Julie saw she
needed the pillows plumping up behind her.

"There, that better? Are you stuck?"

"Course I'm bloody stuck. Flipping leg's nailed down and as I'm attached to the bloody thing… Oh, sorry Julie, I'm annoyed. Annoyed at being here, annoyed at having been knocked over, annoyed at having gone to bloody France."

"My, my, you *are* in a strop! Here, I've brought you something to read. If you haven't forgotten how to read?" The book was one she'd read and enjoyed, a light hearted rather romantic easy read which didn't tax the brain, although it did tweak the imagination over the sexy bits.

"Thanks. I might be doing a lot of reading soon. I'm going to stick with the English degree, if they don't shut the door before I get there. God knows how long I'll be stuck in this thing."

"English? Thought you were going all History of Art?"

"Nope. Done with drawing – look where it's got me. Busted leg, now they've slit it to stick a pin through me, and suppose I can't properly walk or dance or run again? What use is that?"

Julie, at first surprised, was now shocked, but too intelligent to argue at this time. "At least you're still here, which you mightened have been if luck hadn't been around? My mum didn't get that option." Not realising what she'd said until she saw tears in her friend's eyes. "*Oh, Jo! I'm sorry!*"

"Don't be. You're right. I should be the sorry one. Yes, you're right, but I'm not drawing any more. I just don't feel that way. You can have that one of you in France. And the nude one in the studio, if you like."

This wasn't Jocelyn. Not the girl she'd begun to love like more than a sister. She'd love to have the drawings, of course, but didn't they mean anything to her friend – love girl – any more? She changed the subject, talked of Trish and Betty, the return of Robert out of the blue, and was about to say about going back to the dance school but discretion stopped her just in time. She didn't want to talk of Nigel, and as Jo didn't, he wasn't mentioned. Then conversation became a little desultory, and Jo's eyebrows drooped a time or two.

"I'd best be off, Jo. Can I visit again?"

"Love you to, Julie. I miss you about, actually. Sorry about all this. Thanks for the book." She closed her eyes again, helplessly sleepy once more, and when she next came to, Julie had gone. She cried a little, then drifted back to sleep.

* * *

Jocelyn was in hospital for three whole weeks, until her wound had healed sufficiently and her doctor had checked that the bones were knitting well. He was quite unexpectedly pleased at the x-ray, personally supervised the plaster casting, ensuring she'd have adequate manoeuvrability on the ankle joint, but couldn't let her use her knee joint just yet, though he promised her that if she was good, he'd arrange that in a week or two. Both her parents came to collect her in the Jaguar, thrilled to be getting her home again. Jo, in turn, was seeing her home in a new light, as a return to a paradise she'd lost and then regained. She was home just in time for her eighteenth birthday, though understandably her Mums had said the party had been postponed. The biggest problem had been keeping Nigel away, not that she wanted that specifically, but couldn't bear him to see her so immobile and useless, and anyway, it was too close to the start of his next year in Medical school. She managed to talk to him every few days, which was something, but the disappointment in her was plain to see.

Julie had worked wonders, patiently fielding all the outbursts of rancour over her situation, smoothing down the antipathy to her drawing, giving her as much love as she could. Once she had taken Robert in with her, but that hadn't been a good idea. Quite a few of her, and her parents' village friends, had popped in, including Reg, the postman; Mike, who amazingly, planted a kiss on her forehead, and even the local Vicar.

Now she was back. Her bed had been brought downstairs into the sitting room, despite her protestations, with the promise she could return to her own room by the end of the week if she behaved and didn't crash about.

"Crash about? Me? You must be joking. I'm back to where

I was a month ago. Hop about, yes. And I'm not going anywhere."

"Don't you want to go up to the studio?"

"No point. I'm not in a mood to draw."

That was the body blow to her parents, this sudden aversion to continuing her drawing. David had been commissioned to talk to the university admissions people and all the necessary procedures had been completed for her to start at Reading as soon as she was fit. They felt they could do no more, it was her choice and not theirs, though David was more than sad at the lack of interest in the studio they had spent so much love and care on creating.

"Do we have to do any more about the birthday party?" Eleanor, sitting on the edge of the bed in nothing but bra and pants, watched David sorting out his sock drawer. "That's the third time you've done that this week! Haven't you got enough socks?"

He crammed the rest of the loose pairs in and shut the drawer. "Don't think so. She'll see it as all a bit academic. She's had her presents, her friends are all at college or about to go, the studio seems to be past history. That idea of taking her on a day out to see the two Tate's is a dead duck, and she'll think we can't even properly take her out to dinner. Shame Nigel's in Edinburgh, about as far away as he can get, poor chap, Julie's off tomorrow, and, oh damn and blast the whole mess!" He grinned at her.

Eleanor rolled onto her back and waved her legs at him. "Take my knickers off then, see if that gets you into a better mood!"

* * *

Jocelyn was not asleep. She should be, for it was gone midnight. She'd heard her parents, upstairs, but thought nothing of it; her mind was on her abandoned eighteenth birthday party. When she should have had a wonderful time, last Saturday, here it was, her birthday proper tomorrow, and nothing. Bloody bloody nothing. At least she could move around now, and her leg had stopped aching, though it was itchy beyond belief. The long thin flat rod was a real treasure, at least she could scratch.

Julie had given her another book by the same author as that other one; she'd enjoyed that and the latest one augured well. A girl not being able to start a baby had found a soul mate and the two of them had designs on the husband. With the opening all about a tree being blown over, she could relate to that. Idly, she cast Julie in the role of soul mate, but she didn't think she'd want to share Nigel with her. Far too dangerous. Nigel, way up in Edinburgh. Hope he misses me. I miss him.

With a table lamp as a bedside reading lamp, she picked up the book and worked her way through the bit where a mysterious bloke seems to be stalking the orphan girl. After another chapter, her eyes were growing heavy, and she nearly dropped the book twice from sleepy hands. Ultimately she gave up, and just managed to switch her lamp off before she fell asleep.

* * *

At first light, now shortly before seven, David heard the phone go, and struggled to find the bedroom extension before it woke everyone else.

"The Old Vicarage." Goodness knows how he managed to say it properly whilst still half asleep, and who on earth wanted them at this hour? At least Jo was safely tucked up downstairs, so it wasn't about her.

He was wrong.

"Sorry to phone at this early hour, but it's Nigel. I'm catching the eight o'clock flight out of Edinburgh. You couldn't meet me at Bournemouth could you? Surprise the young lady?"

SEVENTEEN

Jocelyn couldn't understand why her Mums was quite so chirpy. She'd been concentrating on the garden restoration after the storm, which had taken all her spare time over the past couple of weeks in between shop duties, and visits to the hospital; happily it was just about back to normal. Nothing much had been said about the failed birthday party; every time the conversation had drifted that way Jo got the feeling her Mums was more disappointed than she was, so on the actual day she'd anticipated a real glumness. Her beloved Pa had given her one box to open, her Mums another; to her delight she found she was the proud possessor of another beautiful set of lingerie *and* a real slinky clinging silky dress in pale blue with a necklace in turquoise stones to match. She'd wanted to try it on, unable to quite see the sense of it when Mums said "Save it for later." There was something in the air, she was sure. Her Pa had apologised for having to go out for a while, said he'd be back for lunch, and they would be going out to dinner, hopalong girl or no.

After one or two queries about not sketching any more, neither parent had mentioned it again, though her early portraits still had pride of place in the house. She'd had a long chat with Felicity on the phone, agreed the magazine could organise another print run of her 'White Dress'; after all, it was money. But that was that; she'd had no urges and doubted she could do anything worthwhile. Instead, she read, discovering an interest in some obscure 1920s authors, and never once ventured up to the orchard. (David had been left wondering what to do with the studio, but Eleanor told him to bide his time. "It'll keep, let's just see.") So now it was Birth Day, and she was an adult of about three hours.

Why did her Mums keep glancing at the drive every time a car drove by? She didn't normally. And no phone call from Nigel, which was a bit off. Julie'd phoned; she'd had quite a few cards, including one from old Mrs Parsons, hand-made with a bit of fabric on a sketched figure, showing the old lady hadn't lost her touch. The best thing was a little parcel from Edward and Dylys, a leather bound copy of a Victor Hugo and a lovely inscription: 'To an angel girl who delights us both – lose not your talent nor your youth.' It didn't quite rhyme, but as good as. At least Edward didn't admonish her for drifting away from painting or drawing. Perhaps he'd guessed her *Inspiration* had left her.

"Do you want another drink, dear? Coffee? Or a cold drink?"

"Mums, I've only just finished breakfast. Why do you keep grinning to yourself like that?"

"Grinning, dear? Well, it's your birthday, why shouldn't I grin? Got to be happy about something, can't be miserable on your *birthday*."

"Mums, I love you, but you haven't said what's going on. I know there's something. What's Pa doing out anyway? He's never out on my birthday!" Which was nearly true, David had always made it a rule to spend the day at home with his daughter when it was her official birthday. A bit like the Queen, only hers was always on the Saturday nearest to the date, this year the day *was* a Saturday.

"Nothing's going on dear, he just had to pop out to collect something. He'll be back anytime."

She looked at the time again. There and back, he'd said, three hours maximum. Nearly eleven; should be soon. "Why don't you have a hop round the garden, see what you think to the new shrub – the one next to the yew trees?"

Jocelyn looked at her mother sideways. She'd definitely got something going on, but what could she do other than humour her. "So okay, Mums. I'll hop round the garden. I might even have to learn how *not* to hop when this comes off," she said, darkly, and went. Eleanor watched her go, and hoped everything was going according to plan. If she'd insisted in her changing early into the new glad rags she'd have smelt a rat, dressed as she was in that old skirt and raggedy blouse she really was no sight for a boyfriend either, but at least she had a bit more colour to her now.

A mere ten minutes later and the Jaguar purred into the drive. Jo was nowhere to be seen. Maybe she *had* gone further, up to the old orchard, which would be great if she had. The car doors were carefully shut, with a velvety clunk, and the occupants looked extremely furtive. Both slid into the house. Eleanor's carefully timed plan had worked. She waited a minute or two before setting off to find her girl. She actually found her in the old barn, sitting on one of the old tables, practising her ankle flex.

"All right, darling?"

Jo was getting far too many 'all rights?', and sort of snapped 'Of course' before relenting, sliding down from her perch to put her arms around her mother.

Eleanor clasped her tight, and hugged her. "You can come in now. Don't need to stay out all morning. Then you can have that coffee you asked for."

"Did I? Oh, all right." Definitely something peculiar happening. This wasn't her Mums at all, being so vague and presuming. With her mother as a better support than her crutch, they managed the journey back across the lawn easily. The beech tree, now two thirds its size, seemed to stand aloof, as if to say, it wasn't my fault. She was glad Pa hadn't taken it all down.

"Just pop into the sitting room, Jo, and I'll bring your coffee through. Your father's home…"

Jocelyn did as she was told, and her father was standing by the window. "Pa! What have you been up to? Where have you been?" She advanced into the room, and felt two hands round her eyes.

"Guess who?"

"*Nigel*! Oh, *Nigel!*" She couldn't spin round quite the same, but she did her best, and fell into his arms while David executed a strategic retreat. "What are you doing here, how did you manage this, oh, *Nigel!* Nigel! It's so good to see you!"

She had to stop, because she was being kissed and she loved it, being held, and loved, and kissed again. "Hmmm-mmmm – oh, it's lovely being held. I've missed you. Thought about you. Wanted you with me, but told Mums not to tell you about the storm 'cos I didn't want you to..."

"Shhh. I know, you silly girl. I know, and I love you for caring. But you mean so much I couldn't, just couldn't *not* see you on this day of all days. So I flew down, special sanction, and I'm back late tomorrow. Your father picked me up from Bournemouth, and here I am. So how's my wounded soldier girl?" He held her at arm's length and surveyed her, all of her, to remind himself of shape and delight and the colour of her hair, the dimpled cheeks and the few freckles and the taste of her, pulling her back towards him and kissing her again.

"Loving you being here. It's made my day, Nigel."

A cough from the doorway. "Your drinks!" Her father, with a tray, and *glasses!*

"Mums said coffee?"

"Champagne, Jo, for a very special birthday girl. It's the recognised thing, you know."

She was smiling now, a radiant, happy, back to normal girl, and with glasses clinked, she had the toast – "To the best girl in the world," and beamed at them all, and drank, and nearly choked on bubbles, and they all fell about laughing, and had another glass each, so she had to collapse in an undignified way onto the settee, with Nigel pulling her to sit upright again and smoothing her skirt back across her knees for her, as a gentleman should. She was giggling now, and feeling more than a little light headed, and kissing bits of him while Mums dived back into the kitchen to regain her composure while her Pa sat down and looked as though he wanted to say something.

"Will you sketch, draw, or paint again, Jo?"

She wasn't thinking any more, the champagne had gone to her head, or her knees, she wasn't sure, but it felt as though the plaster had fallen off. "Dow-nnt know, Pops, wheys?" She was sure she wasn't drunk, but it felt peculiar. Nigel was looking at her strangely.

"Why is your father asking that, Jo?"

"She stopped when the tree collapsed on her. Blamed the whole thing on her drawing, don't know why." David had to do the answering.

Jocelyn's mind clicked back into gear. "Because if I hadn't drawn things, I wouldn't have gone to France, wouldn't have fallen down a staircase, and wouldn't be limping around like a Long John Silver."

"Well, at least you've read R.L.S. That's no logic, Jo, not with a talent like yours. You draw like a angel, and it would be wrong not to use what you have, for heaven's sake."

"Well that's what's happened, and if you want me to stay happy, stop going on about it." She made to get up, but Nigel held onto her. "Let me *go!*" He relinquished his hold, and she struggled up. "If you want to be useful, help Pa get my bed back upstairs. Then I'm going to change and look beautiful for you. Go on. I'm going to talk to Mums."

* * *

Hearing her daughter becoming more definitive than she'd ever known her to be before, Eleanor's attitude was at first defensive and then aggressive. "You shouldn't blame your drawing for this misfortune, dearest, and taking it out on poor Nigel isn't fair on him, not after him coming all this way just to see you on your birthday. That's not being adult, it's being childish. You could have been under that tree even if you'd never lifted a pencil to paper in your life, and maybe another second might have seen us without a daughter at all, and that doesn't bear thinking about. You thank your lucky stars it wasn't any worse. Your father and I are bitterly sorry that you've been damaged, as well you know, but to compound that misfortune by giving up on your drawing isn't either fair on yourself or us. After all we've been doing to support your change in direction, building the studio, encouraging you, even prepared to keep you at home until you can make your name, as I'm sure you would, and you just chuck it because of an *accident?* It's not the Jocelyn I know and love, nor is it likely

379

to be the one your Nigel's fallen in love with, so snap out of it, girl!"

Jocelyn had never had her mother talk to her in quite that way ever before, and reeled under the onslaught. She had been going to try and get her Mums on her side, to stop anyone going on at her, though the champagne had gone to her head and she suddenly wasn't sure about anything, not with her Mums getting cross at her like that. She stood and stared at her Mums, who had gone quite red. Then she'd had enough, and crumpled into a chair, sticking her leg out, wishing she could fold it under her like she'd always done in this, her favourite basket chair, and burst into tears.

Instantly, Eleanor was contrite. "I'm sorry, Jo. I shouldn't have gone on at you, 'specially on your birthday." She wished she could have hugged her, but it didn't seem quite right. "Can I come and help you change? We are going out tonight, a special birthday dinner, just for you! Please?"

Jo sniffed, and rubbed at her eyes. "It's not fair!"

"I know, life isn't always fair, Jo, but others are far worse off. You still have your hands, your arms, a decent leg, a lovely shape and a gorgeous head of hair, and all our love. And Nigel's too, by the sound of things. And Julie's, who's lost a mother! Please let me help you?"

Jo allowed herself to be shepherded upstairs, passing Nigel and her father on their way down from reinstalling her bed in her room. With red eyes and looking very much the worse for wear, she couldn't even look at him, and Eleanor shook her head slightly at him as if to say 'leave her', so he had to content himself with just patting her arm as they crossed. David gathered his wife was doing her 'mother hen' act, and was quite content to leave her with the situation.

* * *

It took Eleanor the best part of an hour to put her daughter through the shower, get her into all her new clothes, brush her newly washed hair back into lustrous shape, and make sure she was in a better frame of mind. Her last minute brief was

"Look pretty, my Jo, if it's only for your father." Jocelyn had to think about her response. She'd been pampered by her beloved Mums, and despite the telling off she'd had, now had a warm sort of inner glow that made her feel different, certainly much more comfortable with her world than hitherto.

"Only seventy-five percent pretty, Mums. This isn't pretty," half lifting the plastered limb, though admittedly the rather swish folds of her new birthday dress now hid most of it.

"No, darling, it's not, but *you* are, and I'm proud of you. Go and give Nigel – and your father – a treat, then we'll be off to have a lovely meal."

She was getting quite good at moving up and downstairs now. Eleanor watched her go. A small smile of satisfaction crossed her features. Amazing what a new dress, (and the bits underneath, she wryly added to her thoughts), a cosy shower and a bit of loving attention will do to a girl. "*I ought to know*," recalling some distant memories of her own, she concluded to her reverie, and slowly followed.

* * *

Jocelyn was expecting to go to their usual place, the Italian restaurant, but no, her father turned left at the crossroads. She didn't say anything, sitting cosily in the back of the Jaguar, with Nigel loosely holding her hand, but she did notice the half smile her Mums was keeping under control.

"Pa – where are we going?"

David, concentrating on the bend in the road and keeping his eyes forward, gave her a very unsatisfactory "Wait and see". So she kept quiet and felt Nigel squeeze her hand, ever so gently. It was taking some time, they must have gone miles. There was the Manor on this road, but that was all she could think of, and they wouldn't be going there, it was far too posh a place, surely…

"Pa! Here?" They turned into the gates; past the lodge house, and the fine gravel drive that led to the Jacobean stone

Manor. Something about four seasons, oh gosh, *really?*

It was a dream. Being greeted as though they were royalty, staff in pristine uniforms, she wished she hadn't got the crutches, but they didn't seem to notice, and the man who seemed to be in charge shook their hands, and her father inclined his head to listen to him as he obviously said something important, then her Pa's face broke into a grin, as they were ushered towards double doors on the left. Her Mums led her forward, Nigel close behind, she had to pause a moment while two of the Manor girls opened both doors simultaneously, and-- and...

"Happy Birthday! Happy Birthday Jocelyn!" echoed round the room, full of people, all holding glasses up, toasting *her?* She scarcely felt her Mums's hand, leading her on, or Nigel's little kiss, but her eyes were misting, and she had to stop while she wiped them with a free hand, crutch under her shoulder. Then her father was taking her crutches, and holding her and her Mums was there, and she was between them and everyone was smiling at her. She couldn't believe this was happening, to *her?*

"All your friends, my darling girl. It's your birthday party! Happy Birthday, angel. It's our surprise. Hope you enjoy your evening!" Then she had a glass, and so had her Mums and Pa, and Nigel, and there was a toast, from the Manor's *Maitre'D,* "*To Jocelyn, at her coming of age at Eighteen. Health, Happiness, and Success in all she does.*" She couldn't help it; tears were streaming down her cheeks. Nigel was offering her his large pristine white hanky, and she was dabbing her eyes, and laughing and crying and smiling, and oh, she could feel her chest muscles hurting with the full emotion of it all. Then there was this big velvet and mahogany armchair, so she could sit down, and see everyone around her. There was Julie, and Trish, and Brendan and Betty with her step-mum, there was Edward and Dylys, even Reg the postman, and old Mrs Parsons, others of her school year, a guy in uniform – oh, yes, from the Base! Two or three people she didn't know, but her Pa seemed to, even his boss from the business was there, and two of Mums's friends from the shop, with some of their closer neighbours; even Mike and his girlfriend. All talking at once, and the noise seemed to be getting louder, as the waitress girls circulated with more wine, or was it champagne, 'cos it sparkled; then wonderful little canapés.

"Jo? Hope it wasn't too much of a shock for you, but it wouldn't have been a surprise otherwise. Everyone has come, pretty well. It's not actually a dinner party, more a sort of buffet do, but then we couldn't tell you that either, could we?" Her Pa was whispering in her ear.

She turned her head back and kissed him, a real proper smoochy kiss; because she loved him and it was so much like him to dream up something like this. "It's super, Pa, it really is! You and Mums, organised all this?"

"With a little help from our friends! Now, enjoy yourself. Nigel will look after you, but you're not to stir from your chair, do you hear me? It's on wheels, so Nigel will push you round. It may be a long evening, and I'm not having you on your feet all night, all right?" He grinned at his rhyme. "And then there's someone you need to meet. I'll bring him across in a little while. Have fun!"

* * *

She felt like a princess, with her subjects paying homage. All she had to do was sit there, and Nigel kept her plied with nibbles and kept her glass topped up. He was very thoughtful and caring, 'cos he told her his bottle was largely lemonade so she didn't get drunk. It was a bit burpy, though, and she wondered how long it would be before she had to explore the ladies loo. No doubt Mums would step in when required. All the chats she had! And the jokes, and the compliments, and the commiserations about her accidents. What she liked best was Edward, with his wonderful way with words.

"My dear Jocelyn!" She would always be 'his dear'. "You look absolutely radiant! I wish I had time to paint – in this chair, the dress, and that hairpiece - (She'd put her heirloom on, luckily, or had Mums's suggested it?) – my little French peasant girl turned Princess! Remember our conversation

383

about you turning artist? And here you are; an artist and an art form at one and the same time! Charming, utterly charming! I must congratulate you, on your success. I'm insanely jealous, your own exhibition!"

She looked at him, puzzled. "What do you mean, Edward? *My own* exhibition?"

"You mean you haven't been approached? Oh, my dear girl, I'm sorry. I can see I've let the cat out of the bag. Here, wait a minute!" He looked round the room, spied the person he was looking for, and beckoned. A tall, well-dressed man with a shock of greying hair and rather lined features excused himself from his partner and approached them. "Charles. May I introduce Miss Jocelyn Danielleson, your potential exhibitor? Jocelyn, this is Sir Charles Carpenter. He owns the Lythguard Gallerie in London. It appears she hasn't been made party to your offer, Charles, and I've rather stolen your thunder. My apologies."

This Sir Charles had a somewhat severe smile, but it was a smile. He picked up her hand, and gave a slight bow as he brushed the back of it with his lips. "I am charmed, Miss Danielleson. May I take the liberty of calling you Miss Jocelyn?"

She nodded, unsure of all this. Nigel had gone off in search of his own comfort, so she was left by herself. Where was Pa? Edward was with her, though.

"Edward introduced me to your talent, Miss Jocelyn. He and I are old friends, and knows my likes and dislikes when it comes to the art world. Maybe he wishes I would like the more colourful concepts of his style, but there we are. I happen to prefer the finer, more detailed work, of which yours is a fair example."

Edward snorted; a very un-Edward like noise. "Fair be damned! Excellent example more like! Give the girl her credit, Charles! You know she's talented as well as I!"

Jocelyn looked from one to the other. "I've given up drawing."

"*You what?*" Edward looked astounded. "You cannot, my Jocelyn. You just cannot!"

Sir Charles raised eyebrows as bushy as Edward's. "Really, Miss Jocelyn? And may I ask why, when I am about to offer you a week's selling exhibition at my Gallery?"

"It's given me nothing but grief. That accident on the ferry coming back from France, then that led to me being knocked over and nearly killed by our tree. I may not be able to run about like I used to, and I've got a scar, and maybe one leg shorter than the other. I just don't feel like it any more. And if I don't feel right I can't draw. The *Inspiration*, as you called it, Edward, just isn't there. The last thing I did was of Nigel, and he's got that." She felt her tears coming back, and sniffed.

Sir Charles looked at Edward, and he looked round for Jo's father. Then Nigel was back, and Edward introduced him. "Sir Charles, this is our Jocelyn's escort. I believe she saved him from a rather nasty situation a wee while ago. Nigel, sorry, I can't recall your surname?"

"Haversed, Sir Charles. Nigel Haversed. I'm at Edinburgh, doing Medicine. Jo – Miss Danielleson - actually saved my life. I was hanging up in an oak tree all tangled up in a parachute harness, and probably would have strangled myself, but she climbed up and cut me loose. She's a great girl, and I love her."

Sir Charles was intrigued, fascinated even. "Well, now, Miss Jocelyn. I'm sure a young lady of your obvious calibre is not likely to allow a comparatively trivial matter of a fracture to alter her entire life? This may not be the time or place to consider the matter in detail, but please allow me the honour of calling on you at home so I can at least place my proposition to you, with your parents, of course." In his book, young ladies were not adult until they were at least twenty one, but he couldn't admit to that nowadays.

Nigel was holding her hand again, and her Pa had come back to her. He'd obviously met Sir Charles, or so it seemed, because Edward didn't do introductions. "Sir Charles. I see you've been introduced to my daughter. Thank you so much for sparing the time to come to our little celebration."

"Not at all, Mr Danielleson, not at all. My pleasure, I can assure you, and to meet a very courageous and talented young lady. I am somewhat dismayed, though, at her declaration not to take up her pencil again. This would be a great loss. I have just asked if I may call, at your convenience, and discuss my proposition in greater detail?"

David touched Jo's shoulder, and she half turned her head to him. There was an unspoken request, an appeal, in his gaze, and a question in his eyes. She had to say yes, if only for him, and she gave him the right to answer in her little nod.

"Please, Sir Charles, it would be *our* pleasure. Do let me have some idea of when you may be free, and I'm sure we'll be delighted. Would Edward be able to join us?"

That's Pa, being clever and devious, she thought, as Sir Charles turned to Edward with his unspoken question. He would be happy to be party to any discussions if it were appropriate, he said, and it was left like that. They moved away, and Jo followed them with her eyes.

"You didn't say, Pa!" It was an accusing tone of voice, but he only smiled.

"I did say I wanted you to meet someone, only half an hour ago, Jo, but Edward beat me to it. Never mind, I think you scored a hit with the chap. He's very influential, I believe. Edward showed him a copy of your print, and it went from there. Now, Felicity wants to say hello."

She was lurking, with Betty in tow. All the others seemed to be quite happy in chatting around, but she guessed they were only waiting their turn to pay homage, for that's what it seemed like; her stuck on this throne-like chair. She'd have to get up and go the rounds, even if Nigel had to give her his arm, though she was sure he wouldn't mind. Better than being stuck behind her like a pageboy.

"Hi Felicity. Thanks for coming. Hi, Betty. How did you do?" She referred to the exams, but that was a wrong move. Felicity beat her to the answer.

"It's very nice to be here, Jo, and thank you very much for inviting us, it's a super party. Maybe it's not the occasion to talk exam results, though. Another time?"

"Oh." She looked at Betty, who pulled a face. Like that, was it? "Right. It wasn't me that did the inviting. All my parents' idea, I didn't know anything about all this. Rather a big surprise."

"Just as well. We were sworn to secrecy. Rather like a 'This is Your Life' thing. We haven't got a Red Book lurking about, have we?" She glanced at David, who shook his head.

"Don't think so. Not this time. Give her a year or three, after she's been shown at the Royal Academy."

Jo was adamant. "I'm not drawing, Pa. It's English for me, once I can get to Reading."

David was unconvinced, but sane enough not to argue at this juncture. "We'll see. Felicity had some news?" Which gave her the opening.

"That's right. The magazine – that's me, really, you know – is going to sponsor another run of your print of 'The White Lady', with your agreement, and we thought some of the proceeds could go to the Air Ambulance, sort of a thank you for getting you off that boat so quickly. What d'you think?"

Jocelyn nearly, but not quite, burst into tears. The whole episode she had tried to sweep into the back of her mind, get it shoved well and truly into the waste bin, and here was Felicity, putting it back into the forefront. Why couldn't she leave the print, her one and only published print, alone? If there were too many of them floating about they'd lose their value. She had to be polite, though, and so she stalled.

"Can I think about this, Felicity? I've had so much excitement today, I can't think straight, so maybe tomorrow? I do like the idea of supporting the Air Ambulance, certainly, but I don't know that that print is ideal." Why was she speaking so much like an adult, she asked herself? I sound a bit stand-offish, just when she's obviously so pleased with her idea. Well, I *am* an adult! "Maybe there's something else more suitable?" Quite what, she didn't know, trying hard to think, but failing. It was either too much lemonade or too long a day...

Her father came to the rescue. "Perhaps Jocelyn's right, Felicity. Can we give it some thought and come back to you. Of course, the magazine's sponsorship is great, but if Jo can do something else...'

But would she, if her declaration 'no more drawing' stayed firm?

Nigel added his two pennyworths. "Maybe something with a helicopter actually in it?"

Jo shook her head. "I can't draw helicopters! I'll have a look at what I've done so far, and then you'll come up to the Old Vicarage and see?"

Felicity had heard about Jocelyn's stated refusal to draw again, and wondered if this was going to happen, but if that's the way it had to be... "I'd like to. Wouldn't do any harm to have *another* of your drawings published, Jo. I'd support that. Give me a ring. Now, Betty and I have to say 'goodnight', we're trying to get another party in as well. Where's Eleanor – I have to say thanks and cheerio to her."

Eleanor was in a little circle of her own acquaintances, including the venerable Mrs Parsons, and they were well involved in talking the open-air theatre back into being. She broke off mid flow to acknowledge Felicity and Betty's 'goodnight', and the comment that Jo may consider letting another print be published. "Good Lord! If that's the case, things are looking up. Well done, Felicity. We're talking open-air theatre. Any use to your magazine?"

Felicity made non-committal noises, and pulled Betty away. Too much of a good thing, hard on the heels of the garden article, and she wasn't a great fan of these open-air do's anyway, being far too susceptible to midges and mosquitoes to relish deckchairs on sticky and damp summer evenings.

Eleanor looked at Felicity's retreating back and shrugged. "Oh well," she thought. "If Jo's thinking positively, maybe we'll get somewhere." She turned back to her group. "Now, where were we?"

* * *

The evening moved along, the buffet was mouth-wateringly delicious; Jo managed to get out of her chair and move around while most folks were sitting, and with Nigel continuously at her side. There were quite a few nice remarks about him, too, and she was losing her irksomeness over her injury as the evening progressed. No one had even commented on her plaster, but they did like her dress, and by the time their guests were drifting away she was glowing, and not feeling at all tired. Pa had tried to get her to sit down again, but she wasn't having any of it. "No, I'm fine, and Nigel's looking after me. Don't fuss, Pa!"

David gave up after a while, just pleased that all their secret planning and all those phone calls had pulled it off. There was a hefty bill to pay, but then one's only daughter didn't have more than one eighteenth birthday party. Finally, the last guest had gone, and they were being seen out when the nice *Maitre'D* fellow whispered in Jo's father's ear. He looked very surprised, even startled, and she wondered what had transpired, though nothing was said in the car on the way home.

She had a lovely passionate hug and quite a few kisses from Nigel before he went into his room, and then her Mums was waiting to see her safely into bed.

"What did that chap say to Pa when we were leaving?"

Eleanor was not going to be drawn. "We'll tell you in the morning, dear. Did you enjoy your day?"

"I did, Mums. Thank you ever so ever so much. It's been super. After all. I thought it was going to be horrible, but it's been great." She snuggled down. "I shan't want to get up too early."

Eleanor smiled. "Nor will we, darling, but Nigel has to get back, I'm afraid. Sleep well, see you in the morning. Night night."

Jo closed her eyes, and was probably asleep before her mother got into her own room. At some point in the night, whether it was the combination of all the rather exotic foods or the alcohol, or just the stresses of the day was uncertain, but she dreamt.

* * *

She was lying on the grass. It was warm, pleasantly warm, and the little clouds above her were moving slowly across the deep blue sky.

The sound of birds, and a light, whispering soft breeze rustling the leaves of the trees around her. She had one arm under her head as a pillow, the other across her tummy. She wasn't sure whether she had a dress on, she didn't know. She must be on the top of a hill, because the ground fell away below her. There was a vapour trail from an aircraft lining across the sky like a strip of cotton wool, but no sound from up there. Peaceful, peaceful, peaceful, and she smiled in her sleep.

Julie was coming, walking up the hill towards her, with her mother, holding hands. Julie's mum was in a flowing, gossamer white dress; Julie naked, her hair unpinned and floating down round her shoulders. They were smiling at her. Then Nigel was there, he was crouched alongside her, with her sketch pad and her pencils.

"Draw that beautiful naked girl, and her mother, before it's too late, she can't stay long. I'll help you."

Somehow she was sketching, using Nigel's back as a rest for the paper. He was gazing at the lovely naked Julie, but it didn't seem to matter, because she too, had no clothes on. The picture was beautiful, wistful, Grecian, the two women gazing at each other with loving expressions, holding hands. There was a basket of apples alongside them. She drew in the vapour trail in the sky with the fleecy clouds, and two trees in the background, then it was finished, and as she put her pencils down, her subjects seemed to just fade away. Nigel was looking at her, with such love in his eyes, and she stood up, holding his hands, face to face, and then she had a ring on her finger, he lifted it to his lips and kissed it, then he let go of a hand to stroke her forehead. "Wake up, Jocelyn," he was saying. "Wake up."

* * *

"Wake up, darling! It's nearly half past eight!"

* * *

Jocelyn didn't want to wake up; it was so nice on her grassy hill. She stretched her limbs out and flexed her spine, flung her arms out wide. Nigel would love her, she knew he was going to love her, and this was all she wanted.

"Darling! Wake up, darling!"

"Mmmm? What's the time?" The grassy hill slipped away, the clouds had gone. It was her *ceiling!* "Oh, Mums! I've had such a weird dream." What was it Nigel had done? She couldn't focus back, it just wouldn't come clear. She'd been drawing, someone. Who had it been? She frowned. It had been so real, somehow, but what – who – had she been drawing?

Then it clicked. *Julie!* But with someone else, she was sure. But she wasn't going to draw again.

Easing herself up; today her leg didn't ache the same as it did usually when she first woke up; seeing her Mums in her Sunday dress brought the day into clarity. It was Sunday, then. Nigel was going back to Edinburgh, and her tummy did a nasty flip.

"Do you want me to help you dress? Breakfast's on the table."

No, she thought. If my leg doesn't ache, I'll manage. I've got to try and remember my dream.

First she slid the plastered leg out, bent the knee joint, found the floor, then the normal one; flung the covers to one side, and stood up. It was as though she'd never had the break. Surprisingly, she felt great, and would have smiled her heart out at her Mums but Nigel was going. Never mind, he'd be back, and he loved her, was *going* to love her, because she'd had him in her dream, and her tummy did another flip.

Eleanor watched her critically. "If I didn't know you better, I'd say you were hallucinating. Your eyes are moving too quick. Did you say you'd been dreaming? Seems to me you had too much to drink last night, or too many prawn vol au vents. How's that leg of yours this morning?"

Jo stretched, and felt the weight on her plastered leg. "It's fine, absolutely fine, Mums. Not a twinge. Look, I'm going to shower, is Nigel…?"

"He's downstairs, been out for a run, don't worry, the coast's clear. I'll leave you to it, then?"

* * *

Eleanor found David and Nigel at the table. "Don't know what's happened to our Jo, but she *is* bright and chirpy this morning, says she's been dreaming. 'Bout you, I shouldn't wonder, Nigel. And her leg isn't bothering her; it's as if she hasn't the plaster on. Strange, but rather inspiring."

"Good to hear. It was a very good do, last night. Everyone seemed to be having a nice time, I know I did. Well worth the flight. I'm just sorry I have to go back!" Nigel reached for another piece of toast, quite at home with his possible future parents-in-law.

"No gain without pain!" David repeated an oft-used phrase. "She'll miss you, I know, but when she gets herself into her university life it won't be so bad, new faces, new places, new experiences. I'll – we'll – miss her around here. Just hope she stays out of trouble. I do *not* want any more scares. Can I pass you the marmalade?"

EIGHTEEN

Within the week Jocelyn had had the plaster removed and was able to examine her leg critically. The scar wasn't too noticeable, just a thin red line she was assured would fade in time – all she might be left with would be a mere sort of pencil line effect. It took her a few days to get the feel of both legs working properly together again, and because of the dire warnings she may have a residual limp, she did everything she could to keep her posture correct. At the final check before the hospital would sign her fit to go to university, the Orthopaedic guy who'd put her back together was extremely pleased with her. "I wish all my patients were as determined as you are," he'd said, "Now don't go and wreck anything else!"

* * *

The following week she was installed at the university, with a whole new set of experiences to take on board, new places, new faces, just as her Pa had said. Her drawing period, those weeks during the summer, seemed another life away. True, Felicity's insistence over getting another print had been rewarded by her agreeing to let the half sexy one of Julie in the old Satin dress in the barn be used; somehow the two prints together made a beautiful pair, the one helping to sell the other, and she had a tidy sum of money to start her off at uni. Despite earnest entreaties from Edward, she remained adamant she wouldn't do any more, at least, not while she was getting settled into her course. She wouldn't be drawn on the idea of a selling Exhibition either, and David felt he couldn't pressurise her by letting her know that Sir Charles had insisted on making a contribution to the buffet party bill – in fact it was a fait accompli because the *Maitre'D* had simply told him Sir Charles had diminished the bill before he had left the Manor that night. It seemed he was content to bide his time, and the matter was shelved. There was a steady flow of letters from Nigel, and she wrote back almost as much, when she could find time and inspiration in between her course work and lectures, and her growing involvement with the University Dance group as the one Society she decided to join. She really took to her dancing, with a positive determination to banish any thought of residual problems over her accidents, as well as an aid to relaxation after sitting still in lectures. There were two guys who liked to partner her, both older, one she got on with better as a dance partner but didn't like him too much as a person, the other made her laugh and was nice to be with, but didn't dance as well. The other girls in her year that she palled up with sadly weren't much into that sort of dancing, so she was largely on her own every Tuesday night, but she did have a few chats with Julie each week, who was in Leicester on her Business Course. They often had laughs about her idea of modelling.

"You know that drawing you did of me, the one that's being sold for the Air Ambulance?"

Jocelyn, curled up in the armchair of her student flat, the mobile phone stuck to her ear, and wishing she had a proper phone rather than this tinny sounding one, nodded, then realising how stupid that was. "Yerrsss?" What was coming next?

"It's quite sexy, in its way?"

"Yerrrssss?" So what?

"Someone who bought one showed it to the guys in my student wing. They been trying to get me to pose for the art group ever since."

"So why don't you?"

"I don't know. Just don't fancy doing it on my doorstep, so to speak. In case they get the wrong idea. I wish you were here, Jo. I miss you."

"I miss you too, we had some good times." She thought of

France, and before that, when Julie had stayed at home. She stroked her legs, running her fingers over her scar, then up. It felt nice; it always did when she was in the mood.

"Do you speak to Nigel?"

"A lot. He's working awfully hard, though. Shan't see him till Christmas."

"And you don't draw anymore, Jo?"

"Nope. I'm getting quite good at the Foxtrot, though." Change the subject, Julie!

"I don't get enough practice in. There isn't a good group here like you have."

"We're doing some demonstrations now. I'm in the team."

"After your accident, Jo, that's some going."

"I know. I'm pretty pleased myself. It's going to be great when I can show off to Nigel."

There was a reflective pause.

"Better go, Jo. I've still got some work to do for tomorrow. Take care."

"And you. Love you, Julie. Speak again soon."

* * *

She climbed out of her chair and went to put the kettle on. The rooms she had were so small compared with home, just the one chair, but it at least it was cosy. She curled up again to wait for the kettle; it took an age. She couldn't ring Nigel tonight, but it had been good to chat with Julie. She thought of her, and the barn drawing she'd done, now selling with her 'White Dress' print as a pair for a hundred pounds each. Well, we're both pretty girls and we show our legs, so why not? Idly, she picked up a pencil and doodled on a piece of A4. Without realising, she'd remembered Julie and her figure, then like the shutters on a window being violently flung open, the stark vision of her dream, that weird night when her leg suddenly got better came vividly into mind. She nearly flung her pencil away. "I don't want this!" Then it was as though the pencil had a mind of its own, sticking to her fingers, and she added the figure of Julie's now dead mum, just as she'd seen it in her dream. The kettle was steaming away, she'd left the lid off and the automatic trip wouldn't work; she had to get up again and switch it off. She made herself a cup of coffee, got out her biscuit tin, put it down by her chair, and curled up again. She had thought she'd read her latest paperback; she treated herself to a new one every week, but instead she picked up the A4 sheet again and looked at it.

The two faces, looking at each other, the flowing lines of the Julie's mother's dress, the way she'd just captured Julie's figure in about ten lines. It was telling her something, and she leant over to prop it up on the bookshelf in front of her. As she sipped away at her coffee, and munched her way through her entire nightly ration of four ginger nuts before she knew what was what, the composition grew on her.

"Damn. DAMN!" She spoke out loud, and closed her eyes, screwing them up, but she could still see the picture. She swung round, and picked up her novel, tried to pick up the story. The girl who seduced a guy because she was lonely had managed to get him to live with her, and…, oh this wasn't going to work. It was gone ten. She'd go to bed. Her little divan was cosy enough, and she generally slept well, even if she didn't bother with any nightwear, the central heating was usually far too hot, despite the thermostat, but she daren't leave the window open, for some latecomer would try and get back into the student block without passing the porter's lodge. Trouble with being on the first floor above the cycle racks. Luckily, another chapter of her book sent her to sleep, and she just managed to switch the light off before she crashed out.

When the dreary grey morning woke her as normal, around half seven, there was no recollection of yesterday evening's doodling, until she saw the thing, still sitting on the bookshelf. At first it annoyed her, then it intrigued her, then she got up from her cornflakes and more coffee to retrieve it, propped it up on the cornflake packet and stared at it for a long time.

"Okay, Julie. You win. I'll do it. *Then* the boys will be after you!" First sign of madness, talking to yourself, oh yes, and she must be mad to go back to sketching. She'd better be careful, no more accidents because of drawing, please.

* * *

In the two hours between lectures at lunchtime she cycled into town, down the hill, fully aware it would tire her out to pedal back, but she had to, she'd got no choice. She'd no paper, and only a couple of pencils. Stupid, really, when there was all that lovely stuff her Pa had bought her, sitting back at home in the studio, gathering dust, but she just had to go, she knew if she didn't it would get on her nerves and annoy her, and wouldn't do anyone any good. The art shop was very helpful, and because she was a student she got twenty percent off the paper, and a free crayon pencil for every two others she bought. Fully equipped, with the precious cartridge paper in a loose roll and wrapped, she tied it onto the bike and struggled back to her lodgings. She'd be back at seven, even after one more lecture and dining in; as she slammed the door after laying the paper on the table with weights on each corner to take the curl out of it, she had a weird feeling of anticipation stir within her tummy. She even whistled her way down the corridor to the drama theatre that doubled as a lecture hall, causing one of her acquaintances to ask if she'd won the Lottery. "Nope," she'd replied, "Not yet, but you never know."

The middle-aged woman who talked about Post Reformation changes in ideology – quite what that had to do with Literature she still had to find out, had a fascinating sense of humour, and the hour and a half went quickly enough. Then it was Hall for dinner, nothing special, the usual banter and she sidestepped that ginger haired bloke who seemed always to be trying it on without giving offence, and got back to her rooms without being followed.

The biggest problem was a drawing board. An easel would have been ideal, but she daren't go and borrow one, anyway, it would have taken up too much space. Then she had an idea and tried lifting the top of her table. It came away from its legs surprisingly easily, just pegged into the frame, and there she had it, a trifle cumbersome, but when propped on the armchair arms, it wasn't too bad. The light was going, though, so it would be a lamp lit job. Soft, she said to herself, it'll look softer, and then she turned the heating up, and stripped to her pants. Quite like old times, recalling her activities last June. No Mums to shout at her here!

Inspiration, that's what it was. Squaring her naked shoulders, a newly sharpened brand new pencil, and with the doodle – cartoon, she remembered Edward called them – as a guide, she set to work.

At half past eight she drank a glass of water. At ten o'clock she felt peckish, and ate today's and tomorrow's biscuit ration. At eleven her hands felt sticky, so she had a quick strip wash, but she went back to the board. Just after midnight she heard noises, and checked she'd locked the door, but it was only the two girls from the other side of the corridor coming back after a night on the razzle. They'd asked her to join them, but it wasn't her; the nice thing was they didn't hold it against her.

By a quarter past one her concentration had virtually gone, and she was not getting the dress right, so she had to give up. Leaving everything just as it was, she tumbled into bed not bothering about getting out of her pants, just pulled the duvet up and fell asleep straight away. At seven she woke, briefly wondering why she'd still got her knickers on, before tumbling off the divan and going to open the curtains. A thinly disguised sun was doing its best on the October day, just adequate light to let her see what she'd done. She scratched her head, feeling crumby and desperate for a shower. That meant a trot up the corridor to the communal shower/bathroom, always an effort, nothing like those at home. Oh, for a proper bathroom! The picture was there, but without the detail. The outline shape of the two women were in place, and she'd got Julie's face and figure fleshed out. It had been the dress on Julie's mother that wasn't right, and she knew she'd have to erase quite a bit. Itchy fingers got her going, and the rubber took quite a pounding, but it just had to go, and carefully, so as not to spoil the surface. Certainly a good quality paper, with a nice satin finish. Her BB pencil glided on beautifully and before she knew it the dress was there. The hands, clasped, slightly wrong angle, so more erasing, then the fingers seemed a bit thin, but the second time she got them right.

"Bloody heck!" She swore, unusually out loud. It was half past nine, and she should be at her first lecture of the day by now, and she wasn't even dressed. She flung an old shirty blouse on, pulled on a tatty pair of jeans, and ran. This was a specialist talk by an outside lecturer, so the room was full, and squeezing in at the back didn't attract any comment. Halfway through she realised her blouse buttons weren't all done up, and as she'd left her bra off in her haste, wondered if anyone had noticed, and almost giggled aloud, turning her involuntary noise into a cough. A few heads turned, but that was all. Set free forty minutes later, and not sure that she'd learnt anything she didn't know or didn't need to know, she had an hour and a bit. Back in her room, she took the blouse off again, remembered to lay her bra out where she could reach it, and set to work once more. Keeping an eye on the time, additional shading on Julie's figure emphasised those 'delectable' curves as she muttered under her breath, "*Wish she was here, so I could get her in properly.*" Then it was another quick dress and frenetic dash to the second (and last) lecture of her day; there wasn't anything else after that, and now, after that hour interlude the light coming into her room was just about right. Suddenly she remembered this afternoon she'd promised she'd play squash with Anthea, the bouncy girl from the flat above her, but now she'd far rather carry on here, so she slipped upstairs to see if she could cry off. Anthea's eyes popped.

"Jo – you can't go about like that!"

"Oh, heavens. I'm sorry, I get carried away. Whoops!"

"What do you mean, carried away?"

"I'm drawing, get so involved with what I do, I get a bit, like I said, carried away." Not bothering with putting everything back on merely to nip up a few steps didn't seem a problem to her, but obviously to Anthea. "Sorry, hope I haven't offended you."

"No, Jo, not at all, but I didn't think you were as scatty as that! What do you draw?" She had a wry smile. "It's not a self-portrait is it?"

Jo's response was factual and said without thinking. "That's how it all started," and before she knew it, Anthea had pulled her into her room and shut the door. Talking to a semi-naked girl out in the corridor wasn't her.

"Here – put this around your shoulders." Anthea passed over a flimsy cottony thing that looked like a beach wrap. "Can I get us both a tea? I'm a bit into fruit teas so name your flavour."

Well, it was nice to have friends around, and Anthea was as pleasant a girl as any, not at all brash like some of them. "You're very kind, but I shouldn't stop long else I'll lose my light."

"So okay, I'll make the tea in mugs then maybe I can come and have a look at what you're doing? Unless it's too racy?"

Jo was stuck with her. She couldn't say no, otherwise it would seem far too impolite. "Sure, and sorry about not sticking to the squash, but I didn't know I'd be doing this at the time; it's like, well, acting on impulse? Or while things are fresh in your mind? I thought I'd managed to give up drawing after my accidents, but this has, er, sort of crept up on me unawares, and I've got to do it else it'll bug me." She took a proffered mug, sipped and found camomile a little thin, but at least refreshing. Why was she saying all this? She thought she'd kept her sketching under wraps. Anthea, a fluffy haired brunette with a rounded figure not too unlike Betty, gave the impression of being a homely sort of a girl with mothering instincts and seemed to be encouraging her.

"Sounds intriguing, Jo. I didn't realise you had an artistic side."

"Neither did I until I was about to leave college. Then one evening I just did this sketch, and it turned out rather well, and it went on from there. I've had two drawings published as prints."

"*Really?*" Anthea sounded genuinely impressed. "So what are you doing an English course for?"

"That's what I studied for, took exams for. Drawing was an accident. So was falling down a ship's staircase." She stuck a leg out and showed her scar, still a vivid red line that pulled every now and again, especially after an energetic dance session. "Then I got clobbered by our beech tree, hit by a lightning strike and had to have it plated and pinned. I vowed I'd not carry on drawing 'cos all it did was to get me into trouble."

"That doesn't seem right if that's what you can do so well, Jo."

Jocelyn shrugged. "Being an artist may not pay all the bills. A degree in English might."

"Don't you be too sure. Too many degrees floating about out there and lots of competition. Not too many artists who can draw well, methinks. Can I see, Jo, or would you rather keep it unseen?"

"If you don't let on, Anthea. I'm not looking to set up a portrait studio, you know!"

Anthea's laugh was as bubbly as her personality suggested. "Why not? Better than part-timing as a bar maid!"

"Is that what you do?"

"Ah ha. They like the busty girls behind the bar, and it's quite fun."

Jo's glance ran over Anthea's front. She had more there than most, certainly, but not in her mind excessive. "Something I could never do. Pull pints, I mean."

"Not a lot to it, but pays well. Now, do I see?" She put her mug down and stood up. "Next time, keep your shirt on!" She laughed again, and Jo had to smile with her.

* * *

In Jo's estimation the drawing was about halfway finished. She wanted it to be good, as an obligation to Julie and, with a bit of a tug at her tummy, as a sort of memorial to Julie's mum. She hadn't really known her, only met her only a couple of times, but the detail in her mind was as clear as clear from that strange dream, and it was all down there, on paper,

401

unbelievably. Whether it was accurate only Julie would know, once she'd seen it, whenever that would be. In the meantime it was a drawing; a mother and daughter, with overtones of a Grecian study, curvaceous, loving expressions, and as she stood back and let Anthea have a glimpse, she could hardly believe what she'd drawn. After so long, having vowed she'd not draw seriously again, and here it was, shouting 'phenomenal!' at her, her best work yet.

Anthea gazed at the life study with a degree of awe. She'd made no prejudgement, she wasn't that sort of girl, but hadn't anticipated this. Her instinctive reaction was to step forward and look more carefully at the faces. The younger girl had a wistful, sad expression, her eyes wide and focused on the elder woman, who seemed to be looking beyond her into the distance. The flowing dress of the woman cleverly masked some of the naked figure of the girl, though the influence of the nude came through and gave the pair a stunning sense of power.

With her head on one side, she stepped back a bit, narrowed her eyes to see the perspective and how it might look finished. There wasn't a suggestion of a backdrop as yet, but her mind told her it shouldn't overwhelm the figures. She'd been to a few art galleries and her History degree course took in something of early painters. This was a beautiful study. She turned to look at Jocelyn, standing there in such a dishevelled unflattering semi-unclothed state, with lips tightly compressed, eyes as wide as her subjects. Jo's unspoken query went with the raised eyebrows.

"I can see why you've had some prints published, Jo. This is powerful stuff. Drawn from memory? You've not had anyone here to sit for you? I think it's great." An understatement, Anthea knew, for the more she looked, the more the figures became alive to her, giving her the shivers. She looked around, for somewhere to sit.

Jo woke up from her own private reverie. Watching Anthea's reaction had been inspirational, and she knew she'd achieved what was being asked of her – though who had done this telepathic asking she didn't know. "Sorry, Anthea, I haven't got an easel so I had to use the armchair to prop the table top I've used as a board. Bit sort of make-do, I guess. Here, have a sit on this." She pulled the small plain chair over that she'd sat on to draw; Anthea moved it so she could sit and gaze at the depiction of the two female figures. It was disturbingly magnetic, drawing her into the intense emotively charged composition.

"Tell me, Jo?"

Jocelyn sat on the edge of her divan bed, hands together flat between her thighs, and with head down, studied her knees for a while, thinking. Should she voice her thoughts, expose her own emotions, in case she ruined the empathy between her and her telepathic vision of her dream subjects, or use Anthea as a sounding board to find out if it made sense? The memories of the orchard dreams she'd shared with her Mums, and then with Nigel. Neither had pooh-poohed them, but Anthea didn't know her, they were merely fellow students sharing university lodgings. She wasn't a schoolgirl any more; she was an adult, well, a probationary adult, sort of, in her mind, until she was twenty-one. She had to firm up her own thoughts now, with no Mums close by to use as that sounding board. Her own girl. So here goes:

"One of my best friends at school, Julie," she nodded at the younger, naked girl on the left of the picture, "She and I became very close during the last few months, especially as Julie's mother – the one on the right – was killed by driving into the back of a rubbish skip lorry that stopped unexpectedly. It affected her more than I realised; 'cos her father wasn't too involved with her, we, that's my Mums and Pa and I, sort of adopted her as a sister cum daughter. We went to France for a week together with my art teacher and his ..." she wasn't sure how to describe Dylys, "Partner. She was my college head of year. They've sort of, er, got together. We..." again, she wasn't sure how to describe the feelings she had for Julie. She tried, "Became closer friends. But I've also got Nigel, and he's become part of my life. Anyway, I had that accident I told you about, on the ferry coming home, when Julie and I were racing each other for the stairway; she's been great, we've been good for each other, and then I had this intense dream one night, about this – and I just knew I had to draw what I'd seen in the dream. I've drawn her before, of course, several times, but never her mother. Which is what's so strange, because I feel I know her so well. It's uncanny, Anthea, and I'm a bit scared of it all. I've had picture dreams before, and there's another sitting in the back of my mind I've been trying to bury for ages, but it keeps popping up. Weird." She looked up, and saw Anthea still absorbed in the two figures. Had she heard what I've said, or what? Jo wondered, stood up, and began to get properly dressed. She'd lost her mood, and the light was moving round towards the increasingly early dusk.

Anthea couldn't detach herself. She'd heard all what Jo had said, and maybe understood how there was such a depth of what was possibly emotion – certainly involvement – in the representation of these two superbly drawn figures. She felt privileged, and an afternoon on the squash court would have been no match for this. She shook her head, as if to clear her thoughts. "Powerful, Jo, very, very, powerful; I shan't get this out of my mind. I can see something of what you say in all this. Thank you for letting me see it."

"I'm glad I did. I needed to open up, I think. I want some fresh air." She'd pulled on her thick comforting woolly sweater, and zipped up her skirt. "Care for a walk?"

"Hmmm. Yes, okay. I'll just pop up and grab a coat, change my shoes. Won't be a minute."

* * *

With Anthea gone, Jo took some deep breaths, and spoke out loud, looking at her picture.

"Hope you didn't mind, Julie. But the entire world will see you, like this. You're beautiful. And your mum." Why had she said that? Something was going on inside her, and she didn't quite know what. She had a sudden urge to talk to her father, and making sure she had her phone as she picked up her coat, shut the room door behind her and joined Anthea as she came down her stairs.

404

They walked out across the playing fields, into the parkland beyond, the early evening mist starting to rise off the meadow to drift amongst the large Horse Chestnuts, bringing yet more leaves falling silently down; whispering into the muted autumnal twilight.

"You're a strange girl, Jo. I don't mean that unkindly, but you are. Did I hear you say you don't drive? And you're not into computers? Have you never been to a nightclub?" Anthea, looking slantwise at her companion, envied her the colourful mass of curls and the complexion unsullied by make-up.

Jocelyn, her mind on the strange mix-up of thoughts introduced by Anthea's interest in her and the evident tremendous impression the drawing had made, didn't anticipate the questions. Being called strange was a new one. Nigel had called her a weirdee! Her opinion that being into computers and nightclubs and having hang-ups over which car you owned was stranger. "Sorry, Anthea. I've not had the need to drive, but my Pa doesn't think it would take me long to learn, with the hand and eye co-ordination an artist has. I don't like noise so nightclubs are out, and computers bore me because there's precious little skill required – once you know the keys and the functions. If they stop you being creative and *talking* to other people, that's not good, let alone the hours you spend hunched up staring at a screen, which isn't good either. I'd rather lie on my back and stare at the sky, at least the brain can do its own thing – and that's how I started getting the mental images I draw from. Does it make sense?" She kicked at a pile of leaves, sending them into a whirl before they settled back on the path. The lights across the park had come on, and the air had a feel of rain. The last bird song echoed above them, the rumble of traffic below the university grounds jarred into the senses when the evening should be quiet to allow the day to lull itself to sleep. The path turned the corner of the park, past the wrecked remains of the flower displays in the beds; the gardeners had gone home without clearing up.

Tomorrow the beds would be apparently empty, merely raked soil hiding dormant spring bulbs.

"I suppose so. Maybe we've come to think we *have* to use computers because they're there. You can draw on them, you know."

Jo snorted in a very unfeminine way. "Oh yeh? Like what I do?"

"No, Jo, not like you do, but then your drawings convey a real sense of life and emotion – at least the one I've seen this afternoon does. I'd love to see your others." Then she had to say what had been in her mind for the last hour or so. "Would you draw me?"

Jocelyn laughed. "I thought you'd never ask! Of course I will. If only to say thanks for talking to me, being so understanding, giving me tea. And, by the way, I've been offered gallery space for a week to show off, but I've not taken it up because I thought I had got drawing out of my system." She breathed in, deeply, loving the familiar smudgy scent of leaf mould. "However, I realise now it's bigger than me. I've brought my phone because I'm going to have to give my parents the best news out." Her eyes watered, and she rubbed at them with a knuckle. "Watch this space." Crossing the path she plonked herself down on a bench, gesturing Anthea to sit alongside her. As Anthea was about to protest, she shook her head. "Bear with me. Don't go. We'll get a pizza or something, maybe then I'll see what inspiration I get to draw you, if you have the time to sit." She sought no reply as she let the phone do its thing. Anti-computer or not, she knew her phone.

"Mums? Hi. Are you eating? – Oh, right – No, I'm in the park, with a friend. *Her* name's Anthea! No, nothing's wrong, I'm fine. Listen, I thought I'd let you and Pa know I'm drawing again, and how! You'll love it. I can't explain on the phone. Can you think if Pa could come and fetch me home for the weekend; I need to use the studio?– Mums! – *Really!* – Oh, all right. Yes, Anthea's seen the drawing. Hang on." She turned to Anthea, sitting on her hands on the end of the bench, staring across the grass at a dog-walking couple. "Tell my Mums what you think of the drawing, here." She offered her the phone.

Anthea, surprised, took a hand from under her thigh and tentatively said "Hello?"

Eleanor heard the uncertainty in Jo's friend's voice. "Hello, Anthea. I'm Eleanor, Jo's mother. Is she behaving herself? Good, she ought to. You've seen her draw! Lucky you; she'd given up before she started at Reading, I'm glad to hear she's picked it up again. What's she doing?" Eleanor heard Anthea's description and the evident awe in her voice, and wondered at the choice of subject. "Well, I look forward to seeing it. Thank you, Anthea. Maybe you'd like to come down some time and visit us? We've plenty of room; it's an old Vicarage with a paddock and an orchard and a big barn, and lovely gardens, even if I say it myself. Right oh. Bye."

Anthea returned the phone to Jocelyn, and heard the parting exchange of love and kisses. Lucky Jo, with a mother like that; her mother was far too brassy and direct.

"Well, we'd best get back before it gets too cold – or wet. Come on." Jo led the way back across the grass. "Pizza or home-brewed spaghetti?"

* * *

The two girls became much more relaxed with each other's company over Jo's home-brewed spaghetti, albeit in Anthea's kitchenette, the better place since Jo's table top was playing an infinitely more artistic role than hosting two pasta bowls. Anthea even sacrificed her only remaining bottle of red wine and the conversation mellowed and turned to more girly topics.

"You mentioned a Nigel?"

"*A Nigel?* Anthea, he's *the* Nigel. I found him in a tree." Jocelyn's conversation was becoming more than mellow under the influence of the red wine.

"'*You what?*" Anthea leant back onto two legs of her chair and nearly fell over, recovering only by putting out a hand and grabbing the table.

"Found him in a tree. He did a parachute jump from a Hercules and missed the D.Z.; Pa and I just happened to be in

407

the right place at the right time. I shinned up this oak and cut his cords so he didn't get strangled. Saved his life, so they say. He's a medical student at Edinburgh; his father's a Vicar. He's lovely."

"Who, Nigel or the Vicar?" Anthea giggled. She hadn't a clue what a Hercules was, guessed it was a plane and decided not to reveal her ignorance of that or the meaning of 'Dee zed'.

Jocelyn saw the funny side of her comment and giggled too; the pair of them started laughing till the tears ran. Anthea recovered first. "You said you'd draw me!"

"So I did. I might not draw very well if I've had two glasses of wine."

"You've had three! Doesn't matter. See what happens."

Jo had brought her pencils up with her, surprisingly thoughtfully, and looked around for paper; she'd not thought to buy another sketch pad.

"Here – use this."

'This' turned out to be the back of one of Anthea's large plain notebooks she used for block diagrams. A bit too shiny and hard, but it would have to do. "How to you want to pose, then?"

Anthea was feeling rather light headed and a wee bit silly. She peeled her sweater over her head and leant behind to unclip her bra. "Like this?" She stuck her chest out and turned her head sideways.

"Far too Greta Garbo. I'm not into sexy poses. Here, sit cross-legged on the table, put a hand behind your head, the other across your boobs. No, I don't like that skirt. Take it off. I know. Put a knee up and hold it with both hands linked. *That's* better. Can you stay put?"

Anthea leant her chin on her knee, wasn't sure what she looked like but was past worrying. Jocelyn used the softest pencil she'd got and sketched away furiously for ten minutes, catching the soulful expression in her sitter's eyes, glossed over the shadowy bits and scrubbed in the bouncy hair.

"There. Tenner for ten minutes. Watcha fink?" She handed the book over. Anthea carefully unwrapped herself and eased her leg down before sliding off the table. What a way to spend an evening!

"That's not bad, Jo. I can see it's me, and you've been very discreet. I could even show this to my mother! I think my father might like it better, though." The giggle hadn't gone away. "I'll pay you the tenner, Jo. It's worth it!"

"Don't be silly, I was only joking!"

"No, I mean it, Jo. Just sign it."

Jocelyn was instantly reminded of Felicity and the idea she'd expressed about her drawings becoming valuable. "Okay. At least I can buy a good pad. Thanks, Anthea." She did a flourished signature in the corner; thought nothing more of it, and took her leave; she was bushed.

* * *

The following morning, early, just before it got light, her mobile bleated at her. Stretching a near numbed arm from beneath the bedding to grab it sideways, she barely managed a "Hello?"

It was her father.

"Thought I'd catch you before lectures or whatever. Look, try and catch a train, Jo, there's one at just gone seven out of Reading. We'll meet you at Salisbury. Much better than me doing the round trip. Don't worry about the fare, I'll pay. How's things? Your Mums says you're drawing again. Great news, girl. You can bring your Anthea if you want to. Have you heard from Nigel?"

She blinked to clear the sleep from her eyes, and rubbed an itch. "He rang me day before yesterday, Pa. He's fine, but I wish we were nearer. I miss him. I'll have to leave my bike at the station, but it should be okay. Pa, can you see if Edward can spare me an hour on Saturday? I've got this drawing I want him to see. I'll have words with Anthea, but I doubt she'll come. I'll let you know. Thanks for the call. Bye."

What a bore today would be. Three lectures, a discussion group, a meeting with her tutor, and she wanted to get on with the drawing. She rolled onto her back and stared at the ceiling. Should she skip the first lecture because that would give her three hours clear? Then she could have lunch at the Union and go straight to the debate thing? A glance at her watch told her she might just get a shower in before anyone else, so she kicked the covers off, picked up her things, and risked the corridor. No one saw her, and the water was still scalding hot. Lobster like, she scrubbed herself dry, flung the towel round and retreated just in time. Her door closed just as the next early riser came past.

Over breakfast – a simple bowl of nutty cornflakes and two slices of toast – she tried not to let her conscience trouble her, glancing repeatedly at her half-finished drawing. Lecture, drawing, drawing, lecture.

The drawing won, and she knew then she was committed. Not bothering to dress, Edward's *'Your Inspiration, my dear Jocelyn!'* came back to mind. She smiled within herself, dear Edward, little did you know! And Dylys, great friend now, so caring when she'd had that accident. She wondered what Nigel would make of all this, her saying one thing, and then doing the opposite – would he think her scatty or just the strange weirdee?

She took up her pencil and picked up on Julie's mother's dress again.

NINETEEN

The train was crowded, but then it was a Friday night. Anthea, at the very last moment, had changed her mind and asked if it wasn't too late, could she accept the invite? So there they were, squashed into the space by the luggage racks, far too intimately for comfort but there was no choice until after Basingstoke, watching the lights flash by. It was dark, and dismally wet. Anthea's involvement had at least prevented the bike ride, for she'd sweet hearted one of her mates to give them a lift to the station, much to Jo's relief because the precious drawing, rolled and wrapped in a begged sheet of polythene, might have otherwise suffered.

The train rattled on; Jocelyn closed her eyes, letting the sway of the carriage lull her. The stop at Basingstoke relieved some of the pressure, but it wasn't until Andover did they get a seat, and then it was just minutes to Salisbury.

"There he is!" She stopped herself shouting 'Pa' at the top of her voice, weaved her way through the disembarking passengers and caught his eye.

"Jo – lovely to have you home! Here, let me have that." David relieved her of the roll and saw a girl who must be her friend standing behind. "You'll be Anthea? Glad you could come. The car's this way. You'll have to run, I'm sorry I forgot a brolly." The Jaguar was parked at risk on double yellow lines, but they made a take-off before any problem arose. Jocelyn relaxed, happy to be going home, while Anthea watched the traffic and the adroit way Jo's father took the car into the country.

"I love your car, Mr Danielleson. How old is it?"

David smiled into the mirror. Not any girl would ask, or know a vintage Jaguar specifically. "Old enough, Anthea.

She's twenty. Not quite an adult. Are you a car person?"

"My father has a little MG. He lets me drive it when we go to car rallies. I wear a scarf over my hair, he has his tweed cap, very 1950s, but loads of fun. Mother stays at home, she can't abide open tops. We've got a Peugeot as well. I'd rather like an MGF, but probably not a good idea nowadays, I suppose."

She lapsed into a reflective silence, aware Jocelyn was looking bored.

* * *

As they turned into the drive, crunched over the gravel Jo knew so intimately, the feelings she had were overwhelming. She was back home, about to hug her beloved Mums; she could sleep in her own bed, she could run up to the orchard, yes, *run,* and re-live all the memories of *the* summer. Reading was a million miles away. And there was her Mums, waiting on the doorstep! Out of the car, not waiting for Anthea, a skip across the path, and a fling of arms around her.

"Mums! Oh, *Mums!* It's lovely to be home!"

Eleanor felt a tear. Such an expressive daughter, such a precious daughter, and yes, it was lovely to have her home, even for a couple of days. She'd only been gone, what, five weeks? "Jo, my darling, it's lovely to have you home. Now, hadn't you better introduce me?" Anthea had brought her little case in with her and clutching Jo's drawing in its roll, looked a little bemused. She'd never managed to work up quite the same level of enthusiasm for greeting her mother after a wee time away from home.

"Sorry, yes," Jo relinquished her mother and turned back to Anthea. "Anthea, meet my Mum. Mums, Anthea has a room above me. She's reading History, and she drives her fathers MG!"

David overheard, coming back after tucking the Jaguar away under cover. "Ah, yes, but it is an easy car to drive, and I guess you don't use it for shopping trips?"

"That's true. Mrs Danielleson, it's very good of you to invite me. I've only really known Jo for a couple of days, properly, that is, so…"

412

Eleanor interrupted her. "Not at all, Anthea. I gather you've been party to the restoration. But, come on in, it's getting chilly and we've supper on the go. Then we can see what our girl's been up to."

Anthea wasn't immediately sure about the comment 'restoration', but after a lovely supper of a bangers and bean casserole with a warm red wine as well, and feeling distinctly as though she'd fallen on her feet in palling up with Jo, she heard the story properly. Then Jo set up her easel, unrolled the new picture very carefully and clipped it onto the board. Still nowhere near finished in her estimation, but it still looked good. She stepped back and let her parents have a good look. A silence, and she looked from one to the other but neither of her parents said a word, until her Mums got up from her chair, and hugged her.

"Jo! *Oh, Jo!*" Eleanor looked into her daughter's eyes. 'That's Julie, and her mother? How did you manage such a lovely drawing? It's beautiful! Oh, my darling girl, you're so clever!"

"Not clever, El, she's brilliant! I think that's inspired. I don't know what Edward will say when he comes tomorrow, but I think that's certainly the best I've seen you do. Well done – and I'm thrilled to think you've started to draw again. What was your inspiration, Jo?" Her father didn't quite understand why his girl started to flush up. He wasn't to know that the word 'inspiration' was an euphemism for being semi-naked in this context, though there was certainly more to it with regard to the 'Mother and Daughter' picture.

Jo explained her amazingly detailed dream, the one she'd had the night after her birthday party, forgotten then remembered with such clarity at Reading, how she'd doodled and the cartoon she'd drawn triggered the creation of the picture now pegged in front of them. "It's not finished. I need to talk to Edward – you rang him, Pa?"

"I did. Pleased to call tomorrow, he said, but I, or you can, Jo, need to confirm. And that's not all. Remember Sir Charles? And that we had to back out of his request to call, after your rather unexpected and somewhat disastrous 'retirement', albeit temporary, from the drawing scene, which was a bit embarrassing to say the least after Edward had talked you up? Well, he's still in touch with Edward over his idea of getting you to exhibit, and it wouldn't take more than a phone call to put that back on track. Any thoughts?"

Jocelyn's tummy did a silly flip. Just like the time when she was called to Mrs Summers' study at college and she hadn't known why; a mild dose of the panics. She had been standing by the easel, but now she collapsed into the nearest chair, and buried her curls in her hands. Decision time! Looking up again, they were all gazing at her, her Mums with a sort of smile; her Pa with raised eyebrows and no expression, maybe he was a wee bit cross with her; Anthea wide eyed and maybe intrigued at all this. Leaning back in the chair, she thought of Nigel. What would he say? But it wasn't up to him; she was still her own girl.

Her reply then: "Okay, Pa. Let's give it a whirl. I can't really let you lot down, can I? And I have a feeling this," – gesturing at the easel-mounted drawing – "is going to be good." It came as a rush of relief to her, with the agony of the past couple of months swept aside in just that couple of seconds. She *would* draw again, and how! The world would know a Danielleson print as an investment, something to be prized, loved, gazed at, and maybe even as inspiration for other things; she blushed again with the 'other things' giving her feminity a twitch.

"Darling?" Her Mums loving smile. Great.

"I'm fine. Relieved, actually," and got up from her chair to stretch. "Early start in the morning. You ring Edward, Pa. I'm for bed. Anthea – thanks for your support." Crossing to the door, she presented her friend with a kiss on her cheek before disappearing, and they heard her taking two stairs at a time before her bedroom door shut.

* * *

"I'd better follow suit, Mrs Danielleson. It seems like it's been a long day. Thank you so much for asking me down; if I've been of help to Jo…"

"Oh, you have. Any encouragement to get her back to drawing – and to think we were less than sure that this is what she should do! Now look at this! Wonderful!" Eleanor knew she'd be seeing the posed couple in her sleep. "Are you ringing Edward now, David?"

He looked at his watch. "Don't see why not. Then he can plan his day. You two go on up. Shan't be long."

* * *

Edward was delighted, David could tell. "I'll call around eleven thirty, if that would be convenient? It will give dear Jocelyn time to feel at ease with her studio again. May I say it is with profound relief I have heard this restoration to sanity. It would have been such a disaster for her not to utilise her talent."

"And Sir Charles?"

"I'll try and contact him in the morning. Meanwhile, I'm full of anticipation. Your description of her new project sounds very intriguing. Till tomorrow then. Goodnight and thank you for your call."

* * *

Once in bed, Eleanor snuggled up to him. "Happy?"

"Happy. I'd never have imagined how relieved I feel she's doing this; after all the agonising we had over the original sketches? Maybe our girl's going to be famous!" He leant over to switch out the bedside lights, and then wrapped his arm around her. "You never did any more about your painting, El. Maybe you ought to, so daughter's fame will rub off on you?"

"Hmmmph!"

"Sorry. Cuddle?"

"Hmmmmm…"

* * *

Jo, in her own bed, slept soundly, dreamlessly, and woke with the light. This was no summer morning, but a dull October day, a slight breeze just enough to stir the smaller branches of her Mums's garden trees. She stretched in front of the window, reliving her summer dashes to the orchard, including that never to be forgotten one in the pouring rain, which brought the costume collection into mind, and she wondered what had happened to the open-air theatre project. It would be nice to think it would happen, if only for old Mrs Parsons. She turned back into the room, a girl with an eventful day ahead of her.

Deciding what to wear took a bit of time, particularly as she fingered the gorgeous dresses she had on the hangers. The Burgundy one, her Pa's exam week gift; the 'White Dress' that was now famous; the blue one her parents gave her only six weeks or so ago; all beautiful. She took down the green one she'd worn at that party, reluctantly put it back, and decided on the old college skirt; she'd put that loose jersey thing on as well. "I have to look sort of presentable, I suppose, if Edward's coming." And her thoughts caused her to chuckle as she slid her nightie off and clipped a bra round her. "No naked sketching today, my girl!"

She heard the shower start, and guiltily recalled she had a guest. Oh, well, Anthea's an undergrad, she can look after herself. Dressed, she made her way downstairs, gave her Mums a 'morning!' kiss and went out to sniff the dampness of the early autumnal air.

* * *

Oh, it was so magical, Mums's garden, after the confines of the far too regimented campus. Here you could imagine the plants talked to you, told how much they loved growing here. Silly girl! She caught herself being far too childish, or was she? Without warning, memories of the garden party came flooding back, her first meeting with Nigel; what an impact he'd had on her life, and *that* wasn't childish, oh no, that was different. Nigel! Oh, Nigel! There was the beech tree, less majestic, but still the tree where she'd sat and drawn Felicity. So much had happened under that tree. Her drawing, yes, the lovely little tea parties they'd had, the dreadful, dreadful storm, and down there, on the grass, just there, she'd lain and thought she was going to die, but her Mums had come, and…

* * *

Eleanor was about to call her for breakfast, saw her daughter staring at the ground over by the tree, realised she was deep in thought, and left her. Jocelyn was her own person now, no longer the schoolgirl; she was shrugging off the vagaries of adolescence, now she must be thinking her own way through the puzzles of life, and coming up with her own decisions. So be it.

* * *

…She'd said she wouldn't draw again, because of how she'd imagined her life had been ruined by the accidents, but here she was, without any of the problems the medical people had uttered such misgivings over, apart from the scar, still a reddish purpley line – and if the tree could survive without a major limb, then what was she doing, muttering about just a healed limb? Looking up into the branches, seeing the colour change and the leaves about to fall, nature doing its thing with no help from anyone; Spring would bring another crop of leaves and caterpillars for the blue tits; the wound would gradually callus over, life will go on. She'd draw, oh how she'd draw. The secret project, the Apple Tree picture, she'd start it today. She must. It was in her, stirring deep down, all those months, all those hours with idle thoughts, sharpening in her mind, fizzing up like the bubbles in her Mums's lemonade. Yes!!

But she'd only got the weekend? She kicked at the handful of fallen leaves, suddenly impatient and cross with the constraints of the decision *she'd* made to go to Reading. She should have stuck with the risks and the joys and the uncertainties of being her own person. What would Pa say if she announced she'd forego the degree and just draw? She grinned up into the tree. "You know, don't you?"

* * *

"Half past eleven, Jo. That's what he said. And he was going to try and get Sir Charles over. So I hope you're all psyched-up! Quite an important day methinks. Did you know what you were letting yourself in for, Anthea, giving Jo your support and company this weekend?" David, spreading marmalade thickly across his toast, looked at the two girls.

Anthea, with a very good night's sleep and a wonderful shower this morning, was all bright eyed and bushy tailed, ready for anything. "I don't think I quite knew the significance of all this, I must say, but Jo's certainly got my support. I do know that I'm thoroughly enjoying the change of scenery. I'm looking forward to exploring your garden, Mrs Danielleson."

"Oh, do call me Eleanor, please. Are you a gardener?"

"Sort of. Not very seriously, but I've done a little at home. Not like this, though."

"Well, we'll try and show you what's what before our Jo's Mr Petersen turns up. You might have to amuse yourself whilst our guests are here, Anthea, if you don't mind. What do you need to do, Jo, before they come?"

Jocelyn already had her day mapped out. "I'm taking the 'Mother and Daughter' up to the studio to work on that; perhaps it would be best if they came there? After lunch I want to see about getting either a large roll of paper, the sort the photographic people use as backing, or, if the bank account will stand it, a piece of proper canvas – something I can use for a mural sort of idea I need to start. Tomorrow I'll sketch out something of the basis of what I have in mind, and then we'll go from there. Oh, and I suppose we'd best put the other things I've done in the lounge or dining room or somewhere so this Sir Charles can see them. If he comes." She was quite sanguine about it and her father was impressed.

"What size, Jo?"

"At least six feet by four, I should think. I'll have to have either a frame or a backing board. And I'll have to check what's up there in the way of usable crayon. It'll be a paint job eventually, once I get the detail in place."

418

"So what's it going to be?" Her Mums was intrigued.

Jocelyn didn't think she could explain her project all that simplistically, largely because she didn't know quite how it was going to turn out herself; the dream was there, the detail would come, she knew it would, the inspiration would not go away, not now. "Suffice it to say it's about life, Mums. From conception to decay; based on the orchard, and the life of an apple. I've had it in mind for ages, but didn't know how to go about it until now. So, if you don't mind, I'd best get started. If you're not doing anything else, Pa, can you help me get the studio up and running again? Mums – you'll show Anthea round while…"

"Yes, dear, we'll have a nice morning pottering about, won't we, Anthea? You happy with that?"

"Very, er, Eleanor. I'd like to see the studio that Jo mentions, though, if I may."

"We'll end up there, before Edward comes. Right, everyone had enough breakfast?"

* * *

David was certainly happy with Jocelyn's organising. To have his daughter back home was great, to have her wanting to use the studio brilliant, to think that she'd got some new project inspiring, and all in all he couldn't have wished for more. The autumnal scent to the orchard was evocative, and because he'd not been up for a few days, there were a few more apples on the grass. There wasn't going to be a huge crop this year, but what few there were tasted fine. He picked one up, inspected and polished it on his sweater before taking a bite.

"Jo?" He offered another to her, but she was standing with narrowed eyes, peering at the space where she used to lay for hours, eons ago, or so it seemed. The roll of cartridge paper was under her arm.

"Er, what?"

"Apple, Jo? They're quite sweet."

"Thanks, Pa. Maybe once I've got going. Best get this clipped down first. Got the key?"

419

* * *

It was if she'd never been away. True, she'd hadn't spent much time up here before the French trip and the accidents, in fact, she recalled, it was with Nigel that time... and she had a twitch and had to ease her bra up to cover her feelings. There was a thin layer of dust over everything. Her easel stood, like a forgotten sentry, waiting patiently and uncomplaining for relief; in this case for a nice new sheet of paper on which the embryonic 'Mother and Daughter' drawing was about to take on a life full of emotion, emergent love and filial understanding. Jocelyn turned back to her father. "You know how much Julie meant – means – to me, Pa? Did you think it wrong? When I have Nigel as well?"

David drew breath. What a question to suddenly drop on him! Of course he knew the girls were close, but how close was close? What did this daughter of his mean? He watched her clip the paper onto the board, and took in the fulsome beauty of her, the teenager turned thinking, caring, and suddenly decisive, adult.

"How can it be wrong, Jo?"

She put the last clip in place, smoothed the paper almost tenderly, a lover's touch? "Girls loving girls, Pa? More than just being *friends?*"

"Depends, Jo, different people see relationships in different ways. If you *love* someone, it doesn't automatically mean you get involved in ways some see as abhorrent. *Loving* is more a deeper form of caring that you express in behavioural levels above the norm. Your love for Julie is expressed here, Jo, and it's her mother you've shown, not yourself. I think your feelings for Julie are to be envied, in a way, because not only do you acknowledge their depth, but also you express them perfectly. And provided you know the difference between that love and the love you feel for Nigel, I don't consider you have a problem. You're not pining for her, are you?"

Jocelyn laughed. Good old Pa, absolutely on the button! "Good heavens, no! I miss her company, yes, and it would be wonderful to have her close by, but I don't *pine* for her. Not like I miss Nigel sometimes. Not always," she paused and thought, "P'raps it's because I know we'll end up together in due course and everything will be okay. We do talk, Pa, you know!"

"I'm sure you do. Now, do you need me as company, or should I disappear?"

"I'll be fine, Pa., except it's a bit chilly. You didn't put the central heating in!"

"No more we did. I'll get a gas heater organised. Leave you to it, then?"

"Okay. Give me a whistle when Edward turns up."

* * *

He'd been right. And her inner girl was happy. She could see her beloved orchard through the studio glass, the mellowness of the season softening the trees shapes against the greying sky. It might rain later, she thought, but right now I have all the light I need, and the space, and the *feel*. The inspirational declaration of her inclinations towards Julie; the knowledge that those inclinations wouldn't supplant her growing feelings for Nigel, absent though he may be, and that Pa was right, it was Julie's mother who was holding her. She felt she could talk to the pair of them as she augmented the composition with deft strokes that surprised even her, and she wasn't even tempted to discard any clothes, bra or top, but then it was jolly chilly, standing here, and she chuckled. How long age was it that she'd had that silly, fanciful dream – or hallucination – when she'd been told, in her mind, presumably – to strip off? There – how does that feel? She added in some rounder shading to a thigh, carried it down onto the lower leg, making her just a trifle more seductive. Then back to the bust line, accentuating the valley. Careful, girls, don't get too sexy! The Grecian-style dress needed some more work. "Perhaps I should have got Anthea to model a dress?" It took a while before she was happy with it, then moved away to consider the background. "What do you think, girls? A bit more garden? Some balustrading, maybe, an urn, with a spiky leaved plant?" She changed to a softer pencil, blunted the end on her sandpaper and tried. "Hmm, not bad. Yes. Fancy a bit of pavement to rest your feet on?" After that comment she frowned. Talking out loud on your own might be misconstrued, even if her subjects were so much part of her thoughts. "Sorry, girls. Don't answer back, will you?"

She'd been there at least the hour and a half. Mums was supposed to be bringing Anthea. She looked at her watch, frowned again; it was just after eleven. Crunch time was looming, but no worries. This was good, she knew it; she could see it 'cos the girls were smiling, and she had a glowey feeling. Let 'em come! With another, sharper, pencil she accentuated the eye lines and the mouths, then using her thumb, softened down the shading on the mother's face. That's about it, then. A sudden bit of a breeze caught the orchard, the trees moved and a few more leaves drifted down, another three apples or so fell, and a brief glint of sun shafted light across the grass. With a flourish, she signed the right - hand corner 'Jo D' and added the date, Roman fashion. Putting her pencil down, she stood back, stretched, and blew a kiss at the finished drawing.

"Love you, girls. Hope you like yourselves." Through the window, away to the left, she saw not just her Mums and Anthea, but the whole tribe. Pa, Edward, and in an expensive looking coat with hat to match, that must be Sir Charles. "Oh, Lord. Here we go then!"

* * *

"Sir Charles! Edward! Welcome to the Orchard Studio! Thank you for coming." This she directed more towards Edward. He gave her an ever so slight bow, and a smile and a wink, as if to say, *Not at all.*

"Miss Danielleson, or may I call you Miss Jocelyn? I'm pleased to be here, after being held at arm's length for so long! I could say I'm pleased that you've come to your senses, but that sounds far too pompous!" But you've said it anyway, thought Jo, so get on with it! "I gather you're giving us a private showing? May I?" He stepped into the studio and gazed at the work on the easel, as Edward eased himself alongside, giving her an encouraging squeeze on her arm as he passed.

Her parents linked arms and Anthea stood behind them, discreetly quiet. Sir Charles paced back, then forward again, peered at the detailing, stood back again, and raised his eyebrows at Edward. Edward glanced at Jocelyn, observing her impassive face. Here was a matured girl, a confident girl, and though he could tell Sir Charles was impressed, she wasn't to know and yet she was so self-assured. He'd only to glance at the drawing to see what was in her mind and how she'd achieved what she had, near technically perfect. Perspective on the background was a trifle short, the dress a teeny bit heavy, but nothing to detract from the overall. He nodded at his friend. Sir Charles would love to own this, he knew, let alone display the piece in the Gallery.

"Miss Jocelyn. Edward was right. You have talent, and this is as good a demonstration as any. Tell me about it. What inspired you, who were your models, and how long did this take you?"

"Drawn from memory, or more correctly, from a dream; no models as such. She," Jo nodded at the figure of Julie, "Is my very special girlfriend from college, and she's being embraced by her mother, who died – was killed – in a road accident about four months ago. The inspiration came from this very vivid dream I had; I knew I had to create the picture as I saw it in my mind. It took me about, guessing, about eighteen hours, something like that. It had to be finished here. It wouldn't have worked, otherwise." Jocelyn looked at her parents, and suddenly, inexplicably, burst into tears. It was her father who enfolded her in his arms, and as she buried her head in his sweater, stroked her glossy curls, hugged her, whispered; "Love you" into her ear, as Edward drew Sir Charles outside and Anthea sat down on the log, unsure of quite what was happening. Eleanor felt very near to tears herself and had to wipe her eyes. Was this emotional demonstrative grief for

Julie's lost mother, sadness for Julie's absence, something about Nigel, or what? Her Jo was sobbing, and David was getting her to sit on the stool.

"There, there!" He spoke the classic comforting noises; "Why the tears, my darling girl? Your drawing's wonderful. They must think it's great, so why?"

Eleanor moved to take a hand; lifted it to her lips. "What's wrong?"

Jocelyn raised her eyes to her mother, with a wisp of a smile. "Nothing's wrong, Mums. Relief, knowing I've done what my dream said. That's all; well, sort of. I just love what I've done. Stupid, isn't it? Sorry. Couldn't help it, it just came over me. Whatever must they think?" She eased herself down off the stool, gave her father a kiss, then her Mums. "Sorry. Weak moment. I'll be all right."

Outside, Edward and Sir Charles were in avid conversation, breaking off as Jocelyn emerged. Edward stepped forward. "Jo, my dear girl, don't for one moment feel embarrassed. I completely understand; you won't be the first great artist to feel submerged in emotion over aspects of their creativity, it's perfectly natural. I can imagine a profound sense of relief also has something to contribute. Sir Charles?"

"Absolutely, Edward is quite right, and I'm confident this will not be the last time, Miss Jocelyn. Please, let me congratulate you on an outstanding work. If, and I may be presuming, you intend to sell this piece, I would take it as a great privilege to be given first refusal. What would you say it is worth, Edward?"

"Two thousand?"

"Undervalued, my dear Edward, I'm sure we could retail this at five. I would offer three, Miss Jocelyn, were you to consider selling. But at least, please do give me the honour of allowing me to exhibit this alongside your other works – which I've already seen in the house – in my Gallery? A new artist of your calibre and – pardon me – youth does not appear every day – or every year, come to that!" He was smiling at her, and not down to her.

David and Eleanor reached for each other's hands, and

waited. Jocelyn went across to the log, sat down alongside Anthea. She seemed bemused by it all, sitting on her hands, turned to look at Jo. "Aren't you going to sell? Three thousand pounds – for less than twenty hours? Jo!"

"I shan't sell, Sir Charles, at least not at present. I have to let Julie see this. If she agrees, I'll let you sell prints, like we did before. If you pay me a holding fee, I'll certainly give you first refusal. *And* you can exhibit it, but on one condition." She was being exceedingly brave, but she had had another inspiration.

Sir Charles face was a picture in its own right. He did not normally expect budding young artists to negotiate in this manner, let alone stipulate conditions, and he sniffed but then laughed. "And this condition?"

"You also exhibit my new mural in pride of place. It'll just be titled 'Orchard'. About six, no eight foot long, four foot in height. Not sure about the medium, probably poster paint or something, I'd like to discuss this with my tutor." She glanced at Edward, a query in her eyes.

"My dear Jocelyn! You've not…?"

A slight shake of her head stopped him. "Of course, this has still to see the light of day, but provided I have the right materials, and light, and time…" She tailed off. Should she suggest she resigned her degree course now, or later?

Her father caught the drift. "You can't be serious!"

"Hmm. I think so. Sorry, Anthea, you might find you've got a new occupant of the room downstairs. I wasn't really enjoying the lectures anyway, and Mums's cooking is infinitely better, and with these gardens, and such a super place to work, and with the best tutor around, and Nigel can come and stay at Christmas, can't he, Mums?"

"You're sure?"

"I'm sure. Look…" She pointed back at the drawing, where the freakish mid-day sun had caught the easel in the studio window. "The girls will be agreeing. And with what I can earn, we'll be better off anyway. Think, Pa, no fees to pay!"

TWENTY

Three weeks later, on a very grey and windy November day, a large van arrived at the Old Vicarage, its driver complaining bitterly about the paucity of the address. He'd been up and down the village, until some kind soul had finally put him right, having looked at the address on his sheet, laughed, and said – "Oh yes, Orchard Studio, that's young Jocelyn's place. Try the Old Vicarage." He lugged the long cardboard roll out of his truck; got a signature, a cheery smile and directions on how to escape from the village back into what he disparaging called 'civilisation'.

Jocelyn had been left on her own; Pa at work, Mums at work, and really, she mused, I'm at work too. Her studio was her world, a cosy, bottle gas heated world with just her self and her *'Inspirations'* to quarrel with, and occasionally one or other of her old friends. Betty, poor girl, hadn't made the grade, but with her interest in horticulture was now working at the garden centre the other side of the town, Trish (full of wedding plans) had been up twice, and dear Felicity, obviously curious, had come and persuaded her – not that she needed much persuading – to do another portrait, this time full length. She daren't tell Pa how she'd posed, at least, not for that one, and Felicity had taken the finished drawing away having paid cash. Jocelyn asked no questions, but had a sneaking feeling it might end up in her bedroom.

University life was but a dream, and she had no regrets. Home life was infinitely more comforting; no running the gauntlet for the shower, no worries over lecture times, and no dodgy meals. The only down side was leaving the dance team, and though she'd vowed to go to the one Julie'd described in town she'd never got round to making the trip. Not being able to drive let alone having her own wheels was becoming a disadvantage, and she vowed she'd get Pa to teach her once the weather improved in the Spring.

It had been a stroke of luck she'd gone down for a hot drink and coincided with the truck's arrival. Now she had the roll, and lugged it back to the studio, full of eager anticipation of the task ahead. The roll had been the gift of Sir Charles, dear man, who had known where to go to get what she'd described. The problem would be getting it set up, and though she'd had an idea or two, she wasn't sure of the feasibility. After a lot of cogitation, she left it alone until her father came home.

"A word with Mike, I think. He'll know." So the buck was passed on down the line, and late the following day another truck – this time a full blown lorry – turned up with a large sheet of something Mike had called 'EmDeeEff'. The following day was Saturday, and Pa had a whole weekend off, so she commandeered him.

The sheet of the MDF nearly filled one wall, placed strategically opposite the window. Then she realised she'd be working in her own shadow, so they had to rethink the layout, so she could get the light sideways. It wasn't ideal, but it would just about work. The jolly thing was so heavy at nearly an inch thick, but at least it didn't bend. The next job was putting the paper on, and it had to be so carefully done. Eleanor was dragged up from the house to help, and eventually, between the three of them, they managed to stand the roll on its end and lay what her Mums called a 'vertical carpet.' It was such lovely paper, too, very thick, sort of glossy, but not shiny. "Contradiction in terms, Jo," had said her father, "But I know what you mean." So there it was, a blank canvas – "It isn't a canvas, Mums, but I know what you mean," she'd said, and they'd all laughed.

Then it was suddenly all very serious. She knew what it cost, because Edward had told her. He'd helped her choose her charcoal. It had to be charcoal, pencil on this would take forever, and she needed to work quickly, not for completion's sake, but to get the right effect. Tomorrow, she'd start first thing Sunday, and she prayed, yes, *prayed,* for a bright sunny day.

That night she rang Nigel, unusually, for Sundays and Wednesdays were their evenings for chatting.

"I start tomorrow, Nigel." He knew what she meant. "Think of me."

"I do, constantly. You're going to do a great job. I saw one of your prints yesterday, in a shop in town; gave me quite a thrill."

"Really! You wait till you see 'Mother and Daughter', Julie as you've never seen her before – at least, not as far as I know!"

"Can't wait. Is that going to be your 'métier?"

"What'd you mean?"

"Well, drawing ladies with no clothes on, not that I object, you understand, but…"

She laughed at him. "Whatever pays, Nigel. Art is one thing, but I need to pay my way. You wait till you see what I'm going to do. It's in my brain, and it's *not* naked ladies. *I* might be when I get to the difficult bits, 'cos that's when I draw best, but I'm trying to get out of the habit. We'll see. Now, when do you come down?" She got him to promise he'd visit the second week in December, straight after leaving Edinburgh. She knew it was a heck of a way but he'd come by train. His car was still in Norfolk.

When she went to bed that night, she couldn't sleep for a heightened sense of anticipation, with bits of her planned composition flitting through her brain like pictures from a moving train. She tried staying on her back, then on her side with legs tucked up, then straight and on her front; hands under her head, down beside her; she tried almost every position and still couldn't get comfortable or dozy. In desperation, she flung the covers off and lay naked; giving the opportunity for her 'inspiration' to work, but all she got was goose pimples and so dragged the duvet back. Getting warm again must have worked because the next thing she knew was a grey mist of light giving some semblance of a dawn.

This was the day. She scrambled up, padded to the window. A mist hung over the garden, wreathed around the shrubs and trees and the lawn had the pearl drop dew; the damp air was dragging the leaves silently down and the world was eerily quiet. A magical moment, this, the slow awakening of an autumnal day. She couldn't help herself, instinctively drawn to be part of this magic, she slipped quietly downstairs, hesitated at the back door, turning the key softly, stood on the threshold and felt the rush of cool air tingle away at her, the fine hairs on arms and legs rise to hold her warmth, then she was away, dancing across the lawn, wet footed and spraying dew as she went, paused at the edge of the shrubbery to look back at the sleeping house. Mums will kill me! she thought, and a huge surge of love for the place, her parents, the whole thing of being her and what she was. A solitary early feeding blackbird ran for cover, and she laughed.

It was Sunday. The day when she was to reveal her thoughts to that pristine acre of paper, and here she was, starkers, messing about in the shrubbery, giving a blackbird an eyeful. Totally mad. Somehow the cold wasn't bothering her now; she hesitated, took several deep lungfuls of the damp air with its tang of decay, and ran on, bounding like a roe deer across the paddock, revelling in the awareness of what she doing, that she *could* do this, when ten weeks ago she could barely hop. A triumph over adversity, that's what it was, and she was celebrating her freedom and total lack of restraint. *She'd draw, oh how she'd draw!* The studio door was unlocked, just as well for she'd not thought of the key. The door creaked a bit; the air was stale and room smelt with mustiness from its age. The intense whiteness of her blank paper stared at her, and she shivered.

Here goes! She picked up a stick of charcoal and the first tree was there. Then the next, and before her eyes the orchard appeared, sketchy outline, broad sweeping strokes, no hesitation. The backdrop to the figures she knew would emerge as the day progressed. She shivered again, and looked at her arms; those goose pimples making her look awfully old. This had to be the maddest thing out, not eight in the morning, yet here she was, starting the most momentous thing in her career – all six months of it, if that, and she giggled – not a stitch on, and fingers now as sooty as a sweep's, which somehow had got charcoally marks on her thighs as well. Daft, plain daft, but she'd remember this moment for the rest of her life. The old coat that Pa had given her as an overall lay draped on the stool, so she shrugged it on, a comforting feel and redolent of her father's use. Sitting on the stool, she surveyed the results of her half hour's dash to get something down, and was happy. Unconsciously she wiped her hands on the tops of her thighs and made more of a mess, but it felt nice and she rubbed, quite vigorously to warm herself, thighs then down her legs.

"Jo! Jo-oh!" Her Mums's call across the quiet of the grass startled her. She got up, and looked out.

Her mother was standing at the paddock gate. "Darling! Do be sensible! You haven't had any breakfast yet –oh!" She saw naked legs under the floppy coat. "Jo! You're mad, girl. Come on down and get dressed!"

The spell had been broken. The world was beginning to spin again, the first rays of sun were catching the tops of the trees and the mist was lifting. Well, she was feeling a little hollow, and the prospect of apricot jam and croissants and steaming hot coffee was too much to bear.

"Coming!"

Her mother turned and disappeared. She didn't want to see a scruffy half-naked daughter prance over the paddock.

* * *

The shower was maaarrvelllous! Such luxury! Her heart was singing, singing as she pulled on her old jeans and a tatty blouse, no questions about underwear, please, Mums, she said under her breath; she skipped down the stairs then remembered her father was still likely to be in bed. Back she went, and with no ceremony, heaved the covers off the recumbent form. "Pa! Breakfast! I've been up *ages!*"

David groaned, and rolled over. Daughters! "Go away! I'm not decent!"

"I'm not looking, and anyway, so what? I've been up to

the studio starkers and it doesn't bother me! Great, in fact. Liberating! Come on, breakfast!"

"All right, masochist. I'll be down."

* * *

"Why do you do silly things like that, Jo?" Eleanor poured another cup of coffee and pushed it across to the errant daughter. "Not only will you catch your death; it isn't decent. Imagine if there'd been someone about!" She contrasted Jo with her father, who would be still in bed if it weren't for her.

"Cos it was just so lovely and peaceful, Mums, and it makes me feel good. Doing something, okay, daring, but *different*. And no one sensible would be about that time on a damp November Sunday morning, now would they?"

"Very true," interjected her father, from behind the paper. "Which makes you self described non-sensible."

"Pa! I shan't get you out of bed again if you're like that! Oh, let me be! It's day one of The Project and I need to stay in a good mood. Come and bring me sandwiches at lunchtime and see. Give a whistle just in case I've stripped off again!" She slurped the last of her coffee, pushed her chair back, stretched, shook her hair and disappeared.

Eleanor gave a despairing look at her husband. "Will she ever get out of this silly habit? Anyone would think we brought her up in a nudist camp!"

"If she draws best like that, El, leave her. It's her life, and she's no exhibitionist, not in that sense. Anyway, she's got a nice figure and a delight to look at, so where's the harm?"

Eleanor brooded, and muttered darkly under her breath.

"What was that?"

"I said you think yourself lucky I don't follow her example!"

"Huh. In the right place, etc. etc."

She leant across the table, tweaked his paper, and as he moved it, gave him a gentle tap on the cheek. "Would you like me to start now?" She unbuttoned her blouse.

"Oh, like that, is it? Sunday mornings and all?"

431

Jocelyn was back at work. The weak sun was doing its best, and with the reflected light from the vast expanse of paper, it was good enough. She'd thought to bring a dampened cloth with her to keep fingers cleaner, but even so, her jeans would suffer. Her blouse buttons were already undone; any moment now and she'd ditch it. The last of the outline trees were in place; a critical survey and repetitive glances through the window confirmed it was about right. Now for the tricky bit, positioning her figures. She wasn't sure about the first group. She'd not drawn anyone younger than herself, but this needed a tiny tot. She left a space, moved into the centre, and made a few tentative swiggles. "Here – here, another there, another towards the bottom, those two close together. Talking to myself again, well Mums says I'm mad, so what? How many's that? Another – hmm. Shouldn't crowd them. Right." Satisfied, she stood back and pondered.

"How far over for the next group? 'bout there, methinks"' and did two more light circular swirls.

Gradually, the paper began to fill with meaningless twists and curls of charcoal, overlaid on the firmer outlines of her trees. A sudden brainwave brought a blunt B pencil into play, lightly naming her swirls, giving each one a name. Now she was sure she wouldn't miss out on any part of the concept and worked steadily on, only conscious of the passing hours as the sun moved round, low in the sky. As requested, Eleanor brought up a plateful of sandwiches for them both, whistling as suggested to show willing, but Jo still had her jeans on, even if the blouse was flapping around her bust. They sat companionably on the old log, and munched.

"Too cool for lemonade, now, Jo. Tomato soup in the flask. Not too strong."

"Hmm. Just right, Mums. It's lovely up here, isn't it?" The sun on the hedgeline showed the yellows and oranges of the hawthorn leaves changing colour and the wisps of seeded grass heads. A straggling blackberry had just about lost all its fruit, but some sloes were still evident. Another apple flopped onto the grass. The next sharp frost and the trees would be bare skeletons.

"What's Pa doing?"

"Putting the lawn mower to bed. Cleaning and sharpening and oiling, you know the sort of thing."

"What about the open-air theatre, Mums?"

"Mrs Parsons has got a good bunch of enthusiasts together. They'll be deciding soon what to do. I'm sorry, dear; I thought I'd told you."

"You may have, but I've forgotten."

" 'Midsummer Night's Dream' is the obvious choice. I've said yes, you know. Next July. Is that all right?"

Jocelyn glanced sideways. Her Mums was being quite serious; she'd thought the idea had gone away, not that she minded."'Of course, Mums. Whatever. Should be fun."

"How about being Titania?"

"Me? Titania – Queen of the Fairies? Get real, Mums. I'm an artist, not an actress. I might paint the set for you, but lying around looking like something out of a Pre-Raphaelite painting ain't me! Now Julie – she'd do it. Better figure than mine."

"There's nothing wrong with your figure, my girl. Boobs to die for, as the saying is. I can see 'em."

Jo pulled her blouse back together. "Sorry, Mums."

"Don't be. Whatever you do, Jo, so long as you're not flaunting yourself, it's fine. If it helps you."

Jo gave her Mums a kiss on her cheek. "Ta. You're a great Mums. Go and give Pa a thrill, I'll come down for tea." She was surprised to see her mother go bright red. "Did I say something?"

Eleanor got up, collected the debris and looked down at her daughter. "You wait until you have a husband. It's amazing what can happen after Sunday breakfast." She walked off, with an open mouthed Jo staring after her. Glory be! Jocelyn shook the crumbs off her jeans. Well, well. Lucky old Pa. Or Mums? Who gets the kicks? Her own girly bits twitched, and inevitably she thought of Nigel.

Nigel was reading the Sunday paper in his digs. He'd breakfasted late, after a strenuous Saturday. At least he hadn't lost his skill at Rugby, although nursing some bruises. Nice to hear Jo's voice last night; he thought of her, seeing her in his mind working away in her studio. He was still unsure whether quitting her university course had been the right thing, but she had had the promise of a possible place on the next year if she wanted to. They'd been very good about her decision, it seemed. Julie and her late mother on a print? That he looked forward to seeing. Julie was a lovely girl, gentle and deep thinking. He could have fallen for her as well – but Jo was much more fun and bouncy and just as pretty, in fact, more so. Strange how Jo had seemed to be so attached to her – girly friends; some would point fingers at their relationship, but he was sure it was all okay. He put the paper down and stared into space. He'd love to see Jo again, hold her, tell her he loved her, kiss her – stroke her... stop it, he said, feeling manly urges. What had he got on next week? He switched the computer on, and trawled the cheaper airline pages.

* * *

The afternoon wore on, the sun sinking ever lower; the daylight ebbing away, leaving that velvet blue haze on the shadows in the orchard and bringing a deepening sense of calm. Jocelyn stepped back from her paper acre, buttoned up her blouse and called it a day. She was tired now, both mentally and physically exhausted, never having worked for so long on one picture, and flopped onto the stool, yawning. Would that there had been an opportunity to bring power up here so she could have had light direct onto the board!

Her work was growing vague as the last direct rays from the reddening sun dipped below the treeline, to take on a mystical air of its own. As she stared at it, the trees seemed to sway in a sudden breeze, and the figures she'd drawn appeared to move, as though they'd woken and started to talk to each other. She shook her head, dispelling the thought. 'Imagination!' She slipped off the stool and without a backward glance, shut the door behind her. Before going back across the paddock, she took a slow walk round the orchard itself. The air was now chilly and had a steely taste, with the elements of autumn decay and mustiness, of dried grass, rotting leaves and the sharpness of the nettles and brambles. Deep breaths, swinging her arms; tossed her hair back and stood quiet, leaning back on an apple tree bole, letting herself absorb the tranquillity of the place. It seemed years since she'd lain on the grass – over there – and thought about this idea. She couldn't have dreamt she'd have actually managed to start it. All that had happened – yet the orchard was still the same, albeit six months older. Would it work? Maybe. She pushed herself off the tree, and went back to the house.

* * *

All through the following week, Jo worked on, getting herself more and more involved in the complexity of what she was trying to achieve. She had to crave some time from her father to take her into town to top up her supplies of charcoal and pencils, and mulled over the medium she would use to add colour to her work. After a lot of soul searching she finally plumped for poster paints, largely on the grounds of cost, for she had a lot of ground to cover – but she could also thin them out and highlight the detail over the top once dried.

"Don't you want to let Edward see how far you've got?" Her mother, trying to be supportive and yet not too involved, could see Jo was driving herself and her temper might be getting short. She ate, drew, and slept, that girl; even her beloved father was becoming concerned.

His question was more matter of fact. "Won't the paper sag when it's wet?" David didn't know much about such things, as he would have been the first to admit, but the problem seemed an obvious one.

Jocelyn, fortunately, wasn't feeling too stressed out at the time as the first section of her *tour de force* was nearly complete. "I'm keeping it as dry as I can, Pa, and only doing a bit at a time, spread across. It seems to work, and the paper is such super quality. I hate to think what I'd have done without Sir Charles' help. You haven't come up to see?"

"I'll be the first in the queue when you've finished, Jo. Are you all right up there, on your own for so long?"

"Mmmm. Sort of; I talk to myself rather too much."

* * *

By the end of the first week she didn't feel the same urge to paint in *dishabille mode* now that the concept was taking shape, and what with wearing the old warehouse coat of her father's and hair tied back with a scruffy scarf her mother had given her, she looked very inch a paintress. It was in such a state that she was found by Nigel.

"*Nigel!* Whatever…!" She couldn't finish, finding herself being kissed, and loving it.

He held her, squeezed her; kissed her again. "I love you, Jo. I came all the way from Edinburgh to tell you. I've missed you. Thought so much about you; I couldn't help myself. Do you mind?"

She was clinging to him, bright eyed, with a damp brush precariously held in one hand in dire danger of daubing him; flabbergasted, caught so much by total surprise her mind went all in a whirl. She'd not heard him come. She couldn't think, other than carefully letting the brush slide onto the floor before burying her head in his chest. "*Nigel!*" She felt tears, eyes pricking; it was silly, all too girlish for anything. "*Oh, Nigel.*"

He stroked her hair, below her band, and stated the obvious – "You look a bit of a scruff," which made her smile.

"I wasn't expecting you! At least I was dressed. But *why?*" She still couldn't comprehend. He'd not said anything on the phone on Thursday when he'd last rung.

"I told you. I came to say I love you, I've missed you, and it's mad and I needed to see you. So here I am. Jocelyn Danielleson – I *love you!*"

There was a dawning realisation he meant it, every single little word. I – love – you! He'd flown what, six hundred miles, hired a car, driven another sixty miles, crept up on her,

436

smothered her in kisses where she wasn't wet with paint, and declared what she knew in her heart of hearts was all she needed.

"You're mad, Nigel!"

"I know. I told you I was. Your mother thinks I'm mad too, if it's any consolation. She told me to tell you it's time for tea. Your father's come home as well." He was still holding her, and kissed her damp and grubby forehead.

Trying hard to come to terms with the admixture of delight, surprise, shock even, her heart was going in true Peter Sellars fashion – boomity-boom – and the adrenalin rush was making her dizzy.

"Nigel, why didn't you say?"

"Because I wanted to surprise you, I guess, and you'd only have tried to stop me coming which would have made us both cross, so here I am."

She struggled now, to break free and breathe. "Oh, *Nigel!*"

"That's me. Let's go and get you de-loused. I'm taking you out for dinner. Best dress job. Come on." He took a hand and gently pulled her towards the door.

"Just a minute, I need to wash my brushes." The routine brought sanity to her mind, as she rinsed out the brushes, dried them with kitchen roll, put the tops on paint jars, and took a long look at where she was with the painting. It was working, even after her surprise interruption she could tell it was working.

"What do you think?"

"Jo, my darling, I'm not looking, not at the moment. I want to see it tomorrow, in full daylight, and after we've found out where we both are – no, it's not a criticism, and certainly not any lack of interest; it's just not the right moment. I'm sure it's fine. Really. Come on." He let her go first, then shut the studio door behind them and collected her hand again, leading her back to the house.

* * *

Eleanor and David were ensconced in the kitchen, with the

teapot already on the go.

David stood up, offered Nigel his hand. "Good to see you again, Nigel, even if it is a surprise. I hope that Edinburgh will forgive you your desertion? And Jo?" There was a wry smile there, seeing his daughter's flushed face.

"No lectures 'till Wednesday. I've skipped a Rugger match, but that's all. It's good to be here, and please accept my apologies for landing on you without warning. I just had to come, you see."

Eleanor's reaction had been one of startled happiness when he'd driven in earlier. If the lad had taken it into his head to come all this way to see her girl, then truly it meant something. She'd hoped Jo would appreciate his efforts, and judging from her current appearance, she had. "Do you want tea now, Jo, or would you rather shower? Nigel – you sit here. I'll get you a mug."

Jocelyn looked at her parents in turn, sensing their quiet satisfaction, and managed a smile. "I'll go and shower. Won't be long."

* * *

When she'd gone and they heard the shower running, Nigel explained. "I couldn't manage another month without seeing Jo; she's been on my mind every day. I'm sorry if I seem so abrupt at just turning up."

He was repeating himself, but it seemed important. "I hope I didn't embarrass anyone."

"No, I don't think so. What was Jo's reaction?" David spoke for them both.

"Amazement, I think. Flabbergasted. Pleased, I hope."

"Oh, yes, she'll be pleased, but I think she's in a state of shock. And she'd been working on that painting non-stop for days, so she's rather burnt out, but she won't give up. Treat her carefully, Nigel."

With a rueful smile, he nodded. "I'll try. It is all right for me to take her out to dinner tonight? I phoned to book a table at the Italian place. We won't be late back, I promise."

She came down in a dressing gown to have her mug of tea, hair all wrapped up in a towel, snatching a few of her Mums scones before retreating back upstairs; "I'm going to have a few minutes' kip, Nigel, if you don't mind. Relax and get myself in better social condition. The painting rather winds me up..." and she went, without waiting for a reply. After a suitable time interval, Eleanor took him up to the guest room and left him to wash and change. Jo's door was firmly shut.

An hour later, she emerged to find them all in the sitting room. Her picture of Julie and her late mother was still in pride of place above the fireplace; Nigel had been riveted by the sheer beauty and expressionism of the piece, but as she entered the room, his heart did another little leap. She'd taken great care to get her hair just right, the heirloom hairpiece in place; she'd added a touch of make-up, and chosen to wear the Burgundy dress. It was a touch shorter on her now, but showed her figure to the perfection he'd remembered. She did a curtsey. "Like it?"

"You're stunning, Jo." Tears came to his eyes. She was a gorgeous girl. He met her eyes; she blushed and dropped her gaze. Eleanor and David watched the by-play, and caught each other's glance. This was their daughter, a very desirable young lady, grown up to become someone else's love. They would lose her into another person's care, Nigel's, before too long, and there was nothing that would prevent that other than some disaster which would bring much heartache in its train.

* * *

After the couple had gone, Eleanor crossed the room and sat alongside her husband, cuddling up to him. David slid his arm around her, and they let time go by without saying any word. What would be would have to be. Before too long, Eleanor detached herself, and got up. "I'm going up, David. Leave the door off the latch. They'll shut it." He watched the sway of her hips and the shake of her hair as she left the room.

They loved each other, deeply, and would need the comfort of that love to help them over this incipient and inevitable change in the structure of their lives.

* * *

Eleanor sensed a subtle change in her daughter's demeanour at breakfast. Nigel, too, was more withdrawn, though as polite and as thoughtful as always. Jocelyn's eyes were different in some way, more mysterious, and something of the light-heartedness of her chatter had gone; she was more reserved. Her attitude to Nigel had changed, too. She seemed protective, almost possessive, towards him, and when she touched his arm to offer him the marmalade pot, there was a little flutter of the eyebrows she'd not noticed her do before. They hadn't been late, as Nigel had promised, though there had been some time between the car on the gravel and the sound of two bedroom doors shutting; she'd heard them even in her calmed after glow state. She didn't think either of them would have 'misbehaved' but there had been a change, even if it wasn't inspired by first-time loving.

"Do you want to go to church this morning?"

Jocelyn looked at Nigel at her mother's query.

"Why not? Jo?"

She shrugged, and then thought; it wouldn't hurt. "With you, Mother? What about Pa?"

Eleanor caught her breath. Jo had called her 'Mother', for the very first time. Her little girl had vanished. "He – he's walking the garden, Jo. You'll have to ask him. Yes, I'll be pleased to go with you. Go and ask him. Jo."

Her daughter went. Nigel looked up at her mother, saw a glimpse of a tear, and reached for her hand. "Mrs Danielleson – Eleanor – I've something to ask."

She knew it, then. "Go on. Though isn't this something you normally you say to a girl's father?"

Nigel had to laugh. "I believe you both already know. I would like – I want to marry Jocelyn. When we both know it's the right time. She's said yes."

In the darkness of the garden, beneath the tree that had nearly killed her, she'd heard him ask, knew that he would, knew that she'd say yes, and felt his hands go round her, holding her, feeling the stirrings of need and desire, wanting him to make her a woman, yet holding herself back and aloof in her strength and belief in her love for her parents and for her own sense of what she was, a girl with a project still to fulfil. When her painting was finished, when she was sure it was right, then, and only then, would she allow him to make love to her, and she knew exactly of the how's and where's and when's that would be. The dreams were becoming reality. The spell, the magic, it was all there. She'd thought of Julie, and had nothing but a returning sense of peace. Their love wouldn't go away, but it wouldn't alter her love for Nigel, either. The drawing said it all. Julie had been – was still – loved by her mother, too. Nigel had kissed her, caressed her breasts, made her senses move her to almost the point of surrender, he'd looked into her eyes, and she'd known his desire for her was as strong as hers to give way, but they hadn't. Somehow, the garden was protective, and the orchard, dark beyond the shrubs, brooded, clutching its own secrets and the naissance of the Apple girl's picture.

* * *

Jocelyn found her father by the barn. As he heard her approach, he held out his hands. With incipient pricking at the back of her eyes, she ran, and he caught her, swung her off the ground and back on her feet.

"Jo?"

She nodded, not trusting herself to speak.

"Yes?"

She nodded again, wiped her eye, reached into the pocket of her skirt. The little maroon box with a simple gold ring and one, just one, emerald. David looked up into the trees, and saw himself, asking Eleanor for her love; now his daughter, a physical and beautiful representation of that love, was treading the same path. He swallowed, held his stomach in to control his emotions.

"You're a lucky girl, my Jo. A very lucky girl."

She buried herself in his old tweed jacket. A muffled "I know," and a sob.

"Hey, hey. You're supposed to be happy!"

"I am. But you and Mums – mother."

"We knew, Jo. One of these days, it had to be. You're far too pretty a girl to be left with aging parents." He chuckled, relieving the tension. "He fell into your lap, didn't he?" Something they'd never forget; ironically the coincident distant drone of a Hercules across the Plain made them both laugh. "Let's take you to church and show you off, then. I take it Nigel wants to formally ask me for your hand before you're entitled to wear that?"

She nodded again, heart too full to answer.

TWENTY ONE

Nigel needed to get back to Edinburgh before Wednesday, so Jocelyn had to relinquish him on the Tuesday morning. Her ring was there, a symbol of his declared love, a constant strange feel on her finger she'd take ages to get used to – a very odd sensation. Sunday had been a bit weird, but a beautiful moment when, walking through the gate into the churchyard, Nigel had stopped them, taken Jo's finger, and slid the ring on. Under the eyes of her parents he'd kissed her, held her hand and they'd walked on and into the church.

She'd been desperately self-conscious; how many people had offered them congratulations and good wishes she couldn't remember. On the Monday evening, nervously, she'd rung Julie, and told her. She got a disappointingly muted reaction, until Julie had virtually said she'd known.

"Known?"

"Yes. Gut feeling? Pretty damned obvious, really. You're a lucky, lucky girl, Jo. I wish he'd fallen for me. How's the project?" She'd changed the subject.

"Fine, but I've had three days off, so I hope I can pick up my train of thought again. Nigel's going back tomorrow, but it won't be long before the end of term. I'll have to go to Norfolk to see his parents, but we'll have Christmas together here. You'll be home soon, too – then you can see the painting. It's massive!"

"I thought you said something about the one that brought you back to sense – me and my mother?"

"So I did. Sorry, I forgot in the excitement. It's the candidate for another print, Julie, but I won't say yes until you've seen it and said it's okay. It's very, er, revealing."

Julie had laughed, a gurgle of a laugh. "When haven't you

been showing off my sexy bits, darling Jo? It's a wonder I haven't been asked to do a Page Three! That's an idea, might get some money. Anyway, must dash. Speak soon. Byeee."

* * *

And now he was off. Another hug, another tongue seeking kiss, a stroke down her thigh, and he'd shut the car door and was away before she could shed another tear. She stood alone in the middle of the drive, the drive she'd raked so assiduously before that garden party, and listened as the exhaust note died into the mind-hugging silence of the day. Not a breath of wind, nothing. The scents of the autumnal decaying garden rose around her, hanging in the air. Engaged! She was *engaged!* She had a *fiancé!* A doctor's wife to be. Gosh. And she laughed. 'Gosh', what an old-fashioned school girlish expression!

She turned on her heel, scuffed in the gravel, and went indoors.

* * *

Back into her scruff kit, clean scarf around her hair; and now in front of her board; the last but one group to do. With fresh enthusiasm and the change in status to bolster her on, she worked assiduously for the next three hours. Hunger pangs reminded her she'd had no lunch, but never mind, a good supper would put that right. The last few brush strokes to complete that group and it would do for today. She knew this last group would be trying and more emotional because it represented life's end, the final piece of her saga. The trees behind that group were already there, stark, leafless, branches drooping; the fallen log even, half rotted. And that little pile of decaying apples, all so sad. But it had to be, no getting away from it; the end of life was inevitable. Julie knew, she'd lost her mother. Reflecting on that episode, now she had the strength of her decision to spend the rest of her life with Nigel behind her, it didn't seem quite so bad. Her mother and father too, taking things in their stride. How different it all was from the beginning of the year!

Her ears weren't attuned to the approach of anyone – she'd not heard Nigel, so now she hadn't heard Edward. A slight cough made her jump and whirl round, long camel brush splattering fine drops over the painting.

"My dear girl, I'm so sorry; I should have made more noise. Your mother gave me the permission to approach." He stepped forward and scanned the huge painting in front of him, ignoring her. What would he say? All the pointers he'd given her during that fateful week in France, some she'd remembered, other things she should have done and maybe gone her own way; but this was *her*, her own style, her dream now realised, for better or for worse. Better or worse – out of the marriage service she knew, and thought of Nigel. Definitely better; she could have found a lot worse in the way of boyfriends – no, he wasn't a *boyfriend*, he was her *fiancé!* She loved the word rolling around her mind. She hadn't told Edward, but then she hadn't seen him since whenever. This was the first time he'd seen this…

There he was, just staring at it, scanning left to right and back. Then a few steps forward to peer closely at some of the detail, before spinning round and reaching for her, taking her hands.

"An allegory. My dear Jocelyn, it's a *wonderful* piece of work; so eminently thought provoking and such masterful design. A *Tour de Force*, an absolute masterpiece. Not finished yet, I see. How long…?"

"Did it take me? Six months; from conception – short-term pregnancy, unless it takes me another three months to say 'Finished', which it won't. Conceived on the grass, over there, while I was still a schoolgirl and nearly took my knickers off." He looked shocked; she laughed, but was nearly hysterically beyond caring. He'd liked it, praised it, and she'd become suddenly, remarkably, deliriously happy. "Virgin birth, Edward. No one else involved; just me and my near-naked inspiration. That's what I do, Edward. I take my clothes off to draw. Big sense of freedom of expression. And it's worked.

Look!" She pointed at one of the groups, to where she was, nakedly standing with others clustered around. He peered at the group, and saw the likeness of Julie, and one or two other college girls, and even boys.

"There's a bit of the French school here. And the trees – more Paul Nash; no, even Monet. Such a bewildering eclectic style. All from the mind of a..." he stopped and let go of her hands. "My apologies, I was about to say schoolgirl, but no, my dear Jocelyn; from the mind of a thinking, daring, wild spirit. This is a long step from the self-portrait, is it not?" He examined the scenes in front of him. "Birth – ah, before that! Really, Jocelyn!" he coughed, and she laughed. She'd enjoyed doing that bit, made her feel quite – well, the word *was* inspired!

She took over: "Childhood. Work, and a bit of play; couple here again; more like 'happy married bliss' I hope; then old age, and ultimately, death and decay, seen in this heap of rotten apples? Is the apple blossom right here?"

"Certainly. I like this touch."

The bees going into the flower above the couple on the grass, though she had been uncertain about the changes in scale, and asked.

"No, not at all a problem, quite the reverse. And this apple," where she'd painted in one particularly special fruit, with a wasp about to attack it, "that's life, to a tee! A lot of thought here. And this is you as well? And isn't that your Nigel? Or at least the young man who followed you – us – to France?"

"My fiancé. We've just got engaged. Look," and she showed him her ring.

He beamed at her. "Well, what a delight! My earnest congratulations! May I inform Dylys? She *will* be thrilled for you, of that I am sure. Any date in mind?" He'd been sidetracked, and just as well.

"Oh, not for some time. Nigel has to finish qualifying as a Doctor – of Medicine – and I have still to make my name. Maybe two years. We're still young, yet. Well, I am. Nigel's about three years older. You know he's the one who I rescued?"

"I do indeed. Very appropriate. Highly unusual, but most inspired – no, over use of the word. Motivational? Certainly that bit. Ahem. Well. I do believe this will, as you put it, *make your name.*"

"You approve?"

"I do indeed. But, forgive me, this is on paper. It will need backing and stabilising, and it must come out of here before it rains. That is essential. All this work, it must not be spoilt. Jocelyn, we should get this into proper conditions, and fast. Will you allow this to go to Charles's Gallery? I know he will be amazed. How long to finish?"

"Another day, maybe day and a half, but yes, I would like some more light. It's a bit grey now. How do you think we can move it, then? I can't roll it up like it came."

"Indeed not. I'll talk to Charles. Leave it with me. Are you finished for the day?"

"Well, yes. I'll just clear up." She went through her routines, as Edward watched. How she had changed! A hesitant schoolgirl knocking on his door, asking about becoming an artist, borrowing fixative and watercolours, to a brash young thing throwing herself around and – sadly, damaging her legs, leg rather, then a moody wimpish thing with no colour; suddenly blossoming and taking on a maturity beyond her years, with talent to match. He was proud to know her.

"I'll go on down."

"Okay. Won't be long." With Edward out of the way, she scrutinised the damage done with her flinging droplets, but nothing untoward. Just the sad bit to do. Tomorrow. She shut the door, and stood, looking over the orchard. Her secret project, no longer secret, but finding favour. She felt ten feet tall, and whispered, across the darkening grass. "Thankyou! Spirit of the Apple Trees! Thank you!" There was a sudden stirring in the near leafless branches, as a wayward breeze rippled through the trees, and another couple of the last apples fell, as if to acknowledge her thoughts.

* * *

447

The following week, after several telephone conversations with first Sir Charles and then a representative of a specialist firm of Art movers, a big white truck arrived in the drive with four sturdy chaps in dark sweaters and jeans. David took some hours away from the Showroom, Eleanor swapped her shift at the village shop; they'd invited Mike just in case, and Edward came as well. Amazing how he could manage to get time away from the college, Jo thought, and then chuckled to herself, as she knew Dylys was still technically his boss. She'd finished the painting as promised, but with a lot of tears over the final bit. It had been a last minute thought to use Julie's Mum's funeral as the guide, the inspiration, though so hard to call it that. She'd put her white dress onto Julie, and managed her father as a grieving husband quite well. Now it was done.

The removal chaps knew what they were doing. They'd brought a roll of very fine muslin and pinned it over the paper, carefully rolling it out and stretching it as they went, making the paper secure against any movement, then another roll of paper, and finally, lifted the whole heavy sheet. The little party of onlookers stood outside, watching as the board emerged, and broke into a spontaneous clapping. Jocelyn felt like crying again, but bit her tongue.

The board was carried in solemn procession down the paddock, across the lawn, and into the waiting truck, lashed firmly to the gratings on the sides. Then the doors shut, the guys climbed back into the cab, and her three – no four weeks' work – had gone. Drained, that's how she felt, drained. Mother – somehow Mums was no longer her – had managed to put a sort of high tea cum buffet together, and they stood around in the sitting room eating sausage rolls and sipping tea, with a sense of total anti-climax. That was it, all over. Project complete. She could do with a holiday.

"Mother? Pa – father? How about a few days off?"

"Have my cottage if you like," Mike overheard, "Down on the coast. Bit out the way, like, but you're welcome. This time o'year needs an airing. Just give us summat towards power."

* * *

So it was, the Sunday following, David drove them down to Cornwall. Not the usual time of year to go to Cornwall, late November, but the roads were clear, and happily, dry. The cottage was down a track, in a little combe-like valley, just a mere couple of hundred yards from the sea, and never quiet. The sound of the breaking waves, or just the swell, was ever present. Jocelyn, tired from the journey but more so from the relaxation of time no longer spent painting, took in her surroundings, found her bed, and curled up. She was asleep in minutes.

Eleanor only had to put a few groceries away in the cupboard while David heaved their cases upstairs to the small bedroom overlooking the sea, before she was done.

"Jo?"

"Leave her. Let's go explore." It was late afternoon, and the sun was dipping low, a slight breeze brought a chill up from the sand. "Coats?"

"Here. Put a sweater on, Dave."

* * *

The steps down to the beach, such as it was, were concrete and spalling. Then it was sand, strewn with debris from the tide, a few shells, an odd length of orange rope, and a broken fish box.

"Not like Mike, those steps. Smell the sea?"

David took her hand. "Aye. Nice for a change. At least we're away. Not quite Majorca?"

"Nope. But if it's quiet for our girl, so much the better. I'm happy. You?"

He nodded, and tucked his arm around her. "You, me, and the sea. Love me?" A deep breath as a hand found his. "Mmmm. We've been lucky, you and I."

"Even…?"

He knew what she meant, and hugged her tighter. "Our Jo's worth three. That's what I say, we've been lucky. I'll miss her."

Eleanor looked up at him. He was staring out to sea, not

449

seeing. "I know. She won't desert us, you know that. And Nigel's a super lad. He'll look after her."

They'd walked to the end of the beach, where the rocks jutted out into the swelling tide.

"What would she do if she was on her own?"

"Funny question. She won't be!"

"If anything happened to us? Or Nigel?"

David went cold. "Whatever do you mean, Eleanor?"

"Her painting. Lots of things she's painted have happened. Others haven't. Yet!"

"Oh! You think she's clairvoyant?"

"She's had some weird dreams."

"Let's go back. Before it gets too dark to see."

"Okay."

* * *

Back in the cottage, they lit the fire in the only downstairs room, and the flames soon warmed them. David got out the bottles of wine they'd brought with them, and Eleanor dug out biscuits and some cheese. There was a sound from upstairs, and Jo appeared, in just a dressing gown.

"Caught you! Some for me?" She edged down the narrow stairs, and flopped alongside her mother. "Hmmm." She nuzzled up against her. "You smell all salty!"

"That's because we're by the sea, silly." Jo got a kiss and a pat on her knees. "Did you have a nice nap?"

"Mmmm. Dreamt." She wriggled a bit and closed her eyes again. "This is nice. Cosy. Do you think the garden will be all right?"

"Strange girl. Of course it will. November, remember." Eleanor laughed. "Poetic. David, pour the girl some wine. Then we'll all have an early night."

Jo opened her eyes, nudged by the glass proffered. "Thanks, Pa." Thinking of her dream, she stirred, and attempted to sit straight, so her mother had to lift an elbow for her. Then she could take the glass, and sipped. "Fruity. Like my dream. What's it like, being made love to, Mums?"

David spluttered. "Don't answer, El, on the grounds it might incriminate you. Whatever made you ask, daughter?"

"Well, I don't know, do I? Apart from..." then she shut up, wondering if she'd said too much.

Eleanor started to go red. She'd not said anything to her husband about winding up her daughter's feminity. "It's all a bit subjective, Jo. Depends on your partner. If he's tender, and caring, and wants to make *you* feel good; and you're all soft and warm and wanting him, it's the nicest feeling in the world. And if you get it right, it's wonderful. But if all he wants is his satisfaction and you're not in the mood, it might be bloody terrible. Then you just have to let it happen and not think about it, I suppose. I'd like to think you'd never have that problem. Enough. Another day. I'm going to bed, and so should you. We'll explore in the morning. Go on, you," she pushed her daughter off the settee and watched her climb the stairs. "Night, night!"

"Night, Mums, Night, Pa."

They couldn't discuss what Jo had asked; the walls were only plasterboard, but David found the nice bits to cuddle and they soon went to sleep. Jo lay awake a little longer, imagining things and feeling a bit strange, but she too succumbed and slept dreamlessly for the first night in ages.

* * *

The morning broke clear and chilly; the sea below sullen and deep grey green, with not much of a wind to roughen the waves. Jocelyn was the first to stir. Tempted by the idea of running naked along the beach, she clambered out of her rather too soft bed, slung a dressing gown round her, padded carefully downstairs, and eased open the door. A cool draught made her re-consider. Perhaps if it's warmer tomorrow? Instead she put the electric kettle on and made a mug of coffee, however the temptation of the concept proved too strong, so she drank her coffee a bit too quickly and burnt her tongue, before taking the path to the beach. At least there won't be anyone else about at this time, she reasoned, reaching the steps. The tide was out, and the beach sands swept clear and unsullied. Dressing gown off, then her cotton nightdress, and the chill air swirled over her, bringing out the goose pimples all over, and making her reddish fair fine hair stand on end over arms and legs. "A jog down to the water and back," she told herself, and set off at a steady lope. Behind her the hill rose to meet an orange tinged sky as the sun began to climb, and a faint shadow started to jog along in front of her. She reached the tide's edge, and twisted sideways to take the line of the water, getting feet damp and sand clinging between her toes. "It's not too bad now I'm moving!" She swung her arms round and round to get the circulation really going. Her hair was bobbing all over the place, matching swinging breasts. "It's great!" She thought of a poem she'd once read:

> First Light reveals unblemished lengths of smoothened beach
> Where nought but sea birds wheel and search
> On stilts, the edge of water, pools in rock
> For nature's bounty, eat, cry and then rejoin the flock.

She knew it went on, something like:

> She, hand to eyes, surveys the total emptiness
> And laughs aloud at joy of life and wind's caress
> Runs, naked feet and blouse undone
> To water's edge, and waits, a vision, for the sun.

That was her, and yes, she was laughing at her wantonness and lack of even a blouse. The strains of the past month had vanished, leaving her soul clear and happy, knowing she'd achieved all she wanted. Her parents, asleep in the cottage behind, would be blissfully unaware their daughter had slipped out; her future husband would be stirring in his lonely single bed and have first waking thoughts of his lovely auburn haired creature running amok on a Cornish beach – dream on, she giggled. I'd best get back.

* * *

Collecting her clothes from the rock where she'd left them, she picked her way carefully back up the path. Oh! Her mother was up!

"*Jocelyn!*" An apparition had appeared at the door. "*Gracious, girl!*"

Jo grinned. "It's rather fresh, out there, but wonderful! You should try it!"

"What, run about starkers, in *November?* Not likely. I shall never comprehend your mind, Jo, all I can hope is Nigel appreciates what he's getting! What if someone saw you?"

"Then they did. I'm only a girl, mother, and I'm not ashamed of what I am. It's just I feel so *free,* with no clutter, nothing to stop the wind getting at me; all my thoughts are as clean and pure as the freshness of the day. It's like taking a cold bath, only heaps better. Now, if the inquisition's over, I'll go and use the bathroom. Pity there's no shower. Father getting up?"

Eleanor looked at her. She stood tall, firm, less freckled now, straight shouldered, well-endowed bust, a waist to be envied, and swelling hips with... well, yes. Just that fading scar on her leg, but otherwise, nicely shaped, and perfect toes. That's what comes of running free. Jocelyn Anne Danielleson. Her daughter, *Her* daughter!

"I'm very proud of you, Jo. What you are, what you do. I couldn't have wished for a better child." Her eyes watered. "Go on, go and get your father up. Breakfast in ten minutes."

Jocelyn heard and saw; she too suddenly felt emotion welling up. "Oh, *Mums!*" The two women clung to each other, kissed, and Jo wasn't a child, just a daughter; she was another woman, a friend, and would always be so. That was the defining moment, a subtle change in their relationship, and something Jo would keep in her mind forever.

* * *

The room was filling up. The buzz of conversation transformed into a muffled roar, or so it seemed. She was nervous, an unusual phenomenon for her, but all these people, dressed to kill, most of them; people she didn't know from Adam, apart from her friends and, naturally, her parents. And Nigel; he'd gone to fetch another glass of apple juice; she couldn't possibly handle any alcohol with a twitchy tummy. Here in London for an Exhibition preview night; a far cry from that lovely week in Cornwall only a month ago, or the weekend before Christmas in Norfolk, feeling so at ease with Nigel's parents. Now, at the start of a new year, here in Sir Charles's Gallery she was nervous, really nervous.

"You look ravishing, my dear Jocelyn, absolutely ravishing. A painter's dream! I love the way your hair is done!" It had been piled up on top like a film star's, she'd thought, but it wasn't bad. She'd insisted on wearing the Burgundy dress, as a tribute to her parents, but the hemline had to be lowered; she couldn't believe she'd grown another inch since June. Edward – her ever-supportive Edward – took her elbow.

"Come and meet a few people, my dear, before the melee gets too intense." Shepherding her adroitly through the crowd, he sought and found a group he knew. "Angela, Jules, Mr & Mrs Rianow – may I introduce our paintress? Jocelyn Danielleson – these reprobates are part of my early set. Friends really, but we all are hopelessly critical of each other's work. Ah, here's Nigel."

He'd been struggling to find her in the crush. The Gallery wasn't all that large despite its mish mash of rooms and Sir Charles evidently had quite a mailing list of those who habitually turned out for free drinks.

Edward added his comments, "Nigel here is Jocelyn's intended. She found him in a tree," so she had to recount her tale all over again, and receive the same adulations. It was getting a little boring, therefore somewhat of a relief to hear the banging on a table or something that prefaced Sir Charles's introductions.

"Thank you all for coming. I hope you all have managed to keep your glasses full; there will be some canapés circulating shortly. Now, I have something especially fascinating to reveal to you this evening. I am privileged to have been introduced to a brilliant young girl – lady – whose talent at drawing from life has already begun to be known, through the medium of two prints that are currently available. The originals of these are here on display in this Gallery. Tonight we show one of her latest drawings, now also newly available in print, a study of a young girl and her mother. Sadly, the mother was tragically killed in a road traffic accident, but the drawing has been completed from an incredible, almost telepathic, memory. This in itself is remarkable, but the depth of feeling in the drawing shows a rare sense of displaying emotion. I commend this work to you.

The same artist, who I am extremely pleased to say, is here with us this evening, has recently completed a major work of Allegory, based on her shrewd and fascinating insight into life. The backdrop of an apple orchard, together with illustrations of the stages of the development of fruit, is echoed by studies of the various stages of human life in all its joys and sorrows. And this, ladies and gentlemen, accomplished by a young lady barely out of college. May I first reveal her work?" He signalled to the two members of the Gallery staff standing guard on the drapes over the painting on the wall to his left. They let the drapes fall, and Jocelyn's 'Apples and Life' was there, vibrant with colour and intensity of feeling.

"May I..." he had to raise his voice against the hubbub of comments amongst the assemblage. "May I introduce to you the originator of this beautiful and thought provoking work. Miss Jocelyn Anne Danielleson." He stepped to one side, and started the tumult of clapping. Jo was led forward by Edward, who raised her hand, kissed it, and stepped back. She was on her own.

Nervously, looking at a sea of faces, with a slight cough, she felt she could only manage a few words.

"Thank you, all of you, for coming to look at this project of mine. Thank you, Sir Charles," she looked at him, and he smiled encouragingly back. "My thanks also to Mr Peterson, who suffered me as a pupil at college, but has since become a great friend and ally. My greatest thanks..." she looked for her parents, finding them at the side of the room and her father raised his hand to show her they were with her. Her tummy contracted with emotion and her voice cracked as she went on "are, is, are," the audience had to laugh a little at her stumbled grammar, "to my parents, Eleanor and David, who believed in me. No girl could wish for more. I hope you like my work."

More clapping, some polite, some enthusiastic; she was temporarily forgotten as the critics moved forward en masse to scrutinise and comment on what she'd done. But Nigel was there to put his protective arm around her and lead her to one side and into the other room, now nearly empty, where six of the other drawings she'd done were mounted and where three people stood in front of them.

"Jocelyn!" A familiar figure, blonde and looking lovely.

"Felicity! I'm sorry; I didn't know you were here!"

"Wouldn't have missed it for the world. Told you I'd not regret my investment. The one in the white dress and the one you did of me? Doubled in value, dear girl. Here, meet my management, Sarah, Catriona; meet Jocelyn, our talented sketcher. We've been talking about you, Jo; hope your ears haven't been burning. The magazine wants some more prints to sell, exclusive and all that. And an article on your aspirations, before Apollo bags you."

"Apollo?"

"Very arty magazine; top-flight stuff, get in there and you're home and dry. Where are your parents, Jo? Oh, and I believe we've met before?" She looked at Nigel, standing passively by as Jo's protector.

"Felicity – meet my fiancé. Nigel Haversted, soon to be Doctor."

"Oh, yes - the soldier in the tree! Pleased to meet you, again, and congratulations. You've swept a lovely lady off her feet, then?"

Nigel smiled politely. "I don't think I shall ever be able to forget that incident, will I? Nice to meet you again, Felicity."

Then they were caught up in more interviews, more offers, more congratulations, apart from one sour old gent whose mores had been offended, but he seemed to be the only defaulter. It just went on and on; not until the wine stopped circulating and the waitresses ran out of canapés did the guests begin to drift away.

Sir Charles and Edward finally caught up with her, now sheltering with her parents.

"An extremely successful evening I think, don't you, Edward?" Edward nodded, but hadn't a chance to comment before Sir Charles went on: "I will be looking forward to the reviews. You've created quite a stir, young lady. Don't be surprised if things take off, but I'll just emphasise our agreement, if I may; the Gallery to have first call on any new work you wish to exhibit, you understand? Maybe this isn't the time to discuss mundane matters, but do you intend to sell 'Apples and Life'?"

Jo hadn't really given it any thought, not having painted her project with selling in mind; she'd done it because she'd wanted to; a mental pressure from her love for her surroundings. No, she didn't think she wanted to sell, if Sir Charles wished it to remain on exhibition; that was fine by her. When the Gallery tired of it she'd think again.

"A very sensible and agreeable answer, Miss Jocelyn, but would it interest you to be quoted the present value?"

Eleanor and David both looked at her, as she pulled a wry face. Value? Well, it cost quite a bit to do, despite Charles's gift of paper, they'd – she had – spent a lot on paint, and then there was her time.

Her father had to ask. "I doubt she knows, Sir Charles, but commercially, is it worth what it cost to produce?" and watched as eyebrows rose.

"My dear sir! Not only is there a substantial offer for the right to exhibit from another gallery, but we've two other offers on the table. One from the management headquarters of a multinational company whose representative this evening thought it exactly right for their dining room, another a private buyer – no names, no pack drill – who has suggested a five figure sum."

"*What?*" David couldn't believe him. Eleanor went pale and put her arm around Jo.

"Mmmm – that's right, twelve and a half thousand. Of

course, it's worth a lot more than that. Are you sure you don't want to sell, Miss Jocelyn? Less my commission, of course, twelve percent. I'm sure we might be able to get you fifteen, possibly more if we held out. And we could always retain copyright. Well?" He was smiling at her.

Fifteen *thousand?* The world spun round her, and she nearly blacked out. Eleanor felt her hand go sweaty, and gripped, hard. "Jo. It's all right." She led her Apple girl over to a chair, sat her down, while the little group expressed concern.

"I'm so sorry, my dear. Bit of a shock?"

"I'll say." She blinked to clear her vision. "I'm okay, folks. Well, it looks like I'll have to get started on another one if they're that valuable. Have to earn my keep!" They all laughed, except Nigel. Was his girl going to start another life? Only time would tell.

* * *

She had become of age. The apples had been pollinated, had ripened and fallen, but her full adult life and growth to maturity had only just begun.

The orchard's trees were being softly covered in snow, drifting down, blanketing the grass where she'd lain, where lovers had loved and lives had been started, where fun and friendship matured and memories were stored and re-kindled, where overall there was a sense of timelessness and peace.

Leaning over the gate she'd vaulted, oh, so many times, she sighed, revisiting her joys and her sorrows, her memories. It was time to move on. Her scarf wrapped closely round, her warm woollen coat hugged about her, she turned and walked slowly back through the snow covered paddock, returning to the house and the post-exhibition party. She'd still be living there, an older and wiser girl, for a year or three yet; the Apple of her parent's eye, her loving and her fruitfulness still to mature.

* * *

After qualifying Nigel would take a partnership in a Medical

Practice only a stone's throw away from Tinsfield, and they would marry in the village Church, with Julie as her Matron of Honour. Oh, yes, Julie married her Robert, as Trish had married her Brendan. Even Edward made Dylys, as he said, still with twinkling eye, an 'honest woman'. *Midsummer Night's Dream* was an outstanding success; and Eleanor's garden joined the ranks of 'Must Be Seen' places. She even found time to re-discover her own talent of painting landscapes in oils, much to Jo's amusement. David realised his ambition of Partner in the Motor Trade Business, and moved Jo's portrait in her Burgundy Dress into an upstairs office.

The 'Apple and Life' mural was finally sold, to be mounted on the Dining Room wall at the London headquarters of that Multi National, and Jocelyn bought her first car. She and Nigel found a lovely little cottage in the village near to his Practice before their marriage, but she still went back to the Old Vicarage and the Orchard Studio to paint regularly until she became pregnant. She continued to sketch – and paint – at home, very happily and successfully, but she never executed another mural. That *'tour de force'* had achieved its undeniable success in promoting her move into adulthood; she'd felt no call, no inspiration, to revisit the need.

The apple trees gradually diminished in number as old age took its toll. Finally, the ancient orchard was cleared for replanting; Jocelyn insisting the tradition would continue. The Studio was dismantled eventually and the 'old order' changed.

Baby Angelina became the delight of her grandmother, let alone her parents. When she was barely two, she had a baby brother, and Grandpa David was overjoyed. Jocelyn Anna called him her Tree Boy, though by now no one, except Nigel and his inlaws, of course, really knew why; whereas Eleanor still called her daughter 'Apple Girl', a name Jocelyn would always, always, treasure.